SUPREME CLIENTELE

SUPREME CLIENTELE

ASHLEY & JAQUAVIS

www.urbanbooks.net

Urban Books, LLC
1199 Straight Path
West Babylon, NY 11704

ISBN-13: 978-1-60162-150-4
ISBN-10: 1-60162-150-7

First Trade Paperback Printing January 2007
First Mass Market Paperback Printing May 2009
Printed in the United States of America

10   9   8   7   6   5   4

Distributed by Kensington Publishing Corp.
Submit Wholesale Orders to:
Kensington Publishing Corp.
C/O Penguin Group (USA) Inc.
Attention: Order Processing
405 Murray Hill Parkway
East Rutherford, NJ 07073-2316
Phone: 1-800-526-0275
Fax: 1-800-227-9604

SUPREME CLIENTELE

Chapter 1

All in Da Game

"Your room number is 810," the desk clerk said as she handed the keys to King. He looked down at the beautiful lady who stood at his side. His six-foot frame loomed over her as he reached around her waist and kissed her lightly on the cheek. He handed her one of the room keys then grabbed their luggage.

"Hold up. I got to use the bathroom," she announced.

King shook his head and replied, "You can't wait 'til we get in the room?"

"No, I need to go now. I'll be right back, daddy. Just hold the elevator for me."

King waited impatiently at the elevator and glanced around occasionally, looking for Zya. He spotted her coming out of the restroom and couldn't help but stare. He admired her perfect body as she walked toward him. Her honey-colored hair was identical to her skin tone, which gave her a unique look. Zya demanded attention every time she entered the room, and she knew it. She strutted across the floor with a model's precision, and with every step, her plump ass shifted its weight from side to side. King's manhood began to harden with every step she took, anticipating what was about to go down when they reached the room.

"You ready, ma?" King asked as he stared at Zya's lips.

"Yeah, I'm ready," she said as she circled the red lollipop she was sucking. King led the way to the elevator.

Just as the elevator door closed, Zya pounced on him. She took the sucker out of her mouth and walked up to King. They were standing toe to toe. She gently grabbed his crotch in search of his dick, and when she found it, she caressed it while tongue-kissing him. King could taste the cherry flavor from the sucker, and his dick was standing tall and firm. Zya drove King crazy. He dropped his bag and tightly palmed her ass with both hands. Zya began to moan while softly stroking him through his jeans, making him grow. The sound of the bell and the door opening stopped their brief ecstasy.

"This is the floor," King said in a husky tone that let Zya know he was horny. He picked up his bag and stepped out of the elevator. King reached their room, and Zya stood behind him with his rod in her hand, still rubbing him. This would be the first night that King got some from Zya, and he was more than ready. That was the main reason he let her tag along with him on a brief business trip to Baltimore.

King opened the door and walked into the room.

He put the duffle bag full of re-up money under the bed as Zya closed the door. King rushed over to Zya and picked her up off her feet, holding her up by her ass. They passionately kissed and made their way to the bed.

King laid her down and took off his shirt. He then removed the pistol he kept on his waist and put it under the bed. He forcefully ripped off Zya's shirt and bra, exposing her big, brown nipples. He put one of her breasts in his mouth and began playing with her nipple with his tongue.

Ooh shit, Zya thought as she palmed the back of his head, looking down at him tickling her nipple.

Zya pushed him off of her and stood up. She did a striptease for King. She slowly dropped to the floor and quickly came back up, showing how she could work her body. Then she slowly slid her panties from under her skirt. Zya, without losing eye contact with King, walked over to the chair backwards and sat down. She opened her legs, and placed one of them on the desk, exposing her neatly trimmed vagina.

"Come here, daddy," she said as she slowly began to rub her clitoris. King quickly stepped out of his pants and walked over to her. He dropped to his knees, preparing to go to work. He was about to show her how Harlem niggas got down.

Zya sat in the desk chair with her legs spread open. She rested her hands on King's neatly waved head and guided him as he pleased her. She slowly moved her mid-section in circles as she grinded against his face. She threw her head back in pleasure as her eyes rolled in the back of her head.

"Just like that, daddy," she whispered, instructing him how to satisfy her.

Just as Zya looked back down at King, she noticed a figure in her peripheral view. A well-built, brown-skinned man crept through the door. He carried a chrome pistol in his right hand and a pair of hand-cuffs in the other. Zya locked eyes with the young thug, but remained silent. As King pleased her, she stared deep into the intruder's eyes, wishing that it was him she was with.

The sound of a gun being cocked startled King, and he immediately looked back at the man pointing a gun to his head. "What the fuck, yo?" King screamed as Zya's juices dripped off his mustache.

"Put your clothes on and get the fuck out," the intruder yelled to Zya. She nodded her head and ran over to the bed to get dressed. King shook his head from side to side, instantly regretting taking one of his hoes on a business trip with him. He knew the two did not mix; while his head was buried in some broad's lap, somebody had been creeping up on him. Zya was a distraction, and he had gotten caught slip-ping.

"Fuck," he whispered as he realized the serious-ness of the situation. King threw both of his hands up and waited for the intruder to speak.

"Yo, where the dough at?" the intruder said calmly as he aimed his gun at King.

"I don't know what you talking 'bout, son."

The man laughed then struck King across the face with his pistol.

"Aghh! Fuck!" King yelled out in excruciating pain as he put his hand over his face. Blood leaked be-tween his fingers and he rocked back and forth on the ground, waiting for the pain to subside.

Without raising his voice, the intruder calmly repeated himself. "Where the dough at?"

"It's in my bag, under the bed," King admitted as he threw his head in the direction of the bed.

"Grab it!"

King knew he had a chance to pop this nigga. He had put his gun underneath the bed with the cash. This was the opportunity he needed. Without even getting off his knees, he scuffled over to the bed. He reached underneath it and frantically began to search for his weapon. The only thing he felt were the money stacks. His hands scurried over the carpet, desperately searching for the pistol. *It ain't here.* Just as the thought formed in his head, he heard another gun cock. He turned around and found himself looking down the barrel of his own gun. Zya stood before him with one hand on her hip, pressing the gun against King's head.

"Looking for this?" Zya asked as a slight smirk formed on her face.

"You trick-ass bitch," King barked as he realized he had just been set up. Zya had begged King all week to let her join him on his business trip to Baltimore. King took this trip once a month and always went alone, except for this one time. He had $60,000 in cash in his bag to cop some bricks from his connect, Poppy, in Baltimore. Little did he know that Poppy would never see that cash. Jules and Zya already had plans for it.

Zya didn't like King's comment, so she struck him across the face with the pistol, causing blood to fly out of his mouth and onto Jules's shirt. Jules followed up by hitting him again in the back of his head.

"Damn, you fucked up my shirt," Jules said as he examined the bloodstain on his white tee. Jules grabbed King's hand and handcuffed it to the bed rails. He then grabbed the bag and headed for the door.

King looked at Zya with total hatred and whispered, "I'm going to find you, and when I do. . . ."

Zya stared King straight in the eyes and blew a kiss at him, before letting out a sexy chuckle. She walked over to him and straddled him. She brought her face close to his ear and whispered, "No, if you find me . . . I'm going to kill you."

King's body tensed up. He wanted so badly to hurt Zya, but he couldn't move. She climbed off of him and looked at his naked body and then focused on his pipe.

"Wit' yo' little-ass dick. What were you going to do wit' that li'l thing anyway? Huh?"

King was infuriated and watched helplessly as Zya and Jules exited the room with all his cash. King tried to get out of the handcuffs, but couldn't. His eyes got big when he noticed Jules walk back into the room with the pistol in his hand.

The two men stared into each other's eyes, but nothing was said. The only sound in the entire room was from King's erratic breathing as he tried to figure out what Jules was going to do to him. Jules pictured King pleasing Zya. The picture of King on his knees with his face smashed in between Zya's legs flashed through his mind, and jealousy overcame him. Jules slowly lifted his gun and fired two hollow tip bullets into King's skull, putting him to sleep forever.

No witnesses, no murder, he thought just before he exited the room.

10:13 P.M.

Detective Lonnie Wade had been sitting in his car, patiently waiting for two and half hours. The anticipation was building more and more as he watched the minutes pass. He was waiting for King, slouched low in his seat and parked in the hotel parking lot, positioned where he had a perfect view of the entrance.

One of Wade's sources tipped him off and told him King usually stayed at this hotel when he went to re-up in Baltimore. Wade even had the room number King was staying in. His source told him that he always went to the same suite. Now the only thing Wade had to do was to wait for King to make the swap then nab him on his way back to Harlem with the dope.

Wade had been on King for months, and he had a pure hatred for drug dealers. He looked at the empty coffee cups and the ashtray full of roaches from the weed that he had smoked over the hours. He believed that he did everything better when he was high. As he puffed on a newly lit blunt, the detective kept his eyes on the entrance, waiting for his target.

Where this nigga at? I hope I got some good information. Wade had been following King for two days, and King finally shook him earlier that morning. That night seemed to be just as futile, and when he didn't see any sign of him, he felt himself drifting into a light sleep. He grew tired and decided to call it a night.

"That's it for the night," he said to himself, as he reached for the keys and turned over the ignition. Just as he was about to pull off, a pearl-colored Porsche pulled up to the front entrance. Wade immediately hit his lights and grabbed his camera from the back seat. He zoomed in on the license plates and began to snap away. He noticed a beautiful woman step out of the passenger side of the car, followed by the driver, King. King tossed his keys to a valet and they entered the building. Wade took pictures of both of them entering the hotel. He zoomed in close on the woman and thought that she looked familiar.

"Damn, she's nice," he whispered to himself. Wade used the camera to zoom in on the woman's curves, and he took a couple of pictures of her ass for personal viewing later.

He quickly focused back on King. He decided to stay for a while longer to see if King was going to leave later that night. Wade wasn't sure if King would make the transaction that night or the next morning. He sat back and opened his glove compartment, pulling out a voice recorder. He pressed the RECORD button and started to talk into the mic.

"King entered the Marriott at 10:15 with a lady with sandy brown hair, five feet seven, and looks to be between the ages of eighteen and twenty-five."

10:45 P.M.

Thirty minutes had passed, and Wade patiently waited for King to leave, or at least turn off his lights. At that moment, he noticed that a car had crept up behind his car, and parked about 20 yards behind him. The driver hit the lights, but no one got out.

Wade stared out his window to see who it was, but he couldn't see through the tinted windows. *Who the fuck is this?* he thought as he lit another blunt and began to puff it.

He saw a man walk past his car, seemingly in a

hurry. The man was so close to Wade's car, it nearly startled him. "What the hell?" he said suspiciously as he picked up his camera so that he could zoom in on the window to King's room.

Wade felt the effects of the marijuana and knew that he was too high to function. He decided he wasn't about to wait any longer for King, and started up his car. *Five more minutes,* Wade thought as he stared at King's window.

10:51 *P.M.*

Wade noticed that the girl who had originally gone in the hotel with King was now walking out with another man. They were walking briskly and seemed to be arguing about something.

They must've made the switch already. But why is she leaving with him? I guess she was a part of the deal too, he thought as he chuckled to himself.

The man and the woman walked past Wade's car and didn't notice that he was snapping pictures of them. They seemed like they were in a hurry, and the man was carrying that same bag, but now you could tell it had something in it.

Wade couldn't make out the man's face. He had a hat pulled down real low, so he could barely make out what he looked like. They jumped in the car and pulled off. Wade stared at the car in his rearview mirror until they were no longer in sight. Wade let the small fish go to catch the big one—King.

Wade was high as a kite, and while waiting on King to come out, he nodded off.

✤   ✤   ✤

"Jules, I kind of feel bad. I mean . . . we could have just robbed him like we planned. You didn't have to shoot him," Zya said, staring at Jules as he swerved in and out of the freeway traffic.

"Zya, it's all in the game. You don't come across capers like this one every day. King was getting money in the streets, and you know money means power. He would have come back for us full force. I wasn't really trying to take that chance. We did what we had to do. You have to trust me on this one, ma. You trust me, right?"

"Yeah, you know I do, Jules, but we could have just left town . . . relocated. I just feel fucked up."

"And go where, Zya? Harlem is home. He would have eventually caught up with us, and that would be another problem. This way, we are scot free. I already have a warrant out for my arrest. With King on us, there would've been nowhere to hide. Just trust me on this one, okay. This is the payday we needed. Now I can cop a couple bricks from Snow and get back on my feet."

"Okay," Zya said as she closed her eyes, trying to forget what had just occurred. She had been playing King from the beginning, and she gained his trust just to set him up. Jules was the mastermind behind the plan and told her, "It's a chance for us to come up." Zya was down for her man, so she did it for him. But now, she not only carried a burden of guilt for deception, but for taking a man's life.

She tried desperately to make sense of the situation and justify what she had helped to do, but all she could visualize was King's lifeless body sprawled across the hotel's bed. *It's all in the game*, she thought as she leaned back in her chair and took a deep breath, attempting to calm her nerves. She distantly heard her favorite song coming out of the speakers. It was Biggie Smalls's song, "Me and My Bitch." It was also Zya's and Jules's theme song.

Zya looked over at Jules, and he glanced at her with a slight grin. "Turn that shit up," Zya said as she bobbed her head slowly to the sounds. Jules turned up the volume, and they bobbed their heads in unison.

Just as the song was ending, Jules remembered he had to make use of the money he just took from King.

"Oh yeah, I need you to take that trip to Jersey and get them bricks from Snow this weekend. You got me?"

"Don't I always? The world is ours, Jules."

"The world is ours."

Wade sat at his desk and prepared for his day at work. He opened his blinds to let the sun in, and strapped his gun in his holster. He sat at his desk, took a sip of his coffee, and picked up his newspaper. He flipped to the front page and read: METS WIN PENNANT. He wasn't a big baseball fan, so he flipped the page and began to look through the paper. He didn't see anything interesting, so he folded the newspaper and prepared to make his rounds through the city.

He stood up, preparing to leave his office when a man walked into the door. He was a black male who looked to be in his mid-fifties. His receding hairline made him look like a taller George Jefferson.

"Lieutenant Jefferson—I mean Lieutenant Jones," Wade said, acknowledging his boss.

The Lieutenant responded, "Good morning,

Wade. Did you happen to see the paper this morning?"

Wade smiled and answered, "Yeah, the Mets won."

The Lieutenant did not smile back. He reached for Wade's newspaper and said, "I think you better look a little closer." He pointed to the photo in the bottom right corner and Wade read the caption: HARLEM MAN FOUND SHOT DEAD IN A BALTIMORE HOTEL. SEE PAGE 5.

"King's dead?" he asked.

Lieutenant Jones answered, "Yep. They found his body last night. He had been dead for two days. We have no leads, and since it was in Baltimore, it's on the Baltimore police to handle that. Less work for us." Wade grew a dumb look on his face as the Lieutenant continued to talk. "Wade, weren't you on King's case?"

Wade hesitated to answer. He was too busy thinking about King's murder. *Damn, I was just tailing this mu'fucka a couple nights ago.*

"Wade!" The Lieutenant barked, snapping him out of his thoughts. "Weren't you on the King case?"

"Yeah, but I guess I don't have to worry about him anymore, right?"

Lieutenant Jones looked at Wade and replied, "I guess not. I guess that's one less killer on the streets. It makes our job easier. But I would have loved to see his face after a conviction. Too bad it ended like this."

Wade was in deep thought and quickly snapped out to agree with Lieutenant Jones. "Yeah, too bad."

On that note, the Lieutenant left the room and Wade walked over to his file cabinet and took out the pictures he had snapped of King the night he died. He took a close look at the woman in the pictures, and knew he saw her before somewhere, but he couldn't put his finger on it.

So, that's what the rush to get out the hotel was for. Y'all killed him and robbed his ass. Bitches are sheisty.

Wade wanted to tell his Lieutenant what he had witnessed the night of the murder, but he knew he needed a warrant, which he did not have, to put King under surveillance. Since the whole police station was already at odds with him, he kept quiet. In a way, Wade was kind of relieved King was dead. It was one less criminal on his list to take down.

The Lieutenant walked back into the room and Wade instantly put the pictures behind his back and looked at Lieutenant Jones.

"Want to go for doughnuts and coffee?" Jones asked.

"Nah, I'm cool. I'm going to catch up on some stuff."

Lieutenant Jones frowned his face and asked, "Wade, is everything okay?"

"Yeah, I'm good."

"All right," the Lieutenant responded and exited the room. Wade took a deep breath and exhaled. He stuck the pictures in his pocket and left his office.

As Wade made his rounds around the city in his unmarked car, he could not get his mind off of King's death. Lonnie Wade rode down the streets of New York and stopped on Trinity Avenue to talk to some of the old friends he had grown up with. Wade rolled down his car window and immediately received love from his childhood friends who stood on the corner trying to make their pay. He didn't agree with what they did, but they were trying to survive, and he understood that. He and his old friends had a mutual agreement. They let Wade know what was happening in the streets. In return, Wade let them know when they were getting hot and needed to lay low. He overlooked their wrongdoings to stay in tune with the streets. This helped Wade find out about incoming shipments and new faces on the scene that were making major moves.

"Yo, what up, kid?" one of the men on the corner yelled out as he and Wade showed each other love.

"What's good, Dill?" Wade replied. Dill looked inside the car, saw Lonnie's face, and threw his hand up to let them know it was cool.

Dill walked over to the car and said, "Jules left town and is coming back on Friday with a major shipment. I don't know how he getting them here. I just know it's coming on Friday. He talking big shit, like he's about to take over the streets with some new shit from Jersey. He fuckin' with Li'l Shay from around the way, and she can't keep her mouth closed. She said he got a spot over there on Lennox in some other chick's name."

Lonnie shook his head and replied, "Good, Good. I've been looking for Jules. He skipped bail a couple of months back. There is going to be a sweep today at four. I advise you to take a break today and lay low."

They both slapped hands and Lonnie Wade pulled off. *Damn, Harlem don't sleep. As soon as one drug dealer's gone, another one wants to takes his spot. Everybody wants to be king of New York. Now this nigga Jules is trying to flood the streets. It's not happening.*

✿ ✿ ✿

Zya sat on the Greyhound, listening to her Mary J. Blige CD, not paying attention to any particular thing. She was on her way back home from picking up some bricks of cocaine from Torey Snow, Jules's coke connect. She closed her eyes and slowly bobbed her head back and forth until she heard a distant voice addressing her and someone tapping her arm.

"Excuse me, miss . . . Excuse me!" a middle-aged white lady said with an aggravated tone. Zya slowly pulled down her headphones and looked at the lady like she was crazy.

"May I help you?" she said.

"Your music is extremely loud. Do you mind turning it down a bit?"

No, this bitch didn't, she thought as she plastered a forced grin on her face. It took all of Zya's willpower not to tell that old-ass lady about herself.

"Sorry about that. I'll turn it down a little," she said as she rolled her eyes and put back on the headphones. Zya was boiling, and knew the lady was uncomfortable sitting by her, because when she first boarded the bus and sat down, she turned up her nose. If this were any other time, Zya would have told her off, but the fact that she had ten kilos of cocaine in her duffle bag humbled her. She didn't want to draw any unwanted attention to herself. She turned down the music and looked out the window.

Zya noticed that the bus had reached New York's Port Authority bus station, and she was home safely. She took a deep breath and waited for the bus to stop. Zya had been taking these trips for Jules once a month, every first Saturday. She went to meet Jules's connect, Torey Snow, from Newark. He would be waiting for her in front of the station, where they would make the switch. He would drive around the block a couple of times then let her back out. It was always a quick procedure. Amir, who couldn't be any older than eighteen, usually picked her up once she got back to New York. He was a little nigga that Jules hired to transport Zya on occasions like this.

Zya was glad to be in New York, safe and sound. She stepped off the bus with a Bible in one hand and the bag in the other. Jules always made her wear "church lady" clothes and tote a Bible when making her runs to Jersey. He said she would be less likely to be selected for random searches. Zya hated her attire, but she knew Jules was right.

Zya entered the station and noticed it was emptier than usual. The bus had arrived a little earlier than expected, so she would have to wait a little before her ride would be there. She couldn't call Jules and tell him to send the whip, because Jules didn't allow her to call him while traveling. He was very paranoid and remained cautious of everything. He was wanted on a two-year-old drug trafficking charge, and was on the run. He avoided using cell phones. He said all cell phones were tapped.

Zya spotted a bench and walked over to it to have a seat. She took off her big church hat and wiped the sweat that had formed on her forehead. She looked around the station and noticed a uniformed police officer walking a hound dog through the station. She immediately grew nervous, and her first thought was to leave the bag and relocate, but they were headed in her direction. She didn't want to look suspicious, so she stayed put. She tried to look as casual as possible, but she had the shakes. She cracked open her Bible and pretended to read as the officer and the dog approached her.

Oh shit, oh shit. I'm caught. Okay, okay, stay calm, Zya. Damn, they're coming my way. Fuck it! I'm about to take off. A bitch ran track in high school. I got a chance.

The dog had his nose buried on the floor and was slowly approaching her duffle bag. "What you got boy?" the chubby redneck said as the dog led the police officer over to her. Just as Zya was about to take off, a loud voice came from a few feet behind her.

"Fuck that shit, man! This is some bullshit!" the man said as he banged on the glass where you purchased tickets. He continued to yell and make a scene. The police officer quickly focused his attention on the man, and put his hand over his gun. The man began to pound on the window forcefully, causing all eyes to be on him. The officer quickly went over to the man to try to calm him down, but the man continued to be confrontational.

"You mean to tell me y'all don't have any routes to Flint, Michigan? My mu'fuckin' brother's funeral is tomorrow! Y'all told me on the phone that I could buy a one-way straight to Flint."

Zya immediately recognized the man's face. It was Amir. He winked his eye at her in the midst of the chaos. As soon as the officer began speaking to an irate Amir, Zya got the hell out of dodge. She picked up her bag and took advantage of the distraction Amir had provided for her. Her heart raced as she hurried out of the station, hoping she wouldn't get caught.

She made it safely outside and began to walk briskly

toward the alley where Amir always parked. When she was finally safe inside his Blazer, she quickly began to take off her shirt and church hat. Just as she finished, she saw a couple of security guards throw Amir out of the station, nearly tossing him onto his ass. Amir continued to yell until they were out of sight.

"This bus station ain't shit. That's why I fucks with them trains. They know how to treat a brotha." When the coast was clear, Amir's frown turned into a smirk, and he ran up the street and jumped into the car. Amir started the car and drove away, his tires screeching as they got the hell out of dodge.

"I'm glad I came in to use the bathroom. That was perfect timing."

"Who you telling? I thought it was a wrap. Good thinking, Amir. I was just about to take off on his ass. Flow Jo wouldn't have had shit on me," Zya said with laughter in her voice as she leaned her seat back and took a breath of relief. "You could have won an Oscar for that little performance. You had them thinking you were about to nut up in there."

"The shit worked," Amir stated, shrugging his shoulders. He turned up the stereo and they both relaxed as they made their way back to home sweet home—Harlem.

Zya and Amir pulled onto her block and noticed all the police cars that had gathered. As they got closer, they realized that the police were in front of Zya's spot.

"What the hell is going on?" she asked as she sat up in her seat and looked at the chaos that was happening at her place. Men wearing NYPD jackets were moving shoeboxes out of the house, and she knew that's where Jules kept all his cash. Then she saw Jules getting escorted out in handcuffs. He still had a blunt hanging out of his mouth as they pulled him out the house.

Amir looked closely at the situation and lightly mumbled, "Damn, Jules," as he realized that the law had finally caught up with him. Zya's heart dropped, and she was in total shock. Zya locked eyes with Jules as Amir maneuvered the car slowly past the scene. Zya's eyes began to water as she saw the police carry her man off in cuffs. She wanted to get out and do something, but she was stuck. She had ten bricks of cocaine in the car.

Zya felt as if someone had just shot a dart straight through her heart as she leaned back in the chair and whispered, "Pull off, Amir."

Look at this pot-belly redneck. I've been waiting here for thirty minutes, and he still hasn't told me what Jules's bond is. Look at him, smirking and shit.

"Excuse me, sir. I've been waiting for you to look up my boyfriend's information for about—"

"He was shipped to Riker's Island this morning. You can take it up with them, but the way his rap sheet is looking, he's not getting out for a while," the chubby officer said with pleasure.

Ain't this 'bout a bitch? He knew all along that Jules wasn't even here. I hate pigs. This is some bull-shit.

"Thank you for nothing," Zya said as she stormed out of the precinct.

What am I supposed to do? I can't go back to the house that Jules got caught in. I have nowhere to go. I

*am going to have to see if I can crash at Vita's spot for
a while. Damn!*

Zya stormed to the curb to flag down a cab and
suddenly became nauseous. She felt a hot flash, and
before she knew it, she was on the ground throwing
up her breakfast. "Oh God," she whispered as she
gasped for air.

After a couple of minutes, she gathered herself
and stood up. *What the hell is wrong with me?* She
managed to hail a cab, and flopped in the back seat.
She told the driver where her best friend, Vita, lived,
and closed her eyes, trying to ease the pain. She
needed to go see Jules as soon as possible.

Chapter 2

Dilemma

Zya waited nervously as she sat in the waiting area. Her stomach was doing somersaults for more than one reason. Jules had only been locked up for a couple days, and her world had been turned upside down without him. She didn't know how long he was supposed to be locked down, and she didn't know how he would feel about her pregnancy.

She looked around the waiting room, and it seemed like every woman in there shared the same story. Everybody seemed to be carrying nine months of baby weight with them. They were all doing the same routine, visiting a baby daddy that was locked up.

Zya could feel the tears building in her eyes as she thought about her own circumstance. She loved Jules, there was no doubt about that. She had done things for him that she would not do for any other, but there was something in the back of her mind that was causing her to have doubts. She didn't want to raise a child without a father. She knew that it would be too hard, and she didn't know if she could do it on her own. She knew the type of man that Jules was, and he was a stand-up type of nigga, but if he did serious time, it would be out of his power. He would have no choice but to be absent from his baby's life.

She also didn't know if she would be able to take care of a child. Jules hadn't been locked up a week, and she was already out on her ass. At nineteen, she had seen plenty of money go through her hands. Jules always kept her with fat pockets. It wasn't uncommon for her to blow a couple thousand on just clothes, and she never once thought about putting any up for a rainy day. She hadn't saved anything because she always thought that the money would come just as fast as she spent it.

I can't even take care of myself. How am I supposed to support a baby on my own?

Zya was consumed by her thoughts of motherhood. She was in love with Jules almost since the first day she met him three years ago, but she was overwhelmed by everything that was happening. She knew that she could stick by him and ride with him during a prison sentence, but she also knew that it would be ten times harder to do with a baby to worry about. Under normal circumstances, it would have been something to celebrate, but with Jules in jail, it felt more like a burden.

"Zya Miller!" the guard yelled, interrupting her train of thought. Anxiety overcame her as she rose slowly from her seat. Her heartbeat quickened, and she had to take a deep breath to calm down.

Will he be happy? What is he going to say? she thought as she walked into the visiting room. She saw Jules sitting in a burnt orange jumpsuit, and she approached him. He smiled when he saw her, and the sight of him put her mind at ease.

I don't even know why I was tripping, Jules is gon' make sure me and our baby is taken care of, she told herself as she sat down.

"Are you okay?" she asked him as soon she picked up the phone.

"Yeah, I'm good now that I see you. Are you okay? Where you staying?" he replied. He knew that Zya would not be dumb enough to go back to her house. He was just glad that she had not been inside when the raid took place. Everything was in her name, though, and once the police realized it, they would be looking for her.

"I'm staying at Vita's," she replied skeptically, knowing that Jules wouldn't be too fond of that idea. Vita lived with her boyfriend, Heavy, and they always had niggas running in and out of their crib. Zya didn't really want to stay there either, but she couldn't be choosy. She had to rest her head wherever she could . . . at least for the time being.

"Too many niggas be through her spot. You know I don't play that shit," Jules said. He was noticeably steamed.

"Baby, it ain't even like that," she argued, trying to reassure Jules.

"No! Fuck that, Zya. Call my li'l nigga, Amir. He'll put you up for a minute," Jules stated.

"Jules, that boy is still staying at home with his mama. He ain't got shit, especially not a room to be offering me," Zya stated.

"Check into a hotel then," Jules replied adamantly.

Zya knew that Jules was hot. He had a jealous streak a mile long, and had been known to smack a couple niggas around who had looked at Zya a second too long. That was one of the reasons why she loved him so much, though. He wanted her all to himself.

"I don't have any money, Jules. I'm broke. I'm not trying to argue with you about this. That should be the last thing on your mind. I love you and I'm wit' you, so let's leave it at that. It's only temporary, anyway, so why trip? It ain't like I love staying with Vita either, but we gon' have to deal with it for now, at least until you get out."

Zya looked at Jules with sincerity, deep sincerity, and saw his anger begin to fade away. The look in his eyes made her feel better about what she was about to tell him. He loved her, and she knew that he did. There was no way he would leave her and his seed on stuck.

"I love you, Jules," she said as she placed her delicate fingers against the cold glass.

Jules put his hand on the glass and took a deep breath before saying, "I love you, too, Zya."

Zya opened her mouth, but no words came out. She looked at her hand pressed against the glass. *I can't even touch him,* she thought sadly. She inhaled deeply then said, "I'm pregnant."

Jules's eyes shot wide open and his head dropped to his chest. He took his hand back from the glass and gripped the edge of the metal table. Zya's heart dropped as she watched the disappointment fill his face, and a hollow feeling formed in her stomach. His actions spoke louder than any words could ever do, and she instantly felt hurt. After all they had been through, she expected more from him.

"You don't have nothing to say?" Zya asked in disbelief. Her voice was shaky from trying to conceal the many emotions she was feeling.

Jules shook his head from side to side as if he was in disbelief. He looked up at her and said, "I got five to nine years, Zya."

Zya dropped the phone, and it collided with the metal table, causing a loud bang to echo through the room. She couldn't believe what she had just heard. It was almost as if her brain refused to process the words. *I've got five to nine years.* The words replayed over and over in her head, and she couldn't stop the silent tears from falling down her face.

What am I going to do? she asked herself. She picked up the phone, but was speechless.

The look on Zya's face made Jules's heart weak. He loved Zya. She was the one woman who was down for him through whatever, and he knew that she felt deeply for him. He was happy that she was pregnant. He knew that there was not a better woman to carry his seed, but he also knew that she needed him to be with her.

"What do you mean? You haven't even been to court yet," Zya said when she finally found her voice. "What about the trial?"

"There's not going to be a trial, Zy. I had an active warrant pending, and they had enough evidence to sentence me to twenty-five years. Me skipping bail only made things worse, so my options were limited. The prosecution offered me a deal to avoid all that. I had to take the five to nine," he said, sounding as if he was trying to convince himself more than Zya.

"Couldn't you have won the trial?" Zya asked, refusing to believe that there was no other way out.

"Zya, I done already been through all that with my lawyers. There's no way around it."

Zya lowered her head, and the salty tears cascaded from her face onto the table.

"There's no way I can take care of this baby by myself. I can't even take care of me. I'm getting an abortion," she said, almost whispering the last couple words.

"No in the hell you ain't! You not about to kill my seed. I love you, Zya, and I'ma be there for you and my child when I get out. That would kill me, Zya. You got to give me something to come home to."

Zya nodded her head as she listened to his words, but the tears wouldn't stop.

"What you gon' do is get on your hustle, and you got nine months to do it," he said sternly. Jules was insistent on getting his point across to the woman sitting across from him. There was no way he was letting her get rid of his child. Even if he wasn't there to support them physically, he would make sure that he gave her the means to support herself. He would supply her with the knowledge she needed to get money while he was away. It would not only benefit her financially, but would keep his spot in the streets on hold while he was away.

"Zya, you gon' have to take care of things while I'm in here. We got a baby on the way, and I need you to be strong. You got to hustle to eat . . . and I got some old debts I need to settle with my lawyers, so you got to hold me down. You understand?" he asked her.

Zya nodded and wiped her eyes. "I understand."

"You still holding that?" he asked her.

"Yeah, I got 'em," she replied, knowing he was referring to the ten kilos of cocaine she had picked up from Torey Snow.

"Time's up!" the prison guard announced as he opened the door to the visiting room.

Zya looked at Jules and asked, "What do you want me to do?"

He knew he didn't have time to explain it to her. They had wasted too much time on other things. He stood up and said, "Wait for my letter."

Zya nodded her head and replied, "I'll be back next Monday."

"No!" Jules yelled out loud. Zya frowned her face, but before she could ask him why, he said, "Come every other Monday. I don't want you to become a familiar face around here."

Zya watched as a guard came and escorted Jules out of the room. He was pulled away so fast that she didn't even get the chance to say "I love you." She got up and walked out of the prison.

By the time Zya arrived at Vita's house, it was dark outside and the street was lined with cars. There was a dice game going down on the front stoop, and Zya already knew what was up. Zya could see that Vita's brownstone was packed on the inside, and she hesitantly made her way into the house. She didn't feel like being around a lot of people, and she definitely didn't want the word getting back to Jules that she was at a house party.

She made her way into the tiny room where she slept, and checked to make sure her goods were exactly where she had left them. She pulled out the duffel bag and began to pull out the bricks, counting each one to make sure that nobody in the house had been in her shit.

I can't afford to take an L right now, she thought as she sighed a breath of relief once she realized that nothing had been touched. The door opened and a Latino girl came bursting into the room with a drink in her hand. The cocaine wrapped in clear plastic was spread out on the bed, and the girl's mouth fell wide open when she saw it.

"Damn, bitch, can you knock?" Zya asked harshly as she got up, preparing to get in her ass. She stopped when she saw the dark-skinned dude enter the room after her. Snow stood behind her with a Heineken in his hand, and when he saw the dope on the bed, he leaned over and whispered in the girl's ear, "Let me handle something real fast, mama." There was an awkward silence in the room. The girl looked at Zya with venom in her eyes and rolled them hard, but didn't attempt to leave.

"Bitch, don't get it fucked up," Zya warned as the Latino girl sped up her step and exited the room.

Snow closed the door and said, "Chill out, li'l ma. What the fuck you doing here in this hot-ass trap house with my dope?" He stared down at her with his gray eyes and spoke with a lazy drawl. His skin was chocolate, and his eyes pierced through Zya as if he had known her all his life. Before she could even respond, he asked her, "What's wrong? Where Jules at?"

Zya didn't think it was smart to be broadcasting Jules's arrest, so she replied, "He's out of town. I'm handling his business in Harlem while he's away." Snow was tipsy, and she could tell by the slant of his eyes, so she didn't doubt that he was buying the excuse.

"It don't look like you handling it too well. You up in this mu'fucka with ten kilos of snow on you," he said as he took another sip of his drink.

"As long as you get paid, you shouldn't have no problems with how I conduct mines," Zya replied smartly, with one hand planted on her hip.

He looked her up and down then licked his lips. He stepped closer to her and leaned over to whisper in her ear. "If you were my bitch, I wouldn't have you out here making my money. I'd have you out here spending it."

Zya looked up at him, and for a second, her eyes were stuck on his. The door opened, and the Latino girl appeared with her hand on her hip. She cleared her throat loudly. Snow turned around, and Zya mugged the girl that was standing in her doorway. *Bitch, don't nobody want your man,* she thought. She smiled slyly then grabbed Snow's hand. She pulled his tall frame down to her and whispered in his ear.

"First of all, I'm not anybody's bitch. I'm his woman, and I ride for mines. I'll leave the gold-diggin' up to your little girlfriend," she said. She kept her eyes on the girl waiting by the door, knowing that she thought the conversation was more than what it was.

"Papi!" the girl called out, growing irritated as she watched Zya work her man.

Snow backed away from Zya, and couldn't take his eyes off her as he made his way to the door. She smiled then closed the door behind him.

Zya put the kilos away and made sure they were hidden underneath the bed. She lay down on the bed and tried to block out the music that was playing throughout the house. Vita had Yung Joc bumping extra loud, and Zya grew frustrated quickly. She couldn't even think straight. The rowdy atmosphere was not healthy for her or her baby, and all she wanted to do was get out of the house. Knowing that she had nowhere to go, she went to sleep.

After tossing and turning all night, Zya woke up to the smell of food. She walked downstairs and went into the kitchen, where she found Vita's boyfriend, Heavy, cooking breakfast. The house was clean and showed no signs that a party had just taken place the night before.

"What up, Zy!" Heavy yelled out, shouting for no damn reason. Zya had to laugh, though. Heavy was cool like that. He was one of them loud, rowdy Southern dudes who just didn't give a fuck.

"What up, Heavy?" Zya said as she sat at the bar-style counter. "Where Vita at?" she asked.

"She went to get her toes wrapped or some shit," he replied as he took the salt down from the cabinet and put way too much in the potatoes he was cooking.

"Her toes wrapped? You mean she went to get her hair wrapped?" Zya asked.

Heavy waved the spatula in the air and replied, "Yeah, she went to the salon to get her shit hooked up. Hair, toes, all that good shit."

Zya laughed at Heavy. *This nigga in here thinking he G. Garvin,* she thought as she smiled to herself and shook her head.

"Yo, Zya, I hear you got them thangs on you," Heavy said. Zya tensed up, knowing exactly what he was talking about. She knew that Snow would not have put her business out like that, so she knew the loud-mouth Latino girl had told someone what she saw.

"Nah, you know I don't get down like that," Zya

commented nonchalantly, trying to make Heavy think he had heard wrong. Heavy was cool, but she knew that he was like every other nigga in Harlem; he had his own agenda. He was a small player in the dope game. He was still hustling rocks, but she knew that he had been trying to get his hands on weight.

He barking up the wrong mu'fucking tree, cuz I ain't got shit for his ass. She knew that she would have to find her own place real quick because she didn't trust Heavy as far as she could throw him, and she couldn't throw his fat ass far at all.

"Oh, you know I'm just asking. If you are rolling like that, I know somebody that want some." His country accent made his offer sound friendly, but country or not, Zya could see through the bullshit. Heavy didn't know anybody worth dealing with. He was inquiring for himself.

"Nah, I don't know what you talking about. You know I don't get into all that. I don't make the money, I just spend it," she said, repeating what Snow had said to her the night before. She got up and went back into her borrowed room.

That nigga is asking too many questions. I should find that girl and beat the brakes off her ass for telling everybody my business. Damn! I was not trying to be out here like this. I'ma sitting duck cuz if niggas even think I got these bricks, I'm gon' become a target. Zya knew the game. She had helped set dudes up, so she knew when a situation had the potential to become trouble, and her current situation was not good.

Zya tried to stay low-key as she waited for Jules's letter to arrive. For three days, she anxiously awaited the letter's arrival. She was waiting for Jules's instructions on what to do with the dope, but her patience was wearing thin. She was dead broke and tired of depending on Vita for a place to stay.

"Jules was supposed to write me a couple days ago," Zya said as she sat on the front stoop waiting for the mailman to arrive. She had timed his route down to the second, and knew that he should be arriving any minute.

"Why are you tripping on his letter? You've been running around bugging out ever since you visited him. What's so important about it?" Vita asked suspiciously. Zya hadn't told Vita about the dope she had been left with. Vita was her best friend, but she had seen Vita pull some grimy shit on other chicks, and Zya didn't trust her with a big secret. Vita couldn't hold water and would have her business all over Harlem by nightfall.

"There's nothing important about it. He just promised he would write and he hasn't," Zya said in an agitated tone.

"I don't know why you riding with this nigga anyway. If I was you, I would leave his ass stanking and move on to the next nigga. Hustlers come a dime a dozen in New York," Vita said as she crossed her legs and hit the edge of her cigarette to dump her ashes.

"Whatever, Vita. I didn't ask you for all that. I ain't one of these gold-diggin'-ass bitches. You know I ain't got it in me to be grimy. I was with him when he was out and doing good, so now that he's down and out, I can't be fake. I'ma do the bid with him," Zya said defensively.

"You and every other chick," Vita said smartly.

Zya looked at Vita like she was crazy and replied, "Fuck is that supposed to mean?"

"Nothing, Zya . . . I'm just saying . . . Look, you know you're my girl. I don't want to see you out here stressing over a nigga. I'm just asking you if Jules is worth you giving up damn near ten years of your life."

I'm carrying his baby. I'll wait for however long it takes, Zya thought. She hadn't told her best friend about the baby yet, which is why Vita was so quick to tell Zya to leave Jules alone.

She doesn't understand what I'm going through. She doesn't have a baby to think about, Zya thought, growing angry. Vita was her girl and everything, but there was a limit on the amount of time that they could spend together before Vita got on her nerves. With Zya staying there for the past three nights, she had far exceeded that limit.

They had known each other since middle school and were almost like sisters. They were bittersweet because they fought and made up all the time, just like they were really related. At the end of the day, they always had each other's back.

Jules needs to come through like he said he would. She touched her stomach and felt the morning sickness creep up on her. She still hadn't been to the doctor. She had been so worried about hearing from Jules that it had slipped her mind.

"You'll be all right, Zy. That nigga will be out before you know it," Vita said as she puffed on a Newport, trying to be supportive. The mailman came walking down the street, and he looked down at Zya with a curious look on his face. His route was an early one, and he had seen her sitting, waiting on him, for the past four days.

"Do you have anything for Zya Miller?" she asked him as he stepped up the steps to Vita's house. Zya shifted her weight from side to side as she waited impatiently for the mailman to check. He sifted slowly through the mail until he finally handed her an envelope.

Vita put out her cigarette against the step and stood up. "I'll give you some privacy, Zy," she offered as she got up and walked inside.

A sense of relief washed over Zya, and her hands trembled as she ripped opened the letter.

Zya,

I hope that you are maintaining while I'm in here. I'm sorry you have to carry this on your own. You and my unborn baby mean everything to me. I am going to take care of you when I get out, but I need you to hold me down while I'm in here. I know you feeling it right now cuz all the money I had was in the house during the raid. That shit is state's evidence now. You gotta charge that to the game and start over.

Remember the day I got caught? When I sent you to get them Bibles from that store in Jersey? That's how you going to have to eat until I get out. Those Bibles that you were bringing back are golden right now.

Remember my man Smitty? He's an older cat from Brooklyn. You need to get in contact with him. He's not going to trust you because he is used to dealing with me. We have a phrase that we say. Once you say it, he'll know you're okay. When you call him, say "All work and no play." He will finish the sentence.

*He usually buys two Bibles from me every
month. That's a guaranteed sell. They go for 16,
but I got them on consignment, so you take 12 dollars from every joint and deliver it back to Snow.
That mu'fucka don't bullshit about his money, Zya.
He a mu'fuckin' killer for real, so don't try to pull
no slick shit. You make sure his money is right
every time.*

*You keep 4 dollars from every Bible. You've got
ten of 'em, so that means by the time you sell them
all and pay the connect back, you'll have 40 dollars. That should hold you over for a minute. Use
the money wisely, because that's all you are going
to have to get by.*

*Get out of that nigga Heavy's crib ASAP, and
take care of my shorty. I'll see you next Monday.*

*Julius "Jules" Carter
P.S. Smitty's # 718-886-5419*

Zya folded the letter and knew that Jules was using
"Bibles" as a code word for the kilos of cocaine. She
knew that it was a strong possibility they were monitoring his mail, and Jules took precautions. She also
knew that when he said dollars, he was talking in the
thousands.

She pulled out her cell phone and felt the butterflies in her stomach as she called the number. She
didn't have any time to waste. She needed to sell the
bricks so that she could have some money in her
pocket.

"Hello?"

"Can I speak to Smitty?" she asked nervously.

"Speaking. Who is this?"

"My name is Zya. I'm calling to conduct the business you have with Jules," she said.

"I don't talk to nobody but Jules," the voice on the other end said calmly. Zya heard a click and then the sound of the dial tone. She quickly redialed the number.

As soon as he picked up the phone, she said, "All work and no play . . ."

"Make a dull day," the voice on the other end replied. "Meet me at Junior's in Brooklyn in an hour," the voice announced then hung up on her again.

Zya made her way back into Vita's to pick up the duffel bag full of cocaine. She hoped that Smitty would take all of it off her hands, but she knew that he would only buy two. Jules had made that clear in his letter, but at least it would put a little money in her pocket.

Inside the house, she was surprised to see Heavy standing in her room, looking through her duffel bag. "What the fuck you doing in my room?" she asked as she stormed past him and grabbed the bag out of his hands.

"This is my house. I can come into any room I want to. I thought you didn't get down like that," he said as he eyed the black bag that Zya held in her hand.

"I don't. I'm just holding it for a friend," she replied. "Anyway, it doesn't matter. Don't touch my shit."

He grabbed her by the upper arm and jerked her roughly, causing her to drop the bag and wince in pain. "Look, bitch. I'm letting you stay here because you cool with Vita, but you ain't even paying no rent. I don't charge you to eat the food in *my* refrigerator or to rest your head in *my* house. You can't look out for ya boy?" he asked her in a threatening way.

Zya snatched her arm back and replied, "Look, Heavy, I appreciate that, and when I get some money, I'm gon' hit you and Vita off, but this shit ain't mine."

"You full of shit, Zya. That little Latino chick told me you was holding the bricks." His grasp tightened around her arm.

"Let me go. Nigga, I ain't Vita. You not about to be—" Before Zya could even finish her sentence, Heavy pushed her hard against the wall.

"What!" He yelled as he cocked his hand back and brought it down hard across her face.

"Vita!" Zya called out in pain.

"Vita ain't gon' save you," Heavy said. He mashed his sloppy body against hers and began to touch on her breasts. She knew that Heavy was no good, but she would never expect him to pull no shit like this. She closed her eyes as she felt the tears build up. He grinded against her as he kissed on her neck, and she felt his dick get hard. She felt the tears threatening to fall, but she refused to submit to Heavy's trifling ass.

"You ain't shit, Heavy. You gon' rape me in the house that you share with my best friend? You gon' play Vita like that?" Zya asked in disgust. Her words must have killed the mood for Heavy because he backed up off her and stormed out of the room.

Zya slid down the wall and held her stomach as she thought about what had almost just occurred. *I have to get out of here*, she thought as she finally wiped her tears away. *I have to get this money so that I can leave.* Her face hurt badly in the spot where Heavy had struck her, and she knew that it would be red. She got up and looked into the mirror. Her face was swollen slightly. If Jules wasn't locked up, she would have gone straight to him and told him what had happened, but there was nothing he could do for her now. She fixed herself up as best she could, grabbed the black duffel bag and exited the room. As she walked past Vita's bedroom, Heavy stood like a statue in the door, mugging Zya as she stormed past.

"Bitch, have your shit out by tomorrow!"

On her way out the door, she bumped past Vita.

"Hey, Zy, where you going?" Vita called after her.

Zya didn't reply. She had already decided that she would not stay another night in Vita's house. She loved her best friend, but her man was foul. She wasn't going to tell Vita about what happened because she knew that it wouldn't change anything. Heavy would just lie about it, and the situation would come between their friendship. Zya walked out of the house and took the subway to Brooklyn.

Zya walked into the crowded restaurant and looked around for Smitty. She had no idea what he looked like, and it was hard for her to spot anybody out of the huge crowd.

"What's good with you, mama?"

"You looking for somebody?"

"Damn, where you going?"

All types of dudes tried to spit game at her as she walked through the restaurant. Even with her face red and swollen, niggas were still trying to get at her. Zya ignored the lines as she spotted an older man in a turtleneck and jeans sitting in the back. She made her way over to him with the duffel bag hanging off her arm.

"Sit down," he said to her calmly once she finally reached his table. She sat down and looked around nervously. She didn't know what to expect, and she kept fidgeting. She looked hot, and Smitty sat back and watched.

"Calm down," he finally instructed. "Are you hungry?" Zya nodded her head and they ordered something to eat.

"I have your stuff," Zya said.

"Where is Jules?" he asked her. She gave him the same answer that she had given Snow, and he seemed to buy it because he didn't ask any more questions.

"What is your name?"

"Zya," she replied.

"How much do you have on you?" he asked her.

"Ten," she replied.

"I'll take them all," he said. Zya hadn't been expecting this because she thought that he only purchased two at a time. She wasn't about to argue, though. She had just come into $40,000.

"Okay, Zya, this is how this is going to go. You are going to leave the bag in your seat when you get up and leave the restaurant. It's simple and easy. Don't look back, and don't be nervous. This is just a simple meal between two friends, okay?"

Zya nodded her head in understanding. She liked Smitty. He could tell it was her first time, and he made it easy for her. They ate their food casually, and when it was over, they both got up to leave. Zya did as she was told and left the bag in the seat, and he simply picked it up and followed behind her as they exited the restaurant.

"Follow me to my car," he said. She did as she was told. He popped his trunk and pulled out a present box that was wrapped in birthday paper and had a huge bow tied around it. Zya's eyes got big. She didn't

have a clue what was going on, but she took the box
from him.

"Open it," he said nicely.

She untied the bow and ripped off the paper.
When she opened the box, she found a multi-colored
Doonie & Bourke bag. She smiled at the designer
shoulder bag and looked up at Smitty in confusion.
He smiled back and said, "Happy birthday." His voice
was loud and he stepped closer to her and embraced
her in a hug.

Once his mouth was near her ear, he whispered,
"This little show is just in case somebody is watching.
The money is inside plus a little extra. Tell Jules if he
lowers his prices then there's a lot more where that
came from."

Zya decided to make the trip to Jersey that same
night. She was walking around New York with over
$150,000 in her bag, and she wasn't trying to get
robbed. She made her way to the Port Authority and
got on the departing route to Jersey. It was 11:30 at
night, and she was tired, but she wanted to tie up the
loose ends. She arrived in Newark an hour and a half
later. She picked up her phone and dialed Snow's
number.

"Hello?" he answered on the first ring.

"This is Zya," she said as she stood in front of the
bus station, clutching the designer bag.

"Who?" he asked.

"I work for Jules. I got your money," she said. "I'm
in Jersey."

"Come through," he replied.

❁   ❁   ❁

Snow hung up the phone in confusion. He looked at his diamond bezel Cellini Rolex and saw that it was close to 1:00 A.M. *What the fuck is she doing making a trip to Jersey this late?* He began to get suspicious because Zya's visit was not planned. He had just given Jules the bricks a week earlier. It usually took him a month to move ten kilos. It had only taken Zya seven days. The situation seemed odd to Snow, and he hoped that he wasn't being set up.

He remembered Zya from the party he had attended a couple days ago. *She still had all of the bricks four nights ago. How the hell she get rid of ten kilos in four days?* he thought. He knew that something had to be up. He had done business with Jules for two years, and he had never switched up his operation. His pattern was always the same. He always sent the girl to pick up the package and deliver the money. The times, the places, the locations . . . everything was always predictable with Jules. Now things had changed. He hadn't heard from Jules, and Zya was telling him that she was handling things for a while. Snow didn't know what was going on, but he hoped that he wasn't getting himself into some bullshit.

He waited for Zya to arrive, and when he heard the cab pull up to his house, he grabbed his pistol and tucked it safely in between his couch cushions for easy access. Most niggas don't feel the need to be strapped in the presence of a woman, but Snow wasn't a sucker for a pretty face. He knew that women could be just as deadly. The biggest drug lord New Jersey had ever seen had been a woman, and he wasn't go-

ing to underestimate the one who was getting ready
to step foot inside his house.

Zya rang the doorbell and waited for Snow to open
the door. He answered in a pair of baggy plaid pajama
pants and a white wifebeater. His tattooed arms were
chiseled almost perfectly, and he stood tall in the
doorway, looking down at Zya.

"Come in," he said as he stepped out of her way
and watched her walk into the house. He looked at
her ass as she walked by and admired her perfect pro-
portions.

"Here's your cash. I haven't taken my cut out yet,"
she said. She pulled the stacks of money out of the
Dooney & Bourke and watched as he put the cash
through a money machine and counted it.

"This had to be handled tonight?" he asked her.
He looked at the side of her face and noticed that it
was swollen.

"Yeah . . . I didn't want to carry around this much
money until morning," she said.

He continued to stare at her. He couldn't help
himself. Her beauty was almost hypnotizing.

They sat in silence as the money machine did its
job, counting stack after stack of bills. Zya looked
around Snow's crib and noticed how nice it was. It
wasn't a mansion or anything, but the nigga was definitely living good.

"What's your name?" Snow asked her out of the
blue.

"Zya," she responded. She had been picking up
dope and dropping off money to him on behalf of
Jules for a while, and she couldn't believe he didn't
even know her name.

"Zya, about the other night . . . I didn't mean no disrespect. I was feeling it, and—"

Zya waved her hand and said, "It's not a big deal. I wasn't offended or nothing. Your little girlfriend did more damage than you did."

"That ain't my girlfriend. What damage?"

"Nothing. It ain't your problem. She just ran her mouth about what she saw. A nigga saw an opportunity and tried to take advantage," she explained.

"That's what happened to your face?" he asked her in a sincere tone. She nodded her head. Snow got up from the kitchen table and put some ice in a Ziploc bag. He then handed it to Zya. "Put that on your face."

She took the ice and smiled. "Thanks."

"Can I ask you something?" Snow inquired as he loaded another stack of bills in the machine.

Zya nodded and he continued. "Why your man got you out here risking your freedom doing his dirty work?"

Zya shot him a look that told him not to go there. "I do what I have to do," she said as she stood up.

Snow stared at the feisty woman that stood before him. He was mesmerized by her swagger. She was feminine, but in so many ways, she was a gangster.

The money machine stopped, and Zya took her cut then made her way to the door. He watched as her sexy walk commanded his attention. She was fine as hell, almost perfect in every way. She was gorgeous, classy, and loyal to her nigga. He wanted her on his team. Before she walked out the door, Snow said, "It's late. You need a ride?"

"If I were a man, would you be asking me that?"

Snow smiled and shook his head. Her attitude was intriguing.

Zya stared at his gray eyes and dropped her defenses. She looked at her phone. *It's almost three in the morning, and I don't feel like waiting for a cab.*

She looked at him and said, "Yeah, I would appreciate that."

He grabbed the keys to his silver Aston Martin and drove her back to New York.

"Just to let you know, I'm fucking your girl up when I see her," Zya said as they drove across the Manhattan Bridge.

"Go for what you know. That ain't my bitch," he replied as he did 95 miles per hour, enjoying the feel of his sports car. "Just make sure she don't leave you lumped up like ol' boy did you," he said in a joking way.

Zya hit him hard on the arm and replied, "That shit ain't funny."

"Where am I taking you?" he asked.

"You can just drop me off at the same house the party was at the other night. I got to pick up my things. I'll take a cab to a hotel."

"That's where you staying at? A hotel?" Snow quizzed.

"You ask a lot of questions," Zya said, trying to avoid answering them.

"I'll take you to get your clothes and drop you off wherever you need to go. I think I need a room for the night too. You got me out here at five in the morning."

They drove the rest of the way in silence. Zya leaned back and went to sleep, and Snow couldn't help but to glance at her every once in a while.

They arrived at Vita's house, and Zya used the key that Vita had given her to enter the house. Snow waited at the front door while Zya went upstairs to get her things. She packed up all her belongings then made her way down the stairs. She tried her best to be quiet, but her movement still woke Vita.

Vita came down the stairs. "Zya!" she whispered. Vita turned on the living room light and saw Snow standing behind Zya. She looked at Zya's bags and said, "You leaving?"

Zya figured that Heavy hadn't told her what happened. She replied, "Yeah, girl, I'm out."

"What happened to your face?" Vita asked.

Zya smacked her lips and stated, "Ask Heavy."

Vita acted as if she didn't hear Zya's last statement, and she focused her attention on Snow.

"Wasn't you over here the other night? At the party?" Vita inquired.

Snow nodded his head. "Yeah, ma, I was here."

Vita smiled devilishly at her friend and said, "You must have taken my advice and dumped that chump nigga. I'm glad, girl, cuz his ass got a baby on the way anyway."

Zya frowned. "What?"

"Remember when I went to get my hair done the other day? Some pregnant bitch was in there talking 'bout how Jules takes care of her. She was going on and on about how he be hitting her up with cash, and how he got money put up for her baby. She had to be about nine months. She looked like she was getting ready to pop."

Zya shook her head in disbelief and shock. "No, she was lying. She had to be lying."

"I don't know. All I know is that she was up in there

talking big shit about how Jules always make sure his family is tight. Some light-skinned chick with short red hair. Her haircut was bad as hell, but she wasn't all that cute. She wasn't cuter than you."

Zya didn't believe Vita. *She is lying. She has to be lying. She found out what happened today with Heavy and now she trying to have me stressing.*

"Why you tripping anyway? You look good on his arm," Vita said, pointing to Snow.

Snow could see the look on Zya's face and could tell that she needed to get out of there. He put his hand on the small of her back and guided her out of the house.

Zya remained silent as they made their way to Manhattan. She didn't say a word. She had already decided she was going to see Jules the next day. It was not the Monday she was supposed to visit, but she didn't care. She had to ask him if what she heard was true. Her heart was beating so hard that she could hear it through her chest. She wanted to scream.

They pulled up to the Marriott hotel and purchased two rooms. As they made their way up to the 22nd floor, Snow could see the pain on her face. *That nigga is a fool,* he thought. He didn't see how any man would want to play Zya. She was everything that he wanted in a woman.

They got off the elevator and made their way to their rooms. He helped her take her stuff into her room. She was exhausted mentally, emotionally, and physically and couldn't help but plop down on the bed as soon as she entered the room.

"You okay?" he asked her.

She nodded her head. "Thank you for everything," she said. She got up and followed him to the door.

"I'm right next door . . . if you need anything . . ." he began.

"I'm good. Thanks," she said, almost in a cold way. She wasn't trying to be rude, but the only thing she could think about was Jules.

That nigga better not be playing me, she thought.

Snow walked into the hall, and before she closed the door, he said, "Zya, I meant what I said the other night. If you were mine, you wouldn't want for anything."

She looked up at him and said, "I'm not yours. I have a man."

The next morning, Zya made her way to Riker's Island. She had calmed down a lot. She had been upset the night before, but after thinking things over, she knew that Jules would never hurt her. She was his and he was hers. She still wanted to go see him, though. She wanted to let him know that she had sold all of the dope and was going to pay his lawyers that very day.

She made the long trip to Riker's, and after going through endless security checks, she was about to sign up to see Jules. She made her way to the visitor's room, where the sign-in log was located. When she was about to sign in, she noticed that somebody else had also signed up to see Jules.

Who the fuck is Tisha Moretti?

Zya looked around the room and her heart dropped when she saw the light-skinned girl with the bad-ass short hairstyle. The girl looked exactly the way Vita had described, and Zya could tell that she was late in her pregnancy. Zya looked at the diamonds that cluttered her wrists and fingers and saw the Mercedes

Benz key that the girl was holding, and she instantly grew angry.

Here I am moving dope for this nigga, and she sitting over there carefree, spending up the money that I probably earned.

Zya was hurt. She was struggling, and Jules was taking good care of another bitch. She had thought they were so much better than that, but it was obvious to her now that she was a fool.

I'm Jules's girl on the side. He isn't cheating on me . . . he's cheating on her. She's wifey, and I'm the girl he uses to make runs and do dirt. He's breaking bread with her and buying me a damn outfit every two weeks to keep me satisfied.

Zya realized that she had never actually seen any of Jules's money. He always just bought her things, but he never physically set her up so that she would be straight. Zya's heart was breaking. The girl sitting across the room was glowing. She definitely wasn't more attractive than Zya, but she had something that Zya wanted, and that was Jules. She could feel the tears coming, and there was no stopping them. She got up and rushed out of the room.

Fuck him. It is over for us. He ain't shit. I'm sitting up here pregnant and stressing over him and this baby. He's the one who convinced me to keep this child, and his ass is cheating. I am too through. I don't want shit from him. I'm gon' drop off the money that I owe to his lawyers, fill up his commissary and be done.

Zya was feeling so many different emotions, she thought she was going crazy. She was mad, sad, hurt, betrayed, confused . . . the whole nine. Her heart felt like it had a hole in it. She felt like she was dying.

Why did he have to do this to me? I would have done anything for him.

Zya dropped off $35,000 to Jules's lawyers and put $500 in his prison commissary. *I'm done with him.* She felt so betrayed that she couldn't stop crying. Her tears were endless as she made her way to her destination. She walked into the building and signed in with the receptionist.

"Would you like counseling before making such a drastic decision?" the receptionist asked.

Zya wiped her eyes and replied, "No, and I would like it done today."

She pulled out the $4,500 she had left and threw $500 on the counter. The receptionist picked up the money and handed her a clipboard. "Fill out these forms and we can get you started."

Zya took the forms to her seat, and the first question brought the tears back to her eyes.

Have you ever had an abortion before? Yes or No. If Yes, how many? _____

Chapter 3

Playing Wifey

"The charges were not accepted," the mechanical operator stated.

Jules looked at the phone in disbelief. *I've been calling her for the past two months. She ain't been up here to see me, and now she's not accepting my calls. Fuck is up?* Jules thought. Jules hung up the phone and decided to dial the number again.

"You are trying to place a collect call. Please say your name after the tone."

"Julius," he said clearly into the phone. He waited impatiently as the phone company tried to connect his call.

"The charges were not accepted," the voice repeated. Jules slammed the phone over and over again before he put it back on the receiver.

"Fuck!" he yelled loudly in an enraged fit. He hadn't heard from Zya since he had first been arrested a couple months ago, and he was wondering where she was. His lawyer had informed him that Zya had delivered the payment for his case. She had also filled his commissary, but she hadn't made any effort to come see him. Every time Jules tried to contact her, she didn't accept his call, and all of the letters he had written went unanswered.

Jules was confused. He didn't know what to think. He was pissed off that he couldn't get in contact with his own woman. He was curious as to how her pregnancy was going. He didn't know if he should be upset with Zya or worried about her, because he didn't know what was up. He had thought that she would ride or die with him, but her recent behavior had him questioning how thorough she really was. She had even moved into a new apartment without giving him the address or phone number. He had to have Amir look her new number up in the white pages just to track her down.

I know she ain't trying to leave a nigga stanking in prison, he thought as he became enraged at the idea of Zya trying to play him. *I done spent too much money on that bitch for her to pull some shit like this. When I was on top, she was there helping me spend my money, but now that I've hit rock bottom, she's trying to skip out on me.* He couldn't believe that Zya was trying to pull shady on him. It wasn't in her character to do him dirty, but he couldn't shake the feeling that he had been played.

He had been with Zya since she was 16, and had broke bread with her since the day he met her. Any time he made a move, she made one too. Their relationship was cool because she didn't trip on him like other chicks tried to do. Zya understood the game. As long as he made her think he was out making money, she didn't have a problem if she didn't hear from him for a couple days.

Jules sometimes abused her trust in him and crept out with other chicks, but Zya never suspected anything because her love for Jules ran deep. He knew that he had her head. Even if he did fuck with other chicks, he was positive that she had never stepped out on him with another nigga. Through all his bullshit and game, he actually did love Zya. She was a real chick, and he knew that she would always ride with him rather then against him. She was loyal. That's one of the reasons he didn't have a problem leaving his business in her hands. She wasn't a dumb chick, and had been involved in his operation from jump. She would know what moves to make and when to make them. He was positive that she could hold his spot down until he got out. But now that he couldn't reach her, he was spooked.

The only thing I can do is wait. I don't want to jump to any conclusions and accuse her of some shit she ain't doing. She'll come through . . . she always does. I just have to be patient. She's carrying my baby, and she will do anything I ask her to. She's proven her loyalty to me more than once. She's probably just nervous and trying to lay low. If she was going to pull grimy, she wouldn't have paid my lawyers or put cash in my account. Nah . . . she's good for it.

Jules sat in his jail cell, trying to convince himself that Zya was still on his team. He tried to come up with the possible reasons she hadn't been to see him. He knew he would have to be easy and wait for her to come to him. He just hoped that she did it soon.

* * *

"You have a collect call from a New York State Penitentiary. Will you accept the charges?" the mechanical operator asked.

"Hell no!" Zya yelled before slamming the phone down on the hook.

I don't even know why he's still calling me. Don't he get the picture? she thought as she looked around her tiny apartment. It wasn't much, but it was hers, and that's all that she could ask for at the moment. It had been eight weeks since she had found out about Jules's lies, and she had been in and out of depression. The abortion had been hard on her because after she had calmed down, she instantly regretted what she had done. She had acted in the spur of the moment, and made her decision based on pure emotion. The guilt had plagued her every day since she had the procedure done.

I didn't want Jules in my life, but he still could have been a part of his child's life. He doesn't even know about the abortion. He doesn't even know that I found out he was cheating. Zya knew that he deserved to know about the decision she had made because it affected him too. The only thing stopping her from telling him was the fact that she didn't want to do it over the phone, and she refused to go see him. The love that she had for Jules had turned to hate the minute she had seen the pregnant girl waiting to see him in the jail. It had broken her heart, and she knew that she would never be able to forgive Jules for his betrayal.

He had me thinking things were one way, when all along they were another. I was looking like a fool, falling for his game for three years, when all along he was using me. If he wanted to get money together, he could have just said that. The love affair wasn't necessary. He came at me like he was my man . . . like he was down for me. He told me that he loved me the way that I loved him. That was bullshit. He's the one who was wrong. I don't know why I'm sitting here second-guessing my decision. He didn't hesitate to step out on me. Fuck him!

Zya's rage was strong, but deep down she knew that the only reason it hurt so bad was because she had loved him so much. She thought that it had been real, but now she was finding out that her feelings were unrequited.

A part of her was even jealous of the girl that she found out about. She loved Jules so much, and for so long he had been her world. He had taken care of her, or rather always gave her a hustle to take care of herself. Here she was now, left on stuck, without any money and struggling to get her life back together.

After paying the money Jules had requested for his lawyers and dropping money for the abortion, she only had $4,000 left. She didn't even have a place to live after she walked out of the clinic. She scoured the *New York Times* looking for a cheap place for the time being. When she finally found a guy who was trying to sub-let his apartment, she paid almost $2,400 just to move in.

Her money was running low, and she didn't have a job. She knew that she needed to snap out of her daze and find work, because the little bit of cash she did have left was disappearing fast. She couldn't afford to be depressed. The only problem was, she didn't know where to start. She didn't even know how to make money if it wasn't from hustling. She had never seen legit money. She always thought that it was too hard to make. She wasn't the type to wait tables or work a 9 to 5. She was in love with the fast life, and only had experience earning fast money.

The allure of the game called for her. She couldn't help it. She was in love with quick flips. Jules had turned her out to easy money, and now that he was gone, she knew that depending on that easy money had been a mistake. She knew that she had to get back in the game. If she didn't, she wouldn't be able to survive on her own. She knew that her staying locked and secluded in her apartment was not healthy for her. She thought that the fast-paced drug game would keep her so busy that she wouldn't have time to think about the love she had lost or the horrible decision that she made when she gave up her child.

I have to get back in the game. It keeps me sane. My only problem is that I'm not connected like Jules was. I don't have anybody waiting to buy from me.

She wondered if she could use Jules's connections to establish herself in the game. She got up from her couch and ran to her closet to find the Doonie & Bourke bag that Smitty had given her. She dumped all of her possessions out of it as she searched for the letter that Jules had written her. *I know it's in here. Damn, I just had it!* Her mind screamed as she frantically searched for the paper. *Where is it?* she thought as she moved from her purse to her kitchen table. She found it lying in the middle of the table, underneath the stack of bills that had accumulated in the name of Patrice Spoon.

She had learned her lesson after Jules was arrested. She had been lucky that the police had not been looking for her. She could have easily been indicted under the RICO laws, just because the house was rented in her name. Nothing in her new home was in her name. She had made it a point to put everything under an alias, just in case anything popped off.

Zya sat down in the middle of her bed and unfolded the letter that contained Smitty's number. She picked up her cell phone, but before she could dial the number, her buzzer rang loudly throughout the house.

She walked into the living room and hit the button on the intercom. "Who is it?"

"It's me. Let me up."

She recognized Vita's voice and hit the release button to unlock the door. Zya folded the letter and put it in her purse. *I'll handle that later,* she thought as she rushed to the door to meet her best friend.

Vita walked in looking like a ghetto superstar. Her big Chloe glasses covered almost her entire face, and she had on a short jean skirt. The suede thigh-high boots she was rocking with it set her outfit off.

"You doing all right? I ain't heard from you in a couple days," Vita said as she gave Zya a hug that made her feel ten times better. After Zya got the abortion, she told Vita everything about Jules and her pregnancy. Vita was a good friend and was there for Zya. She came over almost every day to make sure that she got through.

"Yeah, I'm good. I'm just thinking, really, trying to get things back in order."

"That's good. It seems like you're doing way better. I was getting worried about you for a minute there," Vita said in a light tone.

Zya could tell that her friend had been worried about her. Vita wasn't exactly the mushy type, but after Zya confessed everything that she had been going through, Vita made it a point to be there for her friend. She listened to her vent all night if she had to. She knew that Zya had a lot to get off her chest, and sometimes she would stay for days just to let Zya know that she had people in her corner who loved her.

"I'm not a hundred percent stress-free, but I'm better. Thank you for getting me through this, Vita. I probably would have been sick without you," Zya said as she cracked a smile.

"Girl, whatever . . . You already know how we do. If it was me, I would have wanted you to have my back. There ain't no thanks necessary. I've known your ass since the seventh grade. You are my sister." Vita wrapped her arms around Zya's shoulders, and they both dropped a couple tears. They had their ups and downs, but always remained close. Vita was her sister, and Zya loved her as if they had been born and raised under the same roof.

"Shit, you fucked up my makeup," Vita said, trying to lighten the mood. Zya laughed loudly.

Vita's cell phone rang, and she sighed as she looked at the caller ID.

"Hello?" she answered.

"Hey, baby. I need you to cook up something for me. I'll be home in about half an hour. Meet me there, all right?" Heavy said.

"I'm at Zya's crib. I can't right now. We probably finna go get something to eat," she told him. She really enjoyed spending time with Zya, and Zya needed her more than Heavy did at the moment.

"I thought I told you about being over there all the time. Fuck you be doing that's so important? Why you got to be over there twenty-four/seven?" he fussed into the phone.

"Cuz she my girl. Why you tripping? Since when do you have a problem with Zya?" Vita rolled her eyes and put her finger up for Zya to hold on.

Zya knew that it was Heavy on the other end. She hated his fake ass ever since he had roughed her up. She didn't know how far he had planned on going that night. She thought that he was going to rape her.

"Don't nobody got no problems with that ho. Just be home when I get there!" With that, he hung up the phone.

Vita sighed and snapped her cell phone closed. She looked at Zya with apologetic eyes and said, "Zy, I got to dip. My boo is tripping."

Zya already knew why Heavy didn't want Vita around her. He was too afraid that she would tell Vita about what he had tried to do. Zya was already hip to Heavy's game. He controlled everything that Vita did, and he was, slowly but surely, trying to cut Zya out of the picture. Zya's and Vita's friendship was strong, though, and she knew that Vita wasn't having it.

"All right, girl. Holla at me later." She hugged Vita then walked her to the door.

"You gon' be all right?" Vita asked.

"Yeah . . . yeah, I'm good."

Vita looked skeptically but then smiled. "All right, girl. Call me if you need anything," she said.

Zya closed the door and locked it. Vita's visit actually made her feel a whole lot better. She walked into the bathroom and looked into the mirror. She looked tired, and the energetic light that had once dawned on her face had disappeared. She had on a dingy white T-shirt with holes in it, and her hair was a mess.

The stress had really taken its toll on her. She was used to always being on point. Even when she was just sitting around the house, she made sure she looked good.

I can't afford to look good for nothing anymore. She continued to stare at her reflection, but became disgusted at what she saw. *I need to get myself together. I can't just sit around here broke, waiting for some nigga to rescue me. I need to get on my grind . . . even if I have to work a regular job. I can't just sit around here and do nothing. I'm gon' lose my mind if I sit in this house another day. All I do is think about Jules and what could have been our family. I can't do this to myself anymore. I need to work to get my mind off of everything else.*

The next day, Zya woke up and went looking for jobs. She hated the fact that she had to look for regular work, but she figured that it was better than doing nothing. She got up early and put in applications all over the city, from little eateries to clothing stores. She was willing to work anyplace that was trying to pay her. Her paychecks would be a serious downsize from what she was used to making when she made runs for Jules, but she couldn't be choosy. She needed some money, and a small income was better than no income at all.

It was harder to find a job than she had anticipated. Almost every place she went asked her if she had any prior experience, but she had none.

Zya decided to take a break and called Vita to meet her for lunch. Zya's feet were killing her, so she ducked into the closest restaurant she could find. She ended up in a nice Italian spot on West 46th Street. It was the middle of the day, but the place was dimly lit.

It was a decent establishment that had a casual Italian atmosphere. Zya felt out of place, though, because she was the only black person in the entire place, and all eyes seemed to be glued on her. Zya was seated at a cozy table for two, where she waited for Vita to arrive. Her friend walked in fifteen minutes later, out of breath and looking ghetto fabulous as always.

"Hey, girl, what's up?" she said as she placed her purse on the table and sat down across from Zya.

"Job hunting. I've been out here all day, looking for a job. It seems like nobody will give me a break," Zya said as the waitress approached their table. The woman wore a short black skirt with a tight-fitting white top. She had a mini apron tied around her waist, and was popping gum as she waited for them to pause their conversation so she could take their order.

"Hey, ladies. How are you two gorgeous girls doing today?" she said in a sort of whiny way. Her voice was loud and irritating, but she was nice. She looked to be in her thirties.

"Good. How are you?" Zya replied.

"Oh, I'm doing good," she began.

"Marcella, come over here!" a voice boomed from the back of the restaurant. Zya turned around and saw a round Italian guy motion for the waitress.

The waitress stopped and put her hand on her hip and yelled back, "Vinnie, come on! Don't you see me taking these nice young ladies' orders? Hold on a minute. You know you are my favorite customer. I won't leave you waiting long." The man and his table guests laughed, and he nodded his head and blew her a kiss. Zya laughed lightly.

"Oh, don't mind him. He's high as a kite. He's loud and rambunctious, but he's harmless. His tips are lovely, though, darling." She continued to pop her gum, and cocked her hip to the side.

"Are y'all hiring?" Vita asked as she nudged Zya underneath the table.

"Oh yeah, we're always hiring. These young girls can't always keep up with the crowd, ya know? Why? You looking for a job?" she asked, directing her question to Vita.

"Oh no, honey, I don't do regular jobs," she said vainly. "The nine to five thing ain't for me, but my girl Zya needs a job."

The waitress laughed and said, "I hear you, but trust me, sweetheart, this ain't no regular gig." She focused her attention on Zya. "You looking for work?"

Before Zya could answer the question, a handsome young Italian guy in casual black slacks and a black Armani shirt walked up to their table.

"Excuse me, ladies," he said before turning to the waitress. "Marcella, you know Vinnie will only let you serve him. It's not good business to make him wait."

"Meechi, I was just talking to these ladies here." She pointed to Zya. "This one's looking for a job."

He looked down at Zya and said, "What's your name?"

"Zya," she responded.

"Your name reflects your beauty," he said. Vita smiled and bumped Zya underneath the table.

Zya smiled and replied, "Thank you."

"That smile will make you a million bucks in this restaurant. Have you ever waited tables?"

"No."

"You will learn quickly, I hope. You start tonight. Be here at 7:00 P.M. Don't be late." He began to walk away from the table then turned back and yelled,

"Marcella, their lunch is on me. Before she leaves, give her a uniform and hurry up and get to Vinnie!"

Marcella looked down at her with a smile and said, "Congratulations, girlfriend. Meechi likes you, and he doesn't like anybody."

"Was he serious? Did I really get the job? Is he the boss?" Zya asked, surprised at how easily she had gotten the job. She was glad that she had picked that restaurant. She was in the right place at the right time, apparently.

"Yeah, he and his dad own the place. No offense, but he usually wouldn't hire a black girl. That's how I know he likes you."

Zya didn't know if she should be offended, but she honestly didn't care. *As long as I can take his checks to the bank, I'm good.*

Marcella finished taking their orders and made her way to Vinnie's table.

"Girl, here's to your new job that *I* got you," Vita said as she beamed a smile and raised her champagne glass in the air. Zya tapped her glass lightly against her friend's, and with a confident grin, said, "To my new job."

Zya stared in the mirror and pulled her long hair up into a high ponytail. She kept adjusting it to get it just right. She was nervous, like she was going on her first date or something. She wanted to look good when she arrived at the restaurant. She didn't want to give her boss any reason to fire her. She fidgeted with the tight black skirt then turned around to make sure her panty line was concealed. The skirt was so short that she would have to watch how she picked things up. The waitress uniform was far from cute, but Zya wore it like she was wearing high fashion couture. The tiny skirt hugged her hips, and it was sexy, to say the least.

Her house phone rang, and she rushed to answer it. It was already 6:30, and she wasn't even finished getting dressed yet.

"Hello?" she said as she put one earring in her free ear. She switched the phone to the other side and held it with her head and shoulder as she inserted the other earring.

"You ready? I'm outside," Vita said cheerfully. Vita had agreed to drop Zya off at work so that she didn't have to take the subway.

"Yeah, girl. I'm on my way down." She hung up the phone and went into her room to grab her short apron and put on her black Jimmy Choos. She walked out the door and tied her apron around her waist as she headed to Vita's car.

"You look cute!" Vita yelled as she watched Zya strut to the car. Zya was only five feet five, but she had the stride and the looks of a runway model.

"Whatever. You got jokes," Zya said as she opened the door and got in.

Vita laughed and sped away from the curb, driving recklessly, like all New Yorkers seemed to do. "No, I'm serious. You gon' get hella tips tonight," she said as she chuckled lightly.

It took Vita about fifteen minutes flat to get to the restaurant, and Zya hopped out of the car and rushed inside.

"You want me to pick you up?" Vita yelled right as Zya opened the door.

Zya nodded her head and replied, "Yeah. The place closes at two."

Vita drove off, and Zya entered the restaurant. The place was packed. There were people at every table. The three fireplaces around the room were roaring, and the place was lively with laughter and conversation. The bar area was jam-packed, too, and she noticed Marcella maneuvering in and out of the dining area with large trays in her hands. The place was definitely busy, and Zya scanned the room, looking for her boss.

"You ready to work?" someone behind her asked. She turned around and saw her boss staring her up and down.

"Yeah, Mr. . . ." she began, not knowing exactly what to call him.

"The Mister is for my father. I'm Di'Meechi Castello. Call me Meechi."

An older man walked in the door and stopped when he saw Zya. He looked at his son and said, "Who do we have here?" There was a disapproving tone in his voice, and Zya grew nervous in his presence.

"This is Zya, Pop. She's our new waitress."

"Hello, Mr. Castello," she said sweetly. She gave him a smile and reached out her hand, knowing that she could win him over with her charm. Mr. Castello let her hand linger in the air for a few seconds before he finally returned her friendly smile. He took her hand and kissed it then patted his son on the back.

"Gorgeous girl, Meechi. Good work. Why are you still standing here, sweetheart? I have a restaurant to run," he said as he moved into the dining area and shook hands with a couple of people sitting around the place.

Marcella noticed Zya and came over to her. "Hey, Zya, right?" Zya nodded her head. "Let me show you where everything is at." She popped her gum as she bobbed and weaved around the tables. Zya struggled to move throughout the place without bumping into anybody.

"Excuse me. I'm sorry," she kept repeating as she followed Marcella to the back kitchen. They went through two double doors and entered the busy kitchen. Marcella took her to the back, where an office was located.

"This is the rotation of the tables," she said, pointing to a seating chart on the board. "This is your section. It is the section you will wait every night, unless somebody requests you from my section or from Liz's section." At that moment, an attractive white girl with sandy blonde hair walked into the office, followed by a white guy, who waddled into the room hugging a broom.

"Liz, this is Zya. Zya, this is Liz," Marcella introduced.

"We got a new girl?" Liz asked.

"Yeah, the other one couldn't cut it. Meechi hired Zya earlier today."

"The tips are good," Liz assured with a smile. She winked at Zya and said, "Nice to meet you." She then threw on her apron and rushed out.

"Hi, Zya!" The white kid spoke loudly, but kept his head turned down toward the floor.

"Jesus, Buggy, not so loud," Marcella said harshly. She turned to Zya and said, "He's a little slower than most. He's good for nothing, but somehow he got a job here."

Zya smiled, not wanting to be mean to him. It was obvious that he was slow. "Hi, Buggy," she said as she held out her hand for him to shake it.

He shook her hand wildly and said, "Zya, you're pretty."

Zya laughed and replied, "Buggy, you are very handsome yourself."

"We better get out there," Marcella said as she bumped past Buggy. Zya waved to Buggy then followed Marcella out of the room.

"All you do is take the orders and be hospitable, and you will be fine." They both exited the office, walked through the kitchen, and made their way onto the floor. Zya looked at her section. She had at least fifteen tables, and she took a deep breath before she made her way to the first one.

"Hi, I'm Zya, and I will be your waitress this evening. Can I start you gentlemen out with something to drink?" she asked nicely as she placed menus in front of each person.

"Yes. What's your house champagne?" a stone-faced Italian man asked. Zya grew a blank expression on her face as she picked up one of the menus.

"Umm, let me see." She flipped through the menu, fumbling as she tried to find the page where the drinks were located. "Hold on," she said as she struggled to find the page.

The man grew impatient and said, "Forget it! Just bring us out two bottles of your finest champagne. Ask one of the waitresses who actually know what they are doing."

Zya nodded her head and then went to the bar to fill the order.

Her shift was full of rude customers. She messed up orders and spilled drinks all night. It seemed like the cook would take forever to prepare her customers' meals, but Liz and Marcella's orders were completed quickly. She could feel Meechi and Mr. Castello watching her. *This shit ain't for me,* she thought as she delivered plate after plate of food. She had always thought waitresses didn't do anything, but she quickly realized that she was wrong. She had cussed a couple of waitresses out herself for taking too long with her own meal, and now she regretted it because she was receiving that same treatment. She tried to apologize to her tables for her inexperience, but it seemed like they wouldn't cut her a break. They reported her to the managers and were rude to her. She didn't think she would keep the job for long. If she didn't quit, they were sure to fire her. She knew that she wasn't cut out for it. She leaned against the bar, surprised by the fact that she had a free minute.

"You okay?" Liz came up and asked her as she gave a drink order to the bartender.

"Yeah, I guess. This is just a lot of work. I keep messing up orders and delivering cold food." Zya sighed.

"You're doing better than I did my first day. Don't worry about it. You'll get the hang of it. You just have to move quick, that's all. And don't let these Italian pricks treat you like shit. I will tell them off in a minute if they step too far out of line," she said as she walked away.

Zya tried to make the best of the rest of her night.

The only thing that made the job bearable was the tips. Each table left at least $25, and that was good for the poor service they had received. She watched as Marcella and Liz picked up $100 and $200 tips, but she couldn't complain. It was her first night, and she knew she hadn't done a great job.

Her feet were killing her, and all she really wanted to do was go home. She couldn't wait to crawl into her bed. She looked at the clock that hung behind the bar and saw that it was a half-hour until closing. If she had money, she would have quit after the first hour or so, but then again, if she had money, she wouldn't have to wait tables to get by. Even though she didn't really like the job, she couldn't quit, because she needed the money.

While I'm sitting here talking about quitting, I better hope Meechi doesn't fire my ass, she thought. The restaurant started to clear out, and she began to clear and clean the tables. She hoped that she didn't have to wash dishes. *I don't do dishes. I don't even do my own, so I know I'm not about to bus no suds here.* She continued to clear the tables, and for the first time all night, she noticed the black porcelain boxes that sat on each table. They looked like centerpieces, and she didn't know if she was supposed to send them to be washed or leave them. She picked it up and stopped Marcella as she walked by.

"Hey, do I take these to the kitchen?"

"No, those stay on the tables. That's just a little bit of candy. Meechi doesn't mind if we take a bit either. Meechi lets the customers sample it before they spend their hard earned money on it. Go ahead, help yourself." She hurried off into the kitchen, leaving Zya in the dining room alone.

Zya removed the lid, and when she saw the powder-white substance, she instantly knew what it was. Her jaw dropped, and she looked around. It felt like she had discovered something that had been a secret.

Damn, they got blow just lying out in the middle of the tables. Once she really thought about it, she realized that most of the customers had been acting strange. She had even witnessed a couple people dipping into the boxes, but she had no idea they had been getting high.

She looked around the restaurant. *Fuck did I get myself into?* she thought as she examined the drug. She looked at the cocaine closely and saw that it was poor quality. It was some bullshit that had been stepped on a couple times. She had been around the block enough times to know a good product when she saw it, and the white stuff that was on the table wasn't it. She shook her head and placed the centerpiece back in the middle of the table.

Meechi came behind her and put his hands on her shoulders. She jumped, not knowing that he had sneaked up on her. He squeezed gently and said, "Go home. You've had a hard first day."

Zya stepped out of his grasp and walked around the table to finish wiping it down. "Sorry if I messed up," she said.

"You did fine. We'll see you tomorrow."

Zya took the dishes to the kitchen then waved to Liz and Marcella before leaving. Vita sat parked on the curb, waiting to pick Zya up, just as she had promised.

"How was it?" Vita asked as Zya stepped into the car. Zya sighed and took off her heels. She shook her head from side to side and replied, "Some bullshit.

The only thing that got me going back is the tips. Some rich-ass Italians be eating in that restaurant. Mostly all my tables left me twenty-five dollar tips."

"Damn, twenty-five dollars! You lucky you ain't surviving off my tips. I be leaving chicks like a dollar, if that." They both laughed out loud as they rode down the city streets.

"For real . . . but that restaurant is like a front or something," Zya began to explain.

"Why you say that?"

"It got to be. Right before I got off, I found cocaine sitting on all the tables in these little black boxes. They got coke just lying in the middle of the table like it's legal. People were getting high all night."

Vita looked at Zya like she was crazy, and yelled, "That shit was blow! I thought that shit was some kind of seasoning." Zya burst into laughter. "Z, that shit ain't funny. I ate so much of that shit earlier at lunch! No wonder I've been feeling weird all day."

Zya couldn't help but to laugh. The look on Vita's face was priceless. After she noticed the worried look on Vita's face, she stopped laughing. She knew that it was a sensitive subject.

"You'll be all right. As many niggas be snorting that shit . . . ain't nothing happened to them yet. One time ain't gon' kill you."

"Still, Zya, you know I don't fuck with that shit," Vita argued. Her mom had died when she was in the ninth grade from some bad coke. A small-time drug dealer had been lacing his dope with rat poison. Vita's mother had gotten hold of some. Vita found her mother face down in the toilet after coming home from school, and had never been able to forget that day. She promised herself she would never fuck with another drug. She even stopped smoking weed because of that, and until now had maintained her promise.

Zya could see that she had crossed the line by laughing, so she quickly apologized. "Vita, I'm sorry. I didn't think. You'll be okay. It really ain't a big deal."

Vita nodded her head and continued to drive. The rest of the distance was silent and awkward. Zya knew that Vita was thinking about her mother. She never knew what to say to comfort Vita on that subject, so she left her friend to her own thoughts.

When Zya arrived home, she said goodbye to Vita and headed up to her apartment. Her mind was racing as she thought about the restaurant.

I wonder what else is going down in there. If I didn't know about that, I'm sure there's a lot of other stuff going on that I'm not aware of. Is it safe to work there? I'm not trying to get caught up in anything I can't get out of.

Zya looked at the $500 she had earned from tips. She had waited over twenty tables, and they all had tipped her nicely. She hadn't earned half of what Liz and Marcella did, but she couldn't complain.

If every night is gon' be like tonight, the money alone is worth going back. I don't care what goes down in there. I'm all about my money. I'll walk in and out of there safely every night if I mind my business and do my job.

Each night after that, Zya went to work and did just that, minded her own business. She got better and better at waiting tables, and soon could keep up with the other girls. She got used to the fast pace of the restaurant and fit in nicely by the end of the first month. Zya, Liz, and Marcella had grown close. They were cool to work with because most of the time they were three of the only women in the entire place. Zya worked the tables like a pro, and soon her tips had gone from $500 a night to $2,000 a night. Mostly everybody that came into the restaurant tipped with $100 bills. The Italian vibe of the restaurant grew on her, and she quickly became a part of the family. Zya was getting paid just to be a pretty face and to be hospitable to the guests. She didn't have a problem with it.

Zya walked into work late, and she knew that Meechi wasn't going to be too happy about it. It was Saturday night, the restaurant's busiest night, and he liked for everything to run smoothly. Zya rushed past him, and before he could scold her, she said, "I already know, Meechie. I'm on it. I'm on it." She ran into the back office and clocked in before taking her place on the dining room floor. She noticed that Vinnie, one of the more frequent visitors, was sitting at a table in her section.

That's odd. Marcella usually waits on him.

She looked around the restaurant and found Liz. She walked over to her and whispered, "Why is Vinnie sitting in my section?"

"Marcella is sick, and you know he can't stand me. He said you're the next best thing," Liz said with a smile. Zya shook her head, hoping that Vinnie didn't get too out of control. He was known to be difficult to please, and Marcella seemed to be the only waitress who was able to handle him. Zya walked over to Vinnie's table, where eight Italian men in double-breasted expensive suits sat around. They already appeared to be on their third round of drinks.

It's gon' be a long night, Zya said to herself.

"Zya! How's it going, dark-skinned?" Vinnie asked as he laughed at his own joke. Even though Zya was far from being dark-skinned, Vinnie had labeled her that because she was the only black girl in the place. It used to bother Zya, but she reminded herself that she was there for the money and that was it. She didn't give a fuck about what Vinnie called her, as long as he paid her at the end of the night.

"How are you tonight, Vinnie?" Zya replied with a smirk.

"Bring us another round of drinks. We are not ready to order yet," Vinnie announced. He whistled as she walked away, and Zya ignored him. She walked up to the bar, where Meechi sat talking to the bartender.

"I need you to fill in for Marcella tonight," Meechi said.

"No problem. I've got her section covered," Zya responded.

Meechi shook his head and said, "No . . . I mean after hours." He got close to her ear, and his breath on her earlobe made her arms and back tingle. "Can I trust you?" She nodded but didn't respond. "Good. After work, I need you to wait one table. They have a special reservation." Zya agreed then made her way back over to Vinnie's table with the drinks.

"Have you gentlemen decided yet?" Zya asked, waiting for the men to place their orders. Instead of answering, Vinnie reached underneath Zya's short skirt and grabbed her ass firmly.

"A piece of this nice brown ass would be nice," he yelled out loud enough for everyone in the restaurant to hear. Zya was enraged and embarrassed. She picked up one of the drinks off the table, and out of reaction, flung it in Vinnie's face, glass and all.

"You asshole, don't you ever touch me," she said as she watched the glass hit his face hard. A tiny trail of blood trickled down the bridge of his nose, and he keeled over in pain. He cupped his nose with both hands then stood up in a drunken outrage.

"You black bitch!" he said as he grabbed Zya by the neck. Liz ran over to Vinnie to try and stop him from attacking Zya, but he pushed her tiny frame out of his way. The restaurant was in a frenzy, and everyone stood out of their seats as the chaos ensued.

"Di'Meechi!" Liz yelled. Meechi came rushing out of the kitchen, and he forcefully pulled Vinnie off of Zya. Zya gagged and choked as she struggled to get some air into her deprived lungs. Liz rushed to her side and helped her up.

"What the fuck happened?" Di'Meechi yelled to Vinnie, who now had begun to sober up and had a dumb look on his face. "What the hell was that?" Meechi had his finger pointed in Vinnie's face. "Don't you ever put your filthy hands on one of these girls! The next time you do, I will gut you like a fucking fish!" He then reached inside Vinnie's suit jacket and removed a large wad of cash. "I believe this belongs to the lady." He escorted Vinnie out and cleared the restaurant, apologizing for the incident that had just taken place.

Meechi walked over to Zya, where Liz was standing by her with a worried expression plastered on her face. "You okay?" he asked as he handed her the thick wad of money.

"Yeah, I'm good," she replied as she nodded her head and applied ice to her now red neck.

"Go ahead and go home for the night," Meechi said.

"No, I'm good," Zya replied as she hopped down off the bar and began to clean up.

Meechi nodded and said, "I'll be in the back if you need me. After you're done cleaning, Liz, you can go home." He left the room, and Zya sat down at the nearest table.

She put her hands over her face. *This is some bullshit. I'm not cut out for this. I need to make enough money to get me right for a couple months and then I'm done. These Italian mu'fuckas ain't about to be slapping me around. Fuck that! I'ma work a couple more months so that I can save up $50,000, then I'm done.*

Buggy walked over and began to sweep around Liz and Zya. He stopped in front of Zya and said, "I'll help you cl-clean up." He stuttered badly as he spoke, and began to sweep up the broken dishes.

"Thank you, Buggy," Zya said as she stood up. "You're a good guy." Zya gave Buggy a light hug, and his hands went straight for her breasts. She backed up quickly and said, "Buggy, you can't do that. I've told you that you have to keep your hands to yourself." She didn't yell, but her voice was stern. She wanted to make sure that Buggy got the point. He would always sneak feels when she and the other girls walked past. They knew that he was harmless and didn't know what he was doing, so Zya tried to be patient with him.

"You all right?" Liz asked as she helped get the restaurant in order.

"Yeah, I'm good. I just don't think I'm gon' be here too much longer," Zya said as she grabbed a pail of clean silverware off the cart and began to wrap it in linen. "That was some bullshit. I don't know about y'all, but I don't take too kindly to men grabbing and touching on me. If that shit had happened a couple years ago, I would have had his ass touched. My boyfriend didn't play that," she said, thinking about Jules. She had forced him out of her heart, but she still thought about him from time to time. It had been six months since she had gotten the abortion, and she was finally getting her shit back together.

"Where is your boyfriend now?" Liz asked. She sat down across from her.

"We're not together anymore. He turned out to be a liar. He's rotting in some prison cell upstate."

"Yeah, I can relate."

Zya looked at the white girl with skepticism. *You can't relate to shit that I've been through,* Zya thought.

"What, you don't believe me?" Liz asked, raising an eyebrow. "I'm not as innocent as I look. I've encountered a lying man or two myself."

Zya laughed and changed the subject. "Anyway, I don't need this job that bad for me to be letting some fat-ass Italian jump on me. As soon as I save enough money, this place can kiss me good-bye."

Di'Meechi walked out of the kitchen and saw that the restaurant had been restored to its original condition. "Thank you, ladies. Liz, you can take off and take Buggy with you. Zya still has a couple of things to take care of here."

Liz looked at Zya and asked, "Are you sure? Because I can wait on you. I can drop you off at home."

Zya saw a trace of concern in Liz's eyes and wondered why she was so afraid to leave her there alone.

Liz's anxiety caused Zya to become nervous, but she sucked it up and said, "No . . . no, I'm fine. You go ahead."

Liz pulled out a pen and wrote her number on a napkin. "Zya, call me when you make it home."

Zya took the napkin and placed it into her apron. "I'll be fine," she said as she got up and walked Liz to the main door. She closed and locked the door then walked over to the bar to Meechi.

"Are your guests ready?" Zya asked. Meechi shook his head and replied, "No, but they should be here shortly. Come sit down and have a drink while we wait." She sat in one of the tall stools while Meechi moved behind the bar.

"What will it be?" he asked.

"Cosmopolitan," she replied.

"Zya, I'm sorry about what happened earlier. Vinnie will be dealt with," he said in a serious tone.

What the hell he mean, dealt with? Zya thought as Meechi handed her a drink. She sipped at her Cosmo.

"You are a very special woman, Zya," Meechi said.

"Is that so?" Zya replied.

"Yes. I don't trust too many people to do what you are about to do. Marcella is the only other person besides me and my father that knows about these meetings."

"It's not a big deal. I'm only filling in for Marcella. It's just a dinner reservation, Meechi."

"Zya, whatever you hear or see tonight in this restaurant has to remain inside this restaurant. You are about to serve the most supreme of our clientele.

Do not speak unless spoken to, and do not repeat anything that you may overhear to anyone. You understand?"

"Yeah, I understand," Zya replied.

Meechi looked at her for a minute. He stared so long that it began to make her uncomfortable. "You are a very beautiful woman, Zya. I would hate for something to happen to you."

Zya's face went blank. *Was that a threat? What the fuck am I getting into? What is that serious about a fucking dinner reservation?*

"Come on," Meechi said. Zya stood up and followed him back into the kitchen. He put a code into a keypad on the front of a freezer door, and it opened, causing cold air to be released into the room. The draft made the hair on the back of Zya's neck stand, and she began to get nervous. Meechi held the door open for Zya and said, "Get in."

"What?" Zya said. She looked skeptically into the freezer. There was nothing in there, not even any meat or food. "Meechi, what is this all about?" she asked.

"Zya, you have to trust me. If you don't, there is no need for you to even be here right now. I trust you. Can you trust me?"

Hell no! Zya thought, but instead of saying it aloud, she sighed and replied, "Yes." She didn't know why she agreed. In a way, she was curious to see what the hell was so important.

She stepped into the freezer and cringed as the cold draft stung her skin. Meechi closed the door, and the freezer went black. Zya felt fear creep into her body, and she remained still as she tried to figure out what was happening. The freezer began to move downward, and Zya stumbled as she tried to keep her balance.

"Meechi, what is going on?" she asked.

This is a fucking elevator. Why is it built like a freezer? And where the hell does it lead to? Thoughts raced through her mind, and the fear of the unknown was what she was worried about the most. The elevator came to a halt, and lights came on. Zya couldn't stop the butterflies from fluttering in her stomach. She was nervous, and didn't know what was about to happen.

Meechi walked over to another keypad that was posted on the wall and punched in five numbers. Another door opened, and Meechi stepped out of the elevator. He motioned for Zya to follow, and she hurried out. She was just grateful to be out of the suffocating space. She followed him down a long corridor until they reached a steel door. He knocked and was admitted. Zya hesitated, but Meechi called her name and she entered slowly. She walked into a room that held a bar and a round table, where seven people sat, all staring up at her.

"Where's Marcella?" a caramel-colored woman with a layered, shoulder-length wrap asked. She wore a cream-colored Dolce and Gabbana dress suit, and a huge canary yellow diamond on her middle finger.

Zya couldn't take her eyes off of her. She was gorgeous. She knew that she was somebody important. She sat with her legs crossed and her back relaxed against the chair as she looked Zya up and down.

"Marcella is sick. Zya will be filling in for tonight," Di'Meechi said.

"Check her for a wire," the woman instructed the doorman immediately.

Zya looked in confusion as she held out her arms and was searched thoroughly from head to toe. Her heart was beating like a drum, and she was sure that her uneasiness could be felt throughout the room. Once the security guard gave the okay, the woman spoke again.

"I would like a glass of California Chardonnay . . . Kendal-Jackson."

Zya nodded her head and wrote down the orders for the rest of the men sitting around the table. Before she exited the room, Di'Meechi handed her a piece of paper with the codes and instructions to use the elevator and the keypads. She hurried out of the room and almost found herself running back to the main floor. When she arrived at the bar, her heart was pumping and she contemplated leaving the restaurant.

Fuck this shit. I don't know who those people are or what is going on. Zya rushed to the front entrance and tried to unlock the door. *No . . . no . . . open.* She pulled on the door, but it was locked with a key that she did not have. *Fuck!* She was scared. She didn't want to be a part of shit. She didn't want to know nothing and she didn't want to see nothing. She had known that the restaurant was kind of shady, but this was something totally past that. *They are on some real Cosa Nostra type stuff.* She looked around the restaurant for another escape route, but there was none.

Okay, breathe, Zya, breathe. If I don't get back down there with their drinks, they are going to come looking for me. That woman is already looking at me suspiciously. Zya rushed to the bar to pour the drinks. She kept spilling liquor because she couldn't stop her hands from shaking.

She placed them all on a serving tray then took a deep breath before going back to the elevator. She followed the instructions and made her way back down to the room. She stopped at the door and eavesdropped before entering. The room was silent, except for the blaring television set.

"This is Tamra Gentry reporting live from CNN. Just in, a Cuban freighter was seized at the port of Miami by the local coast guards. Over two hundred kilos of pure Cuban cocaine were confiscated, found in hidden compartments within the crates. If the drugs were not confiscated, it would have made drug dealers millions of dollars on the streets. Miami's Chief of Police will hold a press conference later today concerning the attainment and the big accomplishment in the war against on drugs."

Zya heard the television volume decreasing, and then the voice of the woman in the room. "You took our money but failed to deliver our product! We have been very patient with you, but our patience is running thin. It is very simple. We want the money or the product." The deep, loud voice boomed through the corridor, and Zya held her breath in fear. She didn't want to knock on the door, afraid that her interruption would be unappreciated.

"Someone must have tipped off the authorities, causing them to intercept the shipment. It was completely out of my hands," a male voice said in a pleading way.

"Where is the money?"

"I don't have it. I can get it to you before you have your next meeting. You will have it all in full before next Saturday."

Zya finally knocked on the door, not wanting to

overhear more than she should. She was let in and again, all eyes were on her. She could feel the tension in the room as she placed the drinks in front of each person.

She looked up at a man who was sweating and nervous. The way he stared back at her made a chill run down her spine. His eyes were grateful for her interruption, but also pleading for her to stay. She could feel his fear, and she wanted to get out of there as quickly as possible. She grimaced at the sight of him because one of his eyes didn't have any color in it. It just seemed to be one white ball in his head.

"Did you want a drink, sir?" she asked him.

Mr. Castello, Di'Meechi's father, answered for him. "No, that will be it for now, Zya." He handed her five crisp $100 bills and smiled at her before she exited the room.

"Take care of him," she heard the woman say.

"Wait . . . please I can get your money back," Zya heard him beg. She didn't hear anything else for a while. There was a long silence, and Zya didn't want to walk away, afraid that her footsteps might echo down the hall.

"What do we do now?" a man's voice asked.

"We do nothing," the woman replied.

"Nothing?" another voice asked, his anger apparent in his tone.

"There is nothing we can do. This drought has put us in a compromising position. We are going to have to wait it out until I can find another coke connection," the woman stated, her voice calm and sure.

"But what about the restaurant?" Di'Meechi asked.

"The restaurant will just have to function as a regular restaurant until we can get our hands onto something. The customers will have to find another way to get their highs for now," Mr. Castello said.

Zya had heard enough, and hurried up to the main floor, her mind racing. *I know where to get the goods. While they are waiting for their coke to come in, I could be making a killing. The way these people get high in here, I could make enough money to be set for a while.* Zya thought about the opportunity that had just presented itself. She knew that she wouldn't be stepping on anyone's toes because they had blatantly said that their customers would have to find another source to buy from.

Why not from me? Zya was in mid-thought when Meechi walked in.

"Thanks, Zya. You did good. Take a couple days off."

"Thanks, Meechi. Can I go now?" she asked.

Meechi unlocked the door to let her out. "Remember what I said," Meechi warned as she walked by.

Zya nodded, only half-listening, and made her way home. She was plotting a money scheme in her head, one that was sure to set her up for a minute, and that was all that she could focus on.

She didn't get home until 4 A.M., but she was wide awake. She had already decided that she was going to fill the void the restaurant had encountered, and sell dope to the customers herself.

I have to get in contact with Jules's connect. Torey Snow will have the goods. I know he will deal with me too. I'll sell the dope for cheap so that they will have no hesitation about buying from me. I'll take an L at first, but the more dope that goes through my hand, the more money I will make.

Zya took a shower and then folded up her work uniform. She pulled the napkin with Liz's number out of the apron. She looked at the clock. It was four in the morning, but Liz had been insistent on Zya calling her. Zya had promised that she would, so she picked up her phone and dialed the number.

"Hello?" Liz answered, wide awake.

"Hi . . . It's me, Zya. Sorry for calling you so late, but you told me to call you when I got in."

"Are you just now getting off of work?" Liz asked.

"Yeah."

"What was that all about? Why'd he keep you this late?" she asked nosily.

Zya didn't answer. Meechi had made it very clear that she was not to speak of it.

"Look, I got to go. I'll see you at work." They said goodbye and hung up the phone. Zya's mind was too busy to sleep. Instead, she sat up and counted the money she had made that night. She had plans for it . . . big plans.

I won't have to work in that restaurant for too much longer. In six months, I'll be out.

Chapter 4

Grindin'

Zya had been stashing money up ever since she started working at the restaurant. For almost a year now, she had been saving up her money. She had taken an old shoe box and stashed it in the back of her closet for safe keeping.

Zya knew she had stumbled upon an opportunity last night. Her mind had been turning ever since she found out about the dope drought that the restaurant was experiencing. Zya had $10,000 saved up, and was seriously thinking about using it to cop some work.

I could flip that money three times in a week. The way people run in and out of there to feed their habit, I'd be rich in six months.

Zya went into her room and sat down in front of the closet. She pulled the money out and put it inside her Doonie & Bourke bag. She was about to get on her hustle by any means necessary. Waiting tables at

the restaurant was getting old, and after what Vinnie
had pulled the night before, she was ready to leave.
She knew that if she hustled out of the restaurant for
a couple months, she could save up enough money to
get back on her feet.

There was only one person that she knew who
would supply her with the dope, and that was Torey.
He had dealt with her before, and she had paid him
back so quickly she was sure that he would deal with
her again. She picked up her cell phone and found
Torey Snow's number in her address book. She dialed
the number, and as the phone rang, she could see the
dollar signs forming in her mind.

"Hello?" Snow answered.

"Snow, this is Zya. I used to pick up and drop off
for Jules," she began.

"I don't know what you talking 'bout," Snow said
with a short tone. The line went silent, and Zya didn't
know what to say.

*I know he remembers me. If he don't remember
me, I know for sure he remembers Jules.*

"Six months ago. After I paid you—"

Snow quickly interrupted her and rudely said,
"Look, shorty, I don't know you and I don't know shit
about what you talking about. If you calling about setting up a meeting for the housekeeping position, you
need to put your application in face to face. I don't do
no phone interviews."

Zya heard a click and the dial tone. She quickly became enraged at the fact that he had hung up in her
face. *No he didn't just hang up on me. He talking
about housekeeping . . . I got his face to face interview.* Zya quickly took a shower and dressed. She was
on the first thing smoking to Jersey.

Zya was anxious to get her hands on some dope, and the bus ride to Jersey seemed like it was taking forever. She knew that she didn't have enough money to buy weight. In fact, she didn't want to deal with bricks. That was federal as hell, and she wasn't trying to risk her freedom. She only wanted to buy a couple ounces a week so that she could fill the void in the restaurant while they were going through the drought.

If I'm careful, I can hustle out of the restaurant without Meechi ever finding out. It's the only way that I'm gon' make some real money. The clientele is already there, so all I have to do is let it be known that I've got the product without giving myself up to Mr. Castello and Meechi.

Once Zya arrived in Newark, she caught a cab to Snow's house. She told the cab driver to leave the meter running because she didn't plan on staying long. She simply wanted to make the transaction, discuss future arrangements, and be on her way. She walked up to Snow's two-story Victorian brick house and rang the bell. She tapped her foot as she waited for him to answer the door. After waiting a couple minutes, she rang the bell again and knocked lightly on the door. She grew more and more impatient as the minutes passed.

I know I didn't come all the way out here and he ain't home, Zya thought. There weren't any cars in the driveway, and the house seemed to be still on the inside. Just as Zya was getting ready to turn around to leave, the door opened. An attractive, brown-skinned woman answered the door. Zya immediately noticed the woman's resemblance to Snow and figured that it was his sister. Her gray eyes were identical to Snow's and her body language gave off the same confidence, as if it ran in their family.

"Can I help you?" the woman asked as her eyes slanted down in suspicion. She looked Zya up and down, sizing her up.

"Hi, I'm looking for Snow," Zya replied.

"He's not here right now. I don't think he'll be back for a while, either. Was he expecting you?"

Zya knew that he hadn't known she was coming. When she had called him he acted as if he barely remembered her.

"No, he wasn't. Thank you. Sorry for interrupting you." Zya turned to walk back down the walkway.

"Hey, wait a minute. What's your name? I'll tell him you came by," the woman said with a smile.

"Zya," she replied. "Please tell him Zya came by."

"Zya . . . you his girlfriend or something?" she asked with a curious grin.

"Nah, nothing like that. This is just a business visit."

"All right, Zya. I'll let him know you stopped by."

Zya smiled softly and replied, "Thanks. It was nice meeting you." She walked back to the cab and headed back for Harlem. She was pissed that she had made the trip for nothing. She hated the fact that she was going home empty-handed, and she was reluctant to try to call him again.

It is going to be harder than I thought to get my foot in the game. I thought Snow would be down to deal with me, but he's acting like he doesn't even know who I am. It hasn't been that long. I know he has to remember me. I need to get in contact with him face to face. I know when he sees me, he'll know who I am.

Zya was disappointed, but she knew that she would find her way back into the game. She was a hustler at heart and would eventually get her foot in the door.

Zya made her way home, and as soon as she stepped inside the door, her cell rang.

"Hello?" she answered.

"Hey, Zya. Do you gotta work tonight?" Vita asked. Her loud voice blared through the phone.

"No, I finally got a night off. Why, what you got up?"

"It's a party at the 40/40 club tonight. Big Easy throwing it, so you know it's about to be jumping. Every nigga on the East Coast probably gon' be there. You know we got to fall up in there," Vita said excitedly.

Zya had heard about the party weeks ago. Big Easy was a promoter in Brooklyn and was known for his hype parties. His street team had been passing out flyers for weeks. They had gotten word to all the major cities from Baltimore to D.C. Nearly everybody on the East Coast knew about it. Zya was reluctant to go. Her mind was too focused on making money.

"Come on, Zya. You ain't been out in forever. Your ass is always working. Let's go have fun tonight," Vita said, convincing Zya to go.

"Okay, Vita. Pick me up at eleven."

Vita agreed, and Zya hung up the phone. It was only 3 o'clock, so Zya had more than enough time to get ready. She knew that Big Easy was going to do it up big, and she didn't want to be half-stepping when she walked into the club. Zya took $800 from her purse and put the rest of the money back in the shoe box. She didn't really want to spend the money, but she had never stepped into any club without being the best looking chick there, and she didn't intend on starting tonight. When she was with Jules, she could have easily spent $5,000 on a designer hook-up, but she couldn't afford to do that anymore. She was about to get fresh with $600, and use $200 for spending money.

Zya took the subway to Manhattan and wound up browsing through every store between 5th and Madison Ave. She was shopping at high end stores, but was on a low budget, so she went straight for the clearance racks. She knew that every other chick in the club couldn't even afford to do that, so she was still ahead of the game. Girls in the club would be wearing cheap clothes while they walked the ho stroll for ballers, and Zya wanted to stand out from the crowd. She wasn't a sac chaser or a gold-digger. She never had been and never would be. She was simply going to have a good time. She wanted to make her own money, which is why getting in contact with Snow was so important to her.

Zya tried to keep her mind off of her financial goals and focus on picking out an outfit for the night. She was a professional shopper and could piece together hook-ups better than any of New York's top stylists. She shopped for hours, trying to find deals in the expensive stores, and at the end of the day, she came out with a short, champagne-colored, spaghetti-strapped dress from Christian Dior. The dress was beaded all over, which gave it a sparkle that was sure to stand out in the dark club. It fit her body perfectly, and she knew that she would turn heads. She wasn't looking for a man. A relationship was the last thing on her mind. She still hadn't fully gotten over Jules, but the attention, she figured, couldn't hurt.

Zya headed to the salon and got her hair pulled back with a champagne-colored pin. Loose spirals fell down the nape of her neck, and the natural-colored M.A.C cosmetics that the makeup artist applied had her skin glowing as if she had been kissed personally by the sun. At the end of the day, she looked like she had spent $5,000, but in actuality she had only spent $600 as she had planned. She definitely wouldn't blend in with the broke hoes. She looked like a V.I.P.

By the time Zya finally finished getting ready, it was almost time to go. Vita knocked on her door at ten o'clock, arriving an hour early. When Zya opened the door, Vita stood with her mouth hanging wide open.

"Damn, Zy, you making me look bad," she said with a smack of her lips as she walked into the room wearing next to nothing.

"You look cute," Zya said, knowing that her friend was becoming uneasy about what she was wearing. Vita did that every time they went out. She would see what Zya had on then decide at the last minute that what she was wearing didn't look right. Zya wasn't trying to wait on Vita to find something new to wear, so she added, "For real, girl . . . you look good."

"I thought so too until I saw your supermodel-looking ass," she said, half pouting and half smiling. "Can I look through your closet? I don't think I wanna wear this no more. Please, Zya. I swear I'll be done like that!" Vita said with a snap of her fingers.

"Go ahead," Zya said as she plopped down on the couch. *This girl is about to take all damn day,* she thought.

Vita made her way into the bedroom and immediately plunged into Zya's wardrobe. Zya had so many expensive clothes that it wasn't hard to choose a new outfit. She put on a pair of Zya's short black Prada shorts with the matching cropped Prada Jacket. She left the jacket unbuttoned to reveal her gold lace Victoria's Secret bra. She looked in Zya's full-length mirror and liked the change in apparel.

"Zya, where is your gold Manolo's?" she yelled into the living room.

"In the bottom of my closet, in the gold and black box!" Zya yelled back. "And hurry up!"

Vita bent down and crawled into the closet. *All these damn shoes. How am I supposed to know which ones are which? I don't even see a gold box,* Vita complained silently as she started opening shoe boxes. Vita's eyes bugged as she stumbled across a shoe box full of money. She looked back toward the bedroom door to make sure Zya hadn't come in the room.

Damn, Zya, I know they ain't paying you like this at that restaurant. She began to spark up a conversation with Zya so that she couldn't sneak up on her.

"Zya, what shoes you think I should wear?" Vita said as she took a rubber band off of one roll.

"Girl, I don't know. The party gon' be over by the time you get dressed," Zya yelled back.

Twenty, forty, sixty, eighty . . . two thousand. Vita counted in her head. It took her a minute to respond to Zya because she was counting. Her fingers flipped through the bills quickly as she nosily counted Zya's pockets.

"You hear me?" Zya asked.

"Yeah, I'm almost done! You think its gon' be a lot of niggas there tonight?" Vita asked, not really giving a damn about the answer. All she was concerned about was finding out exactly how much money Zya was working with.

"I don't really care. I'm just going to have a good time."

Twenty, forty, sixty, eighty . . . five thousand. Vita tried to count the money as fast as she could, but she heard Zya get up and head toward her bedroom. Vita threw all of the money back in the shoe box and placed it back in the closet.

"Did you find the shoes?" Zya said, standing in the doorway with her hand on her hip and an annoyed look on her face.

"Yeah, yeah, I got 'em. We can go." Vita's hands were shaking and her voice revealed her nervousness.

Damn, I couldn't finish counting it, but it got to be like $20,000 in that box, she thought, overestimating the actual amount. *If Zya getting money, why she ain't put me up on it? I'm tryna to get paid too,* she thought as they walked to the car. Vita couldn't help herself. She had to ask Zya about the money she had discovered in her closet.

"Zy, don't get mad, but I went through some other boxes in your closet."

"You counted my money, didn't you?" Zya asked, her anger showing in her tone of voice.

"No . . . no, I didn't count it. But how did you get all that money?"

"It's nothing, Vita. I've been saving up my cash from the restaurant. The people in there are big tippers. That's all, okay?"

"Damn, Zya, okay, okay. I was just asking."

"No, you were just being nosy. Let's forget about it and have a good time."

Both girls dropped the subject and made their way to the club. When they arrived, it was 11:30, and the street was flooded with people. It looked like everybody was dressed to impress. The line to the club was long, and they waited for nearly another thirty minutes before entering the club.

The inside of the 40/40 was decorated in purples and different shades of grey. Zya had never set foot inside the Manhattan club, but was impressed by its sophisticated atmosphere and its expensive decor. The club had various levels, and each part of the club had its own vibe. It was so crowded in the club that Zya literally had to squeeze her way through the crowd. As Zya walked in between a group of dudes, one of them grabbed her arm to get her attention. She looked back and saw Amir, one of Jules's old associates. He was looking her up and down, and seemed to be surprised at what he saw. Zya pulled her arm back then smiled and waved, but kept it moving.

"Yo, Zya!" Amir called after her with his arms in the air. Zya wasn't trying to make friendly conversation with Amir. She had stopped fucking with Jules, and she wasn't trying to associate herself with anybody he knew.

"Hey, Zy, somebody calling you," Vita said in her ear, yelling over the loud music as she looked back at Amir.

"He ain't nobody important," Zya replied casually as she continued to make her way toward the stairs. When they finally broke through the crowd, they moved to the second floor. *Damn, it's crowded up here too,* she thought as she looked around for a seat.

All of the tables were taken, but there were open seats at the bar, so she led Vita over there.

"Yo, can I get a strawberry daiquiri with a double shot of rum?" Vita asked the bartender. The bartender prepared her drink, and as soon as it was done, Vita excused herself. "I'll be back. I have to go to the ladies room. Will you watch my drink?" she asked Zya. Zya nodded and continued to nod her head to the Biggie lyrics that the D.J. was playing. Zya sat with her back to the bar as she watched the Pistons versus the Heat on the 60-inch plasma TV.

"You got money on that game?" a voice asked as he sat in Vita's seat.

Zya didn't even look up. She simply replied, "That seat's taken."

"Yo, my man . . . let me get a shot of Remy V.S.O.P and a Long Island for the lady," he said.

Zya turned and said, "Excuse me, but my friend is sitting—" She stopped talking mid-sentence. When she saw Torey Snow sitting next to her, she was at a loss for words.

This must be my lucky night, she thought. *I was just looking for his ass earlier, and here he is.* Her hand began to itch, and she knew that it meant money was getting ready to come her way.

"You didn't know me earlier when I called. Now you buying me drinks?" she asked sarcastically.

"It wasn't like that, shorty. I know who you are. You just broke the rules. I never talk business over the phone," he said. "Cell phones get you nabbed."

Zya nodded her head in agreement. She finally understood why he had acted so funny. "My fault," she said, apologizing for her carelessness.

Snow looked at Zya. She looked even better than the last time he'd seen her. It had been almost a year, and she was still sexy as hell. From her perfectly manicured toes to her flawless features, she had Torey Snow's full attention.

"How've you been?" he asked. Zya turned around in her chair and sipped at the drink that he ordered her. She wasn't trying to spark a personal relationship with Snow. She was strictly seeking out his business services.

"I'm good," she answered. "I'm looking to spend a little bit of money with you, though. That's why I called you earlier." It was her turn to evaluate him as she quickly looked him up and down. She had to admit, the nigga was fresh as hell. He had on Sean John jeans with a tan Sean John jacket resting on top of a crisp white tee. He also wore crisp tan Timberlands with a huge diamond hanging from his left ear. A diamond bezel Rolex rested on his wrist, and he rocked a Jesus piece so blinged-out that the diamonds glistened even in the darkened room. He even had on a diamond pinky ring. His chocolate complexion and grey eyes didn't match, but somehow it worked for him because he definitely looked good. Snow was getting money, and she was trying to get down.

"You didn't come here to talk business, did you?" Snow asked as he finished his drink.

Zya smiled and replied, "No, I can't say that I did."

"Well, then enjoy the party. I got the Remy room for the night. You and your girl come up to V.I.P. and have a good time. Afterwards, we'll talk." He handed her two V.I.P. passes then made his way into the crowd.

* * *

Vita stood over the counter in the parlor area of the bathroom and pulled the tiny package out of her purse. She ripped it open and emptied the contents onto the counter. She used one of her maxed-out credit cards to divide the powdery substance into two lines. The bathroom attendant looked at Vita like she was crazy.

"Bitch, what the fuck you looking at?" she asked with hostility.

The woman jumped and replied, "Nothing, miss. Do you need anything?"

"Do it look like I need something?" Vita snapped back. Under normal circumstances, she wouldn't have been so irritable, but at the moment, she needed a quick fix and the woman was in her way. The woman frowned then turned around and walked into the sink area.

Vita admired the coke before she bent her head down and snorted both lines up her nose. Vita licked her finger then picked up the debris of coke that her nose had left behind. She could feel the tension leave her body as her high set in. The coke made her feel so good, and even though she knew she shouldn't do it, she couldn't help it. The anxious feeling that had invaded her body quickly disappeared, and she looked in the mirror to make sure she hadn't left any traces of the drug on her face. She had hit a line before picking Zya up, but by the time she got to the club, she was feeling antsy and knew that she needed some more.

She had begun hitting blow about six months ago, shortly after Zya moved out. She wasn't addicted to it yet, but it had become a habit that she indulged in frequently. After Zya left, Heavy had been acting real controlling and possessive. He was always worried about what moves Zya made and what Zya was up to. Vita had been Zya's friend way longer than she had known Heavy, so her loyalty always lay with her. She didn't know why he had taken a sudden interest in Zya's business, and it caused tension in her relationship. She and Heavy had started to fight more and more. The relationship was quickly becoming too much for her to bear. Vita found relief in the cocaine that she used, and most of the time, it was Heavy who provided it for her.

It's not like I'm an addict or something. It's only blow. Everybody does it. And I'm not doing it all the time, only a couple times a day, so I'm good. Vita tried to convince herself that she wasn't wrong. She figured because she wasn't smoking crack she was not at risk. What she didn't realize was that cocaine was just as bad as crack. It was the same drug in a different form. Vita didn't notice that she had begun to crave the dope more and more. She only made excuses and reasoned with herself about why doing it wasn't wrong.

Zya walked into the bathroom and called out Vita's name.

"Back here," Vita responded as she looked in the mirror and touched up her makeup.

"You a'ight? You been in here for a minute," Zya asked, noticing a change in Vita's mood.

"Girl, trust. I'm good," Vita replied.

"I got two passes to the Remy Room," Zya said.

Vita hurried and put her makeup back in her purse and said, "Well, what we in here for? Let's go."

As they walked out of the bathroom, the attendant

shook her head in disgust. Zya looked at the girl like she was crazy and said, "What the fuck you looking at?" Vita laughed loudly and grabbed Zya's arm and pulled her out of the bathroom.

"Fuck was that all about? She was looking at you all crazy," Zya said.

"Girl, you know how chicks be. Let's go have fun," Vita replied.

Zya entered the room first and saw Snow chilling on a leather couch that wrapped around most of the room. The room was big, and there had to be a hundred people inside. Everybody was chilling and conversing over drinks and food. Snow was surrounded by his crew and a bunch of women who were trying to be down.

"There go your boy," Vita said, assuming that Zya was interested in Snow. She didn't know anything about Zya's hustle plan, so she had no clue that Zya was simply seeking his services. She planned on chilling off in a corner somewhere until the night was over, but when Snow looked up and motioned for her to come over, she didn't have a choice but to comply. She and Vita strutted over to the crowded couch and loved the jealousy they received when they were invited to sit in the midst of Snow and his crew.

Zya sat down next to Snow. A fat, dark-skinned dude came over to the table and shook hands with him. "What up, Snow? You enjoying the party?"

"Yeah, Easy. You did it big, man. You know I had to come through to support you, fam."

Big Easy told Snow to get at him after the party and then walked away.

"Y'all want something to drink?" Snow asked them.

"Hell yeah," Vita replied.

Snow motioned for the waiter and pulled out a diamond-encrusted money clip with nothing but hundred dollar bills in it. "Let me get a couple bottles of Patron," he said as he placed two hundred dollars on the waiter's serving tray.

The liquor arrived, and everybody was having a good time drinking and chilling. The envious vibes evaporated from the air, and even the women in the room were talking and laughing. Zya sat next to Snow and knew they looked good together. She could tell by the way everybody in the room treated them. If their interaction was under different circumstances, Zya might actually be interested in Snow, but she knew that it could potentially be bad business to get involved with him. She didn't want to mix business with pleasure.

After finishing the liquor, everybody was feeling good and having a nice time. Snow leaned over and got close to her ear.

"You look good tonight," he said smoothly, his deep voice sending chills up her spine.

Zya leaned back and looked in Snow's face. *Yeah, this nigga is feeling it,* she thought as she blushed from his compliment.

"Whatever, boy. You feeling it. Every chick in this room probably looks good to you right now," she responded playfully, still sitting close to him. He smiled, and his perfect teeth made Zya smile back. He was sexy, there was no denying that, but she knew not to cross that line.

"Nah, I don't fuck with skeezers. Just you," he said in a low, confident tone.

"Just me, huh?" Zya replied, shaking her head from side to side.

"Yeah, shorty . . . just you."

Zya was in awe of the man. She was not the type of girl that fell for game, but Snow's game was tight, and he had her interested. *Too bad I can't see what he's about*, she thought. She was determined to stay focused on the bigger picture.

Vita stood up and looked at her phone. "Yo, Zya, I got to go. It's already 2:30, and you know how Heavy is," Vita said as she grabbed her purse off the couch.

Zya looked at Snow, realizing that she hadn't accomplished what she had set out to accomplish. *Damn, if I leave now, it ain't no telling when I'm gon' catch up with him again,* she thought.

She looked at Snow and said, "I got to go. When can I get up with you? I got some business I need to discuss with you."

"We can handle that tonight if you trying to stay. We'll talk about it over breakfast and then *swap it out* like that," he said. "I'll drop you off at home or wherever you need to go."

Zya looked at Vita and said, "Girl, I'ma stay here for a little while. Snow is gon' drop me off when it's over."

"All right, girl," Vita said as she hugged Zya. "Call me when you get in," she said as she gave Zya and Snow a playful look. "Don't do nothing I wouldn't do."

Zya laughed then sat back down next to Snow. He was actually good company, and she was having the most fun that she had experienced in a long time. They chilled for a couple hours, and when the crowd started to clear out, they got up to leave. Snow put his hand on the small of her back and guided her through the crowd. They followed the crowd outside and into one of the parking garages up the block. She spotted his Aston Martin, and she walked by his side as she made her way to it.

"Yo, Zya!" a male voice called out.

Snow and Zya stopped walking then turned around. Amir came jogging up to her with a serious look on his face.

"What up, Zya? Long time no see," Amir said sarcastically. Zya frowned her face up, not sure exactly what he wanted with her.

"You looking good," Amir said. He looked back at Snow. "You doing a little bit too much for a chick that supposed to be at home."

"What is that supposed to mean?" Zya asked.

"You talked to Jules?" Amir asked.

"What the fuck do that got to do with you?" Zya asked defensively, knowing where the conversation was headed. He was stirring up feelings that she had buried, and she didn't appreciate it.

"I'm just saying. My man's stressing about why you ain't coming to see him. You haven't even taken his baby to see him yet. I guess you too busy out here fucking around with another nigga."

"What? Me fucking around? You need to holla at your boy about that. He got that department locked. I didn't do shit to Jules that he didn't bring on his damn self, so fuck you and him!" Zya said with her finger in his face.

She got this confused look on her face and thought, *Why am I even addressing this little mu'fucka.* She put her hand on her hip and said, "Why are you so concerned with Jules's business anyway? Yo' small-time, corner-hustling ass need to quit riding his dick so hard and make sure you known before you try to step to a bitch like me. Don't you ever try to check me about shit that I do. You better realize who the fuck I am, nigga. I'm Zya, and everybody out here know how I get down. Can you say the same about you?"

Amir got a salty look on his face and watched as Zya stormed off. "I'm just saying. He got a right to know about his baby, yo!"

"There is no baby! I got an abortion, so since you acting as the little messenger boy, you can tell Jules that he ain't got to lose sleep over that no more."

Zya walked all the way to Snow's car without saying a word. Jules's little worker had managed to turn her good night bad in less than five minutes. Zya was so mad she was near tears.

How dare that ugly-ass nigga get up in my face talking about what Jules needs to know. I needed to know his lying ass was fucking another bitch, but I didn't. This nigga got me out here destroying my mind and body with an abortion because he wasn't man enough to be faithful. Fuck him! Zya thought. She could feel the tears of anger slide down her cheeks, and she turned her body toward the window to conceal her face from Snow.

He had heard what just went down, but felt that it wasn't his place to step in. He figured as long as the little dude didn't get crazy then he shouldn't intervene. Besides, it looked like Zya was handling the situation just fine on her own.

"You okay?" Snow asked.

"Yeah, I'm good," Zya whispered. "Look, I'm sorry I lied to you about Jules being locked up. He told me not to tell everybody, so I didn't."

"I don't care about that man business. I already knew anyway," Snow said.

"What? How?"

"Zya, the streets talk. Harlem knew about Jules's arrest almost as soon as it happened. I heard about it a couple days after you gave me that whole story about him being out of town. I just figured you had your reasons for lying. That's your man. You did what he asked. Ain't nothing wrong with that."

"He's not my man," Zya stated softly as she looked out of the passenger window.

"So, why are you still out here trying to hustle for him?" Snow questioned.

"Please, I'm not doing anything for him. I'm in it for me. Jules left me broke and pregnant. After I found out he had gotten some other girl pregnant, I was done. I got an abortion, paid him what I owed him, and left his ass alone." Zya wiped the tears from her face. She didn't know why she told Snow what had happened. She just needed to get it off her chest.

"Real talk?" he asked her as he turned her face toward him.

"Real talk. But I'm good, though," she said as she nodded her head.

"You don't deserve a nigga like that. There are a thousand niggas out here who would die to have you on their arm," Snow said sincerely. Zya smiled and blushed, but didn't respond.

He pulled into a 24-hour restaurant, and they ate an early breakfast together while they arranged their business.

"So, how much the ounces going for?" Zya asked as she ate her omelet.

"Seven-fifty," Snow replied.

She frowned and replied, "I'm trying to buy in

bulk. I need a better deal than seven-fifty. I'm gon' keep coming back again and again, so you gon' get constant money from me."

He had to smile at her business savvy. He sat back in the booth and asked, "How much are you trying to pay?"

"Six hundred," she proposed.

Snow was intrigued by Zya, and because of that, he consented to her proposal. She would be the only one of his customers getting the dope for so cheap. He looked at her and the smile on her face was worth the $150 loss.

They finished their breakfast then Snow took Zya home. He followed her up to her apartment and she went into her shoe box to get his money. She only bought five ounces to start off. Snow told Zya that he would have the dope delivered to her in a couple of hours, and the transaction was complete.

"Thanks, Snow," she said. "I'll be in touch."

I'm about to get this money, Zya thought. *I'm finally in the game.*

Jules sat behind the glass and watched his old worker pick up the phone. Amir had been loyal to Jules, and ever since Jules had been locked up, Amir made sure that he visited frequently.

"What's up?" Jules said.

"Shit, man. I just came up here to give you some news," Amir said. "I know you got a lot on your mind right now, but I thought you should know what was going on with your girl Zya."

Jules sat up in his chair and leaned close to the

glass. Amir had his attention. He hadn't heard from
Zya in almost a year, and her absence had hurt his
pride and enraged him.

*That bitch didn't even have the decency to bring
my baby to see me. She didn't even send a picture.*

"Yo, how my shorty doing?" Jules asked.

"Man, I saw her with some nigga at Big Easy's
party last night. That bitch was talking reckless like
she had beef with you or something."

Jules was steaming, but he didn't let Amir see.
"What about my kid, yo?"

Amir shook his head and replied, "She got an abortion. Jules, man, I'm sorry. You shouldn't have had to
find out like this."

"What the fuck do you mean?"

"There is no baby. She said that she got rid of it.
When I asked her about it, she got to popping off at
the mouth and telling me that you ain't shit. She was
on some 'Fuck Jules' type shit, nah mean?"

Jules's heart dropped, and he couldn't believe what
he was hearing. The one woman he loved and would
have given his life for was now abandoning him. The
thought of her was the only thing that kept him
strong in jail. His eyes began to water, but the sadness
he was experiencing suddenly transformed into rage.
Jules stood up from the table and threw the metal
chair at the glass, causing it to crack.

"You tell that bitch I'ma see her ass!" he said right
before the guards subdued him. "Bitch! That fucking
dirty-ass bitch!" He yelled as he kicked and fought
the guards restraining him. They pulled Jules back to
his cell, and once he was there, he sat down and
pounded his fists against his head.

She killed my seed, yo. We were supposed to be a

family. Why the fuck didn't she tell me? I'm in here thinking she's riding for me, when all along she has been running around with another mu'fucking nigga.

Jules was hurt, but he felt anger more than any other emotion. He would have never expected Zya to cross him, but she had, and now he was left in jail wondering why.

The next night, Zya walked into work with a new attitude. She was there to get busy, and nothing was about to stop her from making her bread. She had two ounces in her apron packaged up in grams. She was carrying 56 grams of cocaine on her, and it was the best feeling she had ever felt in her life. She knew she was about to make money. She looked around the restaurant and saw that Marcella was not at work.

"Where's Marcella?" Zya asked Liz. She hadn't been at work in a couple days, and that was odd for her. She usually never missed her tips.

"I don't know. Meechi says she's been sick lately," Liz said as she rushed off to cover her section. Zya walked into the back to punch in, and she found Buggy sweeping the office.

"Hey, Buggy," Zya said nicely. She liked Buggy. He was a sweet guy, but he didn't have it all. He was almost mentally retarded, and most of the people in the restaurant treated him badly. He didn't really do much in the restaurant. He usually swept the floors and performed other small duties around the place. Zya had grown fond of him, though, and always went out of her way to be nice to him.

"Hi!" Buggy said as he continued to sweep the floors. He always walked with his head down and had a crippled walk. Zya walked past him, gave him a high five, clocked in, then made her way onto the floor.

Zya saw Vinnie and his associates sitting at their usual table, and she approached them. *He buys more dope than anybody in this entire restaurant. I have to fuck with him,* Zya thought as she walked over to his table. Vinnie sat back in his chair when she approached, and puffed on his cigar.

"Zya, my favorite girl," Vinnie said. Zya grew a suspicious look on her face and replied, "Since when?"

"Since forever!" Vinnie announced. He pulled out some money and peeled off five hundred-dollar bills then placed them on her tray. "About the other night . . . I apologize. I had kicked back a couple drinks and . . ."

Zya smiled. She had Vinnie right where she needed him to be. "Vinnie, it's okay. I think we can work something out." She took the five hundred dollars and put them in her apron. When she pulled her hand out, she pulled out one gram of cocaine. She put the small package in the palm of his hand and whispered, "Taste that and let me know when you want some more. I've got that for you all day for thirty-five dollars a gram if you spread the word."

Vinnie looked at Zya in amazement then kissed her once on both cheeks, "My girl!" he said almost proudly.

Zya walked away and continued to wait the rest of her tables. Not even an hour had passed since she had given Vinnie the free sample, and he had already spread the word. It seemed like every table she waited on knew that she had grams for sale. The good thing about Italians was that they loved their highs, and when they purchased the goods, they usually bought ounces. She sold through the entire two ounces in a couple of hours. She had to rush home on her break to get more. By the end of the night, she had run through the whole five ounces. She walked out of the restaurant with $7,000.

I just made a $4000 profit in a day. Snow had only charged her $3,000 for five ounces, and she had flipped them in a day, earning $7,000, and that wasn't even including her tips. And because she was supplying her tables with the goods, her tips grew tremendously. She ended up going home with $11,000— seven G's from product and four G's for service. She had stumbled upon a gold mine, and knew that she was about to get rich.

That night, she got off work at 2 A.M., and was on the 2:30 bus to Jersey. She didn't give a damn how late it was. There was no way she was going to work the next day without any product. It had sold too well for her to miss any money. When she arrived in Jersey she took a cab to Snow's house. It was late when the cab finally pulled up to Snow's house, and she hoped that he would still be up.

"Keep the meter running," she instructed as she crawled out of the back seat. She walked up to the house and rang the bell. It took him a couple minutes to answer the door. Snow was shocked to see Zya standing before him with her work uniform on.

"I need ten more ounces," she said eagerly.

Snow looked at her like she was crazy and said, "I ain't trying to tell you what to do or nothing, but you might wanna make sure you get off the five you bought last night first, li'l ma."

Zya pulled a fistful of bills out of her Dooney & Bourke and replied, "They're gone. I sold them all today."

Snow was amazed. He had never seen a woman who possessed so much hustle. The more he was around Zya, the more he realized that she was not an ordinary woman. Snow invited Zya in and hit her off with more product. He was definitely impressed.

The next day when she went to work, she got rid of them just as easily. Her product was selling like hot cakes, and she went back every night to re-cop from Snow. Vinnie had done as he'd promised and spread the word. Every customer that entered the restaurant became her clientele. She was moving ounces so quick that even she couldn't believe it. When a customer bought more than a half-ounce, she simply borrowed small take-home boxes from the kitchen. She put the coke in them to make it look like her tables were simply taking home leftovers.

Zya did this routine day in and day out. She managed to run this operation solo and without anyone noticing. She never asked for days off, and as each day passed, her pockets grew fatter and fatter.

She had easily made a nice profit, but she spent it just as quickly as she made it. She decided to keep her apartment to avoid the hassle of putting a new one in someone else's name. She did, however, purchase a 2007 Dodge Charger and customized it to her tastes. Zya was getting money, and she wanted the entire city to know it. She stayed blinged-out, and even though she wasn't whipping a Benz, her car was far from average. The money and the hustle had become addictive, and she loved the fast pace of the game.

Months passed, and Zya got more and more money. She didn't think that Meechi knew she was serving his customers, and as long as management didn't find out, her operation would continue. He did, however, wonder why everybody had started to request Zya as their waitress. Everybody in the restaurant wanted Zya to serve them, and her clientele grew every day. Snow's dope was so good that once you tasted it, you had to come back for more. There was no one-time buy. Once you got it in your system, you wanted more. The pleasurable experience that Zya provided the customers is what allowed her to eat, and she was eating good.

Ain't nothing gon' stop me from making this money.

The money was blinding Zya, and though she said she was only going to hustle for six months, she never stopped. She couldn't stop if she wanted to. She knew that she had the best hook-up with the restaurant. She didn't have to do anything. All she did was deliver the product. A quick and simple transaction was all that she did. The drug sold itself, and the restaurant provided her with a perfect, low-key location. All she had to do was sit back and collect her money. As long as Meechi didn't find out, she was cool. She knew that she had the perfect set-up, and she couldn't give it up. The money was lovely, and the fact that she didn't have to search for customers had her hooked. She didn't negotiate prices and didn't have to deal with the bullshit that came with the game. Her customers were willing to pay whatever she was charging because her product was so good. Her shoe box full of cash quickly turned into fifteen shoeboxes full of cash as the money continued to pour in. She couldn't leave the game alone. She was too good at it.

This money is too easy to give up. I'm gon' get it until I can't get it anymore. The world is mines.

Chapter 5

Bona Fide Hustler

Bills of different denominations were scattered all over Zya's kitchen table. She smiled as she counted her profit from the restaurant. She moved, at the least, five ounces a day at the restaurant, which made her a nice profit daily. She neatly placed her money into five hundred dollar stacks. She began to count the different piles.

Eleven, twelve, thirteen . . . Damn, I got about thirteen thousand right here. Not bad. I could get used to this shit, fa real. I never knew coke money could come so fast. Another couple of months of this and I can be set for life!

Zya grabbed a stack of bills and gave them a long kiss. She had never had this much money before, and she couldn't believe that it was all hers. She had also built a good business relationship with Snow, and her credit was good with him. She got to a point where she was going to re-up every other day. At first Snow grew kind of suspicious. He had never seen a woman move coke like her, not a woman.

Just as Zya was practically drooling over her cash, a brilliant idea entered her thoughts. *I wonder if Smitty would deal with me without Jules. I could sell it cheaper than what he was getting it from Jules and run through more bricks, which means more money. Sell it cheaper and make less for every transaction, but in the long run, I would get more money because I would sell them more frequently.* Zya pieced her plan together in her mind like a game of chess. Her hustler instincts kicked in, and she was plotting to get more money. The little money that she just got from coke seemed small now that she saw the potential of the dope game.

Zya tore up her apartment looking for Smitty's number. She opened all of the drawers and looked underneath everything that could be looked under trying to find Jules's letter that contained Smitty's number. After an hour of searching her entire place, she gave up. Exhausted and frustrated, she flopped down on her couch and thought long and hard about how she could get in contact with Smitty. That little piece of paper was her only connection to him.

Think, Zya, think. How can you get in contact with Smitty? I got it! I'll make his ass look for me. I need to contact Big Easy.

"Yo, yo, yo this is Big Easy at Power 105, where we play nothing but the hits. Ladies and gentlemen the jump-off is this Saturday at nine o'clock. Julius Carter aka Jules's release party is going down at Club Arlenes.

It's going to be on and poppin', and everybody who's anybody is going to be there. My man is coming home. He beat the case, and the streets gotta show him love. Welcome home, baby!"

Zya smiled as she turned down the radio and listened as her plan went into effect. She had taken a small portion of her money and put it into promoting a "release party" for Jules. She knew Jules would not see the light of day anytime soon, but used him as a pawn in her chess game.

Fuck it. He's used me, and now I'm about to return the favor. I'm out for self right now. Jules had a lot of customers with the coke, and I know all of them. Shit, I was the one who usually delivered it to them, but always in public places and never at their spot. I can make some key connections at this party. If they ask for Jules, I'll tell them that his prison release was postponed and it was too late to cancel the celebration. This is my chance to network, and then I could really start making money. I can hook up with Smitty and everybody else that fucked with Jules. The world is mines.

Zya had dollar signs in her eyes, and knew that the money she was getting out of the restaurant was only the tip of the iceberg. She was aiming for the sky.

Wade sat at his desk with his feet up. He was listening to the radio, and what he was hearing grabbed his full attention. Big Easy was announcing Jules's release party.

What the fuck are they talking about? I put that nigga in jail myself, and he ain't getting out no time soon. This must be a mistake, Wade thought angrily as he picked up his phone and called the front desk.

"Yeah, Mona, this is Wade. Do me a favor. Look up some info on Julius Carter. Tell me his release date." Wade waited a few minutes in silence for the information to come back. Mona gave him the information that he already knew.

"So, he isn't even eligible for parole for another three years, right? Yeah, that's what I thought. Thanks." He hung up the phone and wondered why a release party was being thrown for a person who wouldn't see the streets for at least another three years. Wade made a mental note to go see what was going on at the Arlenes club that Saturday. He turned down his clock radio and put his gun and badge on. He was about to hit the streets for his daily rounds. He always stayed in tune with the streets.

Just as he was about to get ready to leave, his door opened. It was Felix, a rookie cop.

"Yo, Wade. Jones wants to see you in his office ASAP."

"What the hell does he want me for?" he asked.

"I don't know. But he looks mad as hell. What did you do now, man?"

"Who knows? I'll be there in a minute. Thanks," Wade said just before Felix closed the door and left Wade to himself.

"What the hell does he want to see me for? It's always something, shit!" Wade muttered as he headed to see what Jones wanted. When Jones called him into his office, nine times out of ten it was to chew his ass out for doing something. The last time Wade was called into Jones's office, it was to put him on probation with the force because he shot two unarmed dealers in a drug bust. That incident cost them the case, and Jones was infuriated. The time before that, a couple bags of weed were found in Wade's squad car. Jones called Wade in to confront him, and Wade was still high off the two bags at the time. So, Wade was pretty much on thin ice. Wade's badge should have been taken a long time ago, but his ability to infiltrate drug rings and take down kingpins was undeniable. He was NYPD's best.

Wade knocked on Jones's door hesitantly, and heard his lieutenant's voice.

"Come in."

Wade stepped in and watched Jones as he focused on the files that were in front of him.

"What's up, Lieutenant Jones?"

"Have a seat. I have a new case for you. Now, this target is unlike any you have ever been assigned to. This target is ruthless, as well as the most intelligent drug dealer New York has ever seen. That's not the best part. She's a woman."

Wade sat up in his seat because now Jones had his undivided attention. In the bottom of his gut, he knew who Jones was talking about. Jones slid Wade the profile of the target, and when Wade saw the target, his heart skipped a beat. He knew exactly who it was. He listened as Jones continued.

"This is Anari Simpson aka Tony. She is believed to be one of the top distributors of cocaine in the U.S. She is believed to be the mastermind and top supplier of Supreme Clientele."

"Supreme Clientele?"

"Yeah, an inside source has informed us that Supreme Clientele is a roundtable where only the top drug distributors around the country are allowed. Tony is believed to be the ringleader and an active member of the table. Many people believed she died seven years ago, in a car explosion in Flint, Michigan, but these pictures prove otherwise." Jones tossed pictures of Anari walking with bodyguards into the restaurant. "This is her walking into Stello's in the wee hours of the night three weeks ago. It makes sense for her to come out of hiding seven years after she faked her own death. The statute of limitations just expired, meaning we couldn't arrest her for fraud for faking her death."

Wade looked at the picture of Anari, and rage overcame him. He knew who Anari was. Actually, he knew her well. She was involved in the slaying of his favorite cousin, Tiffany Davis about six years back. She was found hung in her apartment in Jersey. The Jersey police labeled it a suicide, but Wade was close to his cousin, and knew she wouldn't kill herself. It was the little details surrounding her death that led him to believe Anari was still alive and responsible for the murder. Anari and Tiffany had been at odds with each other for a long time, so that created motive. A book was found by Tiffany's body, entitled *Dirty Money*. It was a biography about Anari's life and their beef. Another suspicious thing was Tiffany had a lipstick stain on her cheek. It was obvious that someone had kissed her wearing lipstick.

Forensics couldn't prove that the kiss had come from Anari, and it went down as a suicide. The Greeks used that tactic, and called it the kiss of death. They kissed their enemies after they killed them as the ultimate sign of disrespect.

Shortly after his cousin's death, Wade tried to go

after Anari, but to no avail. She was virtually untraceable. Even though it went down as a suicide, Wade had a feeling in his heart that Anari was behind it and somewhere smiling.

Wade's hands began to shake out of pure hatred for Anari as he stared at her file. Wade knew he had to conceal his emotions to avoid getting taken off the case. Jones would not allow him to take the case, knowing that it would be personal. Jones tossed more photos at Wade and continued to brief him.

"That man that you are looking at is Jimmy Castello. He owns Stello's, the place we believe the roundtable meetings are held."

Wade rubbed his neatly trimmed goatee and asked, "Stello's . . . the fancy Italian joint, right?"

"That's right. We also believe Castello is a member of the table. Castello used to be a henchman for Capone in his early teens back in Chicago. In the late seventies he got convicted of extortion. He got out about ten or fifteen years back, and I guess he couldn't fly straight. The person you see standing next to him is his son, Meechi. He's a dumb, arrogant little fuck. He thinks he can't be touched because of his father. He's a piece of shit, and he runs the restaurant. I think he will be the weak link, so target him."

"Damn, they on some real Mafia shit, huh? I thought that shit was just in movies."

"Nah, my boy, this shit here is real. The FBI has been on this case for a while now. They have sent four undercover agents there, and all of them either come up missing or they ask to be pulled out before they can even build a case.

"When the FBI said they needed someone who thought like a criminal and someone who could match their wits, I recommended you. The chief has been on my ass about getting rid of you, but I always put my ass on the line for you. You have to get a conviction on Anari Simpson. She is by far the biggest drug lord the East Coast has ever seen. And how does that make us look? She's a woman," the lieutenant said in exasperation.

"I'm on it," Wade said as he grabbed the files and headed out of the office. Just before he reached the door, Jones spoke.

"And Wade."

"What's up?"

"Cut off those damn cornrolls and pull up your damn pants. You look like the criminals you chase."

Wade let out a small chuckle and replied, "The same traits y'all hate me for are the same ones that y'all need me for."

Wade exited the office and began to think. *I can't believe this bitch resurfaced. She killed Tiff, and now I'm about to put her behind bars for a very long time, fa real! Fuck that bitch! Where do I start, though? I thought Supreme Clientele was a myth. My niggas around the way talk about it, but I never believed them.*

Even rappers would lie in songs and claim that they were connected to Supreme Clientele, but everyone knew Italians didn't fuck with black people too often. Wade thought hard about how to approach this, and he came up with an idea. He was going to smoke her out of her hole, shake things up a bit.

He rushed back into Jones's office and said, "Do you think we can get a search warrant?"

❊ ❊ ❊

Tonight was the night of the fake release party, and Zya was looking forward to putting her plan into action. She was on her way to pick up Vita. She didn't tell Vita the real reason for the party, and she played along as if she had forgiven Jules and really was throwing him a bash. Telling Vita her hidden motives would have been the equivalent of putting it on primetime CNN. Vita couldn't hold water, and Zya knew that there was too much at stake for her to take a chance on telling Vita.

Zya reached Vita's place and blew her horn as she pulled into the driveway. Not a minute after Zya pulled up, she heard the sound of Heavy's speakers shaking the ground. He pulled his truck up alongside the curb and hopped out with another guy. Heavy noticed Zya waiting in the driveway and sarcastically spoke to her as he walked by.

"What's up, Zya? Long time no see, huh?"

Zya threw up her middle finger and shook her head from side to side. Heavy laughed at her sincere gesture and continued to walk toward the house. Zya blew her horn again, letting Vita know she was becoming impatient.

I hate that country-ass nigga. He gon' get his one day. He got the nerve to speak, like he didn't try to rape me. What a clown.

Zya saw Vita coming out of the house, still putting on her heels. As Vita scuffled to the car, Zya noticed that Vita had lost a tremendous amount of weight. She almost didn't even look like herself. *Damn, she's Whitney Houston skinny,* Zya thought as she stared at her friend's physique.

Heavy looked at Vita like she was crazy as he watched her walk down the steps. "Fuck you think you going?" he asked her loudly as he gripped her arm tightly.

"I told you Zya was throwing a party tonight for Jules," Vita replied.

"What I tell you about that girl?" Heavy asked in a low voice. Vita snatched her arm away from him. "Did you think about what I said?" he asked her.

"Heavy, yeah, I thought about it! Damn, we'll talk about this when I get back."

At that moment, Zya blew her horn and smiled sarcastically at Heavy as she watched Vita walk toward her car.

"Hey, girl!" Vita said in exasperation as she got into the car, shaking her head.

"Hey. You ready?"

"Hell yeah. I'm 'bout to get my party on. I can't believe Jules is getting out."

"I just found out today he won't be released for a while. He got into some shit up there and got some time added."

Vita looked at Zya with concern. She knew that Zya was trying to be there for Jules, even though he had played her. "Damn, girl, are you okay?"

"Yeah, I'm good. The party must go on, though. I spent too much money on this celebration to cancel it."

"I feel you, girl. Let's get the fuck out of here before Heavy starts tripping."

Zya pulled off and they headed toward Club Arlene's.

The party was semi-crowded, just like Zya expected it to be. She wasn't there to party anyway. It was strictly business for her. At the beginning of the party, she instructed Big Easy to get on the mic and tell everyone that Jules got a little bit of time tacked on for a fight. At first, the mood grew dull, but after Zya bought everyone a round of drinks, they quickly forgot about Jules.

Zya sat at the back of the club, waiting to see some of Jules's old coke customers. She glanced over at Vita dancing with a man. Vita was working it, and had dude against the wall, grinding her ass into his crotch. Zya looked at the man's face and immediately recognized him.

"Bingo. Black Ty," she whispered to herself as she made her way over to him. Black Ty was a young hustler who used to cop from Jules a while back. Zya remembered driving Jules over to his spot a couple of times. His big-ass lips made him easy to spot.

Zya tapped Vita, letting her know she wanted to cut in. Vita started dancing with another nigga that stood to her right, and Zya start backing that ass up. She turned around and met eyes with Ty.

"Oh, shit! What up, Zya?"

"What up, Ty?"

Ty stepped back a little while dancing with Zya. He didn't want to disrespect his man by being all up on his lady. Zya grabbed his hand and pulled him right back on her ass. She grinded on him, feeling his pipe begin to grow. Ty grabbed Zya by her waist and gently pushed her away.

"Damn, girl, you trying to have me beefin' with Jules, huh?" he asked as he licked his lips and looked her up and down with a lustful gaze.

"Nah, it ain't even like that," she said as she stopped dancing and turned toward him. "I do have to holla at you about something for a minute," Zya whispered in his ear seductively.

"What's up?"

Zya grabbed Ty's hand and led him to her table at the back of the club. They both sat down, and Zya had Black Ty's full attention.

"You still moving weight, right?"

"Yeah, you know it. That's why I came. Since Jules been gone, it's been hard to get my hands on some decent shit."

"That's what I'm trying to tell you. It's back."

"It's back? I thought Jules was still locked up."

"Nah, nah . . . I got the same shit, but for a cheaper price," Zya said as she pointed to herself. She continued, "I'm letting them go for fourteen a pop."

"Fourteen?" Ty said with raised eyebrows.

"Fourteen!" she confirmed.

"And it's the same coke Jules had?" Black Ty asked, trying to make sure he wasn't falling for the okey-doke.

She could see Black Ty becoming more interested, so she continued to hustle. "Yeah, and I'm getting down to my last couple bricks, so if you going to jump on it, you better do it quick," Zya lied, trying to get a sell.

Ty sat there in silence for a minute. It seemed like he was thinking hard about what he was about to say. He did the math in his head and knew that he couldn't beat it. "You can't beat fourteen a brick. Fuck it, I want four. How quick can you get them to me?"

Zya wanted to jump up and down right there, but she kept her composure. She reached into her purse and grabbed a pen. She wrote her number on a napkin and slid it to Ty. "Call me tomorrow night," she said as she got up and walked away from the table.

She had just made her first connection of the night, but it wasn't her last.

"Like I said, I'm down to my last ones, so you better jump on it," Zya said, kicking the same game she had used all night.

"I'll go and get the money now. I need them, Zya, badly," Roc said. He knew that he was getting a deal, and he didn't want to let the opportunity slip out of his hands.

"Nah, it's cool. Just use the number I gave you and call me tomorrow night."

Zya walked away from the bar, leaving Roc with his nose wide open, hoping that he could get down. Throughout the night, Zya discussed business with at least ten different niggas about the coke, and they all wanted in. Each one was Jules's old customer. Everybody was a bit hesitant to deal with her at first, but after they heard the offer she was making, they knew it was too good to refuse. Her sales pitch got better and better with each conversation. By the end of the night, Zya had become a certified hustler.

At around 2 A.M., the party began to wind down and people started to leave the club. Vita and Zya sat at the back table and watched as the club's light switched on and the dance floor became vacant. Everyone was going toward the exit, but one man was entering the club.

Zya looked closer and noticed that it was Smitty. He stuck out like a sore thumb. He was twice the age of most people in the club, and he wore a black silk shirt with gators to match. Smitty was an old school, fresh-ass player who was well respected. A toothpick hung out of his mouth as he smoothly walked across the room, looking for his old friend. Zya watched as Smitty scanned the room.

"I'll be right back," Zya said to Vita as she slid out of the booth and headed toward Smitty. Smitty spotted Zya coming toward him, and he flashed his pearly whites at her.

"Hey, lovely. Where's the man of the hour?"

"Oh, you didn't hear? They on some bullshit and trying to keep Jules in on some bad behavior shit. He got into a little scuffle a couple days ago," Zya lied.

"That's just like a nigga to hate on someone before he gets free."

"I know," Zya agreed.

"I was really looking forward to seeing my man too. He's missing a lot of money right now. Know what I mean?"

"Really? He told me to holla at you. I lost your number, but you know what they say."

"What's that?"

"All work and no play . . ."

Smitty paused for a minute, trying to figure out what Zya was trying to say. He got the picture and then smiled while finishing Zya's sentence. "Makes a dull day."

From that night on, Zya supplied Smitty his bricks.

Snow drove through the streets of Jersey in his snow white Benz, the same color of the product that enabled him to buy the luxury car. He inhaled the weed smoke as he banged 2pac's "Hailmary" out of his sub woofers.

"I ain't a killa, but don't push me. Revenge is like

the sweetest joy next to getting pussy." Snow rapped along to the lyrics and watched as all eyes were on him as he cruised the city streets. At 27, he supplied the suppliers with the best cocaine from his overseas connect. He was in a comfortable situation and was getting a lot of money out of the streets. The last couple of months he noticed an increase in his income, and knew the main reason behind it: Zya.

I don't know how she does it. She re-ups every three days. I have never seen anyone move weight so quick. She's moving weight like a nigga out here. Maybe I need to relocate and get some of that Brooklyn money. If Zya is moving them bricks like she is, I know I can get crazy money there. Yeah, that's not a bad idea. Maybe I need to give Zya a call and see what's up. I'm glad she's on my team, Snow thought.

Zya had been buying bricks left and right. The way Zya was moving coke, everyone was happy, because everyone was getting money. Snow even lowered his prices for Zya. She was his number one customer, and he wanted to keep her happy.

Actually, Snow wanted to do more than supply Zya with bricks. He wanted to supply her in the bedroom. He grew more and more attracted to her over the past few months. Having a beautiful woman around him was nothing new, but Zya's demeanor set her apart from the rest. She was so gangster, and that's what turned Snow on the most about her. She matched his wits, and he had never seen anybody hustle like her. It was like she was born to move coke. Every time she cashed Snow out for his product, her flipping through the money got him aroused. Snow told himself that he would never mix business with pleasure, but with Zya, he was willing to make an exception.

"Damn, girl, go easy on that blow," Heavy said as he laughed at the sight of Vita indulging herself. He sat on the couch with a blunt in his mouth, making smoke circles.

"Shut the fuck up, Heavy," Vita said as she hit another line of what she thought was cocaine.

He had been giving her powder heroin, telling her that it was blow. Heavy had discovered Vita was cheating on him with more than one person. He felt like she was on the verge of leaving him for someone else, and his insecurities emerged. The mind control that he once had over Vita was fading, and he wanted it back. Now she yearned for what Heavy had, and he finally regained control.

If Vita didn't have her "coke," she would get physically sick, but she never knew why. She was experiencing withdrawal from the heroin and didn't even know it. She just knew that Heavy's product was the only blow that got her where she needed to be. Heavy had total control over her, and she was helpless. Heavy was done with Vita, but he wanted her to suffer before he quit her.

"I'm serious, Vita. You need to slow down. You just did five lines in under an hour."

Vita hit the last little bit of heroin on the table and looked at Heavy with a runny nose. "Heavy, let me get a li'l more, baby," she begged.

"What you going to do for me?" Heavy asked as he puffed his blunt.

Vita stood to her feet and almost fell back down. She gathered herself and walked over to Heavy. She dropped to her knees and knelt directly in front of Heavy. "I'll suck and fuck your dick so good, you'll never forget it."

Heavy grabbed Vita by the arms and shoved her aggressively. "I don't want any of that dope-head pussy."

Vita began to cry and rub her arms frantically. "Please, Heavy, let me get a little bit," she pleaded, folding her hands, trying to sway him.

Heavy enjoyed torturing her, and he pulled out a bag of heroin and waved it from side to side, teasing her. "Remember what you were telling me a couple of weeks ago? About how much money did you see in Zya's closet?"

Chapter 6

Federali

Zya picked up her cell phone to call Vita, and heard the operator's voice, informing her that Vita's phone was disconnected. "That can't be right," Zya said as she sat at her kitchen table counting money. She hung up her phone and tried again, but got the same response.

Damn, Vita. I would have let you hold something to pay yo' damn bill. She and Heavy must be beefing again. Oh, well. I guess I'll have to go and holla at her a little later.

Just as Zya was about to return her cell phone back to its clip, she felt it begin to vibrate. She looked at the caller ID and saw that it was Snow calling.

"What's up, Snow?" she answered.

"Zya, they on deck," Snow said, informing her that he had the bricks.

"Oh, okay, so I can pick them up tonight."

"Yeah, that'll be good. When can I be expecting you?" he asked.

"Tonight when I get off work."

Zya hung up the phone and smiled because she knew more money was headed in her direction. Snow had just got back from seeing his Cuban connect, and he had picked up another shipment. People had been calling her the last two days for weight, but she had to wait on Snow to return.

Zya and Snow became close in the midst of dealing with each other. Snow offered her a partnership, and they were both getting bread together. Zya loved his prices, and she was kind of feeling his style too. Even though it had been a while since she stopped messing with Jules, she still wasn't ready to be involved with anyone. She told herself she was all about making money right now. But every time she came into contact with Snow, she thought about what it would be like to be his woman.

Zya glanced at the clock and saw that it was nearly time for her to go to work. With the drug money coming from the restaurant and from the streets, Zya had accumulated a lot of money. Some weeks she got so much money, she wouldn't be able to count it all. She just grabbed a shoe box and dumped the money into it.

She walked to her room and opened her closet. She had removed all of her clothes from her closet, and only shoeboxes filled the space, shoeboxes full of money. It was barely enough room to put the box in her hand inside. She managed to squeeze it on the top, and then she closed the door.

I need a safe, because this shit ain't going to work,

she thought as she fixed her hair, preparing go to work.

It had been three months since she got connected with Jules's old clientele. With her low prices and good dope, she had made three times as much as Jules ever made monthly. Zya was on top of the game and making a name for herself.

Zya went under her bed and grabbed two ounces of coke and stuffed them into her purse. Earlier, she had put a gram of dope in each baggy, and they sold like penny candy. This was an everyday routine before she went to work. She usually had to run back home to get more, so she contemplated taking more to save the trip.

It ain't worth the risk. I'll just come back if I need more, she thought as she headed out of the door to work.

An hour later, Zya was at Stello's, waiting tables. She had only been at work forty-five minutes, and she managed to slang an ounce and a half. *Damn, I need to ask Meechi to let me take my break early so I can run home. I only have a half left, and the night crowd haven't even came yet.*

Zya went to the bar to put her food order in. Just as she pinned the receipt on the order board, Meechi stuck his head out of his office and called her.

"Zya, come here for a minute."

Zya wanted to wait on her customer first and also put up the dope she had left before she went into Meechi's office. "Okay, I'll be there in a second."

Meechi's face expressed anger, and he raised his voice. "No, I need to see you right now. Come here," he said as he ducked back into his office.

Zya took a deep breath and walked into Meechi's office. She saw Meechi sitting behind his desk, staring at her. "What's up, Meechi?" Zya said nervously.

"I have to talk about what you've been doing in my restaurant."

Damn, I'm busted. He's going to fire me, but I don't give a fuck. I already made ten times as much in dope money in here than what he's paying me. I don't know, these Italians are crazy.

Meechi stood up and walked over to Zya. He reached in his inner coat pocket, and Zya's heart skipped a beat.

"Meechi, please don't shoot me," she said.

Meechi looked at Zya like she was crazy as he pulled out a white envelope. "What the fuck are you talking about? I just wanted to commend you on doing a good job. All the customers rave about you, and I wanted to show you that I take care of my hardworking girls. Here." Meechi handed Zya the envelope full of hundred-dollar bills.

"Thanks," she said as she finally exhaled and tried to stop her heart from beating one hundred miles per hour.

Meechi sat on top of his desk and lit a cigar. He noticed Zya's nervousness and laughed, "What did you think, I was going to kill you or something?" They both laughed, but Zya wasn't laughing at Meechi's comment. She was just happy she didn't get caught selling her own product out of the restaurant.

Zya put the envelope inside her apron and said, "Well, I have a lot of customers waiting. I'm going to get back to work." She started toward the door.

Meechi spoke to her just as she reached the door.

"Zya, I need for you to serve the roundtable tonight. Can you do it? Marcella called in sick again."

"Sure, Meechi."

"Oh yeah . . . and, Zya."

"Yeah?"

Meechi's smirk turned into a frown before he spoke. "I want a ten percent cut on the dope you're moving out of my fuckin' restaurant. I know about everything that goes on around here. Remember that. You're a hustler. I like that. We can't supply the customers right now, so I don't see anything wrong with you making some pocket change. Ten percent from now on. Got that?"

Zya nodded her head and left the office.

Fuck, fuck, fuck. How long has he known? I guess I wasn't being slick after all. Well, at least now I don't have to sneak around here with the coke. This could be a great business move.

On her break, she had made her usual trip to her house so that she could re-up, and at the end of the night, Zya had sold all of her coke. She watched as everyone at the restaurant prepared to go home for the night. She sat at the back table and began to count her earnings for the day once most of the staff was gone. She took out Meechi's ten percent and put it to the side. She didn't mind giving up a percentage to him because it could have been much worse.

I am glad that he only asked for a cut. I thought he was about to dead me right then and there. Them damn Italians don't play when it comes to money.

Zya was supposed to stay back because that night

was the night of the Supreme Clientele meeting and she told Meechi that she would serve them. Liz was the last staff member to leave, and she saw Zya at the back table. Liz walked over to Zya, and she was so busy counting her money, she didn't even notice Liz approaching her.

"Oh my goodness. How did you get all of that money?" Liz asked as she stared at the stacked of hundred- and fifty-dollar bills on the table.

Zya was startled by her unexpected company, and had no time to conceal her cash. It was too late. Liz had seen all of her business. Zya, at first, was annoyed by her nosiness, and smacked her lips to let it be known. Zya quickly lightened up and tried to cover up her attitude. She searched for an excuse.

"Girl, Vinnie gave me a five thousand dollar tip tonight. I guess he felt guilty for how he's been treating me."

Liz grew a look of skepticism on her face, but just played along with Zya. "Yeah, I guess it was due. What are you still doing here?"

"Meechi asked me to serve another private dinner tonight. I need the extra money too."

"You're not the only one. I wish he would let me do a couple of them private parties. Marcella started doing some private dinners and bought herself a new car within a month. Lord knows I could use the extra cash. You know, with the kids and all."

Zya knew that Liz had three kids, and felt sorry for her. Zya grabbed five one hundred dollar bills off of the table and handed it to Liz. "Here you go."

Liz's face lit up when she saw the money Zya was handing to her. "I cannot take this, Zya."

"Take it, Liz. You know you need it. Besides, the

way Vinnie acts sometimes, he should give all of us big tips."

Liz dropped her head and humbly took the money. "Thanks, Zya. I owe you big time for this. I could really use this money."

Before Zya could respond, Meechi stepped out of his office and yelled, "Zya, make sure you lock up once everyone leaves."

Liz looked at Zya and said, "I guess that's my cue. I'll see you on Monday, and thank you again."

"Later," Zya said as she stuffed the money in her purse and followed Liz to the exit. Zya locked all four deadbolts and flipped over the CLOSED sign. When Zya turned around, she saw Meechi leaning against the bar.

"Got my cut?" he asked.

"Yeah, it's right here." Zya reached into her purse and pulled out the envelope. She walked over Meechi and handed it to him. His eyes got big when he peeked inside the envelope.

He handed the envelope back to Zya and said, "Honey, I said ten percent, not your whole take."

Zya handed the envelope right back to Meechi and responded, "That is ten percent."

Meechi grinned and the stuck the envelope into his inner coat pocket. "You're amazing. You know that, right?"

Zya threw her hands in the air and shrugged her shoulders. "I know, I know. What can I say?" she asked as she boasted playfully. They both laughed, and Meechi went back to his office.

"The meeting starts in about a half an hour. Grab a bottle of our best wine from the back."

Before Zya could reply, Meechi closed his office

door. Zya put her purse behind the bar and went to the back, where the wine was.

It's dark as hell back here. Where's the light switch? she thought as she rubbed the wall right by the room's entrance. As she searched for a switch, she heard movement within the room and grew very tense.

"Who's there?" she yelled as she continued to search for the light switch. After a few seconds of frantically searching for it, she found it and flicked it on. *What in the hell?* She saw Buggy standing in the corner, looking terrified.

"Buggy, are you okay?" she asked and she went toward him.

"I . . . I got lo-lost. Zya, I want to go . . . go home," he stuttered as he shook timidly.

Zya walked over to Buggy and gently grabbed his arm. "Come on, Buggy. Let's get you home." She led Buggy to the front exit. She grabbed him by the shoulders and looked directly at him and whispered, "Buggy, you can't be roaming around here like that, okay? You know Meechi doesn't allow anybody in the back."

"Okay," Buggy said, not knowing what he had done. Zya looked back to ensure Meechi wasn't coming, and unlocked the doors.

"Buggy, go home, okay? I will see you tomorrow."

Buggy smiled from ear to ear and waved to Zya as he exited the restaurant. Zya watched as he walked across the street to the apartment he stayed in. Zya locked the doors once she saw he was in.

I feel sorry for him. He must have been scared back there, not knowing where he was at. I'm glad I found him when I did.

Zya quickly got back on task and returned to the back room and grabbed a bottle of Cristal from the cellar. She returned to the bar and put it on ice. That's when she heard the back doors being opened, and then she heard the noise of the elevator going down. *That must be them coming in now*, she thought as she went to the kitchen and prepared some finger foods for the guests.

Zya waited a couple of minutes to let the round-table get settled, and then she prepared to go downstairs. She grabbed the paper that had the security codes written on them for access to the room. She went to the freezer and searched for the keypad. Once she found it, she pushed in the code, *11, 28, 84. Bingo!* she thought as the freezer lights came on and the elevator began to move downward.

When the elevator stopped, Zya opened the door and saw the long, narrow hallway that led to the roundtable room. She grabbed her order pad from her apron, so that she could remember all of the orders, and started toward the room. The closer she got, the clearer the conversation became. Zya heard and recognized the voice that was speaking. It was the woman she saw at the table the last time. She was speaking calmly and clearly.

"We have to do something about the cocaine drought. We have no connect, which means no product. We are losing a lot of money right now with the drought, and we just took a loss from that one-eyed bastard. We need some coke. Not that bullshit, either. We need some pure cocaine. My connect is tapped out, and he has no idea when he is going to get more." She spoke with so much confidence that

Zya knew she was the most powerful person in the room.

Damn, they killed that man with the fucked-up eye. That's messed up—before Zya could even finish her thoughts, she heard someone coming toward the door. She quickly got out of her eavesdropping position and tried to look as normal as possible. The door cracked open, and she pretended to be just about to knock.

"Oh, there you are. The guests are ready," Meechi said as he opened the door completely and stepped to the side so Zya could enter.

Zya walked in, and all conversation seemed to come to a screeching halt. She looked around the room and noticed that six people were sitting at the table, all of whom were looking directly at her—all of them except for the woman who sat at the head of the table. The woman gently tapped her temple with her index finger, looking as if she was in deep thought.

It was an uncomfortable silence for a couple of seconds, so Zya quickly began to write everyone's orders down. The only person she noticed that she knew by name at the table was Mr. Castello. She went from person to person, taking orders. The woman was her last stop.

"And what would you like to drink, ma'am?" Zya asked as she held her pen to the pad.

"What's your name?" the woman asked as she looked up at her.

"Zya," she responded.

"Okay, Zya, give me a glass of Dom," she said as she looked Zya in the eyes and smiled.

There was something warm about the woman's eyes that welcomed Zya. She wrote her order down and went toward the door, but before she exited, she heard the woman's voice.

"Zya, I like those Manolos you rockin'. They hot!" the woman said as she looked down at the $500 pair of shoes Zya wore.

"Thanks," Zya said as she smiled and walked out of the room. Before she closed the door, she heard the woman say, "Damn, Castello, how much do you pay your waitresses? I want a job here." The whole room burst into laughter, and Zya headed upstairs to get the drinks for Supreme Clientele.

The next day, Zya was having a good day at the restaurant. It was a Saturday night, and she had already moved a couple ounces before the night crowd even came. Nothing could have messed up Zya's day—nothing except what was about to happen.

"Get on the fucking ground!" a police officer yelled as he pointed his nine millimeter directly at Zya. A swarm of police officers rushed into Stello's all at once, completely ransacking the place. There were police everywhere, telling everyone in the restaurant to get on the ground. Even the cooks and customers had guns in their faces.

Zya fumbled her plates in her hands and dropped them on the ground, causing them to shatter into little pieces. She dropped to the floor with her hands up in the air. She lay face down on the ground, right next to Buggy. She glanced at the door and watched as more police filed into the building with their guns drawn. The last man to walk in was a man that looked to be in his mid-twenties and wore braids to the back. Zya knew he was a police officer because he wore a bulletproof vest that had NYPD stamped on the chest.

He took his time walking in while smoking a cigarette. He dropped it on the ground and stepped on it as he began to look around, giving orders. "Check the back. You, check behind the bar. Tear this mu'fucka up until you find something. Let's go!" he yelled as he walked over to the officer that was putting Meechi into cuffs.

Meechi smiled arrogantly and didn't appear to have a worry in the world. "Where's your search warrant, officer?" Meechi said with a smirk on his face.

"Shut yo' bitch ass up. I'll do all the talking. Where are they?" Wade asked calmly as he stood directly in Meechi's face.

"Right here," Meechi said as he gave Wade a pelvis thrust, indicating his balls.

Wade gave Meechi a shot to his mid-section and watched as Meechi fell to his knees. Wade knelt down to get on Meechi's level and began to whisper in his ear.

"I know what's going on here, and if you cooperate, you won't rot in jail for the rest of your life."

Meechi burst out into laughter without responding to Wade's plea. "Oh, what, you don't like the food here? Next time you visit, ask for me. I'll make sure your plate gets my special sauce," Meechi said, fully enjoying himself.

"Get him out of here," Wade said as he walked away and began to scan the room.

Zya looked over at Buggy, and he had a blank expression on his face. He didn't even realize what was happening. Zya whispered to him, "It's all right, Buggy. Just be still, okay?"

"O-okay," Buggy stuttered as he stared aimlessly.

Zya felt sorry for Buggy, but she really should have been thinking about her own situation. She had two ounces of cocaine in her apron. *I got to get this shit off of me. I can't move my damn hands because of these handcuffs.*

Zya began to think about how she could get rid of the dope, but she was in a sticky situation. The man with the braids ordered all the people in the restaurant to be taken down to the station. The police officers took everyone down, even the cooks and customers. They weren't going to let anything slip in between their grasp. They even loaded Buggy up in the police wagon. Lonnie Wade was about to find out something, one way or another.

Meechi sat in the interrogation room with Wade and Lieutenant Jones over his left and right shoulders, talking in his ear at the same time. They were trying to break Meechi, but he wasn't budging. They were not getting any information out of him, and they were growing frustrated. Meechi sat there smiling, and never answered any of their questions. The only thing he would say was to joke about how bad their breath smelled. He knew they had nothing on him, and Meechi was enjoying himself. The more fun Meechi had, the more infuriated Wade became. Wade couldn't take Meechi's arrogance any longer, and he snapped. He grabbed Meechi by the collar and got right up in his face.

"Listen up, you ol' pasta-eating mothafucka! I used to smack up niggas like you back in the day. You think you can hide behind yo' daddy like you own the world, but you have another thing coming. I know about the drugs and the operation you're involved in. It's only a matter of time before you and Supreme Clientele go down," Wade said as he released his grip and forcefully pushed Meechi.

Meechi's cocky smirk never left his face. "Supreme Clientele? What the fuck is that? Oh, that old Ghostface album *Supreme Clientele*. I liked that album. You niggers sure know how to do that rap music."

Wade couldn't control himself. He rushed for Meechi, but Jones grabbed him just before he reached him. Jones pulled Wade out of the room so he could regain his composure.

Liz sat in the interrogation room, crying, looking at the pictures of Marcella's dead body.

"We found her body three days ago in a Dumpster," he stated. "This could have easily been you, Elizabeth. The people you work for are animals. Help me get them. Help me bring justice for your friend." Wade knew the pictures would make her break. Wade sat next to Liz, pretending he genuinely felt bad for her, but he was just trying to squeeze her for information about the restaurant. She cried and cried as she saw her friend's lifeless body, and Wade knew he had her right where he wanted her.

"This is what they do to innocent people after they're done using them. We need your full cooperation to help take these people down. They killed your friend. What do you know about the meetings that go on there?"

Liz managed to talk to Wade between her sobs. "I don't know. They don't tell me anything. Marcella used to serve the after hour meetings. They wouldn't let me do them, so I don't know what goes on. I just know that when the meetings take place, the restaurant closes down early, and they send everybody home except for the waitress serving them."

Wade continued to grill her. "So, who started to wait on the table after Marcella stopped?"

"They had Zya doing it."

"Zya?"

"Yeah, she's the black waitress."

Wade looked at Jones and nodded his head, signaling him to put the black waitress in an interrogation room for him to question.

"Don't worry about anything, sweetheart. We are going to take the scumbags down and bring them to justice for what they did to your friend."

Wade exited the room and entered the one next to it. He looked through the two-way mirror and saw a beautiful sister waiting at the table. She was twiddling her thumbs, and he could tell that she was nervous. He stared at her beauty, and had a feeling that he knew her from somewhere. He stared at her closely and tried to remember where he had seen her before.

She is fine as hell. How is something so beautiful into something so ugly? Where have I seen her before? She is the wifey type I would take home. I'd tear that shit up every night. She would be my queen, and I would be her . . . King! That's where I saw her. Wade smiled and rushed out of the room and headed to his office. He had just taken a big step closer to his ultimate goal—Anari.

❈ ❈ ❈

Zya sat in the interrogation room sweating bullets. She had been arraigned and charged along with all the other workers in the restaurant. She had been sitting in the bull pens for three days, and she didn't know what to do. They had all been stuck with a bullshit charge: conspiracy to commit an illegal activity. The police had searched her and found the cocaine stashed in her apron, so she got hit with possession as well. She nervously played with her fingers and looked at the mirror that hung on the wall in front of her. She knew that it was a strong possibility that someone was monitoring her from the other side.

What am I supposed to do? Think, Zya . . . think. I need to get out of this shit. They are on some bullshit right now, for real.

Zya thought about calling Snow, but didn't want to connect the dots for the police. She doubted that she was under any serious investigation, but if she was, she wasn't going to lead the police straight to Snow. *Why did they come busting into the restaurant anyway?* she thought as she waited impatiently.

Wade put his hand on the doorknob of the room Zya was being held in and was about to go in before he heard Felix's Latino accent. "Yo, Wade! Are you ready to go in with the next waitress?" Wade threw his hand up, signaling Felix to yield. Felix stopped dead in his tracks and watched as Wade entered the room alone.

Wade watched as Zya played with her fingers, and she was noticeably shaken up. Without saying a word, he walked to Zya and tossed some photographs on the table in front of her. Zya looked down at the photos and her heart dropped at the sight. She couldn't believe it. There it was in front of her, pictures of her entering the Baltimore Hotel with King, and another one was with her exiting with Jules on the night of King's murder. Zya knew that she had to remain calm.

"What's this supposed to mean?" she asked as she crossed her arms and rolled her eyes at Wade.

How in the fuck did he get those pictures? I have to play it cool. Those pictures don't mean shit. If they do, he wouldn't be showing them to me. I would already be in jail. Something's got to be up, Zya thought as she confidently stared at Wade.

Wade looked at the two-way mirror and said aloud, "Let me get some privacy." He leaned against the table, standing right next to Zya.

I knew someone was watching on the other side of that mirror, she thought.

Wade stared at Zya for a second and then spoke. "Yeah, you're right. Those pictures don't mean anything right now. But when you add these ones, they mean a lifetime sentence behind bars." Wade tossed pictures of King lying dead on the hotel's bed. Zya grimaced at the sight and turned her head, trying not to look at them. Zya felt the burden of King's death on her heart, and knew that she had played a part in that brutal set-up. She flipped over the pictures and screamed, "Fuck!" She knew she was in a bad predicament.

Zya quickly tried to defend herself. "He gave me a ride to the hotel to meet my boyfriend. I didn't have anything to do with that murder."

Wade slammed his hand on the table, scaring Zya and making her jump. He was ready to cut the bullshit and expose his hidden motive.

"Stop fucking playin' with me, shorty. There were two sets of fingerprints found in that room. Now, I

can run your prints and compare them to the ones
found in the room. You and I both know what little
discovery I will find. But I don't want you. I could
care less about the little hustle you got going on. I
want Supreme Clientele. I want Anari Simpson."
Wade lowered his voice and continued. "Now, you
have a decision to make. Do you want me to run your
prints or do you want to cooperate?"

Zya knew she was in an unfavorable position, and
she couldn't think of any possible way out of it, so she
responded, "No, I don't want you to run my prints."

"What do you know about Supreme Clientele?"

"I don't know anything. I just take their orders and
serve a couple of drinks, that's all."

"Where are the meetings held?"

Zya wasn't willing to tell Wade any good information, so she just played a part. *I'm no snitch, but I
guess I can just feed him some bullshit to keep him off
my back.*

"They have the meetings in the front dining area."

"Well, I need to know everything. I want you to tell
me what they say, what they do, and what they look
like. Listen for names, dates, places, everything! Do
you fucking hear me?"

Just when Wade was about to speak, someone
walked in the room. What Zya saw confused her. It
was Buggy—not the Buggy she knew, but he was
walking upright and did not have that dumb look on
his face that he always had.

Zya spoke. "Buggy?" *What the hell is going on? I
thought he was retarded. He's a fuckin federali! I
can't believe this shit.*

Wade smiled and looked at Zya. "Meet Agent
Matthews. He is with the FBI and is an inside infor-

mant currently working undercover. He is going to be working closely with you and—" Wade didn't even finish his sentence before Lieutenant Jones came in.

"Wade, let her go. Castello's lawyer just came in and dropped nine hundred thousand, posting every single person's bail. Ain't that 'bout a bitch? The fucker just dropped nine hundred thousand in cold cash on the front desk," Jones said as he shook his head side to side and placed his hands on his hips.

"Fuck!" Wade yelled as he hit the desk. He bent over and whispered in Zya's ear. "You have a week to tell me what you're going to do. If you don't cooperate, I'm going to put you away, just like I did your little boyfriend."

Chapter 7

Heavy Trouble

Zya massaged her wrists softly, trying to remove the tiny bruises that the handcuffs had caused. Castello's lawyers had gotten all the charges against her dropped, but she was still in a bad situation.

I can't believe this is happening. This shit can't be happening to me. I helped set up King because Jules needed me to. I'm so fucking stupid. I helped that nigga kill somebody, and now I'm the one who is getting ready to take the fall for it. I risked my life and freedom for him, and he couldn't even be faithful. My loyalty to him is what got me in this situation in the first place. I have to choose between a murder charge and snitching.

I can't do no jail time. That shit ain't for me, I already know I wouldn't make it one day. But I can't snitch either. That is the number one rule of the streets, and I would be breaking it if I did what Lon-

nie Wade asked me to. If I do cooperate and Supreme Clientele finds out . . . I'm done.

Zya stared out the window to her apartment and a tear slid down her face. She never expected that she would be in a position like this, and she didn't know what to do. *I can't go to jail,* she thought. *I'm not built for this shit,* her mind told her as she slid down against the wall and put her head in her hands. She was kicking herself for being so stupid. She had done dirt, and it seemed like karma was coming for her.

She had known what the consequences would be if the shit ever hit the fan, but she honestly hadn't expected to be caught. She knew the game and knew that when things got hectic you were supposed to take the jail time and keep your mouth shut; charge it to the game and keep it moving. Zya couldn't do that, though. There was no way she was willing to do prison time for a murder that wasn't her idea to begin with.

It wasn't even a part of the plan. It was only supposed to be a robbery, and now I'm sitting here thinking about how to get out of a damn murder charge that I didn't ask to be a part of in the first place. She couldn't believe that she had been so stupid. She had seen other girls get played by niggas before. It wasn't odd for a dude to talk sweet in a girl's ear just so he could use her. Zya was usually the girl who peeped game, but with Jules, she couldn't see through the bullshit. She had been blinded by her love for him. She realized now that Jules had used her, but it was too late, the damage was already done. He had taken advantage of her loyalty and gotten her involved in something serious. No matter what she chose to do, her life was getting ready to be changed forever.

Zya didn't know what to do. She was stuck between a rock and a hard place. She needed an escape, a way out of the dilemma that she had been forced into. She picked up the phone and called the only person she could trust. She was scared, and her heart was pounding as she waited for him to answer his phone.

"Hello?" Snow answered after the fifth ring.

"I need help," Zya whispered as she gripped the phone tightly and closed her eyes.

He could hear the shakiness in Zya's tone and knew that something was wrong. She was so strong and level-headed most of the time, but this time was different. Just the sound of her voice let him know that something serious had gone wrong.

"What's wrong, Zya?" he asked.

Zya felt the hot tears grace her face. She hated the fact that she had lost control over her own life. Her destiny was in someone else's hands, and the only thing she could think to do was run. *I have to get out of here. I have to get out of New York. I can't go to jail . . . but I'm not a snitch either. I have no choice. I've got to run.*

"Zya? Zya, what's wrong?" Snow asked, his deep voice reflecting his concern.

"I have to get out of here. I have to leave New York," Zya announced in a frightened tone. She got up, ran into her bedroom and frantically pulled her suitcases from underneath her bed.

"Leave New York? Whoa, mama. Slow down and tell me what's up."

Zya continued to stuff clothes into the suitcases. She knew that she wasn't going to be able to take everything, so she tried to get the things that were most important. She ran back and forth from her dressers to her suitcase as she tried to explain herself to Snow.

"Something happened. I killed somebody," she began.

"You what?" Snow exclaimed in disbelief.

"No! It wasn't like that. It wasn't my fault. I got caught up in a murder after I helped Jules set up this nigga named King."

"Damn, Jules the one who had King hit?" he said.

"Yeah, but we weren't supposed to kill him. We were only going to rob him. Things got out of hand and Jules shot him."

"What the fuck that got to do with you?"

"Now some detective claims he saw the entire thing. He has pictures of me going into the hotel with King and coming out with Jules. He says that he's going to charge me with the murder. I know me and you still got business to take care of, but right now I need to get out of town," Zya said.

Snow had heard about King's murder, and now that Zya was telling him the details, it all began to make sense. He was surprised that King had been caught slipping. He was notorious in New York, and Snow was convinced that it had been a professional job. Now that Zya admitted she was involved, Snow knew what had gone down.

Jules used Zya to get close to King. After she earned his trust, she set King up to be robbed. Whether it was planned or not, King's trust for Zya got him killed. I just hope that I'm not getting myself into the same situation.

"I'm on my way over. Don't do anything until I get there. Just be cool," he instructed. He wanted to keep

Zya as calm as possible. After hearing her story, he realized that he didn't know exactly what she was capable of doing. He would have never expected murder from the woman he had come to know. *Maybe I don't know her as well as I thought.*

Snow jumped into his car and made his way into New York. He knew that Zya was hot—she was under investigation for the murder of King—but he couldn't stop himself from driving toward her house. She had bricks that he needed to take off her hands, but in the back of his mind, he knew it was more than business. He was drawn to Zya, and knew that he could not turn his back on her. It was something about her that he couldn't get out of his system. He didn't know if it was because she had made it clear that he couldn't have her, or if he really was attracted to her. All he knew was that she was different from any woman he had ever met. On top of her beauty, she was smart and loyal.

Her loyalty to Jules is what got her in this situation in the first place. She was ridin' for the wrong nigga, Snow thought as he made his way to LaGuardia Airport. *Ain't no way she should have had to hustle for herself. Jules done fucked it up for every nigga now. She don't trust nobody. I'm gon' help her get out of town and get right, so that I know she's straight. The way she helped me get money, I owe her this.*

Zya paced the same back and forth pattern in her apartment for three hours, waiting for Snow to arrive. *He's not coming. I got to get out of here. He ain't gon' show,* she thought as anxiety hit her. She was scared. She had never been so afraid in her life, and she didn't want to hang around any longer than she had to. Her bags were packed. All she needed to do was count her money and pack it up, then she could get the hell out of dodge.

Zya pulled one of her heavy suitcases from her bedroom to her front door and was about to go get the other one when she heard a loud knock at her door. She jumped at the loud noise then crept to the peephole. Torey Snow stood on the other side of the door, and she sighed deeply, trying to calm her nerves before she opened it. She clicked the locks, opened the door, and stared into the eyes of her partner in crime. Snow could see that she had been crying. Her eyes were red and her hair, which usually flowed neatly down her back, was disheveled. Snow stepped into her home and closed the door behind him.

"How did you get into the building? It's supposed to be locked," she said.

"The door was broke. I just walked right up."

Zya stood toe to toe with him and said, "Thank you for coming. I'm not trying to get you involved in no hot shit. I just didn't know who else to call."

Snow stared down at Zya. She looked so fragile and weak. He moved her hair out of her face. He was star struck by her beauty, and at that moment, wanted nothing more than to keep her safe.

"I didn't think you were coming," Zya said as she looked down at her feet and wrapped her arms around herself.

Snow lifted her head so that he could look in her eyes. "I don't know what type of nigga you used to fucking with, but I do what I say I'm gon' do. My word is bond. You can trust me."

Zya nodded her head as she walked to her couch. She sat down and said, "I just need to get out of here. I can't believe I got myself into this shit."

"How did you get into this?" he asked, wanting to know if he was doing the right thing by helping her.

"I was dumb. I met Jules when I was fifteen, and he basically showed me how to hustle. From the very beginning, he taught me how to cook and cut dope. He schooled me in everything. I loved him so much, I just wanted to be with him all the time. He was always in the streets, though, and the only way that I could go with him was if I was helping. So I did! I became good at hustling. I made runs for him, I cooked dope for him, and I did whatever he asked me to. I never thought about what the consequences would be. I was so dumb I didn't realize that our relationship was nothing but business, sex, and broken promises. We never did things like normal couples. The only thing that I ever did with Jules was make money and fuck."

Snow sat back, listening to Zya's story. She told the uncut version and left nothing out, admitting everything to him.

"King began to become a problem for Jules. When King came to town, Jules lost money. That's why he stopped copping from you for a couple months. It was because King was taking his business. One day, we were out and King tried to holla at me. Jules saw it, but he didn't get mad like he usually did when niggas pushed up on me. He decided that I should get close to King so that I could help set him up. He asked me to get with King so that he could catch him with his guard down, and I did it, no questions asked.

"But the night of the robbery, Jules changed the plan. He shot King because he said that he would eventually come back for us. I didn't know that it was going to happen like that. I swear to God, Snow, I had no idea.

"After that, Jules got nabbed and I found out I was pregnant. I went to visit him one day and some other girl was sitting up in there, nine months pregnant, talking about she was going in to see Jules. She was well taken care of while I barely had a roof over my head. He was probably cashing her out with all the money I was making for him.

"I got the abortion the same day, and you know the rest. Now I'm here." Zya leaned against her bar-style counter and felt like a weight had lifted off of her shoulders. She vented to Snow. It hurt to think about everything she had been through, and she couldn't help but to let it out.

He walked over to her and embraced her tightly. *That nigga fucked her over,* he thought in disbelief. He would never understand Jules' logic. He knew about the other chicks that Jules had messed with, and they were all hoodrats that every nigga in the hood had dug out. Jules had played Zya, a girl that every nigga in the hood wished he could have.

"Zya, I know Jules hurt you, but you got to let me in. I'm not him," Snow said as he held her in his arms. Zya felt good in his arms. It felt like she belonged.

Snow pulled two tickets and two booklets out of his coat pocket. He handed them to Zya. Zya read the tickets. *Mexico!* She looked at Snow and said, "Are you serious?" He had purchased her a one-way straight flight ticket out of the country, and had some-how gotten her a fake passport.

"You said you wanted to get out of town," Snow said.

"Are you coming?" Zya asked as she held up the second ticket and raised her neatly arched eyebrows.

Snow looked at her seriously and replied, "Do you want me to?"

Zya did want him to. She had been feeling him for a while, but didn't know if she could handle another relationship right now.

"I don't know. I just don't want to get into the same type of situation I just got out of," she said in a low voice.

"Zya, I've been checking for you since I saw you at your girl's house with the bricks laid out on your bed. I'm feeling you, and I ain't about them childish games. If I'm with you, I'm gon' be with only you. I want you to be my woman. I'm trying to make you my queen. I want to be the nigga that take care of you. No questions asked, I will give you the world. Jules was your boyfriend, Zya. I'm trying to be your man. You were built for me, Zya. Even my sister like you, and she don't like anybody," Snow said with a laugh.

Zya had to laugh too. "Okay," she said as she nodded and smiled.

"Okay what?" Snow asked.

Zya repositioned herself and straddled him. "Okay, I want you to come with me. I have been feeling you too. I was just so afraid that I might get hurt again."

"Do you trust me?" he asked as he stared at her with his light eyes.

Zya nodded her head and replied, "I trust you."

"We gon' get out of town for a while so that things can cool down. I'ma take care of everything. I got you, shorty. I'm not gon' let nothing happen to you."

Snow's words melted Zya, and for some reason, she believed him. *I can't deny my feelings for him. I do want to be with him, and I trust him. He won't hurt me,* she thought as she moved her face closer to his. She slid her tongue into his mouth and kissed him slowly but passionately. His hands automatically moved to her backside, and she rotated her hips against him.

BOOM!

At that exact moment, the wood on her door splintered as three masked men entered her apartment. One carried the sawed-off shotgun that had damaged her door, and the other two carried black guns with long noses. Snow reached for his pistol, but was unable to get to it in time. One of the intruders pulled Zya off of Snow by the hair, and another one pointed a pistol at Snow's head.

"Uh-uh," the masked man said to Snow as he saw him reach for his weapon.

The guy who had Zya pointed the gun directly in her face and said, "Open your mouth!"

"Don't touch her," Snow said calmly, keeping his composure. He knew that if he panicked, he would frighten Zya, and he knew that in order to keep her safe, he had to keep her calm.

"Nigga, you shut the fuck up!" the gunmen said.

"Bitch, open your mouth!" Zya's gunman yelled as he jammed the steel in her mouth, causing her lip to bust. "There you go," the gunman said. "Just like sucking a dick." Zya gagged from the long nose of the gun.

The third intruder ran to the back of the house. "Yo, it ain't no shoeboxes back here. There's a safe!" he yelled to the front of the apartment.

"What's the combination?" Zya's gunman asked her as he removed the gun from her mouth.

Zya remained silent, but Snow began to talk in a calm, low voice. "You idiot mu'fuckas know y'all just signed your death certificates, right? Even if I don't make it out of here, I got niggas that will hunt you down in my place. Y'all niggas is dead."

"Didn't I tell you to shut the fuck up?" Snow's gunman hit him hard across the face with the butt of the gun.

"No! Stop it!" Zya screamed as she tried to free herself to get to Snow.

"Bitch, what's the fucking combination to the safe?"

Zya still didn't talk. She just stared at her attackers with cold eyes.

"What's the combo to the safe?"

There was no way she was giving up her cash. "Fuck you," she stated loudly in defiance.

Zya's gunman loosened his grip and skeptically said, "Heavy, man, let's just get out of here."

"Heavy!" Zya shouted in disbelief. She knew that he didn't like her and that he was upset that she hadn't put him on, but she would have never expected him to rob her.

"Stupid mu'fucka!" Heavy yelled at his partner. "I told you no names!" Heavy walked back and forth, rubbing his head in anger. "Fuck it!" he yelled as he removed his mask.

"You think this is a game?" he asked Zya, staring in her eyes. He rushed over to Snow and hit him repeatedly with his gun. *Whack! Whack! Whack!*

"Heavy, no!" Zya screamed as she struggled to break free. "Stop!" *Whack! Whack! Whack!* The sound of the gun slamming against Snow's head and face made Zya's knees go weak.

"Bitch, give me the combination!" he yelled as he hit Snow over and over again. *Whack! Whack! Whack!*

"Okay! Heavy, okay! Stop!" she begged.

Whack! Whack! Whack!
Whack! Whack! Whack!
Whack! Whack! Whack!

Zya fell to her knees, her heart breaking as she watched Heavy hit Snow repeatedly and forcefully with his gun. She heard the crunch of bone against steel and could almost feel the pain herself. "Stop it!" she screamed at the top of her lungs. "Stop! I'll do anything. Just please don't touch him."

Heavy stopped the pistol whipping and turned toward Zya. He had Snow's blood splattered on his shirt. Zya looked back at Snow, who was passed out, his blood leaking onto her white couch, and his face a swollen and unrecognizable pulp.

"What is it?" Heavy asked.

"Thirty-four, twenty-eight, thirty-one."

Heavy took off for the bedroom and told the other gunman the combination. Zya's eyes flooded with tears as she watched Snow's body lose its life.

"If he dies, I swear to God I'm goin' . . ." she said coldly to the gunman who had his gun pointed at her.

"Shut the fuck up, bitch! Your ass ain't gon' do shit," the gunman interrupted, disregarding her threat.

Heavy and his henchman came running into the room with three duffel bags full of money. He walked up to Zya and whispered in her ear, "You should have just let me fuck." He ran his hands along her breasts, and she cringed at his touch.

"Come on, man, let's go!" the other two intruders

yelled as they exited the apartment. Heavy smiled devilishly and then ran out behind them.

Zya ran over to Snow. "Snow! Snow! Wake up, please, wake up!" Zya tried to lift him up from the couch, but she couldn't. She picked up her phone and dialed 911.

"Nine-one-one, what is your emergency?"

"I need an ambulance. Somebody's hurt. I need help. Please!" she yelled between her delirious sobs.

"Okay, miss, we are tracing your call now. An emergency dispatch unit will be at the address you are placing this call from in approximately ten minutes."

Zya hung up the phone and held Snow in her arms. "God, please let him be okay," she pleaded as she rocked him back and forth. There was so much blood. It was everywhere, and she hoped that he would be okay. *God, please help me. You just brought him to me. Please don't take him away.*

Zya didn't notice that EMS had arrived until they pulled her off of Snow.

"Are you all right?" they asked her. Besides a cut on her lip from the gun being jammed into her mouth, she was fine.

"Yes, just help him! Please hurry!"

The paramedics loaded his body onto a stretcher and she grabbed her keys and asked, "Where are you taking him?"

"Bellevue," a paramedic said as they rushed out of the apartment.

Zya was frantic, and her nerves were bad as she sped toward First Avenue. *Please let him be okay.* She sped into the emergency parking lot and hopped out of her car. She ran into the building and went to the nurse's station.

"I need to see Torey Snow!" Zya said. The nurses looked at her in bewilderment. She was covered in blood, and her lip was busted and swollen.

"What are you looking at? I need to see Snow! Torey Snow!" Zya yelled. One of the nurses came from around the desk and led her through two double doors and into an examination room.

"Please, I just need to make sure he's okay," Zya pleaded. The nurse put on gloves and nodded sympathetically. "Okay, but first we are going to make sure you are okay."

The nurse removed Zya's bloodied shirt and saw that she looked worse than she actually was. All of the blood had been Snow's. The nurse applied three stitches to the corner of her mouth and gave her some ice for the swelling then she helped her clean herself up.

"Here's a gown. That shirt is too bloody to put back on."

Zya took the shirt and asked, "Can I see him now?" The nurse nodded and then led the way up the hall to Snow's room.

Zya put her hand over her mouth when she saw him lying in the hospital bed. His face was swollen badly, and although the doctors had cleaned him up, she knew that he was hurt. She stood next to him and watched over him. His eyes were closed, and Zya felt guilt for what had happened.

If he wouldn't have been there trying to help me, this would not have happened.

A doctor walked into the room and looked at Zya. "Miss, are you okay?" he asked her.

Damn, I must look pretty bad too. She nodded her head and asked, "How is he?"

"Well, he has a very serious concussion and a broken jaw. We're trying to make sure that there is no hemorrhaging, so we're are monitoring him right now. He will be in here for at least two days."

"Can he wake up?"

"Yes, he will wake up in a couple hours or so. The pain medication that we injected is what is causing him to sleep so heavily. He will be sore, however, but once that jaw heals and the concussion is gone, he will be fine."

Zya sighed in relief and held Snow's hand to let him know she was there. She couldn't believe what had just happened, and in the bottom of her heart, she knew that Vita had helped Heavy set her up. Vita was the only other person who knew that she kept money in shoeboxes at the bottom of her closet.

I trusted that bitch. I've known her since seventh grade, and she gon' pull something like this . . . for Heavy's ass. She was like my sister. When I see her ass, it's curtains for her.

Zya knew that she wouldn't be able to bring harm to Vita because she had been close to her for so many years. She didn't understand how Vita could try to hurt her, especially for a nigga. She thought that their friendship was special, and that they were better than that. *I guess I was wrong.* She was pissed off by Vita's betrayal, but more than that, she was hurt.

Zya felt a presence in the room, and she looked up to see Lonnie Wade in the hallway, watching her. Zya's heart skipped a beat as she got up and walked out of the room.

"Are you following me?" Zya asked him angrily as she followed him up the hall. He stopped at a coffee machine and began to put money inside.

"I just thought you should know that I am on your every move. You can't run from this, Zya."

"I wasn't trying to!" Zya lied. She just wanted Lonnie Wade to disappear from her life.

He pulled Zya into one of the hospital's closets and pinned her against a wall. "Sure you were, Zya. I was one of the officers called to the scene that just took place at your house. I saw the suitcases. You are going to help me bring down Anari. If you don't, your pretty little self will be rotting in a prison cell for the murder of King. Think about it," Wade said in a threatening way as he pulled out one of his cards and held it close to her lips. "I guess I don't have to question you about what happened tonight. I'll just write it up as a robbery. But I better hear from you . . . and soon." He opened the door and left Zya in the closet alone.

She hated Wade. She hated Vita. She hated Heavy. She hated Jules. Everybody in her life was creating turmoil right now, and all she wanted to do was leave. The one person who she was beginning to trust had gotten hurt because of her, and she was trapped in a city where everyone was out to get her.

Zya walked out of the closet and went back to Snow's room. He was the only person she cared about at the moment. She sat down in the chair next to his bed and held his hand as he slept. She tried to wait for him to wake up, but hours passed, and she too dozed off.

She felt Snow squeeze her hand in the middle of

the night, and she woke up instantly. She turned on the small lamp on the stand next to the bed and looked at him with worry written all over her face.

"I'm here," she said as she held onto his hand.

Snow's jaw was broken, and it hurt him to talk. "Did they hurt you?" he asked as he gripped her hand tightly from the pain.

"Shh, don't talk. I'm fine. I'm just sick from worrying about you." He sat up in the bed and removed the IV from his arm.

"What are you doing?" Zya asked.

"We're getting out of here. I'm gon' get you on the first flight to Mexico, and I'm gon' go handle Heavy," he said. He winced from the pain that shot through his face as he talked.

"No, Snow, you need to stay here. The doctor said he needed to make sure you weren't bleeding internally."

"Zya, them niggas is dead, yo," Snow said loudly, rage filling his eyes. He had never been touched before, and now that he had, he knew he would have to make examples out of Heavy and his goons.

"I know, I know, but I need to make sure you're okay first."

"What about you?" he asked.

"I don't have any money to go anywhere now. I'm gon' have to grind it out until I have enough to skip town," she said.

"You know I got you," Snow replied.

"And you know I can't accept your money. I got to make my own, Snow."

He didn't like what Zya was saying, but he respected it. After much convincing, Zya persuaded him to stay the full two days in the hospital. She stayed with him all day and all night, and they grew close in that short time. Snow liked how Zya wanted to take care of him. In fact, he liked everything about her.

"You got to give me some pussy now. A nigga done got pistol whipped for you and shit," Snow said with a smile, trying to lighten the mood.

Zya laughed loudly and smiled at him. "The going rate for this is worth more than a pistol whipping," she said playfully.

Zya was feeling Snow. She was feeling him a lot, actually, but knew that she would have to put him on the back burner after he got out of the hospital. She didn't want to. If it was up to her, they would be on a beach at that very instant, sipping on daiquiris, but it wasn't up to her. Her life was in the hands of Lonnie Wade, and she knew that he didn't have her best interests at heart. Something told her that he had something personal to gain from this investigation, and she knew that it was not going to be easy to get rid of him.

I have to get my paper back up so I can get out of town as soon as possible. She was dead broke and would have to start from scratch. That meant she had to get her work on consignment. All of the money she had was taken in the robbery, so she didn't have a choice. Even though she was sure that Snow would try to hit her with free bricks to get her back on her feet, she would not accept them. Their feelings for each other didn't change their business relationship. She was determined to keep business and personal life separate. She didn't want any favors from anybody, not even Snow. When she made it to the top, she wanted it to be because she hustled and fought her way there, not because her boyfriend placed her there.

She began to come up with a hustle plan in her head. She knew that the two days she was taking off work to be with Snow were days that she could be hustling in the restaurant, but she felt like it was worth it. She felt like his predicament was her fault. *He was only trying to help me,* she thought. So, she decided to stay by his side until the doctors let him go home.

While Snow was in the hospital recuperating, she called into work, but she knew that she would have to go back to work as soon as he got out. Her life was still at stake, and she knew that she was going to have to answer to Wade, sooner or later.

Chapter 8

Snakes in the Grass

Anari had her chauffer park in the back of Stello's. She had never visited the restaurant in the daytime, but because of recent events, she felt a meeting with the roundtable was urgent. Before she exited the tinted limo, she put on her big shades that covered most of her face, and a silk head wrap that concealed her hair. Her new French manicure graced the door handle and she exited the limo. She walked to the back entrance and knocked on the door. A man looked through the peephole and let Anari in. Anari went straight to Meechi's office and knocked on the door.

"Come in," Meechi said as he sat at his desk, talking on the phone. Anari pulled off her sunglasses, exposing her face. Meechi quickly hung up the phone when he noticed Anari's face, and gave her his full attention.

Anari had a displeased look on her face as she sat down in the chair in front of Meechi's desk.

"What the fuck is going on?" Anari said calmly as she seductively crossed her legs and rested her folded hands on her knee.

"I don't know. They just busted in unexpectedly. They don't have anything, though, but someone is talking. They mentioned Supreme Clientele, and the detective asked about the meetings."

"We have a rat somewhere."

"I know."

"Where is your father?"

"He went back to Chicago, just until things calmed down."

"I don't blame him. But shit doesn't stop now. We need to find the inside rat and handle that situation. There is too much money being lost right now with us having no coke," Anari said with a serious look on her face.

She wasn't going to let a raid stop the operation. There was too much money to lose by shutting down. Anari had been in the dope game for a long time and had seen hundreds of millions of dollars pass through her hands. The money was just as addictive as the dope that she sold. She knew that she was taking a loss, but there was nothing she could do. The last couple months, her connect had been without dope, which meant she was without it. Anari kept thinking about her empire slowly going down the drain, and that only fed her desire to find another connect. She had worked too hard to establish herself in the drug game. *I'll be damned if I fall off because of a fucking drought.* Anari's first priority was to find the police informant, within the restaurant.

"Who do you think is the rat?" Anari asked as she leaned back in her chair.

"Well, there are only a few people that know about the meetings," Meechi said as he reached out his hand and began to count. "There's only Liz and Marcella. I caught Marcella talking to Liz one night about the meeting, so I got her taken care of. Liz, she is a good girl and goes to church every Sunday. She wouldn't say anything. And there's Buggy, but he's a fuckin' retard. Oh yeah, and there is Zya. She's the black waitress that served us the other night."

"What do you know about that Zya chick? Could she be snitching?"

"No fuckin' way. Forget about it! She's just as dirty us. Ya see, she's been pushing coke around the restaurant. You know, since the drought. If you ask me, she kind of reminds me of you a couple of years ago," Meechi said as he played with the toothpick that dangled out of his mouth.

"Is that right? Where do you think she gets her coke from? Is it any good?"

"Probably not. She's from the fuckin' ghetto," Meechi said as he laughed at his own joke.

Anari grew slightly offended and replied, "I'm from the hood, Di'Meechi. Don't get it twisted. For the last couple of years, I've had the purest shit that hits this country, so that don't mean shit!"

Meechi knew he had pushed Anari's buttons, and tried to lighten up the mood. "Sorry, Anari. No disrespect. I just don't think she has the quality that we are looking for."

"Just to make sure, let me talk to her. Set it up for later on tonight."

"Okay," Meechi agreed as he nodded his head up and down.

"And Meechi, take care of the other waitress and fire that retarded kid. I'd rather be safe than sorry," Anari said as she got up to leave the office. She didn't want to kill Liz, but it was all in the game. This was the life she had chosen, and there was no half-stepping; either you do it all the way, or don't do it at all. Anari wanted to keep the grass cut, because then the snakes would show.

Wade rode through the city streets, collecting his thoughts. Lately, the only thing he could think about was revenge. He remembered how close he had been with his deceased cousin, Tiffany. He laughed as he pictured them in the bar, getting drunk as hell together and trading "yo' momma" jokes, and when he first told her he was going to be a cop. She talked for days about him becoming one of the "others."

Then he remembered when he was the one called to the scene when she supposedly committed suicide. He had just talked to her the night before, and everything was going good with her. He knew that she couldn't have killed herself, and it tugged at his heart. The only thing he could remember was her naked body hanging there with a lipstick mark on her cheek. He couldn't get the image out of his head.

He missed his cousin a lot. The sad feeling he was experiencing instantly transformed into rage when he thought about who was responsible for her brutal death. He wanted Anari to suffer for what she had done, and now that he had a chance to get her, he wasn't going to miss.

Wade looked in his ashtray and saw his half-smoked blunt and picked it up. As he began to light it, his phone rang. He put the blunt down and answered his cell phone.

"This is Wade," he said.

"They found the waitress's body in the water last night," Lieutenant Jones said on the other end.

"Fuck, fuck, fuck! They killed Zya," Wade yelled as he hit his steering wheel repeatedly. He knew that Zya was his only connection to Supreme Clientele. She was the only person that could get close to Anari.

"No, not Zya Miller. Elizabeth Fulton, the other waitress," Jones said as he corrected Wade.

Wade was relieved that the key to the case was still safe and sound. "Damn, they got to her. She had three little boys at home. What was the cause of her death?"

"A single shot to the back of the head. After she was shot, her body got tossed in the river. Her body was spotted by the boat unit."

Wade picked up the blunt and hit it then hung up the phone. He knew if they found out Zya was cooperating, she would be next. *It's only a matter of time before they sniff her out. I have to find out as much as possible before they find out.* Zya was only a pawn in Wade's chess game, and he had no problem sacrificing her. But before he did, he wanted to get the most out of her.

Zya took the money from the short, bald-headed Italian and slyly slid him a small bag filled with coke. He had just copped three grams from her. Zya walked away while stuffing the money into her apron when Meechi approached her.

"Let me see you in my office right now," he said sternly as he grabbed her elbow.

"All right, damn. "

Zya walked to Meechi's office and saw the woman she had served at the roundtable leaning on the edge of Meechi's desk. She also noticed another man from the table sitting to her far right.

"Take a seat, Zya," The woman instructed as she opened her hand and waved it over the chair nearest to her. Zya walked over and sat down, her heart beating fast. She didn't know what they wanted from her, and she grew uneasy.

They found out about Wade's proposition. I'm all fucked up now. Damn, I knew they were gon' find out. I'm not trying to be mixed up in this shit, Zya thought as she sat down and crossed her legs.

"My name is Anari, and I hear you got a little clientele in here."

"Yeah, I get a lot of requests."

"Nah, not that kind of clientele. You know what I'm talking about. Coke clientele," Anari said as she studied Zya.

Meechi must have told her, and now she's mad because I'm cutting in on some of her money, she thought before saying, "Just a few grams here and there. Just to make a little extra cash on the side."

Anari wasn't about to beat around the bush, so she put her cards on the table. "Do you have any on you?"

Zya pulled a baggy containing three grams and handed it to Anari. Anari ripped the bag open and poured the coke on the table. She dipped her pinky in the coke and rubbed it on her gums to see how numb it would get. The quicker her gums got numb, the better the product. To Anari's surprise, her gums numbed up instantly. She called the man in the corner over to test it out, and he bent over the product and hit a line.

Snort! Snort! The man immediately stood up straight and threw his head back to prevent his nose from running. "Damn, that's some good shit. I can't feel my fuckin' face," he said jokingly as he imitated a scene off of a movie.

Anari chuckled and then looked at Zya. "Can you get more of that?" she asked as she pointed at the coke.

Zya spoke before even thinking. "Yeah, I got it all day. What you need?"

"Let's start off light. How soon can you get me two?"

Zya smiled, knowing she was about to get paid. *Hell yeah, I can get them in a couple of days. You ain't said shit but a word,* she thought as she tried to conceal her excitement.

"Okay, so you want two bricks? To you, I'll sell those twelve a piece. That'll be twenty-four thousand for both of them."

Anari and the man laughed at Zya so hard, Zya grew kind of offended.

"What's so funny?" Zya asked as she looked around, trying to see what she had missed.

Anari cleared her throat and said, "I want two hundred kilos. Can you handle that?"

Zya was so embarrassed, and to save face, she confidently replied, "Yeah, I can get them. I need about a week to discuss things with my partner."

"So, it's official. I should be hearing from you in a week or so then."

"All right, then," Zya said just before she got up and exited the room.

What the fuck did I just do? How in the hell am I supposed to get 200 kilos of cocaine? I've never even seen more than twenty at a time. I'm always running my damn mouth, trying to be Miss Big Shot. How could I say I didn't have them, after they were laughing like I ain't a hustla or something? I gets down for mine. I need to call Snow and see what he can do. Damn!

Chapter 9

Well Connected

I hope I didn't just agree to something I can't deliver. Two hundred kilos is not an ordinary order. Niggas on the street don't be messing with bricks like that. They are talking about messing with millions of dollars of weight. They got me out here federal as hell, Zya thought as she drove her Charger across the Manhattan Bridge. *I hope Snow is able to fill this order. They don't seem like the type of people that understand when it comes to breaking agreements. I told them that I could get it. I hope I'm not made out to be a liar.*

Zya knew that she had just stepped into the major leagues. The thing is, she didn't even want to be there. The Supreme Clientele roundtable intimidated her. She didn't even like waiting on them at their meetings, so now that they had requested her services, she was on edge. She didn't want to make a wrong move, because she was afraid that the price to pay would be her life.

Zya had done the math in her head, and because they were buying so many kilos, she was only going to charge the roundtable $10,000 for each one. Snow was able to get the bricks for $5,000 a piece, so that meant that she and Snow would make a $5,000 profit to split between them for every brick they sold. Supreme Clientele was going to pay her two million dollars for 200 kilos of cocaine. *Damn I'm gon' make a killing,* she thought. A half a million would be her profit. She had never seen that much money in her life, and she was ready to get it. The more she thought about the money she was about to make, the heavier her foot got on the gas pedal. She did ninety miles per hour all the way to Snow's house.

Zya felt butterflies in her stomach as she thought about seeing Snow. They hadn't had a chance to have a serious conversation since he was released from the hospital. She didn't know how things were going to be between them, and she was nervous. She was confused about her feelings for him, but there was no doubting that she felt something. Just thinking about him put a smile on her face, and the thought of seeing his face excited her. It was getting harder and harder to keep their business relationship separate from their personal one. Zya was about her business all the time, so if she stuck to her rule, she would never have any personal time for Snow. She did miss him, and wanted to be near him all the time, but she always fought her urges. She tried to stay busy to avoid thinking about him, but his eyes and his smile always crept back into her thoughts. She didn't even call him to let him know she was coming. There was so much money at stake, she didn't want to risk it by talking about it over the phone.

As she drove the rest of the way to Snow's house, she found herself wondering about her life. *I wonder, if I had to choose between money and happiness with Snow, which one would I pick?* she thought. She honestly didn't know the answer. Her relationship with Jules had left a bad taste in her mouth, and it had her not trusting her own feelings. She had been financially dependent on Jules, and when he abruptly disappeared from her life, she was left in a bind. It seemed like money was more important than her happiness right now, because here she was given an opportunity to be happy with Snow, but she was putting him on hold until she could get her money right.

Why can't I just trust him? Why can't I just put my life and my heart in his hands? She wondered. She wanted to do it so badly, but something inside of her was causing her to hold back. She knew that her scars from Jules were not healed yet, and she hoped that she didn't sabotage her relationship with Snow because of it. She didn't want to make him pay for another man's mistakes, but at the same time, she didn't want to make another mistake by trusting Snow too quickly.

When she finally pulled up to his house, she was more confused than ever. She saw his car parked in the open garage and knew that he was home. She wanted a real life, a real love that was long-lasting and unconditional. She didn't want to be used or have a business arrangement that was based on convenience rather than love. *Would Snow be able to give me that even though we were business partners first?*

Zya stepped out of the car and walked slowly until

she reached Snow's door. She rang the bell once and waited for him to answer. She smiled to herself. *This nigga always take forever to answer his door,* she thought as she shook her head from side to side. He finally answered the door, and the sight of him made her heart flutter. His face was still swollen, and the bruises made his dark skin appear purple, but even with all that, he still looked good. It was something about the way he carried himself that attracted her. She loved his swagger, and she had to admit, he was very hard to resist. He stepped aside and held the door open for her to enter.

"How have you been?" Zya asked as she stared into his eyes. She was quickly beginning to learn that his eyes were her favorite part of him.

"I'm good," he said as he stared back at her.

"Are you in pain?"

"Not really. The medicine makes it so that I don't feel it."

Zya's eyes reflected her concern, and Snow could see that something was bothering her. He cared for Zya, and he had let it be known, but the next move was up to her. He wasn't going to chase somebody who didn't want to be caught.

Snow walked into his living room and sat down on his brown-and-beige furniture. His living room was decorated in earth tone colors, and his taste was excellent. There was a silence between Snow and Zya that said neither of them knew what to say.

"I'm sorry I haven't been by. I'm just really trying to figure out what's going on. I don't know if what I'm feeling is right," Zya admitted to him.

"I understand, Zya. Take all the time you need," Snow replied.

"I just don't know what I'm doing anymore. I'm trying to sort stuff out, but I can't. What's more important to you, Snow . . . money or happiness?" she asked him.

Snow shrugged his shoulders and replied, "Money."

Zya laughed and said, "I wish that I was that sure. I know that money is important to me. Not because I'm greedy or anything, but because I want to be able to take care of me, you know? I don't want to have to depend on anybody, but it seems like I'm so focused on getting money that I'm missing out on something that I really want."

"What do you really want?" he asked.

"I *want* to keep my business with you and my personal feelings for you separate. But somehow, they always seem to intertwine. I have to keep business and personal separated," Zya said as she sat across from him with her legs crossed.

"Why does that have to happen?" Snow asked.

"It just does," Zya replied almost in a whisper.

"I won't hurt you," he said.

"I know . . ."

"Do you?" he asked as he stood up and made his way into the kitchen. Zya didn't respond. She didn't know what to say to him. He had been upfront with her about how he felt, and even though she was feeling him too, she wasn't trying to rush things.

After seeing that she was unsure, Snow decided to change the subject. He wasn't trying to pressure her. He knew that she would learn to trust him in her own time. It was up to him if he chose to wait or not.

"I know you didn't come all the way to Jersey to talk about us. So, what's up?" he asked her.

Zya felt bad that he had changed the subject of

conversation. Even though she hadn't come to talk about their relationship, she needed to. *I want to talk about us,* she thought silently. She knew that business needed to come first, so she adapted her usual hustler's mentality and replied, "I need some work."

Snow began to head for the basement, where he stored his dope in an underground cellar he had installed in the house. He stopped dead in his tracks when he heard her say, "I need two hundred kilos."

He turned around to face a smiling Zya. "What's wrong? Speechless?" she asked as she walked sexily in his direction with a confident look on her face.

"Two hundred kilos. That's a lot of bricks. You doing it like that?" he asked as he stared down at her. They stood toe to toe, and the sexual tension was high between them.

She nodded her head, stood on her tip-toes and whispered in his ear. "See, if I mess with you, Snow, one of us is gon' have to leave the dope game alone. I can't give it up. I'm too good at it," she said as her sweet breath danced in his ear.

Snow slid his hands around her small waist and rested them on her ass, pulling her body close to his. "We can be good together," he said. His voice was thick with seduction, and Zya could feel his tension through his jeans. His face was so close to hers that their lips touched when they talked, and he was making her hot. Her pussy was wet, and at that moment, she wanted him to bend her over and tear that ass up, but she knew better than to get caught in the moment. This was strictly business.

She turned her head to the side and closed her eyes. *I can't believe I'm about to say this,* she thought before the words came out of her mouth. "We are good together . . . but for business purposes only, at least for now."

Snow nodded his head and replied, "Okay, okay. Business. Let's talk business then." He led Zya to his kitchen table and they took a seat.

"Two hundred kilos is a big order. I can't just walk into this blind like I usually do. You got to explain the situation a little more."

"Understandable. What do you need to know?" she asked.

"Who are they for?"

"I sell the coke out of the restaurant where I work. That's why I can move it so quick because the customers come to me. But the only reason why I could even do it in the first place is because the owner lost his connect and was going through a drought. They have this roundtable that meets once a month. Snow, no bullshit . . . there are some powerful people sitting at this table. Anyway, they called me into the meeting and asked if I could get more dope. I told them yes."

"Are they good for it?" he asked.

"Yeah, I think so."

"They gon' have to pay half up front," he said sternly. He wasn't willing to take any chances. Ernesto, Snow's connect, didn't play around with his money. Snow knew not to even think about doing bad business with him, and he figured if the roundtable paid half up front, that would at least cover the costs of the dope. His business with Ernesto would be square. They could collect the other half of the money when they delivered the package.

"My connect is going to charge five G's a piece for the bricks."

"And I figured since they were buying so many we could only charge them ten a piece," Zya added.

Snow nodded his head in agreement and replied, "That'll work." He paused for a minute and did the math in his head. He wasn't a genius when it came to math, but he could count and analyze money better than any accountant. "We'll both make five hundred thousand out of the deal."

"Do you think you can make it happen?" Zya asked eagerly. That was exactly the type of cash she needed to get out of town and be set.

"Yeah, I know my man got 'em. Give me a couple days and I'll call you to let you know what's what."

Zya stood up and prepared to leave.

"Zya . . ."

She paused before she exited the front door and looked back at Snow.

"What are you doing about that other situation? Has that cop come around again?" He wanted to know how Zya was doing, but also needed to make sure he wasn't being set up. She was hot right now because of her involvement in King's murder, and he wasn't trying to be her plea bargain. He knew that it was a possibility that Zya was setting him up to reduce her sentence or to walk away with her hands free altogether.

Is she trading her charge for my conviction? he thought. He couldn't put it past her. She had pulled grimy on King. *What makes me so different from him?*

"I haven't heard from him, and hopefully I won't. That is why this flip is so important to me. I need to make this money so I can leave town."

Snow watched her walk out the door, and was unsure of her intentions. Here he was telling her to trust him, and he wasn't even sure if he trusted her fully. He knew one thing for sure. No matter how much he was feeling Zya, if he had to, he would handle his business. If she ever tried to cross him and send him upstate, he would kill her without hesitation. He had no love or tolerance for snitches.

He tried to shake his feelings of apprehension. He didn't want to think that Zya was dirty, but at the same time, he didn't want to bet his freedom on it either.

Fuck it! I'ma roll with her. She hasn't lied to me yet. First thing tomorrow, I'll call Ernesto and put in the order.

That night, Zya lay in bed, restlessly tossing and turning. She couldn't sleep. Her mind was in a thousand places at once. *Damn, a half-million dollars is a lot of money. If I can get that and get out, I'm good. This is the opportunity of a lifetime, a one-time flip that will have me set for life,* she thought. Zya had grown accustomed to making money, but she had never seen it like this. Her love for the hustle made her good at selling dope, and she knew that she was no longer small-time. She was knee-deep in the game, and she couldn't even remember how she had gotten there.

Two hundred kilos, she thought in disbelief. She still couldn't believe it. She closed her eyes and forced herself to relax. *I need to just be easy and relax. I can't do anything until Snow makes the call. I have to wait on him to handle things on his end before anything jumps off,* she thought before drifting into a mind-numbing sleep.

* * *

"Mr. Ernesto says that you are not scheduled to contact him for another month," a female voice explained. Her voice was thick with a Spanish accent, and her broken English was hard to understand.

"I need to speak with Ernesto now. Tell him that he doesn't want to pass up on what I have to offer." Snow listened to the woman as she repeated what he had just said, and waited a while before Ernesto picked up the phone.

"Snow, to what do I owe this unexpected call?" Ernesto asked, apparently agitated by Snow's disregard toward his policy. Carlos Ernesto was one of Cuba's biggest suppliers, and he dealt with so many different people that he put each of his buyers on a specific schedule. He knew who was calling and when. The times never varied, and he left only a small window of opportunity to get in contact with him. He was also familiar with the amount each of his buyers usually purchased. He was thorough when it came to business, and he left no stone unturned when deciding who he would and would not deal with.

"I normally wouldn't call you out of the blue, but I came across an unexpected opportunity that is too good to miss," Snow said. He knew that Ernesto was in love with money, and that his words would pique his interest.

"What opportunity would that be, my friend?"

"I need two hundred kilos."

The line went silent, and Snow waited for his connect to respond. "That is a big jump up from what you usually request," Ernesto stated.

"A special order just came in, and they need it filled ASAP," Snow replied.

"Special?" Ernesto questioned. "Special orders can be a man's downfall," he said firmly. Snow could hear the hesitation in Ernesto's voice. "For years now I have done business with you, and the quantity of your order has never changed. Always twenty kilos. Why is it changing now?"

"Things have changed within my operation. I have gained a partner who has helped me expand my clientele into New York."

"And your partner is the one who has set up this special buy?" Ernesto asked, his voice still reflecting his suspicion.

"Yeah, but I can vouch for—"

"You can vouch for no one but yourself," Ernesto said calmly but sternly. "If you want this deal to go down, I need to meet your partner first." Ernesto hung up the phone.

Snow had expected Ernesto to have doubts about filling such a big order, but he hadn't expected him to ask to meet Zya. He hadn't told Ernesto that his partner was a woman, and he wasn't sure how Ernesto would react once he saw her.

Snow shook his head, grabbed his keys and walked out the door. There was no turning back now. Ernesto wanted to meet Zya, and that was the only way he was going to get his hands on that many bricks.

He hopped in his car and drove the distance into Harlem to let Zya know what was going on. He parked on the curb in front of her apartment building and put his chrome nine millimeter handgun in his waist-line. He looked in his rearview mirror before exiting the car. He ascended the flights of stairs that led to Zya's door and knocked lightly.

Zya opened the door and let him into her home. As

soon as Snow saw the apartment, he visualized the robbery that had happened. He instantly felt rage toward Heavy and thought, *That fat nigga is dead.*

"Did you make the call?" Zya asked, snapping him out of his daze.

"Yeah, you got a passport?"

She frowned her face and replied, "Yeah . . . I mean I got the fake one you gave me. For what?"

"We're taking a trip to Cuba."

Two weeks later, Zya was on a flight to Cuba. They flew to Canada first, since no U.S. planes are allowed to fly to Cuba. She sat next to Snow and thought for sure that he could hear her heartbeat. She was nervous and couldn't stop fidgeting in her seat. *What if the deal doesn't go through? What will Supreme Clientele say if I can't come through with my end of the deal?*

Snow looked at Zya and said, "You all right?"

Zya nodded and replied, "Yeah, I'm good."

He laughed lightly and asked, "Well, can I please have my arm back?"

Zya noticed that she had her arm interlaced through Snow's, and she was holding on for dear life. Embarrassed, she released her hold on him and blushed slightly. "Sorry," she said.

"Calm down. Everything is going to go fine. By this time next week, you'll be a half-million dollars richer," he assured her.

Zya leaned her seat back and opened up the book she had purchased for the plane ride. As she read *Diary of a Street Diva* by Ashley JaQuavis, she tried to calm her nerves. The book was so good that she got through the rest of the flight without thinking about the meeting. The plane landed, and Zya followed Snow off the plane and through the airport.

As they approached Customs, Snow leaned down and whispered, "Let me answer any questions they ask." Zya nodded and stepped up to the Customs inspector with Snow by her side. She was nervous because she had never even seen a real passport, so she had no clue if hers looked legit.

"Passports," the officer requested in a monotone voice. They handed over the information, and the Customs officer reviewed them. He glared down at them skeptically and asked, "What brings you to Cuba?"

"We're vacationing," Snow responded. The skepticism didn't leave the officer's face.

"Around what part?" the officer asked.

Snow grew a blank expression on his face, but Zya stepped up and said, "Havana."

The officer looked the two of them up and down, noticing that they weren't carrying any luggage. "Where is your luggage?"

"We don't have any. I'm making him buy me all new things on this trip. Can you tell me the best places to shop here?"

The officer reluctantly put his stamp of approval on the passports and said, "No, Miss, I'm sorry. You will have to ask someone near your hotel. Enjoy your stay."

Zya and Snow walked away from the Customs department and out of the airport as fast as they could without drawing attention to themselves.

Ernesto had arranged for a car to pick them up, and they were transported to his house. Zya tried to remember the route as they drove through the dirt streets of Havana. If anything popped off, she wanted to know how to return the exact way she had come.

When they pulled up to the 20-foot steel gate that protected the stone mansion, her mouth dropped to the floor. She hadn't really known what to expect, but the gorgeous mansion that stood in front of her was beyond anything she could have ever imagined. The chauffeur drove them up to the front of the house, and she got out and looked around.

She took a deep breath and followed behind Snow as he approached the front entrance. She was dressed in a thin, white Donna Karan sundress that tied around her neck, and her hair blew as the wind whipped it lightly to the side.

Snow rang the bell, and a short brown woman who wore a white maid's smock answered the door.

"Bienvenido, Señor Ernesto le está contando con," the woman said quickly in Spanish, welcoming them to Ernesto's home. "Perseguir me."

Snow nodded his head and followed the woman through the house and onto a patio decorated with exotic floral arrangements and hundreds of plants. Zya sat down across from Snow, and he stared at her across the table. He smiled at how well she was handling herself. The nervous girl on the plane had transformed into a confident woman who was here to handle business, and he was amazed at how easy it was for her to change faces in a matter of minutes.

The sliding door to the patio opened, and a well-dressed Cuban man entered the room. He wore all white, and his shirt was unbuttoned some, revealing his chest hair. He had a Cuban cigar intertwined between his fingers, and as he approached, he said, "Snow, mi caro amigo."

"Good to see you, Ernesto," Snow replied as he stood and shook hands with the man.

Zya stood and Ernesto focused his attention on her. A look of surprise took over his face as he stared at the beautiful, young black woman who stood before him.

"And you are?" Ernesto asked as he took her hand and held onto it gently.

"Zya," she spoke softly.

"My partner," Snow added as he stood back and watched Ernesto kiss Zya's hand before taking a seat at the head of the table.

"So, tell me about this deal that you have arranged," Ernesto said, looking directly at Zya.

She sat back in her chair and crossed her legs then replied. "What would you like to know?"

"Who is on the receiving end of this transaction?" Ernesto asked.

"A roundtable called Supreme Clientele," she answered.

Ernesto looked back and forth from Snow to Zya, and his eye-brows arched in disbelief. "Tony's Supreme Clientele? Señorita Anari?"

Zya nodded her head, and even Snow looked at her in shock. *Damn, I thought she was dead. I've heard stories about some woman named Anari disguising herself with a man's name and taking over Jersey a couple years back. I didn't think that shit was true. The streets talk about her like she's a myth. How the fuck did Zya get connected with her?*

"You must be mistaken. Anari is dead," Ernesto said with an arrogant laugh.

"No, Mr. Ernesto, you are mistaken. I guarantee

you that Anari is very much alive," Zya said in a matter-of-fact tone.

Snow watched Ernesto's face and could tell that he was shocked about what Zya had just told him.

"If you are representing who you say you are, why can't Anari's roundtable get their cocaine from her original source? What happened to her connect?"

"It is my understanding that her Colombian connect is tapped out. That is why she sent us to recruit your services. Supreme Clientele would like to make you their new supplier."

"So, Poe has finally run dry," he stated in amusement, referring to Supreme Clientele's former connect.

"You know him?" Zya asked.

"Everybody knows one another at this level of the game. I always keep up with my competition."

"It seems as though our offer will put you one step ahead of him then," Zya said confidently with a seductive smile.

Ernesto turned to Snow and began to speak in Spanish.

"Poder ella ser confidente?" Ernesto asked. It was important for him to know that he could trust the woman that was sitting before him. He didn't want to fall victim to her enticing beauty. Her looks said that she could be trusted, but he wanted to know if Snow was willing to vouch for her.

"Me creer etas ella poder," Snow replied as he stared at Zya. He gave Ernesto his word that she was trustworthy.

Zya smiled as she stared Snow in the eyes. The two men sitting before her didn't know that she knew how to speak and interpret Spanish very well. Growing up in a foster home in the Bronx, she had become accustomed to the language, so what they thought was a private conversation between the two of them was in actuality one that she could comprehend.

"Me consilidar les etas me poder," she said, finally speaking up on her own behalf. She had predicted that Ernesto would wonder if she could be trusted or not. She assured him that she could be.

Both men looked at Zya in amazement, and Ernesto leaned back in his chair and took a puff of his cigar. He laughed and said, "Never underestimate the power of a woman." He laughed heartily as he blew his cigar smoke into the air and continued. "You, my dear, are quite the businesswoman. You two have yourselves a deal. I will have the product ready in one week. You will need to find your own pilot to fly it into the States." He shook hands with Snow and then began to walk out of the room. He stopped at the door and said, "Zya, contact me if you ever need a job." She smiled and Snow laughed as they prepared to leave the room.

They walked out, and Zya was expecting the driver to take them back to the airport, but instead they pulled up to an oceanside villa.

"Where are we?" Zya asked.

"This is one of Ernesto's villas. It is where I stay when I come here to do business," Snow said as he stepped out of the car and began to walk up the long gravel driveway.

"Okay. Why are we here?" she asked as she got out and ran up the driveway after him.

"We're staying for a couple days," he said.

"I didn't bring any clothes, Snow. Why can't we just fly back tonight?"

"It looks hot for us to cross Customs too soon. We don't want to draw any unnecessary attention to ourselves. If we fly back the same day we arrived, they are going to ask a lot of questions. We don't need that right now."

Zya nodded and followed him inside. As soon as she walked inside, her breath was taken away by how luxurious the villa was.

"Oh my God, Snow, look at this!" Zya exclaimed in amazement as she walked to the back of the house and saw the waves from the ocean washing up on the backyard shore. "This is crazy!" she said excitedly. The night had fallen, and the water looked pitch black against the light sand.

She slid open the screen door and stepped outside. She walked onto the beach, sat down near the edge of the water, and enjoyed the feel of the ocean water as it washed up onto her feet. She felt Snow's presence as he walked up behind her. There was something about him that sent chills up her spine whenever he was around. Snow had an essence about himself, a certain swagger that was very attractive.

He sat down next to her with a bottle of Cristal in one hand and two champagne flutes in the other.

"I can't believe I pulled that off with Ernesto. I was so nervous," she admitted.

Snow shook his head. "Zya, I ain't never met a chick like you in my life. I been getting money for a minute, but I have never seen anything like this. You flip ounces faster than any nigga I know. Fucking around with you, I went from copping twenty bricks to two hundred bricks overnight."

"I don't know. It's just in me, I guess. Getting money is what I do best. It's just like breathing to me.

You know how they say a shark will die if it stops swimming?" she asked. Snow nodded his head, and she continued. "I will die if I stop hustling. I gotta do it to survive, at least until my money gets long. I'm not trying to be in it for the long haul. I want to get enough money so that I can get out of New York and away from the bullshit."

He handed her a glass full of champagne and she said, "To a great partnership." They touched glasses and took a sip.

They sat beachside, talking and laughing with one another as they enjoyed the compliments from Ernesto's full bar. Zya drank three glasses of champagne, and the alcohol had her feeling good.

Damn, I wish I had known we were staying here for a couple days. I would have brought clothes and something to swim in, she thought as she stared at the dark, enticing water. She stood up and slipped out of her dress, revealing her black Victoria's Secret thong and bra.

"What you doing, ma? You feeling good and shit. Put your clothes back on," he said, his speech slow and sexy from the champagne.

"Let's swim," she said as she grabbed his hand and led him toward the water.

"I don't swim," he said as he pulled her close to his body.

She looked up at him and began to unbutton his Sean John shirt. "Please," she begged cutely as she removed the fabric from his broad shoulders, enjoying the feel of her hands against his skin. His shirt dropped to the sand, and Zya rested her hands on his chest. He took another sip of the Cristal and shook his head no.

"Snow, look at that water. Look at this beach. We have it all to ourselves. We might as well take advantage of it. We will never get another chance like this." Her hands moved down to his jeans, and she slowly unbuttoned his pants. They fell around his ankles. She looked down, and a slight smile spread across her face as she noticed how well he was hung. He stepped out of his jeans as she pulled him into the water with nothing but his boxers on.

"Shit," he said as the cold waves washed over his rock-hard abdomen. His six-pack glistened as the water hit his body, and she admired his perfectly chiseled body.

"Come here," she said as she splashed water in his direction.

"You playing," he said as he put his hands up to stop the water from hitting his face. She splashed the water in his direction until he was forced to splash her back. She laughed and screamed loudly as he picked her up and threatened to toss her into the water.

"Okay, okay, Snow, I swear, I quit. I don't wanna get my hair wet," she yelled in between the laughter. He dropped her into the water, and she popped back up instantly, the water running down her body. He grabbed her again, and she flailed her arms, trying to get out of his tight grasp.

"Aww, shit!" he yelled when he felt her elbow him in the jaw. He grabbed his face in pain.

"Oh my God! Snow, I'm so sorry. Are you okay?" she said as she got close to him and placed her hands on his face.

"I'm good, ma. I'm good," he said as he headed up to the shore.

Zya grabbed their clothes off the beach and followed behind him as he walked back into the villa. "Here, sit down," she said. She walked into the kitchen and got some ice out of the freezer. She wrapped it in a towel and got on her knees in front of him to apply it to his face. "I'm so sorry." He stared at her as she carefully held the ice against his broken jaw. Her hair was wet, and her ass devoured the thong she was wearing.

She noticed him staring at her. "Why are you staring at me?" she asked softly with a half-smile.

"Because you're beautiful," he replied.

Zya took the ice from his face and stared back at Snow. He was wearing her down, and no matter how hard she tried to resist him, she couldn't. He put his hand on her chest, feeling her heart beat. "You're nervous," he said in a low and raspy tone.

Zya looked him in the eyes and nodded her head. She was nervous. She had only felt love for one other person in her entire life, and that was Jules. The feelings that were creeping into her heart at that moment scared her. She wasn't trying to fall in love, but sure enough, she was slipping, and there was no catching her balance. She didn't want to love Snow, but she was starting to.

Snow moved his hands softly up her neck. He pulled her close to him, and his tongue explored the inside of her mouth. She kissed him back hesitantly and explored his body with her hands as she felt tingles run up and down her spine. As their kiss continued Zya became comfortable, and her tongue massaged Snow's mouth aggressively but gently.

Snow stopped suddenly and said, "Wait, this ain't

right. You feeling it from the champagne, and I don't want you to regret this in the morning. We can't mix business and pleasure."

Zya's body was on fire. Her pussy was throbbing and dripping wet, but she knew that he was right. She nodded her head and they stood up. "You're right. We can't do this." She began to walk out of the room but stopped when she got to the bottom of the steps that led upstairs.

"Snow?" she called out, knowing he was watching her.

"Yeah?" he replied.

She turned around and felt the desire burning between her thighs. "I want you," she said softly as they rushed toward each other. Zya tackled Snow onto the floor, and he laid her on her back. Her pussy was dripping wet, and her mind was filled with erotic thoughts as she fantasized about what Snow was going to do with the bulge that was growing inside his boxers.

Snow looked on in awe as he watched Zya tease him. Zya parted her pussy lips and revealed her pinkness to him. "No business with pleasure?" she asked him seductively.

Snow's dick was practically ripping the fabric of his boxers. He released his long, black, thick dick from the confinement of his underwear, and he slid her thong to the side and filled the space with his manhood. She kissed him forcefully as he ripped her bra from her body. Her D-cups filled his hands as he massaged them with one hand and grabbed her ass with the other.

"Damn!" he growled as she got on top of him, and then put her vagina in his face while lowering her mouth onto his dick. He dove his tongue into her sweet pussy like it was a hard dick, and she moaned loudly and arched her back as she let him make love to her mouth. He watched her round ass as it bounced up and down on his face, and he almost burst from the sight.

He lifted her off of him because the sex was too good. He was afraid that he would explode at any minute. He picked her up and kissed her passionately as he carried her upstairs to the bedroom. He laid her down on her stomach and eased into her from behind. She moaned and tried to run from the size of him, but he pulled her down gently and began to rock slowly in and out of her, sending a pulsing sensation through her body.

"Snow . . ." she called out as he went in and out of her. She grabbed the headboard in pleasure as he made love to her, and it felt so good she thought she was losing her mind.

He switched positions and lay down as his manhood stood at full attention, teasing her. It was her turn to turn him out. She jumped on him and rotated her hips in circles, riding him at a slow place. He sucked on her nipples gently as she gyrated on his pole. The way she rode him made her breasts bounce up and down, causing him to become entranced in her hypnotic movements. Zya rode Snow like she had invented the position, and it was by far the best pussy he had ever felt. There was so much sexual tension and frustration built up between the two of them, and it made the sex that much more intense.

"Damn, girl," he said as she locked and unlocked her vaginal muscles, making him go crazy. He loved the brief pleasure that he felt every time Zya bounced up and down, causing her ass cheeks to slam against his balls. He grabbed the back of her head and pulled her near until they were face to face. Her eyes were closed, and she bit her lip as she rode his hard, thick dick.

"I love you, Zya," Snow whispered in her ear.

"I love you, Snow. Oh my God . . . I love you so much," she moaned. Snow was laying the pipe, and she knew that her pussy would be forever his. She felt his body tense up, and he curled his toes as her face twisted in utter delight. They both felt the other begin to climax.

"Snow!" she yelled out loud as her orgasm rushed her body.

He touched Zya's hips and pounded her down one last time and then lifted her off of him as he let out an animal-like grunt. His semen oozed out, a symbol of his satisfaction. Snow looked over at Zya, who was staring up at the ceiling. He pulled her near him, and she rested her head on his chest.

"What are you thinking about?" he asked.

"I was hoping that I didn't just make a mistake."

He kissed the top of her head and replied, "You don't have to worry about nothing. I'm here with you and only you. I told you I was gon' make you my queen. Fuck that mixing business with pleasure shit. It ain't none of that. It's just us, you and me. We in this together. We about to get this money, and the only thing you should be worried about is how you gon' spend it."

Zya sat up and smiled at him. He was what she wanted, and now that she had decided to take it to an intimate level with him, there was no turning back. "I don't know anything that could feel better than this," she said.

Snow smirked and replied, "I do."

"And what's that?" she asked as she formed an instant attitude, thinking he was talking about another girl.

"Getting Heavy," Snow replied. "When we get home, I want you to help put the word out. That mu'-fucka been hiding since he stuck you up, but I got ten stacks for whoever can point me in his direction."

Chapter 10

Dope Fiend

"He looks like he's a good candidate. Right?" Zya asked as she stared at the man walking to his car with an ugly pilot's hat on his head.

"Nah, he walks like he's got a stick up his ass. He's probably never done anything wrong his entire life. What about that ugly cat right there?" Snow asked as he pointed across the airport's parking garage at a chubby man who was also wearing a pilot's hat.

"Not him either," Zya said, shaking her head.

They had been sitting in the airport's staff garage for over an hour, trying to find the right pilot to approach. Zya was growing skeptical about their recruiting tactics and began to second guess approaching a total stranger with their illegal proposition.

What if we ask the wrong person and he runs to the authorities? Then the whole transaction would be ruined, Zya thought as she watched a group of pilots exiting.

"First shift must be leaving now," Snow said as he looked at his watch then back at the group of men leaving. One pilot came out, lagging behind, and caught their attention. He snatched the corny pilot's hat off of his head as soon he stepped out of the door, and lit a Newport cigarette. He had his pilot shirt's first two buttons undone, revealing his gold chain and chest hair. He had a certain swagger as he walked, like he came straight off a *Sopranos* episode. He looked kind of cheesy, but he was just what they were looking for. When he thought no one was looking, he took a leak on the side of a car.

"That's our guy!" they both said simultaneously.

Snow hopped out of the car and waited until the man passed the car, and began to follow him. The man was so busy trying to shake the piss off of his shoe, he didn't even notice Snow sneak up right behind him. Snow pulled out his pistol from his waistline and stuck it to the back of the man's neck.

"If you don't want me to blow yo' fuckin brains out, cooperate," Snow whispered as he directed the pilot to his car. Zya had the door already open, so Snow shoved him inside. Snow hopped in the front seat and looked at the nervous man sitting there terrified.

"Here, take all of my money," he said as he tossed his wallet into the front seat. Snow caught the wallet and threw it right back at him, hitting him in the face.

Zya began to speak. "We don't want to take your money. We want to give you ours."

The man grew a confused look on his face and murmured, "Huh?"

"We have a proposition for you. We need something transported from Cuba back to the States."

The man threw both of his hands in the air and began to sweat profusely. "I don't know what kind of game you guys are—"

"Shut that bullshit up. You like money, right?" Snow asked.

The man hesitated before answering, "Well, yeah. Who doesn't?"

Snow nodded his head and said, "That is what this is all about."

He tossed the man a stack of money from his glove compartment and continued to attempt to persuade the man. "That's twenty-five grand. We have another fifty for you after you transport the goods for us. We have the jet already. You just have to fly the mu'-fucka."

The man caught the money, and his eyes almost popped out of his head when he saw all of the hundred- and fifty-dollar bills. He stuttered before beginning to talk. "I-I don't know about this."

"Well, give us back the money," Zya said as she reached for the stack in his hand.

The man threw his free hand up and said, "Now, hold a minute." He looked at the money and flipped through the bills once again. "You say I'll get fifty more on my return?"

Zya and Snow looked at each other and smiled. They knew they had just acquired the pilot they needed for the job.

"Here is how you can contact one of us directly. Both of our numbers are programmed on speed dial," Snow said as he tossed a cell phone into the pilot's lap. The pilot put the money and cell phone in his briefcase and hurried out of the car. Zya took a deep breath then exhaled.

"I hope he calls back. We really need him on our team right now. If we can't find a pilot, the deal is bust, and we gon' lose out on a half-mil."

"He'll call," Snow said confidently as he started the car.

"What makes you so sure of that?" Zya said with uncertainty.

"Did you see his face light up when we dropped that cash in his lap? I knew he was game as soon as he got that look in his eyes. Shit, everyone has a price."

"I hope you are right. Now we just have to sit back and wait on him," Zya said as she put on her designer sunglasses and leaned back in her chair. Snow pulled out of the parking garage and headed back to Zya's spot in Harlem.

Vita smacked her arm frantically with two fingers, desperately searching for a vein. The dope house that she sat in was dim and musty. She was surrounded by all kinds of drug users and junkies, but they all had one common goal: everyone was searching for a high. Vita had just turned a trick with one of the dealers in the back of the dope house to pay for her fix. She still hadn't lost her ass yet, and the drug dealers took advantage of it by exchanging sexual favors for product. She was a hot commodity in the dope houses she lurked in.

Vita injected the heroin-filled syringe into her vein and felt the drug work its magic. The warm sensation slowly crept up her vein, and she closed her eyes as she entered her momentary paradise. Vita's eyes began to water, and a slight smile formed on her face. Vita's addiction had grown stronger and stronger as the days passed. She eventually found out that Heavy had been giving her heroin rather than coke, but by that time, it was too late. She had already become addicted. After snorting heroin didn't get her high anymore, she switched to shooting up, because she knew that she would feel the full potency of the drug. She got a better high through the needle.

After she helped Heavy set up Zya, she hadn't heard from him. With no money and Heavy not there to supply her with her drug habit, she did anything for a fix. She would suck or fuck whoever, just to get the monkey off of her back. What once was a beautiful young lady was now a pitiful dope-head with a bad addiction.

Vita thought every day about how she had betrayed Zya, and she regretted it. She had crossed her best friend just to get a high and some money. The fucked up part about it was she didn't even get anything out of the caper. Heavy manipulated her into giving him the information he needed to rob her best friend, and then after he used her, he split. Now Vita had no one. She had no family, no man, and she had lost Zya, the closest person to her.

Vita sat in the corner with her legs wide open, exposing her vagina to whoever wanted to see it. She had been wearing the same skirt for days, and she smelled badly. She was so high, she didn't care. She just sat there and enjoyed the incredible feeling. That's why she didn't notice who crept up on her and gave her a rude awakening.

❀   ❀   ❀

Zya sat at her dining table and stared at her phone, hoping that it would ring. It had been twenty-four hours since they had approached the pilot, and she had not received a call.

I knew that square-ass mu'fucka wasn't going to call back. I can't see how people are so scared to get money. No big risk, no big reward. People on Wall Street take bigger risks than this on the daily.

Just as she was about to give up on waiting, her cell phone rang. She looked down at the caller ID and she grew disappointed. It was only Black Ty.

"What the fuck does he want? I just sold him a couple of bricks two days ago. I know he ain't ran through them that quick," she said just before answering her phone.

"Hello?"

"Yo, Zya. Guess who I am looking at right now."

"Who?"

"Vita. She over here at one of my dope houses on 140th, knocked out in the corner. She looks bad, too."

"The one I used to drop the bricks off at?"

"Yep."

Zya felt her adrenaline begin to pump as soon as she heard Vita's name. "Keep her there. I'm on my way."

"I got you. You still got ten thousand on her head, right? You gon' break me off—" But before Ty even finished his sentence, he heard a dial tone.

Zya flipped her phone down, grabbed her car keys, and bolted for the door. She couldn't wait to get her hands on Vita. She was so focused on getting to the dope house before Vita got away, she left her pistol. She turned around before she got to the elevator and re-entered her place to grab her gun. Zya was more than ready to see Vita.

Zya pulled up to the house and parked her car two houses down from Black Ty's spot. She grabbed her .22 out of her glove compartment and put it in the holster she kept on her ankle. Zya walked up to the door and knocked. Black Ty peeped out the hole and let Zya in.

Without even acknowledging Ty, she began to scan the room. She spotted Vita over in the corner in a nod. Zya wasn't going to waste any time. She pulled out her gun and fired a round into the ceiling. All of the junkies began to scramble around, and didn't know what was going on. Vita was so high, she didn't even move. She just sat there, drooling from the lips.

"If you don't wanna die, get the fuck out," Zya yelled as she focused on Vita. Immediately, everyone ran out of the dope house, trying to avoid getting their lives taken. Black Ty went on the front porch, leaving her alone to handle her business.

Zya walked over to her former best friend and stood above her. Zya thought back on how they were once two peas in a pod. Now Zya was about to take her life. Zya grabbed Vita up by her hair, yanking her to her feet. Vita didn't know what was going on. She tried to focus her eyes on the person that held her by the head, but before she could realize what was happening, she felt the cold steel of Zya's gun go across her head. Vita fell to the ground, holding her bloody nose. Zya kicked her in the stomach with all her strength, remembering how Heavy put Snow in the hospital.

"Bitch!" Zya yelled as she kicked her in the stomach a second time. Zya circled around Vita, watching her suffer. The more Zya remembered how close they were, the more enraged she became.

"You dirty-ass bitch," Zya said as she struck Vita in the back of the head with her gun. Zya dropped to one knee and grabbed the back of Vita's hair. Zya pointed the gun right at Vita's forehead and asked, "Why? Why did you set me up to get robbed? We were like sisters, Vita!" Zya yelled as tears began to form in her eyes.

Blood was all over Vita's face, and tears began to roll down her cheeks. She began to plead with Zya.

"Zy, I'm so sorry. It wasn't me. It was the drugs, Zya. Them drugs got a hold on me. They got me, Zya. He said he was only going to break in and take the money. I didn't know he was going to hurt you."

"Shut up!" Zya yelled as she pulled back the hammer of her gun, preparing to take Vita's life. But before she killed her, she had to find out if she knew where Heavy was. "Where is that fat mu'fucka? Where is he, Vita? Where is Heavy?" Zya screamed as she gripped Vita's hair even tighter, almost pulling it right out of her scalp.

"I don't know. He split on me right after it happened."

Zya stood up and aimed the gun toward Vita's head. Vita raised her hands in fear.

"Wait! Wait! He is having this thing at the Marriott on Saturday. I heard one of his boys talking about it when I went to get a fix yesterday. They are having some type of get-together. He didn't even recognize me. He was on the phone talking big shit, about the private get-together and the stripper he hired for Heavy."

Zya gripped her gun tightly and put her finger on

the trigger. She looked into Vita's eyes and didn't see the same person she used to be close with. Vita's eyes had no soul. She knew that the drugs were eating at her. Zya looked down at Vita's arms and saw all of the marks where she had been shooting up, and felt sorry for her. *Damn! I can't do this*, she thought. She still loved Vita, but she knew that she had to handle her business. If she didn't kill her, Snow would when he found her. Zya closed her eyes and once again put her finger on the trigger, but she still couldn't do it.

"Please, Zya, please don't kill me," Vita pleaded.

"I never want to see you again. You hear me? You better not be lying about Heavy, either, because if you are, I will find you. Look at you. You're dying slowly anyway. You are not worth it," Zya said as she released her grip on Vita. Zya stormed out of the house and saw Black Ty waiting on the porch, smoking a cigarette.

"I'm not cleaning that shit up. You better handle that, Zya," Ty said as he puffed on the cigarette.

"She's not dead. I'll be sending over someone to give you your money for finding her," Zya said as she walked off of the porch.

Black Ty eyes followed Zya's ass as she strutted to her car. "Yo, Zya, when you gon' give a nigga some play?" he asked.

Without even turning around, she yelled, "When yo' ass can afford to cop more than two bricks a month. You can't afford me." She pushed her alarm and hopped in her car. With that comment, she belittled Black Ty, and he was so embarrassed, but he knew she was right. Zya put money in his pocket. How could he holla at his boss? That's when he realized how big Zya had gotten, and her position—at the top of the game.

He just shook his head and re-opened shop. "That's a boss bitch right there," he said as she pulled off.

Zya called Snow as soon as she got in the car, letting him know that she knew how to get Heavy. She told him she killed Vita, only to spare her life and prevent Snow from going after her. She told him she would meet him at her spot. They had a birthday party to attend.

Heavy had a bottle of Cristal in each hand as he sat back and received a lap dance from a beautiful Puerto Rican stripper. "Move it, mami," he said as he poured the champagne on her ass. He enjoyed his twenty-sixth birthday party with his crew. He wanted to throw a bash at a strip joint, but he had too many enemies to count. He didn't want to get caught slipping, so the Marriott's presidential suite became the private location. Three men were in the room with two strippers. The music was bumping loud, and everyone was having a good time. Heavy looked over at his friend, who was getting head from one of the strippers, and that instantly made him want to get in.

"Yo, what about the birthday boy?" Heavy asked as he got up and took a swig of the champagne.

One of Heavy's henchmen stood up and announced, "Nah, nigga, we got something lined up for you. It should be here any minute now." Just as he finished his sentence, they heard a knock at the door. Heavy quickly pulled out his pistol and grew paranoid. His boy motioned for Heavy to put his gun away, saying, "Chill out. Put the burner away. Damn, man, you never relax."

Everyone began to laugh at Heavy's paranoia, and even Heavy realized that he needed to relax and enjoy his birthday. He smiled and shook his head from side to side. He tossed his gun into one of the dresser drawers and focused on the door. One of Heavy's friends opened the door and presented a gypsy belly dancer with a veil covering her face. She seductively danced while rolling the gigantic cake to the middle of the floor.

Heavy watched closely as the belly dancer seductively moved her body like a snake, and he couldn't take his eyes off of her ass. The dancer sexily pushed Heavy down into the chair and began her show. She turned her back toward him and lightly bounced on his crotch, arousing him.

All the men were talking shit and laughing at how Heavy was so into the lap dance. The belly dancer slowly began to take off her see-through blouse as she pranced around the room. The music was so loud that the only thing clearly heard was the ranting of men. Heavy took another swig of the bottle and watched the dancer's snake-like movement.

The dancer made her way to the door, and Heavy yelled, "Where you going, baby girl? The party is over here," he said as he pointed at himself. The last thing Heavy saw was the dancer's hand move toward the light switch, and he grew excited.

"Hell yeah!" he said. He began to pull out his dick so that he could really get the party started. He continued, "Shit, turn the lights back on. I want to see that ass while I'm hitting it." Heavy heard slurping noises all around the room, knowing his boys were getting head from the strippers. He couldn't take it anymore. He was fully erect.

"Baby girl, where you at?" he asked. The lights came back on, and what he saw almost made him piss on himself. Snow was sticking halfway out of the cake, with two twin pistols pointing directly at him. He looked over at the belly dancer, and the veil was removed, exposing her face. It was Zya. She also had a gun pulled out.

The element of surprise made Heavy and his crew vulnerable. They didn't reach for their weapons, in fear of getting shot. Heavy's facial expression said a thousand words. He was totally caught off guard, with his dick in his hand.

Zya had a chrome handgun pointed at Heavy's boys. Snow began to bark out instructions while waving his gun in the direction of the corner where Heavy was at. "Yo, y'all move over there in the corner. Y'all hoes get the fuck out if you want your life. If any of you call the police, I will find you and kill the people closest to you. After that, I'll blast both of you."

Zya started to pick up the women's clothes, and she threw them toward the door, "Y'all heard what he said. Get the fuck out!" The women didn't even grab their clothes off the ground. The two girls ran out butt naked while they still had their lives.

All of the men stood in the corner with their hands in front of them, hoping Snow and Zya didn't pop off. Snow had his twin Desert Eagles pointed at the crew, while Zya searched them and took off all their pistols. Zya pulled her old gun off of one of the men and said, "This looks familiar. Where did you get it?" Before the man even answered, Zya struck him across the face with the gun. Zya returned to Snow's side after letting out her frustration on the man.

Zya pointed her gun at Heavy and asked him, "Where is the money you took from me?"

"I don't know," Heavy replied with both of his hands up.

"Oh, you don't know?" Zya walked over to the man standing next to Heavy and without hesitation, put a bullet through his skull, causing his blood to splatter on everybody. The man's blood was all over Zya's face, and it was the first time Zya had actually killed anyone. But it wasn't like she expected. She didn't feel bad. She was ready to put another bullet through someone else's head.

She pressed the barrel of her gun to the next man's head and looked at Heavy. "Where is my money?" she asked coldly.

Heavy was noticeably scared out of his mind, and his hands began to shake. "Yo, I don't have it. It's at one of my stash houses."

Snow walked over to him, not believing a word that he was saying. He hit him in the mouth with the butt of the gun, and there was a loud crack as Heavy's jawbone shattered.

"That's what a broken jaw feels like," Snow said as he hovered over Heavy's body. "Where is the stash spot?" Snow asked. Snow wanted to kill Heavy right then and there, but he knew that he needed him alive to take Zya to her money.

The sound of Snow's cell phone rang. He had programmed his phone to make a certain ring tone when the pilot called. It was him. Snow stepped back and answered his phone.

"Hello . . . I'll meet you at the parking garage tomorrow at five." Snow hung up the phone and looked at Zya. "It's done."

"So, does that mean what I think it means?" Zya said as she slightly grinned.

Snow smiled back and nodded his head. Since the pilot agreed to fly the drugs overseas, they had a million dollars waiting for them in Cuba. The measly $100,000 that Heavy had stashed wasn't important.

At that moment, Zya and Snow pointed their guns at Heavy at the same time. The loud shrill of Heavy's voice echoed through the room just before they loaded his body up with bullets all at once. The bullets from their guns caused Heavy's body to jerk from left to right, ripping his flesh one bullet at a time. Heavy lay there dead, with sixteen bullets lodged into his body.

The one man remaining was in shock. He just stood there twitching and staring at the dead bodies in front of him. Snow raised his gun and pointed over to the man, prepared to end his life too. Zya looked in the man's eyes and saw pure fear. She didn't feel the need to kill him, and wanted him to be the one to deliver a message to the streets: Don't fuck with Zya Miller.

"Let him live," Zya said as she began to walk away.

Snow knew it was a mistake, but he followed suit, and they both headed out of the door. Just as they reached the door, they heard movement. It was the man reaching for his gun and aiming it at them. Before the man could let off a single shot, Snow turned around with his gun in his palm and fired hollow tips through his body, reuniting him with his crew.

❖   ❖   ❖

The next day, they met the pilot at the parking garage and made him follow them to the nearest hotel to plan the transport. Zya had paid for the room earlier that morning, so that there would be privacy and no distractions when going over the plan to move the dope. They entered the room, and the pilot began to give them his perception on how the transport should go. He had a whole different outlook on the situation than he did the last time they had met, and seemed way more comfortable. He had a couple days to think about the financial opportunity this job provided for him. The pilot had done his homework, and found the safest flight route to Havana, Cuba.

"All right, here is the shortest and safest path to Cuba. I will first fly to Miami and gas up at this private airplane strip my father owns. After I finish there, I will hit the air around four o' clock, because that is the busiest part of the day for air patrol. On a daily basis, they have a lot of imports and exports from the port of Miami. I won't log in my flight, so there will be no record of the flight. See, if I fly below air patrol radar, they won't detect the plane," the pilot explained as he scrolled his finger from Miami to Cuba.

The pilot looked at Zya and then at Snow, waiting for their approval. They were definitely impressed by the pilot's groundwork, and knew that they had the right man for the job.

Zya leaned over to Snow and whispered in his ear, "I like him." Snow shook his head in agreement, and then told the pilot he was hired. After going over all of the logistics, the rendezvous was over, and Zya and Snow shook the pilot's hand as they prepared to leave.

That's when Snow asked for insurance. "You say

your name was Sam, right?" Snow said as he still held
a firm grip with the man.

"Yeah, my friends call me Sammy."

"Okay, Sammy, I will need a picture of your kids
and your ID. If anything goes wrong on your part,
your family will be receiving a visit from me personally."

Sammy's face went blank, and he was shocked at
the remark, but he knew that they were only covering
their own asses. He respected the game, and pulled
out his wallet and gave Snow what he had asked for.
Sammy exited the room, leaving Snow and Zya there
alone.

"This time next week, we will be able to leave the
game for good," Snow said as he began to roll up the
map.

"You're right. We could leave this game alone. Can
you leave the game for good, Snow?" she asked as she
looked at his piercing gray eyes.

"I don't know. Could you?"

"Nah, I don't think I could. This is the only thing in
my life I have ever been good at. I live to hustle. It's
like it's the only way that I find satisfaction. It's in
me," Zya answered.

"I guess Jules created a monster, huh?"

"No, Snow, he discovered one."

Chapter 11

Supreme Clientele

S now drove to Stello's and parked outside while Zya went in to pick up the money.

"I'll be right back," she said as she got out and knocked on the restaurant door. It was 5 A.M., and the restaurant was dark on the inside. Meechi finally answered the door.

"Are they here?" Zya asked.

Meechi shook his head and replied, "Only Anari. She is the one who handles the connect transactions."

Zya nodded and made her way to the kitchen and got into the elevator. When she got to the entrance of the meeting room, she took a deep breath before walking in.

Anari sat at the head of the table with a champagne glass in her hand. The room looked odd without all of the members sitting around the table.

"Is the money ready?" Zya asked Anari as she stared down at her.

Anari's face was expressionless, and she sat down with her legs crossed, staring up at Zya. "Are you done with the petty street beef?" Anari asked, her voice filled with annoyance.

Zya frowned and replied, "What are you talking about?"

"This beef that you have with your best friend and her boyfriend . . . is it over?" Anari asked sternly. She wasn't the type of person who got involved with bullshit. She was too big for it, and wasn't trying to deal with anybody who wasn't on her same level.

Zya grew a look of confusion on her face. *How the hell did she know about Vita and Heavy?* she thought.

"I know everything," Anari said as if she had read Zya's mind. "How much did they take?"

"A hundred thou," Zya admitted.

Anari chuckled lightly and shook her head in annoyance. "Let me explain one thing to you," she said as she tapped her finger on the table. "What can you do with a hundred thousand dollars? That is not big money. You are stepping into the big leagues now, Zya. All the little shit doesn't matter. That is the stuff that will get you caught up, believe me. Now you have a body on your hands that didn't need to be. I make so much money that I pay people to do my dirty work. That is how you have to be.

"I'm not trying to get involved with someone who does not fully understand the game. I fuck with hundreds of millions of dollars. I don't sweat the small stuff. You will make ten times the amount that was taken from you if you stick with me, but I have to know that you understand exactly what I am saying. The ghetto street shit has to go, because I do not leave loose ends. I cut them quickly. If your involvement with little stuff brings any attention to my organization, I will clip my loose ends, starting with you. Is that understood?"

If Anari had been any other chick talking slick to Zya, she would have beat that ass, but she knew that Anari was not to be tested. She also knew that there was a lot of money at stake. "I understand," Zya replied.

Anari pulled out two large suitcases full of money and handed them to Zya. They locked eyes, and their stare was almost hostile. Zya didn't appreciate the way that Anari had checked her, but she knew that there was nothing she could say about it. *Just make this money, Zya,* she told herself.

"There is a plane waiting on a private landing strip Upstate. Your pilot can fly it across seas."

Zya nodded and turned around to exit the room.

"Be careful," Anari advised.

Zya carried the money to the car, and when she was safely inside, popped the latches to open them up.

"Damn!" Zya exclaimed as she laid her eyes on the most money she had ever seen in her life.

If the roundtable wasn't so connected, I would take this shit and be ghost. Zya turned around in her seat, and Snow pulled away from the curb. They were headed for Cuba. They had the money in their possession, and there was no turning back.

✿　✿　✿

"I thought you said you knew how to fly this mu'-fucka!" Snow yelled as he strapped his seatbelt. The sky had been flashing, and the heavy clouds had turned dark, causing the sky to look like it was pitch black. Zya gripped Snow's hand and closed her eyes as she felt the plane dip wildly as they flew threw the storm.

"It's not me. It's the storm," the pilot said as he struggled to control the plane.

"God, please let this plane land safely. Please let us land safely. If you get us there, I swear I will be in church every Sunday," Zya prayed, trying to calm herself. She wasn't religious or nothing like that. In fact, she hadn't been to church since she was a child, but she knew that God was the only thing keeping their plane in the air.

The flight to Cuba was a long ten hours, and the storm didn't let up until they were on the ground. When they finally stepped down on solid ground, she was relieved, and her worries were quickly replaced with the thoughts of money. Ernesto had arranged to meet them at his associate's landing strip, and he was waiting for their arrival.

"Snow, Zya, how was your flight?" Ernesto asked as he grabbed Zya's hand and kissed it.

"It was good," Zya lied, trying to cut out the chit-chat. She was there for one reason and one reason only: to get the product.

Snow knew that there was no need for small talk. He simply popped one of the briefcases open and held the money out for Ernesto to see. "That look right?" Snow asked.

Ernesto rubbed his hands together and replied, "That looks very right." He snapped his fingers at the group of Cuban men who were standing near the dirt road, waiting by a big rig. The men opened up the back of the truck and began to transport three large crates from the truck to the plane.

A smile formed on Zya's face. *I can't believe that I'm transporting two hundred keys into the border. This shit is bananas. If we get caught, I'm doing Fed time for real.* Zya felt a surge of adrenaline rush her body. She was scared and nervous, but most of all, she was excited. She had just been drafted into the major leagues, and her signing bonus was $500,000.

"Why don't the two of you join me at my villa for drinks?" Ernesto said.

Zya looked up at the sky and noticed that it was clear. "We better get going while the sky is good. Can we take a rain check?"

"Of course, Zya," Ernesto said.

"I'll be in contact," Snow said as he shook hands with Ernesto.

"Zya," Ernesto called out. She turned around and watched as he approached her. "A neck pillow for your flight," Ernesto said as he handed her the U-shaped pillow.

Zya smiled and replied, "Thanks." Ernesto waved goodbye as they boarded the plane and headed back for the States.

The plane finally landed, and now that they were home, they were both eager to make the transaction with Supreme Clientele. Snow had a couple of his henchmen waiting for their arrival at the landing strip. Snow looked out his window and saw the small private airport and smiled. He looked at Zya and said, "We did it."

"We did it."

"This is crazy," Zya answered as she leaned over to kiss Snow. Just as her lips was about to touch his, she jerked back and reached out her hand. She smiled and said, "I forgot. Keep business and personal completely separated."

Snow laughed. "Oh yeah, I almost forgot." They shook hands and then they both stared out of the window as they reached the ground.

Zya removed the neck pillow Ernesto had given her and tossed it to the side. *That pillow was comfortable as hell,* she thought as she rubbed the back of her neck.

Once the plane was on the ground safely, Zya handed Sammy an envelope. It contained fifty thousand dollars, plus a ten thousand dollar tip. It seemed like Sammy jumped out of the plane as soon as the wheels stopped rolling. He wasn't going to wait around for small talk. His job was done, and he knew that Zya and Snow were involved in some illegal activity that could get him thrown in jail for life.

Snow and Zya exited the plane, and Snow immediately instructed his workers to start unloading the crates and place them in the three different vans. Once the crates were all loaded, Zya and Snow followed the dope in a separate car until they reached one of Snow's stash houses.

Once they arrived at the house, Snow helped the men move the crates into the abandoned building, and Zya began to think about what she would do with her half of the money. Zya followed the men in, and couldn't wait to take the goods to Anari so that she could get the rest of their money.

Once the men put all the crates in the house, Snow told them that he would meet with them later, and they left. Zya grabbed the duffle bags that they brought specifically for the dope, and carried them over to the crates. She examined one of the crates, trying to figure out how she would open it. *How do you open this thing?* she thought as she looked for a method.

Snow saw her trying to open it, and insisted that he would grab a crow bar from the basement. He left the room to go and get it, but Zya was eager to see what 200 kilos of pure cocaine looked like, and couldn't help herself. She grabbed her gun and shot off the four corners of the box, making it easy to remove the top. She took off the top and her heart dropped. She wasn't looking at two hundred kilos of dope; the crates were full of neck pillows.

"Fuck!" Zya yelled as she picked up one of the pillows and tossed it against the wall. Zya began to kick the crate repeatedly, letting out her frustration. She yelled for her partner to inform him they just got hit.

"Snow!"

Snow pulled out his gun and bolted upstairs to see what was going on. To his surprise, he saw Zya standing over the crates unharmed.

"Are you okay, Zya?" he asked.

"No, I am not. Your sheisty-ass friend just double-crossed us. He didn't supply us with any dope. He stuffed this mu'fucka full of pillows. What the fuck am I supposed to do? Anari is expecting 200 kilos before the day ends," Zya said as she slumped to the ground with one of the neck pillows in her hand, "and the only thing we have is some fuckin' pillows." Zya threw the pillow against the wall forcefully and dropped her head on her knees.

Snow looked at Zya and smiled lightly. He knew Ernesto kept many tricks up his sleeve. He walked

over to the pillow and picked it up. He began to smile
as he discovered his ingenious Cuban friend's idea.
He ripped open the pillow and found pure Cuban cocaine wrapped in plastic.

"Yo, Zya, look what I found," Snow said as he held
up the ripped pillow.

Zya took her head off her knees and looked up.
She instantly went to the crate and began to rip every
neck pillow, finding more and more dope. There
were two hundred pillows, all containing one kilo of
product.

"Two hundred kilos of Cuba's finest," she said as
she felt a sense of relief. They wasted no time loading
the goods into three different duffle bags. Once all of
the dope was in the bags, they headed toward Stello's
to meet Anari.

They reached Stello's two hours later, and Snow
pulled his car to the back as Zya directed him where
to park. Snow parked his car about ten feet away
from the back door, and they both hopped out to deliver the goods. Just as they grabbed the duffle bags
out of the trunk, Meechi opened the back door.

"Are those it?" Meechi said as he began to look
around suspiciously.

"Yeah, all two hundred of them," Zya boasted as
she looked down at the bag she was carrying.

Out of nowhere, Meechi placed two fingers to his
mouth and whistled. The sound of tires screeching
echoed through the alley, and a black-tinted SUV
emerged out of the dark alley. Before Zya and Snow
could even react, four men jumped out and grabbed
the bags.

Meechi quickly let Zya and Snow know it was cool.
"Don't worry. They're with us. We don't touch the

dope," he said as the men pulled away. Everything happened so fast, before they even realized what had happened, the men were gone.

Meechi stood in the doorway. "Anari wants to see you and only you," he said as he looked at Zya. Zya turned to Snow and then back to Meechi.

"He goes wherever I go. He's my partner," Zya said as she stood her ground.

"Anari is very picky on who sees her face. You will have to come alone or not at all." Meechi turned to Snow and said, "No disrespect to you, homeboy, but that is the rules." Meechi played with the toothpick hanging out of his mouth as he waited for them to make a decision.

Snow turned Zya toward him and quietly told her, "Go in there and handle it. I'm right out here if you need me. You got that thang on you, right?" Snow said, referring to Zya's gun. Zya nodded her head up and down and then turned around to walk into Stello's.

Zya entered the restaurant and followed Meechi as he led her to the freezer. Meechi began to explain to Zya how the transaction would work.

"Everyone is waiting for you downstairs. This is how it works. They have their men take the coke to another location, to make sure it's the whole order and test the quality. If they call back and tell them it's all good, they will hand you your money. Simple as one, two, three," Meechi said. He dreaded telling Zya the procedures. Meechi was slightly jealous that Zya had been able to do business with Supreme Clientele. His father was a part of the table, but even then, he couldn't join. He hated to see a young black girl become affiliated before him. Nevertheless, he kind of liked Zya, and didn't show his envy.

Zya stepped into the freezer, and a chill ran up her spine; not because of the cold air, but because of the colder room she was about to enter, the Supreme Clientele's roundtable room.

Meechi opened the door, and Zya walked into the meeting room. After Zya entered, Meechi left the room. All eyes were on Zya as she stood before the round-table. Nobody said a word, and Zya grew uncomfortable as she waited for someone to speak. She looked at Anari, sitting at the head of the table, calmly tapping her perfectly manicured nails against the red oak wood.

What the fuck is going on? They are just staring at me like I'm a painting or something. I hope all the dope was there. Oh shit, what if Ernesto was short on the dope? They will kill me for coming short. Fuck it, I'm about to ask them what are they looking at.

Zya opened her mouth to speak, but Anari quickly ceased that action by putting her finger over her lip, signaling Zya to remain quiet. Zya just looked at the whole table and looked at Mr. Castello sitting to the right of Anari. He looked like he was waiting on something too. He gently rubbed his temples with his right index fingers while staring directly at Zya. Zya's chest felt like a baboon was on the inside, trying to pound its way out.

I knew I shouldn't have got involved with these crazy mu'fuckas. I'm about to get out of here. No, I can't. They already have the dope, and they haven't paid me my money yet.

Just as Zya completed her thought, Anari's phone

rang. She picked it up and was getting information on the other end. Without saying a single word or revealing any emotion, Anari hung up the phone and looked at Zya. It was complete silence as the two women intensely stared at each other. Anari was the first to speak.

"Zya, we were doubtful that you would be able to deliver such a vast quantity of cocaine, but you have proved us wrong. After much discussion, we have come to realize that you would be a great asset to this table. Your cocaine is superb, and we need that connect. Please have a seat," Anari said.

Zya sat down and continued to listen.

"We would like to offer you the opportunity of a lifetime. We would like to continue our business with you, if you are willing to join our roundtable."

Zya's mouth dropped from astonishment.

"What do you say?" Mr. Castello asked.

Zya smiled and nodded her head in disbelief. "Yes. I say yes."

Anari laughed and began to clap as she welcomed Zya to the roundtable. Everyone at the table joined in with the applause, and then Anari went around the roundtable, introducing each member.

"Meet Khadafi Langston. He is our Midwest supplier, and also one of the most brilliant business minds in the country." Khadafi was a well-built, attractive man who wore a bald head. His salt-and-pepper beard displayed his maturity. Zya studied his neatly tailored suit and blinging cufflinks as he extended his hand toward her. He was the only black man in the room.

"Welcome to the table," he said politely as he kissed her hand.

Anari looked to the left of Khadafi and introduced the next member. "This is Emilio Estes. He controls the Clientele on the West Coast." Zya looked at the man and could tell he was of Dominican descent. He wore a flowered shirt with a wife beater underneath. He kind of reminded Zya of Scarface the way he slumped over in the chair like he owned the place.

He looks just like Tony Montana, Zya thought, almost laughing at the resemblance.

"The next member is Anderson Wallace. He is our legal consultant, and has political connections out of this world. He has seven of the nine Supreme Court Justices in his back pocket. He is what keeps Supreme Clientele untouchable."

Anderson Wallace slightly blushed and spoke. "You make me sound so good, Anari. I just do my job. Hello, beautiful. Welcome to the table."

"Of course you know Mister Castello, the advisor of the Council and owner of this place. He is a seasoned veteran in distribution, and I'm still learning from him after seven years.

"Over to your right is Jimmy Ross from Miami. He is half crazy, but he sure knows how to move blow. He supplies the South with the product." Jimmy Ross was a husky Italian with a cigar hanging from his lip. He nodded his head, acknowledging Zya.

"You already know who I am," Anari said as she grabbed a Cuban cigar out of the ashtray, lit it, and leaned back cockily in her chair, displaying her beautiful smile. "The baddest bitch who ever did it," she said jokingly, causing the room to explode into laughter. Although Anari was just joking, everyone in the room knew she was telling the honest truth.

Chapter 12

Bossy

Zya became a permanent member of the round-table, and she was amazed at exactly how powerful they were. Everybody sitting at the table was connected. From federal judges to nickel-and-dime corner hustlers, Supreme Clientele had a hand in almost every drug transaction going on in the United States. Each member possessed a different asset that was brought to the table. Zya's asset was her connection to Snow and her ability to get her hands on large quantities of coke.

The original order of two hundred kilos quickly increased to five hundred kilos, and it was a transaction that took place twice every month. Zya and Snow made the flight overseas on the same days each month, and their profits proved exactly how big-time they were. What they were making from their business arrangement with the roundtable, combined with what they were earning from the streets, they were certainly "gettin' it." Zya and Snow became a powerhouse in the drug game, and built an empire that was untouchable. She hit Smitty and Black Ty off with more bricks, and she controlled the Harlem drug trade. Supreme Clientele took her to another level.

Supreme Clientele consisted of seven people, including Zya, from different regions of the country. There was no city that their dope didn't reach. They were connected and powerful, and now that Zya had been initiated into the table, she was connected too. With Snow's connection to Ernesto and Zya's connection to Supreme Clientele, together they became responsible for six percent of the drugs being brought into the United States. If you were smoking, snorting, or selling dope in 2007, there was a good chance that you were getting it from them. They were big and everybody knew it.

Zya quickly learned the order of the table and knew that the most powerful person of the bunch was Anari. Her story had been told and retold so many times in the street that she had become a ghetto legend. Nobody knew if a woman named Anari Simpson aka Tony even existed. Zya was one of the lucky few who actually saw Anari, and she made it a point to get close to her.

Mostly everybody in the game gets killed or sent Upstate. She been in it for a minute and is still breathing and on top. Whatever she did, that's what I'm trying to do, Zya thought. She knew that Anari was a good friend to have. She looked up to her. She was one of few women in the drug game, and she was the one calling the shots. She conducted business with a no bullshit policy, and Zya took notes whenever she was in her presence.

Zya knew the order of things. She was sitting at a table of mostly men, so most of the time, she sat back and listened. She didn't do too much talking. She observed everything around her because although she was getting money, she didn't have power or respect yet, and that's what she was seeking. She knew that the members of the roundtable were veterans in the game. They had been around a while, and she wasn't trying to step on anybody's toes with her inexperience. She wanted to earn their respect, and she knew once that happened, she would be just as powerful, if not more powerful, than them.

She had one thing that everybody else sitting at the table had lost, and that was her hunger. She was hungry for the game, and that is what made her hustle so different from everybody else's. She went after the money like no other, because no matter how much she made, it was never enough. Zya took to the streets like a duck took to water. The streets were her habitat, and she knew how to milk them for everything that they were worth.

Anari could see Zya's potential, and made it a point to keep her around. She knew that Zya was a queen pen in the making. All she needed was to be groomed.

She is smart and uses what she has to get what she wants. She reminds me a lot of myself. Her hustle is crazy. She doesn't even realize that she is the one keeping this roundtable on its feet. Without her dope, we'd be stuck, still seeking another connect.

Anari was impressed by Zya and pulled her under

her wings to teach her everything she needed to know about the game. She knew that Zya had to be careful because she was playing in a deadly game that was not meant for women. Emotions had to be thrown out of the window when it came to the dope game.

The only person she can trust is herself. Anari had lived by that rule since the first day she stepped foot in the game. She had given up so much and almost killed the only person she could count on because of it, but she knew that if she wanted to be a part of the streets, she would have to sacrifice, and she did. Anari knew that a hustler's reign usually ended in one of two ways: prison or death. She was trying to be the first one to change that. She didn't want to go out in a blaze of gunfire or be locked behind a cage. *That don't make you a gangsta. That just proves that you did something wrong and wasn't even around long enough to enjoy the money you made,* she thought.

So far, Anari had been careful and precise. She was always on top of everything, and her perfection had saved her life more than once. The more time she spent with Zya and the more she observed her, the more she saw the potential that the young girl had. Zya was only twenty-four, and if she played her cards right, she would be on top of the world before she hit thirty.

Zya and Snow had personally taken over the drug markets in the states of New Jersey and New York. Zya was the brains behind the operation, and Snow was the muscle. With his notorious tactics, they took over any and all operations that were not affiliated with them. They established the perfect drug ring, and nobody made money on those streets except for them. Anybody who tried to infiltrate was quickly forced out, either by gun play or by competition.

Zya made sure that their operation ran like a business. They made sure that other hustlers in Jersey and New York couldn't compete. Ernesto's product was too good. The dope was so good that the fiends had nicknamed it *Supreme* because it was above the rest. Their highs lasted longer and felt better when they purchased their rock from Supreme Clientele.

Supreme reigned in the streets, and everybody wanted a piece of the pie. But Snow's army only consisted of a select few. He didn't trust too many people, and made sure that he only kept thorough people around him. Zya and Snow were getting money, and everybody knew it.

During Anari's reign in Jersey, she was forced to stay low-key because of the fact that she was a woman. Zya, on the other hand, was flashy and also fearless because she knew that Snow's reputation protected her. Everybody knew that she was his woman and therefore was off limits. Niggas didn't even look at Zya for too long, let alone plot to rob her. She was safe in the hood, and was loved because she made sure that everybody ate, as long as they were loyal. She walked around the city like she owned it, and her Acura was quickly traded in for a silver, two-seat, Z-24 BMW, and that was just her weekend car. Zya switched whips like she switched panties, and the fleet of cars from her collection lined up and down the driveway to the 10,000-square-foot mansion Snow had purchased.

The only thing she hadn't changed was where she rested her head. She still lived in the tiny Harlem apartment. She had been so busy making money that she hadn't found the time to shop for a new place to live, and she didn't want to move in with Snow too quickly. Their relationship was good just how it was, and she didn't want things to change if they decided to live together. She didn't mind the cramped space in her apartment, though, because it was filled with cash. The only thing that was in her apartment was her bed and her clothes. There wasn't enough room for anything else. Her apartment was filled to the ceiling with moving boxes full of cash, all hundred-dollar bills. She didn't have room for any other denominations. The boxes occupied every single inch of the apartment, from top to bottom. She was literally swimming in money. She and Snow each had two Swiss bank accounts and money stashed away in the Cayman Islands. They were living good.

Once Anari saw how flashy Zya was, she quickly hooked her up with Anderson Wallace, a lawyer who was a pro at washing money. His laundering services were a lifesaver, and after having numerous conversations with Snow and Zya, he convinced them to start front businesses. They opened over ten businesses, ranging from real estate to record labels. Zya even started her own clothing line. They had their hands involved in anything, and whenever they made a move, it was always to benefit them and improve their position in the dope game.

Snow even went as far as to open up a funeral home. He knew that it would be the perfect investment because it would help them conceal any evidence of any murders they might have to partake in. "No body, no murder," he had explained to Zya. Their business endeavors were wise because they allowed them to cover their paper trail with the IRS. They would never get caught up on a tax evasion charge because every single cent they spent was accounted for, right down to the last penny.

They made sure that they were affiliated with the right people too. Snow suggested that they make contributions to political parties because, he said, "Politicians are the smartest crooks of us all. They never get caught."

Zya was making so much money that it didn't make sense for her to keep her job at the restaurant. She was already a part of the roundtable, so she would still receive a cut from Stello's profits anyway. She was big money, and the word was spreading quickly. Everybody wanted to be down, but Zya knew better.

After her run-in with Lonnie Wade, she began to realize that she needed to watch who she surrounded herself with. She hadn't heard from the detective in a couple months, and she hoped that he had forgotten about her. He had wanted her to do the unthinkable, and that was become a snitch, but now she was directly involved with Supreme Clientele. She couldn't give him any information if she wanted to. She hoped that Wade didn't pop back up because the way she was flashing money, he would know that she knew more than she was letting on. She was knee-deep in the game now, and there was no getting out. She hoped that the cop wouldn't bother her again, and she told herself that she would be extra careful just in case he did resurface.

All I need in this life is Snow, Anari, and my money . . . and I'm good. Fuck the world and everybody else in it.

❖　　❖　　❖

Jules looked at the picture of Zya and felt an intense hatred toward her. At first he didn't believe the things he had been hearing. He thought that his li'l niggas had been misinformed about what Zya had been doing. He tried to give her the benefit of the doubt, but the more time that passed, the more he began to believe that she had pulled dirty and tried to play him. He hadn't heard from her in almost two years. Since her very first visit to Riker's, Zya hadn't stepped foot back inside the prison.

She was pregnant with my muthafuckin' kid and couldn't even write to let me know what was going down. That was my unborn child too. I had a right to know, he thought as he stared at the picture of the woman he used to adore. He was hurt deeply by her betrayal. She had meant the world to him, and he would have done anything for her. When she told him that she was pregnant, it had been the happiest day of his life. He had been looking forward to being a father and maybe even a husband to Zya one day. He had it set in his mind that when he got out, he was going to settle down with Zya and take care of his family.

When she stopped accepting his calls and the visits stopped, he was devastated. They had done so much dirt together, and she had been loyal to him for so long, that he never expected her to turn on him once he got locked up. His hatred for her was driving him crazy, and the only thing on his mind was revenge.

That bitch killed my seed and tried to leave me in here on stuck. He was losing his mind, thinking about her betrayal, and was counting down the days until he was released. His lawyers had been working on his appeal and had informed him that the search warrant that was used during the raid had not been valid.

I'ma be out this bitch in less than a month, and the first thing I'm gon' do is dead Zya's ass. His love for his former girlfriend had quickly transformed into hate. The last time he had seen her had been when he first caught his charge. He had expected her to come every other Monday, but the only visits he got were from his cousin, Tisha. Tisha was pregnant and came to visit Jules often to show her support. Before Jules got locked up, he used to spoil his little cousin, and she felt obligated to be there for him while he was away.

After Jules found out about Zya's abortion, he had to ask Tisha to stop coming. It was too painful for him to see his cousin's newborn baby because it reminded him too much of the child that he was supposed to have. Zya had taken his life from him in the blink of an eye. He had nothing to look forward to when he got out. The only thing he was anticipating was the day he ended Zya's life. Killing her was the only thing that would put his mind at ease. He was not only hurt by her actions, but embarrassed that, in the end, he had been the one looking stupid. He loved Zya, and even though he had not always been faithful to her, she was always the only woman who had his heart. He always came home to her at night, and thought that she had cared for him as much as he did her. When Zya just disappeared without an explanation, his ego was wounded, and his stubborn nature couldn't let her get away with what she had done.

"Is everything in order for the first of the month?" Khadafi asked as he looked around the table.

"Everything my way is in order. Zya's coke is a hit on the West Coast. The customers can't get enough of it," Emilio responded. Emilio ran the West Coast drug market.

"Good, good. The first of the month is our biggest payday nationwide," Khadafi said. Khadafi, the man who ran the Midwest drug market, ran the meeting as Anari and Zya sat back and listened. They didn't have too much to say. Zya knew that her operation was good. She didn't need any directives from anybody. Snow made sure her shit was tight, and the rest of the table was beginning to notice. Anari took a piece of paper and slid Zya a note.

I'm going to Miami for the weekend. Are you available to make that trip with me?

Zya read the note and wrote back: *Hell yeah, I'm down. What's down there? We got business to take care of or something?*

Anari replied: *Nah, this weekend is strictly for pleasure. I'm gon' show you how to really enjoy some of this money you making. You're gettin' money like a don diva. Now you've got to play like a don diva.*

The next night, Snow stood in her bedroom doorway watching her pack her clothes for her weekend trip.

"Damn, shorty, you got to go?" he said as he walked toward her and stood directly behind her.

"Yeah, I need a vacation. Why, you gon' miss me?" she asked him as she cocked her head and smiled.

He kissed her neck and ran his hands up and down her body. "I'm gon' miss something," he said as he turned her around and unbuttoned her pants.

"How much you gon' miss me, daddy?" she asked him as she started to unbutton his jeans.

He didn't respond, but he picked her up and laid her gently on the bed. He kissed her, his tongue caressing every inch of her mouth. His fingertips made her skin tingle, and she loved how gentle he was with her. He always took his time with her, and he made love to her like he aimed to please. He wasn't one of those men who only thought about themselves. Everything he did was to make her feel good. He stopped undressing her and lay down next to her.

"What's wrong?" Zya asked him.

"You gon' be all right this weekend?" he asked.

Zya smiled and replied, "Yeah, baby, I'll be okay. I'm good. Ain't nothing gon' happen to me, so stop worrying."

"If there's any problems . . ."

Zya put her finger up to his lip. "Shh, come here." She kissed his chest and then made her way down. By the time she was done with him, he was satisfied and carefree.

The next morning, Snow drove her to Anari's private landing strip. They were taking a private jet to Miami, and Zya was excited about the trip. He got out of his car and pulled her Louis Vutton luggage out of his trunk. He walked up to the stairs of the jet, where a stewardess took the bags from him.

Anari stepped off of the plane and walked down the stairs, where Zya and Snow stood.

"You must be Torey Snow," Anari said. "It's good to finally meet you."

"You too," he said as he shook her hand gently. He looked at Anari and noticed how beautiful she was. She didn't look to be a day older than thirty. She was so feminine, and as he looked back and forth from Zya to her, he could see a resemblance. He couldn't believe that the woman he was standing in front of was the same woman that the streets feared. Her reputation was so notorious, and to him it seemed like the woman and the myth didn't match.

"Your coke connect has been very helpful," she said.

"So has your money," Snow replied as he kissed Zya on the top of the head. "I'll see you when you get back," he said. "You ladies have a good time."

Diamonds on my neck. Di-diamonds on my grill. I'm bossy . . .

Zya and Anari cruised slowly through South Beach, Miami, as Kelis's hit song blared from the stereo system of a black convertible Mercedes Benz CLK 550. They rocked their heads to the music. They drove down to the port of Miami, and Anari parked the car. There was a huge ship sitting at the end of the dock.

"We're taking a cruise?" Zya asked.

"Nah, this is a casino that I'm thinking about investing in. An associate of mine owns this. It's a floating casino. The boat goes out every night at ten. It's invitation only, though. All of the players are very exclusive."

Zya nodded as she got out of the car and headed onto the boat. When she entered, the only thing she could hear was the sound of the slot machines. It was so alive in the place, and the different shades of red mixed with deep tones of wood made the room seem bright and energetic.

"Damn, Anari," Zya said as she watched everyone in the casino turn around to speak as they walked by.

"They all just think I'm a big spender. No one in

here knows who I am. They just know that I drop a lot of money every time I come," Anari explained as she made her way through the crowded casino. She walked up the spiral staircase that led to the top level of the ship. It was where the tables were located, and she headed straight toward the dice game.

"You know how to shoot craps?" Anari asked.

"Just in the streets. I've never rolled the dice in a casino before," Zya explained as she shook her head from side to side.

"It's the same game, only it's better," Anari said as she stepped up to a table.

A white man in a suit and sunglasses walked behind the dealer's table and handed one of them a briefcase. The dealer popped the latch and opened it up to reveal money that was neatly stacked and wrapped in $1,000 bundles. Zya and Anari were the only women around the entire table, and all eyes were focused on the transaction.

"How much?" one of the dealers asked as he looked up at Anari.

"A hundred thousand. Split it up between me and my girl," Anari instructed. The dealer nodded, and multi-color gambling chips were given to Zya and Anari.

Zya shook her head and said, "Anari, I can't take that."

"Why not? You helped me make it, so help me spend it. Fifty G's ain't shit. I come down here and lose that in an hour. Just enjoy yourself and relax. You've earned it."

Zya picked up the chips from the center of the table and placed them in her rack.

"Hey, excuse me!" Anari yelled as a waiter walked by.

The man stopped walking and said, "Would you like to purchase a drink, Miss?"

"Yeah, bring me a Long Island. Zya, what you drinking?" she asked her friend.

Zya looked at the waiter and said, "Bring me a daiquiri. It don't matter what kind."

Anari placed a $500 chip on the waiter's tray and said, "That's your tip. The drinks from this table are on me for the night. Bring me the bill at the end of the shift."

A round of applause went around the table, and everybody placed their drink orders. The dealers brought the dice down to Anari, and she shook her head.

"Pass," she said. The dealers went to Zya, who was standing directly next to Anari. She put a $500 chip on the pass line and picked up the dice. Everybody held their breath as she tossed them to the other end of the table.

"Eleven!" the dealer shouted as the dice landed. Zya got cashed out $500 from her bet, and then continued to enjoy the game. The liquor came non-stop, and she was feeling good. The alcohol had her talking big shit at the crap table, and she was having a lucky night. The dice seemed to agree with her that night because every time she rolled, she hit point after point. Everybody bet on her, and she was making everybody money that night.

"Give me a thousand dollar hard six," Anari instructed as she placed two black chips on the table.

The dealer placed the bet, and Zya looked at Anari and said, "What's a horn?"

Anari laughed and shrugged her shoulders. "I don't know. It's the only bet on the table that I don't already have, so I said fuck it."

Zya laughed and replied, "Fuck it. Give me a five hundred dollar hard six."

Anari shook her head and looked at Zya like she was confused.

"What?" Zya asked.

"You over there pinching pennies and shit. You got to bet big to win big," Anari suggested as the waiter delivered a round of shots to the entire table.

Zya threw her head back and felt the liquor warm her up as it traveled down her throat. She slammed the shot glass down on the table and said, "You gon' stop acting like you the only one out here getting money. Five thousand hard six!" she yelled as she threw the chips to the dealer.

"Six thousand!" Anari laughed and said.

"Ten thousand!" Zya said as she smiled devilishly around the table. A crowd had formed around the craps table, and everybody was in awe of the two women who were recklessly throwing money out onto the table, trying to outdo each other.

"Final bets!" the dealer called. Zya and Anari mugged each other playfully and burst out laughing.

"A hundred thousand hard six," a male's voice said as he parted through the crowd and threw the money on the table. Gasps broke through the air, and Zya saw a brown-skinned man in an Armani suit and a fresh Caesar haircut step up to the table. He made direct eye contact with Anari, and she smiled without saying a word.

The dealer handed Zya the dice, and she picked them up and schooled them against the table. A crowd had gathered around the table, but nobody spoke. Everybody was anticipating the outcome of the dice. The whole room was frozen with anticipation, and dozens of people crowded the table. She took a deep breath, closed her eyes and then tossed the dice.

"Six the hard way!" The dealer yelled in disbelief and shock. Zya jumped up and down from the excitement, and the crowd roared in applause. Security squeezed the cup of water he had been holding, crushing the cup like Zya had just crushed the casino. They were paid out $100,000 each, and the man who had placed the largest bet was given a $1,000,000 check, written directly from the owner.

"Damn," Zya whispered as Anari grabbed her arm and pulled her away from the crowd.

Zya followed Anari up to the man who had placed the bet. Anari walked up to him and punched him playfully in the arm.

"You get on my nerves. I'm always the biggest player until you walk up in here," she said. He leaned down and kissed her on the cheek.

"Zya, this is Von . . . my husband. Von, this is the girl I've been telling you about."

Zya smiled and shook her head. She couldn't believe that Anari had known the guy all along. "Nice to meet you, Von," she said.

"I been hearing good things about you. Anari talk like she's found a protègè'," he said as he kissed the top of Anari's head.

Damn, she be talking about me like that. I hope I keep impressing her, because I'm trying to do it big like her. She done put in so much work to where she ain't got to do shit now but sit back and collect her money, she thought silently as she looked up at Von. He was mysterious to her. There was a bad scar on his neck, but his face was flawless. He was definitely a fly nigga, and Zya knew that he had just as much if not more money than Anari.

"Y'all ate?" he asked.

Anari shook her head then turned to Zya. "You hungry?"

Zya nodded and Von said, "Good. You can buy since you just won all that money."

Zya laughed and replied, "I got you."

They sat down in the casino's restaurant and ate dinner together. Zya was intrigued by Anari and Von. They were on top, and it was apparent that they were very much in love. "So, how did you guys meet?" Zya asked as their waitress brought out her steamed lobster and crab cakes.

Anari looked skeptically at Von and said, "Should we tell her?"

Von shrugged and said, "She's your friend. Do you trust her?"

Anari looked at Zya and said, "He tried to kill me."

Zya looked confused, but didn't say anything.

Von shook his head and said, "You love to bring that shit up, don't you? It didn't even go down like that. She had a nigga fooled," Von said.

Anari and Von argued playfully as they explained to Zya the story of how they met. Von met Anari several years ago, while she was still haunted by the death of her baby's father. After the tragic murder of her son, Anari was forced into the game. A girl named Shawna had gotten close to Anari so that she could set her up and kidnap her son for ransom. Something went wrong, and Anari's son was killed. Anari was out for blood, but Shawna had love in the streets, and Anari knew that she would be hard to touch. She dove into the game head first to get money, so that when she confronted Shawna, she would be powerful enough to avenge her son's death.

Anari called herself Tony and began to hustle in Newark, New Jersey. While on the hunt for Shawna, her operation began to grow, causing her to step on the toes of Von, who already had New Jersey's drug market on lock. He began to lose money, and put a hit out on Tony's head. Anari's true identity was concealed so well that he didn't know that he had put a hit out on his own woman.

He hired a thorough assassin named Boss Sparks, and it took him a while, but he found Anari and placed a bomb underneath her car. Von found out Tony's true identity and was in disbelief. He was standing outside the car as Anari turned the key. He yelled for her to get out of the car and ran to snatch her out of it. The car exploded just as he pulled Anari from the car, but he was burned badly from the explosion. His right arm, chest, and neck had been burned, but both he and Anari were still alive.

Anari knew that the fire was so big that it would have consumed everything . . . bones and all, so to everyone else, it appeared that they had died in the blaze. Von's DNA was already at the scene from his skin being burnt so badly, so they fled the country together and left everything behind. Von had connections with different men across the country, and it was his idea to form Supreme Clientele, which Anari headed.

"Damn," Zya said in disbelief as she looked back and forth between Anari and Von. *They on some Bonnie and Clyde shit for real*, she thought.

"You are the only person who knows the true story," Anari said. "I hope I can trust you," she added.

"You can," Zya said. Anari had been through a lot, and she finally understood why Anari was so careful about not being seen in public.

"I think I've read a book about y'all. For real. It's this book called *Dirty Money* by this dude and this one girl."

"Ashley and JaQuavis. They are good friends of ours." Von said and nodded. "We paid them to pen the story for us. It's authentic. They wrote it exactly how we told them, to make everybody who read it think that we died in the end."

Zya nodded her head. *Damn, they got off, and now they can't be charged for shit because it happened more than seven years ago. On paper, Anari and Von don't even exist.*

Von got up and dropped four-hundred dollar bills on the table. "You ladies have a good time. I have some business I need to take care of." He leaned over and kissed Anari lightly on the lips and then said, "The next time you come to town, I'll have to show you how to do it up big for real."

"Sounds good," she replied.

"The next time you come to Miami, bring Snow," Von added.

"How do you know about Snow?" Zya asked in amazement.

"I know everybody my woman deals with," he said as he walked away.

Zya and Anari finished their dinner and then gambled for the rest of the night. They didn't leave the casino until one o'clock in the morning. They were drunk as hell as they made their way to Anari's beach house.

"Zya, I haven't trusted anybody in a long time, but you are cut just like me. That's how I know you are worth my time and energy," Anari said as they made their way into Anari's house. "For real. You are a thorough bitch! Stick with me and I'm gon' take you places!" she yelled loudly.

"Shh! You gon' wake up your neighbors," Zya said as she laughed at how drunk Anari was.

"Neighbors? A bitch like me don't have neighbors. I own this whole strip."

Zya looked up and down the street at the luxurious oceanfront houses that lined the block. They could easily cost a million a piece, maybe even more.

"Damn, you own all this?"

"Every single blade of grass," Anari said as she opened the door to her house and walked in. The inside of Anari's shit was plush as hell. Everything was computer operated. Even the sink faucets worked by voice command.

"Damn, you really are untouchable," Zya said.

"So are you. You just don't know it yet," Anari explained. "That's why our friendship should be valuable to you. You are good at this, but I can teach you how to be great at it."

"It doesn't get any greater than this," Zya said as she looked around Anari's home. She couldn't believe that she was actually chilling with Anari. It wasn't on no business type stuff either. They were vacationing like they were friends.

Anari sat down on her couch and put her feet up. "Zya, at the rate you are going, you are going to be bigger than me. There is only one way that could happen. Eventually, you are going to have to make a decision. I can't keep you underneath my wings forever. You are either going to have to kill me to take my spot, or I am going to have to kill you to keep it. That's the game, that's how it goes. I know that your loyalty to me will be tested. One day, you will have to choose between loyalty and supremacy."

"If you are so sure of that, why am I here?" Zya asked.

"Because right now I trust you. I'll handle everything else when we cross that bridge."

Zya didn't understand Anari's logic, but she respected it. For the rest of the weekend, they developed a genuine friendship and understanding of each other. Zya knew that she was in good company, and couldn't believe that she had moved to the top so quickly. She knew that if she let Anari school her on the game, she would eventually become one of the best players in it. Anari's friendship was valuable and Zya knew it.

On the last night in Miami, Zya and Anari stayed up until four o'clock in the morning, eating ice cream, sipping wine, and cracking up off of Jamie Foxx comedy shows.

"I know I must like yo' ass. I haven't done this since my best friend died years ago," Anari said. Zya knew that she had earned the trust and respect of the biggest member at the roundtable. Not only did Anari respect Zya, but she considered her a friend.

Anari told Zya goodnight and faded into the master bedroom. Zya retired to the guest room to go to sleep. She was exhausted, and the liquor was wearing off, causing her a slight headache.

Zya looked out of the bedroom's patio and admired the Miami view. The whole city was before her, and it was beautiful. *The city lights and the ocean are so beautiful. This is the life right here. One day I will be standing on my own patio with a clear view of nothing but water. That day may come sooner than later.*

"The world is mine," she said in a low voice. Zya stripped out of all her clothes as she walked over to the king-sized canopy bed and flopped down, preparing to go to sleep.

Just before she completely nodded off, Zya she saw something sweep past her patio window. She instantly jumped up and became suspicious. *What the hell was that?* Zya thought as she began to search for her gun. Zya, without any clothes on, crept slowly to the patio window with her gun drawn. Her heart pounded in anticipation as she tried to find out what or who brushed past her window. Zya was ready to light up whoever was creeping on her. She counted softly, preparing to shoot whoever she saw outside the patio. She leaned her back against the wall beside the window and held her gun up.

"One . . . two . . . three!" she whispered as she swiftly stood into clear view and looked onto the huge patio. What she saw was not an intruder. Anari had on a silk robe that was completely open, exposing her naked body. She was sprawled out on the table on the patio with her legs completely separated. Von's face was buried into her vagina, pleasing her.

Zya slowly lowered her gun and let out a sigh of relief. She put her hand on her chest and felt her heart racing. Zya couldn't help but to look back at the two on the patio. They had no idea that they had an audience. Zya peeked out of the window, standing out of visible sight, and continued to watch.

Von flipped Anari over, and she was on all fours on

top of the table. Von stood behind Anari, preparing to enter her. Zya couldn't take her eyes off of the escapade. She felt wrong for looking, but it was turning her on. Von's naked, bronze body was lean and muscular, and his ass muscles flexed as his penis searched for Anari's kitty cat. She watched as Von's long, thick penis went in and out of Anari. He reached over Anari and began to play with her clitoris as he made love to her. It was like nothing Zya had seen before. He was taking his time, trying to please his woman. Von moved his hips in perfect unison with his fingers on Anari's clitoris. Every time he entered Anari, he kissed the back of her neck.

"Damn . . . ooh," Zya whispered as she watched closely. Zya's hands, without her consent, managed to make their way down to her clitoris, and she imagined that it was her getting broke off on the patio. She rubbed her clitoris and then she entered two fingers inside her warm and wet vagina. Every time Von went into Anari, Zya's fingers entered herself. Von didn't know it, but he made love to two ladies that night.

"Oh," Zya whispered as her legs began to quiver, almost causing her to fall. Not even sixty seconds later, Zya exploded, and her juices dripped onto her toes. She felt bad for watching them have sex, but it was like a guilty pleasure. She couldn't wait to return home to Snow so she could get hers. Zya staggered over the bed, completely satisfied, and sleep like a newborn baby.

Chapter 13

Addicted

Lonnie Wade woke up to a strange woman lying naked in his bed. He sat up in confusion and looked down at himself in disgust as he discovered the vomit that was covering his clothes. *Fuck!* he thought as he tried to remember the events that had taken place the night before. From the looks of things, he knew that he had brought a girl home with him last night. What he couldn't remember was if he had worn a condom.

Damn, I hope I strapped up. I ain't tryna fuck around and catch something from one of these New York hoes, he thought.

He examined the filth that had accumulated in his downtown apartment. There were empty Hennessy bottles everywhere, and the place reeked of liquor and weed. Lonnie had always been a social drinker, but after the murder of his cousin Tiffany, he became indulgent and began to drink heavily. He had seen a lot of murders and had worked a lot of cases as a police officer, but the day that he was called to the scene of his cousin's murder was the same day that his work began to fuck with him. Tiffany's death had hurt him because they had been so close. He began to drink and smoke heavily after her murder, and his habits affected his work.

Detective Lonnie Wade had been hired into the department because of his ability to get the job done. He graduated at the top of the police academy and was good at what he did. His thuggish appearance and nature didn't change once he put on his badge. He had been born and raised in Brooklyn's Pink projects, and his environment was one of the things that put him above the rest of the rookie cops on the force. He quickly excelled in the department. He stood out because of his ability to go undercover. He was a hood nigga who happened to be a cop, so it was nothing for him to change faces and play a drug dealer to make a case. His cornrows and thuggish demeanor were what the department hated the most about him, but those were the same qualities that enabled him to do a good job and close cases.

After Wade was called to the scene of his cousin's murder, he grew an "I don't give a fuck" attitude and disregarded the procedures of the precinct. He had been reprimanded more than once for using unnecessary force when subduing a suspect, and had also been warned about his drug and alcohol use. Lonnie Wade became a tyrant on the streets. He did what he wanted, to whomever he wanted, when he wanted, because he had a badge that said he could. He was an asshole, and was on thin ice with the police commissioner. NYPD had been forced to settle a couple of civil suits because of Wade's renegade tactics. He had become a loose cannon, and even though he had once been a good cop, his recent actions had forced the department to take action.

I was close. I was so fucking close to getting a good case on Anari. Zya Miller was my way in. With her telling me what was going on during the Supreme Clientele meetings, I would have been able to bring them down.

Wade took a shot of his cognac straight from the bottle then threw it across the room out of frustration. *I'm so close to making the case of my life.* He stood up and felt the room spin beneath him. He was fucked up, and had been for almost three months. Lieutenant Jones had suspended him on paid sick leave after finding Wade passed out in a squad car with an ounce of weed and a couple pints of Henny.

"Don't walk your sorry ass back through these doors until you're clean," the Lieutenant had screamed at him. "Your sorry black ass is a waste of God-given talent. You have all the potential in the world, but you are too busy screwing your life away to use it!"

Lonnie Wade knew that his boss was right, but instead of getting his shit together, he took two steps backward by giving in to his habits. He didn't care about the suspension because he figured, *Shit, I ain't on the clock no more. I can do what the fuck I want to and get paid for it.* Wade was deteriorating fast, and it wasn't until now that he began to realize that he was throwing his life away.

"Wake your ass up," Wade said as he smacked the girl lightly on the ass then laid back down with his body half hanging off the bed. The girl stirred and tossed and turned as she pulled the covers up above her head.

"Get the fuck up and get your clothes on," Wade said with his eyes closed. The girl sat up and rolled over on top of Wade. Wade gagged as she pushed the air out of his lungs. He leaned over the side of the bed and hurled right onto his hardwood floor.

"Ughhhh," he yelled loudly as the alcohol began to come up in large amounts.

Oh, shit. I promise I won't ever drink again, just please . . .

"Ughhhh," he heaved as he tried to control the convulsions of his stomach. "Oh, shit!" he yelled loudly as he rolled onto his back and stared up at the ceiling. The girl was staring at him with a look of disgust plastered on her face.

"Bitch, what you looking at? Put on your clothes and bounce," Wade yelled. The girl smacked her lips and hopped out of bed.

"Nigga, fuck you. You ain't nothing but a drunk. As a matter of fact, you can lose my number," she spit out as she quickly put on her clothes.

Wade was in too much pain to talk. He stuck up his middle finger, and the girl picked up an empty liquor bottle and threw it at him before she stormed out screaming, "Fuck you!"

Lonnie closed his eyes and shook his head from side to side. Things had been bad before, but they had never gone this far. Wade knew that he had a problem. He had a serious alcohol and weed addiction. He was living a reckless and fucked up existence. He had always known that, but the fact that he maintained his job at the precinct soothed his soul. He loved being a cop, and even when everything else in his life was fucked up, he knew that his job would always be there. Now that his job was on the line, he felt lost and foolish. His behavior was putting him in jeopardy of losing the one thing that mattered most to him, and that was his badge. His badge kept him sane and let him know that he was needed in this world. He had always prided himself on being a good detective, but his frequent and abundant use of substances was affecting his career in a negative way. He wanted more than anything to find his cousin's killer, and he knew that if he nabbed Anari, her conviction would be the case that took his career to new heights.

"I got to get myself together," Lonnie stated to an empty room. He could smell the liquor seeping out of his pores, and his tongue was dry from all the weed he had been smoking.

His apartment was a mess. There were soiled clothes from his many hangovers lying all over the place, and trash was scattered all over the floor. "I'm gon' get my shit together," he said as he tried to sit up. He got up and maneuvered his way around the cluttered floor and into the kitchen. His stomach felt like it was riding its own personal rollercoaster, and his head was banging from the dim light shining through the blinds of his apartment.

Damn, I'm fucked up. Lonnie finally made it to the refrigerator and opened it up, hoping that he had something to settle his stomach. The refrigerator was dirty and bare. The only items inside were a bottle of ketchup, some spoiled milk, and a box of baking soda.

Wade slammed the door closed and took off toward the bathroom as he felt his stomach threatening to erupt again. He just made it to the toilet when he threw up, and felt the most excruciating pain of his life. He noticed that blood began to appear in the toilet boil. *What the fuck?* he thought as he continued to throw up. His vomit changed from clear to red as more and more blood continued to come up. *What the fuck is wrong with me?* he thought as he got up and staggered into his bedroom. He had heard that drinking destroyed your liver, but Wade hadn't thought that he was at risk. He didn't actually realize how much liquor he ingested. He never thought he was a drunk, only that he needed to slow down.

Fuck. I need to slow up on this shit. Something ain't right. Wade lay down in his bed and closed his eyes, trying to stop the headache that was causing excruciating pain behind his temples. *I need to see a doctor,* was the last thought that crossed his mind before he passed out from the pain of his intoxication.

Jules walked away from the prison with a smug expression plastered on his face. He mugged each guard as he walked by. His lawyers had finally come through, and his appeal had been granted. The one thing on his mind was getting to Zya. He had been thinking about getting to her ever since he discovered she had played him. *Grimy-ass bitch. She gon' get hers,* he thought as he walked toward the gates, where Amir was waiting to pick him up.

"What's good, baby? You finally out!" Amir yelled as he slapped hands with Jules and embraced him in a quick hug.

"Hell yeah. That mu'fuckin' cop thought he could keep a nigga down just because I had to do a bid. He got another thing coming, cuz I'm back, baby. I'm about to be back on top," Jules said.

"You trying to get back in?" Amir asked.

"Hell yeah. Ain't shit changed. I'ma do me until the day I die. I trap. That's what I do best. Selling drugs paid my bills," Jules bragged as he thought about getting back in the streets.

"A'ight, man," Amir said skeptically.

Jules frowned and replied, "What you mean *a'ight, man*? What's that all about?"

"Shit has changed, man. You been gone for a hot little minute. Harlem is different. The game ain't the same as it used to be."

Jules shook his head and confidently replied, "Nah, nigga. Shit ain't changed that much. Niggas still like to eat, right? I'm about to make all these Harlem cats rich. All I got to do is make the call to Snow, and I'm back in the game."

Amir shook his head, knowing that Jules had been out of the loop while he was locked up. He didn't want to be the one to tell him the news, but Jules saw the look on his face.

"What?" Jules asked.

"Man, Jules, yo' man Snow got Harlem locked."

Jules shook his head. "Nah. I got love in Harlem, baby. When niggas find out I'm out, they gon' be singing a different tune. Besides, how the fuck y'all mu'fuckas gon' let a nigga from Jersey come through and run Harlem? That shit don't happen. Only Harlem cats know how to get down in Harlem."

"Shit, Snow got a Harlem cat on his team."

"Who?"

"Zya," Amir said.

Jules waved his hand in dismissal. "That bitch is dead. You hear me? As soon as I see her ass, his little connect with Zya is finished. That's on my life."

"Nah, man. It ain't gon' be as easy as you think. Zya ain't the same broad you used to fuck with. She is running shit for real. She's getting money out of all the boroughs in New York and in Jersey. Shit, that bitch started fucking with Snow and took over. The pussy must be right, too, because he be deading niggas. Anybody who even looks at Zya wrong gets they shit rocked."

Jules clenched his jaw as he listened to Amir talk. He hadn't known that Zya had started fucking with Snow. His jealousy and rage seethed through him as he thought about Zya and Snow . . . together. *She was probably fucking with him all along. I had her ass making runs to pick up from that nigga, and she was fucking stepping out in the process. I don't give a fuck how big she is. I'ma get to her sooner or later.* Jules was hot at the fact that Zya had moved up in the game. He was even hotter that she was playing wifey to Torey Snow.

"Fuck Snow. That mu'fucka doing shit that I've already done. He ain't doing nothing new. I taught Zya everything she knows. I'm gon' go see Black Ty to see if he can give me some work on consignment."

Amir nodded his head, but knew that Jules was setting himself up for failure. Zya controlled all of the drugs in New York and New Jersey. There was no room for anybody but her and Snow. Even if Jules did cop something from Black Ty, he would still be underneath Zya because she supplied Ty.

As soon as they made their way into Harlem, Jules instructed Amir to drop him off at Black Ty's. He was on a hunt for Zya's head, and he knew that he would have to get on his feet before pursuing her. She was now the queen pen of New York, and he realized that she was going to be harder to touch than he had expected. He needed to get back in the game so that he could get back on his feet. He was going to get to Zya one way or another, no matter how long it took.

"A'ight, Jules. Get at me when you get settled," Amir yelled as he put two fingers out of his car window and drove off.

Jules went to Ty's dope house. He knew that he would be able to find him there because Black Ty stayed in the trap house all day and all night, trying to make his pay.

He walked around to the back door, not wanting to make Ty's block hot. He knew that being on parole, he had to be careful where he was seen. He wasn't trying to get sent back Upstate.

Jules knocked on the door in a rhythmic pattern.

Tap-tap . . . Tap-tap . . . Tap.

Black Ty opened the door immediately and went crazy when he saw Jules. "Oh, shit! My nigga out!" he yelled as he slapped hands with Jules. "You ready to get back on?" Ty asked immediately, already knowing why Jules was standing on his doorstep.

"You already know," Jules replied. He entered the dope house and looked around at the crack heads scattered about.

"I see you still letting these mu'fuckas get high in your shit," Jules commented.

"Hell yeah. When they highs fall off, they already at the candy shop," Ty replied in a joking way. A skinny, fiend-out-looking girl with matted hair and dirty clothes walked up to Black Ty, begging.

"Ty, let me get a pack. I'll do anything, Ty. I'll make you feel good," the girl said as she looked at him with soul-less eyes.

Ty shook his head and replied, "Damn, don't you see me over here talking to my mans?"

"Come on, Ty. You know I'm good for it. I'll do whatever you want . . . even in the butt," she pleaded as she clung to his shirt.

Ty smacked the girl's hand off of his white T-shirt and pushed her away forcefully. She scurried away and huddled in the corner as she scratched her arms frantically. She was scratching so hard that you could hear the skin tearing, and she began to bleed.

"Man, that shit is fucked up. I actually used to want to fuck with that bitch before she got all fiend-out," Ty said as he turned toward Jules to continue their conversation.

Jules looked closer at the girl in the corner, and a smile slowly crept across his face. He couldn't believe what he saw. It was Vita, shooting dope in the corner. *Damn, she out here bad. I know she knows where to find Zya,* he thought as he approached her. Vita looked up at Jules and began to fix her hair out of embarrassment. She kept her eyes on the floor as she rocked back in forth in the corner.

"Hey, Jules. You holding something?" Vita asked with a half-smile. Her teeth were yellow, as if she hadn't brushed them in weeks, and she looked bad.

Jules didn't give a damn about how she looked. He saw an opportunity and took advantage of it. He knew that he would have to give up something to get the information he wanted, so he ran over to Ty and whispered in his ear. Ty smiled and slapped hands with Jules. He grabbed two packs of heroin off the table and walked back over to Vita.

"I can help you out if you help me out," Jules said.

"I'll do anything, Jules . . . anything," Vita said as she opened her legs and exposed her vagina.

Jules had been locked up for three and a half years without any pussy, and even Vita's cracked-out offer was appealing to him. He grabbed Vita off the floor and went into one of Ty's rooms. Vita stood in the middle of the room, still scratching at her bleeding skin as she waited for Jules to approach her. The only thing she was thinking about was getting her high. Jules turned her around and bent her over the edge of a dresser and rammed himself forcefully inside her anus.

"Aghh!" Vita yelled out from the pain of Jules ramming in and out of her asshole. Vita tried to get loose from his hold, but Jules kept grabbing her by the hips, forcing her to take his ten inches. Tears slid down Vita's face as Jules pushed her head onto the top of the dirty dresser.

"Jules, stop!" Vita screamed, but Jules continued to please himself, disregarding her screams. He turned her around and pinned her against the dresser. The drawers dug into her back as he humped in and out of her.

Vita closed her eyes and pictured her mother, dead from her drug habit. She realized that she was doing the same thing to herself, and tears flooded down her face as her best friend's ex-boyfriend fucked her harshly.

Jules finished his business by pulling out of her and emptying his semen all over her naked stomach. Vita fell to the floor and cried as Jules pulled up his pants and fastened his belt buckle.

"Where's Zya?" Jules asked without any remorse for what he had just done.

"I don't know," Vita lied as she shook her head from side to side.

Jules began to head toward the door, and Vita crawled after him, begging for her form of payment. "Jules, what about the dope?"

"Tell me where Zya is and you will get your shit," Jules said as he waved the heroin in Vita's face.

Vita knew that she shouldn't, but she told Jules where Zya's apartment was located. Jules threw the dope on the floor, and Vita quickly scurried out of the room to take a dose of her deadly medicine.

"Junkie-ass bitch," Jules said in disgust as he walked out to discuss business with Black Ty.

After seeing a doctor, Wade discovered that all the liquor he had been drinking over the years had caught up to him. His liver was polluted from years of alcohol abuse, and the doctor had informed him that if he didn't give up alcohol, he would drink himself into an early grave. Wade decided to get himself together, and he enrolled in Alcoholics Anonymous classes. He was determined to get clean so that he could get back to his case. He wanted to catch Anari, and knew that he would not be able to do it if he was not in his right mind. Anari was too smart to be brought down by a washed-up alcoholic cop. He knew that he had no chance of catching her unless he flew straight. Wade even cut off his braids and bought new clothes that were appropriate for work. He still wasn't the suit-and-tie type of cat, but he did buy some slacks and shirts to wear on the job.

Wade went back to the precinct to talk to the Lieutenant about coming back to work. He took a deep breath and knocked on the boss's door.

"Come in."

Wade stepped into the office and said, "I'm ready to come back to work, sir."

The Lieutenant squinted his face and reached for his eyeglasses. "Wade? You look like a completely different person!"

Lonnie chuckled and replied, "That was kind of the point, sir."

"How long have you been clean?" he asked as he folded his arms and stared intently up at Wade.

"Only a couple days, sir. But I'm enrolled in an Alcoholics Anonymous program, and I'm flying straight from now on. You have my word that I am only about the work from here on out," Wade proclaimed with a serious expression on his face.

Lieutenant Jones sighed and threw his pen on his desk. He sat back in his chair and propped his finger to his chin as he thought about bringing Wade back.

Lonnie read the expression on his boss's face. "I know you've heard this story before, but it's different this time. I'm done with everything."

"Even if I bring you back, you're going to have to work in the office for a while."

Lonnie's face contorted in anger. "That's bullshit. I have to get back on the Supreme Clientele case!"

"No, you have to get clean! The Commissioner is already riding my ass because of you. I can't take any more chances on you, Wade."

Lonnie leaned over the wooden desk and stared intently at his boss. "You won't be taking a chance, Lieutenant. You know me. I can clear this case. I can bring down Anari Simpson. Think about how much publicity you will get when our department brings her in. That conviction will put you in the Commissioner's seat."

Lonnie knew exactly what buttons to push to get Lieutenant Jones on his side. Everything in the justice system was political, and if Wade was able to get a conviction on Anari, then everybody associated with the case would excel in their careers.

"I don't know . . ."

"Let me back in, sir," Lonnie stated.

"No drugs?"

"None," Lonnie agreed.

"No alcohol, Wade!"

"Never, sir," Lonnie replied.

"Don't bullshit me, Wade. I'm sticking my neck out for you. Don't make me regret it."

Lonnie cracked a smile and knew that he was in. All he had to do was pick up where he had left off. "I won't, sir. Thank you." Lonnie hurried out of the office before his boss changed his mind.

I just got one call to make.

Zya felt the sun warm her skin as she relaxed in the beach chair on the secluded Miami beach.

"Would you ladies like a drink?" a young white boy asked.

"Yeah, bring me a green apple martini," Zya replied. She looked over at Anari, who was lying on her back with huge sunglasses over her eyes.

"Hey, Anari, you want a drink?" Zya asked. Anari didn't reply, and Zya figured that she had fallen asleep.

"That'll be it," Zya said as she waved the waiter away.

It was their last day in Miami, and they had decided to spend it relaxing on the beach. *I don't think I'm ready to go back to Harlem. It's like paradise down here,* Zya thought as she watched the waves roll onto the hot sand.

Zya's cell phone rang loudly, startling her and interrupting her peaceful moment. She picked it up, thinking that it would be Snow, but when she saw a number she didn't recognize, she thought, *Who is this?*

"Hello," she answered, revealing her irritation.

"I know you didn't think I forgot about you," the voice said on the other end of the phone.

"Who is this?" she asked with an attitude.

"This is Detective Wade. Meet me Friday night at nine o'clock at the abandoned warehouse down by the Hudson River."

Zya's eyes darted to Anari's sleeping body, and she thought about what they had discussed the previous night. *I know that your loyalty to me will be tested. One day, you will have to choose between loyalty and supremacy.* Anari's words echoed in her head.

"I can't do it," Zya said firmly.

"You will do it, or I'll put your pretty ass in prison and let some dyke make you her bitch."

Zya was silent as she weighed her options in her head, frantically trying to think of a way out. *I can't snitch on Anari. She's too powerful. She can't be touched. This nigga don't even know who he's messing with. He's trying to get me to do his dirty work, and I'm gon' be the one fucked up if I get caught.*

Fuck that. I'm not a snitch. I haven't heard from him in months, now he wanna call me up out of the blue and threaten me.

"I can't do it," Zya repeated.

Lonnie Wade smirked in the phone and said, "Don't get cute. You must have forgotten about the pictures that I have, placing you at the same hotel as King's murder. Oh yeah, and we still haven't found the match to those fingerprints."

She was silent, and he knew his threats were working. Before she could say another word, he coldly stated, "This is not a negotiation. Be there."

Zya snapped her cell phone closed and looked over at Anari. Her heartbeat sped up as she thought about what Lonnie Wade was asking her to do. *I don't have a choice,* Zya thought. She couldn't see another way out, and realized that her hand was being forced. She didn't want to turn on Anari, but she wasn't going to jail.

It's either her or me.

Chapter 14

Snow Storm

"I'll call you later, Zya," Anari said as she stepped off the plane and got into the limo waiting at the bottom of the steps.

Zya looked out of the window and saw Snow waiting for her. She smiled at the sight of him, leaning against his Escalade with his arms folded across his chest. She grabbed her bags and rushed off the plane, running across the landing toward Snow. She jumped in his arms when she reached him, and kissed him passionately as he picked her up off the ground.

"I missed you," she said as she looked up at him and wrapped her hands around his neck, rubbing the back of his head.

"I missed you too," he replied as his gray eyes stared down at her. He grabbed her bag off the ground, threw it in the back of his truck, then opened the passenger door for Zya.

"How was your trip?" he asked her.

"It was good. Anari is cool. We got to know each other a lot better. It's more than business between us now. She even went as far as to call me her friend."

Snow nodded his head then turned up his sub-woofers. Rick Ross was blaring from his speakers, and they bobbed their heads in unison as they drove toward Harlem.

By the time they arrived at Zya's apartment, she was exhausted and couldn't wait to get inside and go to sleep. Snow looked up at her window and noticed that a light was shining from Zya's apartment.

"Did you leave your lights on?" he asked her as his brow suddenly dipped low, revealing his suspicion.

"No, I don't think so." Zya looked up at her apartment window and shook her head. "No, I never leave my bedroom light on." She grabbed her bag out of the back seat and ran into her building and up the stairs. She ascended them two at a time, hoping that no one had been inside her place.

Please let my money still be there, she thought. If somebody had broken in, they had come across the biggest payday of their lives.

When Zya reached her apartment, she noticed that her door was slightly ajar, and Snow pushed her to the side as he pulled out his .357. He put a finger to his lips, signaling for her to be quiet, and he walked slowly into the apartment, letting his gun lead the way. Zya stood back with a worried look on her face. She followed Snow through her apartment, gripping the back of his T-shirt in hesitation. After searching the entire house, he relaxed some and put his arm around Zya and kissed her on the top of the head.

"They tore this mu'fucka up," Snow said as he examined the trashed apartment. The many boxes of money were safe and sound, just as she had left them. Her apartment, however, was messed up. It looked like a tornado been through it a couple times, and all of her clothes had been thrown from her closet and ripped to shreds. The mattress on her bed was even cut up, the cotton spilling onto the floor.

"Why would someone do this?" she asked as she looked around in confusion. She was worried because if her money had been gone, then she could have chalked it up as a robbery, but the intruder had taken nothing. The only thing done was destruction to her property, and that told her that it was personal, which meant that their business was not settled.

Obviously they came here looking for me . . . whoever it was, she thought as she stood in the middle of the living room with her hands on her hips. She looked up at Snow.

"What if they come back?" she asked.

"You won't be here, so it doesn't matter. All this shit is replaceable, but the fact that they didn't even attempt to take the money says that somebody has beef with you."

Zya couldn't imagine who she had crossed. She didn't think that she had made any enemies on her way to the top, but now she couldn't be so sure.

"Fuck this. You need to move out of this bullshit-ass apartment anyway. You are getting money now, so you can't be in the hood no more. That makes you too easy to reach. Niggas shouldn't be able to contact you, and they definitely should not know where you rest your head. We're moving you to Jersey tonight," Snow said.

"You're right. I should have listened to you," Zya

said. "I was so busy trying to make it on my own and keep my own place that I was being stupid."

Snow put his hands on Zya's face and said, "I love you, and you gon' be mines forever. Let me take care of you."

Zya smiled and replied, "Okay, Torey Snow. Take care of me then."

Snow laughed then grabbed a box of money and headed for the front door. Before he exited, he said, "From the looks of all this money you getting, it looks like you gon' be taking care of me."

Zya cocked her head to the side and replied, "Ha, ha . . . very funny. Nigga, I know what you working with. You getting more money than me." She grabbed a box and carried it down the steps, following Snow to his car. Zya had so many boxes filled with cash in her apartment that they had to rent a U-Haul truck to transport them from her apartment in New York to Snow's house in Jersey.

Zya had her dope stashed at her house, but left it. She would have one of Snow's goons transport it the next day. She was so geeked to be moving in with Snow. She knew that by living together, they were taking their relationship to the next level, and she was ready to learn everything there was to know about Snow.

When they pulled up to Snow's mansion, Zya got out of the car and stared up at the enormous house that sat before her.

"What's wrong?" Snow asked.

"I don't know . . . It's . . . It . . ." She couldn't finish her sentence, so Snow finished it for her.

"It's home, Zya," he said as he grabbed her hand and led her inside.

Although Zya had been inside Snow's house before, it felt different now that it was hers as well. That night, she kept Snow up all night, just talking about them. She needed to know that he loved her and that he was there with her. She didn't want another fake nigga on her team, just talking good, but not meaning the things he said. Snow assured her that he was a real nigga, and that as long as she did her part as a woman, he would hold her down.

"If I didn't want you here, you wouldn't be here," he assured her.

Zya was close to Snow, and she believed every word that he said. He had her head, heart, and soul. She knew that he would never do her shady because he could see how much she loved him. He was her best friend, and she knew that he would give her anything and everything she desired. He wanted Zya to be happy, and as long as she had him, she would be.

"Baby girl, your man is tired. Can a nigga go to sleep?" he said with a smile. Zya looked at the clock. It was 4 A.M., and they hadn't stopped talking since they had finished moving.

"Sorry," she said with a laugh. "I'm just happy to have you in my life."

He pulled her close and kissed her lips before falling into a fast and comfortable sleep.

Snow wasn't a mushy type of nigga. He loved Zya, but he didn't feel it was necessary to talk about it. He would show her instead of telling her, because he felt that actions spoke louder than words. She had heard Jules when he said it, but she could feel Snow when he showed her exactly how much he cared.

* * *

The next night, Zya's phone rang while she was headed out the door, preparing to attend a Supreme Clientele meeting. She looked at her phone and saw that it was Black Ty and answered it.

"Hello?"

"What up, Zya. I need to get right again," Black Ty stated, calling for a re-up.

"Damn, already?"

"Yeah, I moved through the whole order already. I need four, pronto."

"I see you stepping your game up, but I can't get that to you tonight. I got plans."

"Come on, Zya. If I don't get that tonight, I'll be missing so much money. I need you on this one," Black Ty pleaded.

Zya took the phone from her ear and looked at Snow as he put on his jacket, preparing to make a run.

"Yo, do you think you can drop off four bricks to Black Ty tonight?" she asked.

Snow picked up his car keys and answered, "Yeah, I guess. I was on my way to Harlem to pick up some dough anyway. I'll do it."

Zya put the cell phone back to her ear and quickly said, "Be at your spot at three. The bricks will be there. Since it's so late, tack on ten percent, baby. You know I don't make runs this late."

"No problem, Zya. Thanks. But my spot is getting kind of hot. Meet me at the old warehouse by the Hudson River. You know the old steel factory."

"A'ight," Zya agreed before she flipped down her phone. Zya held up her keys, twisted **off** her apartment key, and tossed it to Snow.

"I have four left in the Frosted Flakes boxes in the

top cabinet," she said before she left the house and headed to the meeting.

Vita's high was coming down as she sat on the couch at the dope house, nodding off. She distantly heard a conversation going on in the next room. She recognized Black Ty's voice, talking to someone.

"I just got off the phone with Zya. It's all set up. She is going to meet me at the old steel factory by the river at three."

Vita heard another man's voice responding, "Good, good. I've been waiting to see Zya for a long time. After tonight, that queen pen shit is over. She's dead. I can't wait to see her face when I pop her ass. This has been a long time coming," the man said.

Vita recognized the other man's voice. It was Jules. *Damn, he is going to try to kill Zya. I should have never turned on her. She has never showed me anything but love. I have to call her before she walks into a trap.*

Vita pulled back the couch pillows, searching for loose change so she could run to the payphone. She searched frantically and managed to scrape up just enough. Vita rushed out of the house and ran to the corner store to try to contact Zya before it was too late.

Snow's all-white BMW crept toward the back of the warehouse. In the back of his truck he had four bricks with Black Ty's name on them.

Where is this nigga at? Snow thought as he circled the empty parking lot for the third time. Just as he was about to pull off, he saw the garage door open. Bright lights shined on him, temporarily blocking his vision. Snow threw his hands up, blocking the light from his eyes. Black Ty emerged from the side of the car, exposing himself. Ty waved his hands, signaling for Snow to pull in. Snow pulled into the garage, and Black Ty shut the garage door behind him.

The tinted windows on Snow's car concealed his identity until he opened the door and hopped out. When Ty saw Snow's face, he was caught completely off guard.

Where is Zya? She was supposed to make the drop, Ty thought in shock. Snow noticed the change in Ty's expression.

"Fuck is yo' problem? You got the dough, man?"

Black Ty began to stutter as he replied, "Yeah, yeah. Where is Zya?"

"She had to handle something. What the fuck you concerned for? You wanted the brick, right?" Snow asked as he walked to the trunk and grabbed the bag containing the coke. Snow walked back to Black Ty and asked, "What, you deaf, nigga? You wanted the bricks, right?"

Black Ty grew apprehensive and took a step back. "Yeah, I still want them," he said.

Snow looked at Ty like he was crazy and then became slightly agitated. "Well, go get the fucking money."

"It's in the trunk," Ty replied.

"Well, go get it, nigga. Fuck is wrong with you?" Snow said as he shook his head from side to side, annoyed with Ty's dumbfounded behavior. He watched as Ty walked to the back of his trunk and attempted to open it. Ty seemed to be having trouble popping the trunk, and Snow looked at his phone to check the time. He noticed his battery was dead and yelled, "Yo, what's taking so long?"

Black Ty looked up and yelled, "It's stuck! Sometimes you have to push the button while pulling up the trunk. Could you reach in the glove compartment and hit that button for me?"

Snow dropped the duffle bag and walked over to the tinted SUV.

"Nigga, you supposed to be getting money. You need to get yo' trunk right," Snow said as he opened the door and stuck half of his body in the vehicle. He spotted the glove box and opened it.

Zya got me dealing with this ol' bum-ass nigga. I can't believe—Before Snow could even complete his thought, he felt the barrel of an AK-47 pressing against the back of his head.

"Move and I'll pop off," Jules said calmly as he rested his index finger against the trigger.

Snow knew the drill. He put up his hands, and Jules instructed him to slide out of the truck.

"Fuck!" Snow yelled as he realized that he had walked into a set-up. Black Ty walked around from the back of the car and couldn't look Snow in the face. Snow just stared at him, smiling. "You know you dead, right?" he stated, addressing Black Ty.

Jules hit Snow in the back of the head, trying to gain his undivided attention. "You need to pay attention to the nigga with the gun!" Jules yelled as he reached over Snow's body and grabbed Snow's gun from his waist. "You won't be needing this," Jules said as he tossed Snow's gun to Black Ty. Snow finally realized who was holding him at gunpoint, and it all started to make sense.

"Welcome home," Snow said sarcastically as he held the back of his head in pain.

"Where the fuck is Zya?" Jules asked as he and Snow faced each other.

"She's at home, waiting for me to come lay the pipe down." Snow smiled at his own witty remark, and Jules struck him again, but this time in the mouth and with more power. Snow fell to one knee and wiped the blood from his mouth.

"We used to get money together. As soon as I got knocked, you pulled that snake shit and started fucking my girl."

"Zya ain't yo' woman, first of all. She's mine. Secondly, she is a grown woman and can make her own decisions. Why you being a bitch and crying because you couldn't keep yo' woman?"

Jules kicked Snow, making him fall flat on his back. "Well, you can have that bitch. Get up!"

Snow staggered back to his feet, and Jules grabbed him by the collar and threw him on the hood of Black Ty's truck, face down. Jules put the gun to the back of Snow's head and said, "Don't worry about that bitch Zya. I'm going to send her to hell right behind you." Jules turned his head so the blood wouldn't splatter in his face as he pointed the pistol toward Snow's head.

Zya sat at the roundtable waiting for the meeting to begin. She felt her phone vibrate on her hip for the tenth time in a row. *Damn, who the hell is blowing me up like this?* she thought as she looked down and saw an unfamiliar number. The same number kept popping up, and she wondered what could be so urgent.

"Please excuse me," Zya said as she stood from the roundtable in middle of the meeting. She stepped out the door to answer her phone. It had been vibrating since the meeting began.

Who is this? My phone has been ringing since the meeting began. It better be good, she thought as she picked up her phone.

"Hello?"

"Oh my God, Zya! I'm so glad to hear your voice."

"Vita?" Zya asked in confusion.

"Zya, don't go to meet Black Ty. It's a set-up. Jules got out, and I overheard them talking about setting you up," Vita said, talking fast.

"What the hell are you talking about?" Zya asked.

"Jules and Black Ty are trying to kill you. Don't go to the warehouse," Vita screamed into the phone.

Zya instantly thought about Snow. She had sent him to make the drop-off to Black Ty.

"Look, Vita, if anything happens to Snow, I'm going to kill you," she said, threatening to kill the messenger of the bad news. Zya flipped down her phone and instantly flipped it back open to call Snow.

Come on, Snow, pick up, she thought frantically. Snow's phone went straight to voice mail, and she tried again, but got the same response.

Zya rushed out of the restaurant and jumped into her car, leaving her skid marks in the middle of the street as she peeled out. She was headed to the warehouse to get to Snow.

"Wade, she just pulled off. She seemed like she was in a hurry," Agent Matthews said, speaking into a walkie talkie. He was parked across the street from Stello's, working the late-night shift of a stake-out.

"Did you see Anari enter?" Wade asked.

"Nah, I just saw Zya come in and rush out."

"Stay on her ass. I'm on my way," Lonnie Wade instructed.

Agent Matthews trailed Zya, and she didn't even realize that she was being followed. He followed her as she got onto the freeway. He could barely keep up with her luxury sports car. He tried to stay close, but the way she maneuvered in and out of traffic at 100 miles per hour, it was impossible.

"Damn, she's got to be doing at least one-twenty," Matthews said as he looked at his dashboard. Zya made a sudden swerve and got off at an exit. She did it so swiftly that Matthews didn't have time to get off. He blew past her and watched as she sped onto the service drive.

"Damn," he yelled as he sped up to get off at the next exit.

"Whoa! Whoa!" Black Ty shouted. "Hold on, Jules. Don't do that shit on my car."

Jules grabbed Snow by the back of his neck and attempted to move him off of Ty's hood. Snow knew he had nothing to lose, so he went for it. He swung around and grabbed the barrel of the assault weapon. Jules tried to shoot Snow, but Snow jerked the gun in Black Ty's direction. Bullets left Jules's gun and entered Black Ty's body, blowing him back, straight off of his feet.

Snow and Jules wrestled over the gun, but a loud crash caused them both to drop the gun. *Boom!* The garage door came flying off its hinges as Zya bulldozed her car through the garage. Her gun was aimed out of the window as she let off four shots, aimed at Jules's head.

Jules ducked and scrambled for his gun, returning fire. He hit one of Zya's tires, causing her to swerve out of control.

After letting off rounds at Zya, Jules looked back to locate Snow. To his surprise, Snow was out of sight. Not until he heard gunshots did he see Snow shooting at him from behind a barrel. Snow had gone to get a hold of his gun while Jules was busy letting off on Zya. Snow and Jules exchanged shots, but no one was hit.

Jules saw the flashing police lights from the garage window and made his way to the back to escape. Jules ducked out the back without being seen by the police.

Snow shot at Jules until he no longer saw him. He then focused his attention on Zya's smoking car. He noticed that her airbag had exploded, and he rushed over to her. He looked in the car and realized that she was stuck in the seatbelt.

"Zya, we have to get out of here. The hook is outside," Snow said as he tried to wiggle Zya's buckle, but it was stuck. Zya tried to maneuver her way out of the belt, and it still didn't work. Snow told Zya to stay still. He put his gun to the belt lock and squeezed. The belt loosened, and Zya quickly jumped out. Snow could hear the doors of the police car slamming as they approached the scene.

"Zya, go through the back and I'll cause a distraction. Get the fuck out of here!"

"Fuck that. I'm not letting you go down by yourself," Zya said as she stood by her man.

"Zya, don't be stupid. I'll meet you at home. I love you," Snow said as he kissed Zya and pushed her toward the back entrance.

"I can't leave you. I'm gon' ride or die. Fuck that."

The police were nearly in, and Snow shouted, "Go now, Zya!"

Zya knew there was no debating, and headed toward the back. Snow ran over to Black Ty, who was barely breathing, and let off two more shots to his chest. He then picked up the bags containing the coke and jumped in his car.

Just then, the police busted in with guns drawn. Snow knew he was no match for the fifty police officers that surrounded his car with automatic rifles pointing directly at him. He saw too many *Cops* episodes to be stupid and try to pull off, so he stepped out of the car with both hands in the air, surrendering.

Wade was the first to get to him, slapping the cuffs on. He looked around and saw Zya watching from the back door. He turned his head, pretending not to see her, and began reading Snow his rights.

Zya snuck out the back, unnoticed, trying to think about how to get Snow out of this predicament.

Chapter 15

Through the Wire

Zya ran into the precinct with a duffle bag full of cash in her hand. Her heels clicked in a frantic rhythm as she approached the front desk. There was already a woman standing there, but Zya stepped right next to her and interrupted.

"I'm here to post bail for Torey Smith," she said, using his real name.

The officer sitting behind the desk looked at her and replied, "I'm sorry, Miss. You are going to have to wait for me to help this lady first. She was here before you." He turned his attention back to the white woman, causing Zya to become even more upset.

Zya didn't care if the woman had been there first or not. She had business to handle, and she needed Snow out of jail. *There is no way I'm leaving him in here.* Zya's eyes reflected her determination and anger. She slammed her hand on the counter over and over and said, "Excuse me."

"Miss, I already told you," the cop said in irritation.

Zya opened the duffle bag and began to place thousand-dollar stacks on the counter top. "I heard what the fuck you said. Now hear what I'm saying. I need to get Torey Smith out of here now!" she yelled, causing a scene.

The white woman standing next to her stepped to the side and said, "Go ahead, help her. I can wait."

The officer looked at Zya in amazement as she continued to place money in front of him. "What did you say his name was?"

"Torey Smith," she said as she stood before him with a worried expression on her face. The officer typed the name into the computer and waited as the system searched the database. He frowned at Zya and shook his head.

"Looks like you came down here for nothing, princess." He picked up a stack of money and tossed it back to her. "He was just arrested tonight. This money is no good until the judge sets a bail."

"What?" Zya asked. "I just set five hundred thousand dollars in cash down in front of your face. Ain't no bail in the world gon' be that high!" she yelled at him.

"Be that as it may, your little boyfriend is gonna have to sit his drug-dealing ass in jail until he can see a judge," the officer stated smugly as he chuckled and turned the computer screen toward Zya, so she could see he wasn't lying.

Zya was enraged. She knocked the computer screen right off the tall counter, and it shattered when it hit the floor. "I want to see Snow!" she yelled as the cop's face turned crimson red from his anger. She was causing a scene, and other police officers had come out to the lobby to see what was going on. "Where is he?" she yelled as the cop subdued her, preparing to place her in handcuffs.

Lonnie Wade walked into the room to see what the commotion was, and ran over to stop the scene when he saw who it was. He couldn't believe that she had walked right into his precinct. He smiled because he realized that he could put his plan into motion sooner than he had expected.

"Shepard, I'll handle this," he said as he unlocked the cuffs and patted the ruffled officer on the back.

Zya looked up at Wade and rolled her eyes. "You fucking pig," she stated as she spit directly in Shepard's face. He lunged for her, but Wade stopped him before he could reach her.

Wade grabbed a stack of money off the counter and threw it at the officer Zya had confronted. "Here's a little something for you. Put the rest of it up, and have it waiting for her when she leaves." The officer thumbed through the money, and a smile spread across his face when he saw that it was all hundred-dollar bills.

"It looks like our meeting just got bumped up," Wade whispered in her ear as he led her into his office and closed the door behind him. "Sit down," he instructed as he placed her forcefully in a seat.

Zya's eyes followed Wade as he walked around and took a seat at his desk. He looked different from the last time she had seen him. He actually looked like a cop. "Nice look," she commented in a joking manner as she turned her nose up in disgust.

"I thought it was time for a change," Wade said arrogantly as he stared at her.

"Now everybody can see that you're not one of us. You're a fucking cop," Zya spat out.

"One of us?" Wade asked, questioning Zya's last statement.

"Cut the bullshit, detective. Where's Snow?" Zya asked.

"He is sitting in a bull pen, waiting to be charged with first degree murder and possession with the intent to distribute. He won't be going anywhere anytime soon."

"What will it take to get him out of here?" she asked.

"Your full cooperation," Lonnie replied as he sat back and put his hands behind his head.

Zya shook her head and stood up as she paced Lonnie Wade's office. Her mind was in a frenzy. Snow had just been caught with two bricks and the gun he shot Black Ty with. She knew things weren't looking good for him.

She knew what she had to do to get him out, but she didn't know if she would be able to go through with it. She didn't even know if the deal with Lonnie was legit. *He could just use me to get Anari and then still charge me and Snow,* Zya thought.

She replayed the night's events over and over in her mind, wishing that she could have changed the outcome. *I should have known something wasn't right. Black Ty never copped more than once a month. He helped Jules set me up,* she thought as she walked the same back-and-forth pattern.

Wade watched her and knew that she was weighing her options in her head. He knew that he had her trapped, so she would have to cooperate. If not, he planned on putting the bracelets on her wrists before she even got out of the station.

Jules is dead, that's my word. How the fuck is he gon' try to get me killed? What he mad for? He's the one who fucked things up for himself. What did he expect for me to do, stay with him after he played me? Now he got Snow sitting up in this fucking jail over some jealous bullshit. What am I supposed to do without him? Snow is my other half. I can't choose Anari over him. I have to be loyal to him.

"There is no other way out," Lonnie Wade stated. "You have to choose. Are you going to save yourself or are you going to save Anari?" he asked as he placed a set of pictures in front of Zya.

Zya stared down at pictures of dead bodies that she didn't recognize. "What the fuck are you showing me these for? I didn't have shit to do with these murders. You can't pin these on me. I don't even know these people," she stated as she slid the pictures back across the desk.

"Calm your ass down. I know you are not involved in these murders. I just thought you should see what type of person Anari Simpson really is. You think she is your friend, but Anari has no friends. You are willing to risk your own freedom for a woman who would not do the same for you," he said as he spread the photos in front of Zya.

"This is what happens to all of Anari's friends. They end up six feet under ground while she remains on top."

He pointed to the first photo of a girl. "This is La'Tanya Morton, Anari's best friend and ex-partner. She is the person who helped Anari build her empire.

If it wasn't for the work that this woman put in, Anari would not be where she is today. When she was arrested for her involvement in Anari's operation, Anari left her in prison to rot. This is how she ended up," Wade stated. Zya looked down at the picture of the girl who was lying in a puddle of blood. "Anari did not even show up at her trial."

Zya turned her head as she sat in the chair with her arms crossed, and Lonnie pulled out the next picture. "This is Deandre Biggs aka Biggs. He was a member of Anari's entourage. After he was loyal to her for years, she shot and killed him." Wade continued to show her photos of people that Anari had supposedly double-crossed, and Zya listened in disbelief as she saw photo after photo of murders that Anari had committed.

"If she did this to some of her closest friends, what makes you think she will hesitate to do it to you?" he asked her, playing the role of the sincere cop. He didn't care about Zya. He just wanted to use her to get the information he needed. Zya was nothing more than a pawn in Wade's game.

"Anari is only out for herself. She has no loyalty to anyone, and if I gave her the same choice that I am giving you, she would not think twice about giving you up and saving herself. So, let's talk options." He reached underneath his desk and pulled out Snow's gun and the two bricks Snow had been delivering to Ty.

"See, since I am the arresting officer in Snow's case, I can make this evidence disappear. On one hand, you can get rid of the photos that incriminate you in King's murder, and you can get Snow's charges reduced. You can make all of these things go away if you help me get Anari.

"On the other hand, if you choose not to cooperate, you will go to jail for the rest of your life, and I will put the gun and the drugs that I pulled off of Snow into evidence. With this much evidence, you and Snow will go to jail for the rest of your lives.

"The ball is in your court. Just think about it . . . no pressure," Wade said as he raised his hands in the air.

Zya dropped her head in defeat. She knew that she really didn't have a choice. She had to go along with Lonnie Wade. She didn't want to, but she had to in order to save herself, and more importantly, to get Snow off. She had to choose between giving up Anari and giving up the man she loved, plus her own freedom. She knew what she had to do.

"I'll do it, but I want to see Snow first," she whispered as she wiped a tear from her cheek. She knew that now that she had agreed, she would have to go all the way. She was playing a dangerous game, and if she was discovered, Supreme Clientele would kill her.

Her response was music to Wade's ears, and he stood with a smile that spoke a thousand words. *Zya is in. Now all I have to do is wait for her to bring me back some information that I can use to lock Anari up for life,* he thought as he motioned for her to follow him. Zya stood up and walked solemnly through the station toward the bull pen that contained Torey Snow.

Wade stopped and looked into the tiny room where Snow was being held and then said, "I'll be right out here. Take your time." He opened the door and Zya walked in.

Snow was sitting back with the handcuffs still on and his legs spread apart. He had a pained expression

on his face, and Zya knew that the cops hadn't taken
him to the hospital yet. He was still bleeding, and her
heart broke as she looked at him.

"Snow," she whispered as she ran over to him. He
looked up in surprise and tried to stand. "No, sit
down, baby. I'm here for you," she said as she knelt
down in front of him and put her hands on his face.

"Are you okay?" he asked her. She nodded her
head and replied, "Yeah, I'm okay."

"Listen to me, Zya. You've got to be careful. Jules
is out, and he thought you would be the one coming
to the drop-off."

"I know, I know. I'm so sorry, Snow. I shouldn't
have sent you."

"Yes, you should have, because you would be dead
right now if it had been you. That nigga is out for
blood, Zya. You have to watch your back from here on
out. You hear me?" Snow asked.

"Yes, I hear you. I'm gon' get you out of here. I promise. Just give me a minute. I have a plan. I promise I
won't leave you in here," Zya said. She kissed him
softly, and Snow lifted his cuffed hands to wipe the
tears off of Zya's face.

"I love you, Snow," she said.

"I love you too," he replied.

Zya didn't want to leave his side, but she knew that
she had to go. "I'm gonna get you out. I swear on my
life."

He kissed her forehead before she stood up and
left the room.

"When is the next meeting?" Lonnie asked her
when she stepped into the hall.

"Saturday," she replied with reluctance.

"Then Saturday it is."

*   *   *

Zya sat in the tinted van, wearing only a bra as Federal Agent Bryson Matthews aka Buggy strapped a wire to her chest. Zya looked at him in disgust and shook her head as he continued to hook up the device.

"Hey, Buggy, it's been a while," Zya stated sarcastically as she mean-mugged him.

He looked at Zya and replied, "Look, I'm only doing my job. These people put poison into our communities. I only do what I think is right."

"Yeah, but you still a fucking snake," Zya responded as she folded her arms across her chest, trying to conceal herself. Buggy shook his head from side to side as he finished programming her wire.

I can't believe I'm about to do this. If they find out I'm wired, it's over. I would rather be sitting in a jail cell than at the bottom of the Hudson, Zya thought as she realized what the consequence of her actions would be if it was discovered that she was working for the police. Supreme Clientele didn't play when it came to snitches, and she knew that Anari would personally take care of her if her secret was ever revealed. She was gambling with her own life by helping Wade, and she hoped that she had made the right decision.

Her thoughts switched to Snow, and she instantly got back on track. *I have to do this for him. I can pull this off,* she thought as she saw Wade approach the van.

Wade hopped in the van and looked at Zya. "You ready?" he asked. She nodded her head nervously and could feel herself panicking. She breathed deeply and exhaled loudly to try and shake the anxious feeling that had invaded her body.

"You can do this. All you have to do is sit in the meetings and act normal," Wade instructed. "What time did you say the meeting starts?"

"Two A.M.," Zya replied.

Wade felt a sense of urgency as he waited for the restaurant to close. Here he was, sitting outside of the place where his cousin's killer did business. He was more than ready to arrest Anari, and he couldn't wait until the day he heard a judge sentence her to prison for the rest of her life. He was so close to taking Anari down that he could taste her conviction.

He turned his attention toward Zya as he watched her button the top of her dress. His eyes lingered on her breasts, and she quickly buttoned up her clothes. They all watched the front of the restaurant, waiting for the lighted OPEN sign to turn off. The cops waited eagerly, but Zya dreaded what she was about to do.

"Its show time," Buggy said as the sign turned off. Zya took a deep breath and listened as Wade began to give instructions.

"Okay, all you have to do is get her to say something about the murders. If you can't do that, then get her to discuss a big drug transaction. Let her lead the conversation, and when you address her, call her by her name. Make sure that you speak clearly, so that the bug will pick up the entire conversation."

Zya nodded her head. "Can you tell that I'm wearing a bug? It feels like you can tell. It's uncomfortable," she said.

Wade looked at her in annoyance and replied, "You're fine. Just get in there and do what you have to

do to save your ass. Remember, if you don't cooperate fully, the deal is off."

"I know what I got to do. Fuck you, Wade!" Zya
said as she hopped out of the van.

Before she closed the door, Wade replied, "Yeah, I
know you wish you could. But we have business to
take care of." The two other cops in the van laughed
at Wade's witty remark. Zya slammed the van door,
and as she walked toward the restaurant, guilt began
to eat at her conscience.

*How could I do this? Anari has shown me nothing
but love and loyalty. Now look at me. I'm wired like a
fucking rat, trying to put her in jail for the rest of her
life. If Snow wasn't depending on me, I wouldn't do
this, but my freedom is not the only thing at stake
here. I have to come through for him. I'm the reason
why Snow is locked up. I sent him to meet Black Ty. I
have to ride for him. He is more important than
Anari.*

She turned around and watched the van ride away
and park on the next block. Zya had so many emotions going through her body. She felt guilt and nervousness in her every step, but most of all, she was
scared.

Zya walked to the back door of the restaurant and
fidgeted with the wire, hoping that it wasn't notice-
able. *Be cool,* she told herself as Meechi opened the
door for her. She made her way down to the meeting
room. Knots formed in her stomach as she walked
down the long, narrow hallway that led to the room.

When she entered, she saw Khadafi standing at a
graphing chart that displayed the rising economy
rates of various countries overseas. The roundtable

was contemplating expansion into the global market. When she walked in, it seemed like all eyes were on her.

"Nice for you to join us," Anari said playfully as Zya took a seat next to her. Zya sat down, and the meeting continued as she tried to act as normal as possible.

Don't think about it, just do it, she thought to herself as she sat next to some of the most powerful people in the country. Her mind was in a daze, and she sat perfectly still as she pretended to listen to Khadafi explain why he thought it was important for them to expand.

"Zya, do you think that you would be able to control the distribution in the Caribbean, since you already have connections in Cuba?" Khadafi asked her.

Zya stared blankly at the graph, her mind a million miles away. She hadn't even heard his question. *Please don't let them find out. I have to do this for Snow.*

The other members at the roundtable stared at Zya as they waited patiently for her to respond. Anari frowned and tapped Zya lightly. "Zya!"

She jumped from Anari's touch and looked around the table. "Yes?" she said as she snapped out of her daze.

"Long night?" Emilio asked with laughter in his voice.

Zya blushed but didn't respond. She looked at Khadafi and replied, "I'm sorry, Khadafi. What were you saying?"

He asked her the question again, and she answered with the knowledge of a seasoned vet, but her voice was a little shaky.

"Are you okay?" Anari whispered.

Zya nodded her head and tried to refocus her attention on the chart. She wanted to avoid eye contact with Anari because she was afraid that she would see right through her. Zya kept bouncing her foot against the ground and tapping her pen on the table. Her heart was pounding, and the room felt like it was one hundred degrees.

Anari could see that Zya was uncomfortable, and she leaned over and whispered, "Are you okay? You don't look so good."

Zya gave her a half-smile and nodded her head. "I'm fine," she assured. "I'm good." At that moment, a waitress Zya had never seen before walked into the room to take their orders.

"What would you like?" the girl asked Zya.

"Cristal," Zya said.

The girl left the room, and Zya could feel Anari staring at her out of the corner of her eye. *She knows,* Zya thought as she fidgeted in her seat.

Anari burned a hole through Zya as she continued to stare her down. Anari could feel that something wasn't right with her friend. *She's too nervous. I've never seen her like this. She can't even keep her feet still,* Anari thought as she observed Zya's body language.

She knows. Damn, I have to get rid of this wire, Zya thought. She wanted to get up and walk out of the room, but she knew that it would make her look suspicious. Nobody ever left the meeting room until the meeting was adjourned, unless there was an emergency.

Zya noticed the waitress come back into the room with the drinks. She had a tray and was concentrating on not spilling the seven glasses on top of it. *She's my way out of this room,* Zya thought.

Zya waited for the girl to come around the table, and just as she was getting ready to place her drink on the table, Zya leaned over and placed her purse directly in the girl's path. The waitress stumbled, and her drink flew from her hand onto Zya's $20,000 silk Prada dress.

"Ohh!" Zya said as she stood up and tried to wipe the drink off of her dress. She knew that she had just ruined her dress, but she would rather destroy that than have Anari destroy her.

"Oh, I am so sorry. I-I tripped. I didn't mean—" the girl began to explain. The fear in her voice was apparent, and Zya looked up in shock. It was the first time that Zya realized that she was one of the people at the table who were feared.

She looks at me the same way I looked at Anari when I first started serving this table, Zya thought, realizing exactly how far she had moved up the ranks.

"It's okay. It was a mistake," Zya said to the girl. She pulled out a roll of money from her purse and handed it to the waitress. "You're fine. I promise, it's not a big deal. I just have to go clean myself up."

Anari watched the entire scene, and her eyes stayed on Zya as she hurried out of the room.

Oh, shit. I got to get rid of this fucking wire, Zya thought as she rushed upstairs and entered the bathroom. She went into one of the stalls and frantically unbuttoned the top of her dress. Her hands were shaking as her fingers struggled to free the buttons. She ripped the wire and the tape from her chest and flushed it down the toilet then quickly redressed and made her way back to the room.

❖   ❖   ❖

"Fuck just happened? I lost the signal. What the hell? That bitch just took off the fucking wire!" Wade yelled as he hit the dashboard repeatedly.

"Maybe something happened," Buggy stated.

"Fuck!" Lonnie yelled out of frustration. "I'll be right here waiting when her ass comes out," he said. He knew for a fact that Zya had taken off the wire. From what he had heard, Supreme Clientele existed and was contemplating making major moves. He had heard another woman's voice, but Zya didn't identify the woman as Anari. He knew that he was going to have to add some fuel to her flame in order for Zya to do what he needed her to do. He picked up the phone and called the precinct.

"Lieutenant Jones. Yeah, this is Wade. Could you look in my desk and pull out the evidence in the Smith case? I didn't get a chance to check it into the evidence log before my shift ended last night." He hung up his phone and said, "Bitch better do things my way from here on out, or her ass will be next." He had just turned in the evidence from Snow's case, so now all Zya had to save was herself.

"Do you think she will still cooperate now that you just screwed her boyfriend?" Agent Matthews asked.

Wade shrugged his shoulders and replied, "She better, or her ass is next."

Zya re-entered the room, and Khadafi asked, "Is everything okay?" Zya nodded and relaxed a little bit now that she didn't have the wire on.

"I know how upset Remy gets when she spills something on one of her outfits," Khadafi stated lightly, referring to his girlfriend back home.

Zya shook her head and said, "I'm fine. No harm done."

"Well, then, can we continue this meeting?" Jimmy Ross asked. Zya locked eyes with Anari, and her cold stare sent a shiver down her spine.

"No, not yet," Anari said as she pulled a small .22 from underneath the table and set in down on top. Every member seated at the table pulled a weapon and placed it in front of them for easy access, while Zya stood up, looking scared and confused.

"What is the purpose of this?" Emilio asked. It was a known rule at the table. If one member pulled their gun then everybody else should follow suit. Shoot first, ask questions later.

"Zya, unbutton your dress," Anari said calmly.

"What?" Zya asked. *I knew she knew. She knows I was wired.*

"Open the top of your dress," she repeated.

All of the men at the table looked on in confusion, but Anari stared Zya down.

"Fine," Zya said as she did as she was told. She unbuttoned her dress and slid the fabric down off her shoulders until only her bra covered her breasts. Anari's hardened expression softened as she shook her head from left to right.

"I'm sorry," she stated loudly. "I'm too cautious sometimes. Please forgive me, Zya. You are a good and dear friend to me. I should have never questioned your loyalty to this table. You would never turn snitch."

The men at the table laughed lightly, trying to cut through the tension in the room.

Zya stared at Anari and replied, "Its okay. I understand."

"Jesus, Anari, you think everybody is out to get you," Jimmy Ross exclaimed in laughter.

"This is a family. No one in this circle would ever betray family," Mr. Castello stated.

"Please sit down, Zya," Khadafi said as he placed his hand on the small of her back and guided her to her seat next to Anari.

Anari apologized again for her behavior, and the meeting proceeded. Zya's nerves were on edge for the rest of the night, but she knew that she had accomplished something.

Anari feels bad for accusing me. She won't come at me wrong again. She trusts me. I'm not going to chance it, though. I will never wear a wire into one of these meetings again. Lonnie Wade is going to have to come up with another way.

Zya felt badly about double-crossing Anari, but Wade had convinced her that if the shoe was on the other foot, Anari would do the same to her. The only thing that was on her mind was protecting her man. She would get Snow off no matter what the cost, and in the process, she would clear herself from King's murder as well.

The next thing on her agenda would be to handle Jules and Vita. There was no way she was letting them get away with what they had done. Jules had tried to kill her, and Vita had helped him do it. She knew how Jules got down, and was aware that he was a killer.

I have to get to him before he gets to me. I can't concentrate on him and Anari at the same time. I have to handle him first, then I can put all my energy into getting Snow off and clearing my name.

Chapter 16

The Monster

Vita sat in Ty's dope house and held a heroin-filled needle to her arm. She wanted to put the needle down, but she couldn't fight the urge. She had been clean for two days, but her will power was running thin. She placed the needle to her arm, but stopped just before it punctured her skin.

I'm just like my mother, a dope fiend. If this won't kill me, the AIDs will. I guess all the trickin' and sharing needles caught up. She began to cry, *I did so much dirt in my life, maybe I deserve to die at an early age. The one person that cared for me, I turned on her for a fix.*

Fuck that. The few years of my life I do have left isn't going to be filled with being a junkie. I am going to fight this and get clean, Vita thought as she tossed the needle across the room, watching as another junkie hurried to the drug and picked it up.

Vita was determined to make the best of what she had left of her life. She was going to go cold turkey and shake the monkey off of her back. She felt her body craving the drug, and excruciating pains shot through her stomach, causing her muscles to tighten up. She crawled into a fetal position while gripping her stomach. The pain was so agonizing, she lost control of her bowels and defecated on herself. She felt so ashamed that she couldn't control her bodily functions, and she cried in the middle of the floor, praying to God that it would stop, but it never did.

Jules stormed out of the clinic and his heart ached. He had just found out the most awful news of his entire life: He was HIV positive. He had been coughing up blood, and went to the doctor a couple of weeks back to see what was wrong. That day, he went back for the results, and the doctor informed him that he had the incurable monster.

When the doctor gave Jules the news, his knees buckled and he almost fell. He couldn't believe what he was hearing. Jules argued with the doctor and told him it must be a mistake, but the doctor told him he was 99 percent sure. He tried to offer Jules programs for him to attend with others in the same situation. Jules snatched the paper out of the doctor's hand and furiously exited the office.

How in the fuck did I get this shit? I can't fuckin' believe I have HIV. But how? I didn't get into that faggot shit in jail, and they test you before you go in, and I was negative. I . . . Vita! That bitch gave me this shit. I am about to kill that nasty whore. She's dead! Jules thought as he jumped in his car and recklessly drove to the dope house where he knew Vita would be. He was enraged, and the only thing he wanted to see was Vita's blood. She had put his life on a permanent countdown, and he wanted her dead.

Zya knew where Vita would be, and she was parked outside of Black Ty's dope house. She couldn't believe that after she let Vita live the first time, she would turn on her again. Vita was the reason that Snow was in jail, and her betrayal had given Wade another tool for blackmail. Zya wanted Vita dead, and she was about to fulfill her own wishes.

She pulled out her pistol and walked into the dope house. When she entered, she saw fiends all around the room, getting high. Even though Black Ty was dead, the show still went on, and his dope house was still poppin'.

Zya scanned around the room, looking for Vita, but didn't see her. She pulled out a hundred-dollar bill from her bra and held it in the air.

"Whoever can tell me where to find Vita gets this," Zya said as she held the bill over her head so everyone could see it. Immediately, everyone pointed toward the back room, trying to be the first to inform Zya where their peer was located. Zya tossed the hundred-dollar bill in the air and watched as the fiends scrambled to get it. She stepped over the wrestling dope-heads and headed to the back room with her gun in hand.

Zya stepped into the room and smelled a foul odor and almost gagged. She saw Vita lying in the middle of the floor, balled up, trembling, and clenching her stomach. All of the emotions that Zya had felt for her friend went out of the window. Her bottom lip began to quiver in pure fury, and she walked over to Vita and pressed the gun to her temple.

Zya looked at Vita and barely recognized her. She was not the same person. Zya didn't even want to say anything to Vita before she killed her. She just wanted to get it over and done with. Zya closed her eyes and prayed for Vita before she ended her life.

Without even looking up, Vita spoke. "Zya, I always loved you. You are my sister, and I know I pulled grimy on you. But that wasn't me. That was the drug controlling me. Just remember me as the girl who used to be your best friend. Remember, we were like Thelma and Louise. Don't remember me as this crack head junkie who turned on you. It wasn't me, Zya. I'm dying of AIDS anyway. It doesn't matter to me if I go now or later. I just want this shit to be over. I love you, Zy." Vita closed her eyes and prepared to meet her maker.

Zya's eyes watered, and against her will, a single tear rolled down her face. It pained her to see Vita like that. Although Vita had turned on her, Zya felt deep in her heart that Vita loved her. She also knew that she loved Vita. They had been best friends since middle school, and Zya's memories of the good times appeared in her mind. Zya quickly tried to escape the thought, and put her finger on the trigger. This was the second time she had Vita at gunpoint, and she knew that if she didn't kill her now, it was a possibility that she would have to do it again.

"I love you, Vita," Zya said.

Vita closed her eyes and braced herself for the blast. But to her surprise, Zya walked out of the room, leaving her there alone to sulk in her own guilt.

Zya walked out of the dope house and decided to let Vita die slowly. She couldn't bring herself to kill Vita. *She is dying of the monster anyway. She has enough demons to battle,* Zya thought as she got into her Benz.

Just as she was about to pull off, she saw a car wildly pull onto the dope house's front lawn. The screeching of the tires was loud and unexpected. Zya focused her attention on who was in the car. She couldn't see the man clearly until he got out. When he jumped out of the car, he slammed the door forcefully, and that's when Zya saw who it was—Jules.

Jules carried a big chrome pistol in his right hand as he ran into the house. Zya cocked back her gun and followed Jules into the house without him knowing. When Zya crept through the front door, she saw no sign of Jules. She just saw the junkies scattered out, using their preferred drug.

At that moment, Zya heard a single gunshot come from the back room. "Oh shit, Vita!" Zya said as she rushed to the back. When she opened the door, Jules was standing over Vita's body with his gun still smoking.

"Vita!" Zya screamed as she saw her friend's body slumped on the floor. Jules had shot her in the chest, leaving her body lying there, motionless.

Jules heard Zya scream, and quickly turned around and pointed his gun at her. Zya had her gun pointed on him also. They faced off in the middle of the room, both aiming their guns at each other. The last time they were standing face to face, they were deeply in love. Now the only emotion they felt for one another was hatred.

The sight of Zya sent a pain through the pit of

Jules's stomach. She was still as beautiful as he remembered, only now, she was his enemy. She had been disloyal, and it was finally time to make her pay. Jules was the first to speak.

"You grimy-ass bitch. As soon as a nigga was down, you did some snake shit and didn't hold me down. I knew I couldn't trust a hood rat." Hatred seethed off his every word, and as Zya looked in his eyes, she could see that any love that they had once shared was now lost.

"Hood rat? Fuck you, nigga. I am far from a hood rat. I always held you down, no matter what. Who took those out-of-state trips for you, huh? Who helped you get your paper? Who helped you stick-up innocent niggas for your gain? Me, that's who! You fuckin' bitch-ass nigga. I held you down from day one!"

"You never held me down. As soon as I got locked up, you killed my baby and started fucking with other niggas. I wanted that baby so bad. All the bad shit I ever did, didn't matter if I could just bring an innocent life into this world. You took that peace of mind away from me." Jules began to think about his newly acquired disease. "Now I can never bring another life in this world. I hate you!" Jules said as he clenched his gun even tighter and jabbed it in her direction as he spoke.

"I had the abortion because when I came to the jail to visit you, I saw that trick you had up there visiting you. I guess you forgot to tell me that, huh? You had it set up perfectly. You even had us coming up on different schedules, so we wouldn't run into each other.

"You already had a baby, so what were you so worried about ours for? You lied to me. I thought you loved me, but I was just a toy to you, your little side chick. Fuck that. I am a queen, and I don't come second to anyone."

Jules's face twisted because he didn't understand what Zya was talking about. "What the fuck are you talking about? I never had a baby by another girl. You were my only woman. I took care of you, Zya. I loved you."

"Stop lying, Jules. I saw the bitch with my own eyes," she yelled. Her voice trembled as she remembered how badly it had hurt when she had seen the other girl visiting him in jail.

Jules lowered his weapon and put his hands on his head as he began to pace back and forth. "Fuck . . . Zya, fuck!" he screamed at her. Tears accumulated in his eyes as he realized what Zya was saying. "You should have asked me about it! We were better than that. You should've come to me like a woman and asked. The girl you saw was my cousin, and she was pregnant with my godson. I was telling her about how you were pregnant, and how I was about to have a shorty, and how our kids would grow up together like we did.

"You didn't stop and think about that, did you? You didn't even come to ask me. You just assumed. It was my fuckin' cousin! You took me through all that bullshit because of something that wasn't even true." Jules used to love Zya from the bottom of his heart, and once upon a time, he would've taken a bullet for her. Now he wanted to put a bullet through her. He continued as the tears came rolling down. "You couldn't fuck with any other nigga. You had to go and fuck Snow. You is a ho, and ain't going to be nothing but a ho."

Jules saw that Zya was in shock from the news he had just given her. Tears flowed down her cheeks as she processed the information over again in her mind.

He didn't cheat on me. Oh my God, I killed our baby and he didn't even do anything. I should have asked him. It was his fuckin' cousin.

Fuck that. He's lying! I saw it with my own two eyes. God, please let him be lying. I should have done things differently . . . Please let him be lying. Zya was going crazy, trying to separate the truth from the lies. If Jules was actually being honest, then Zya knew that she was dead wrong. The decisions that she had made began to haunt her as she tried to clear her head.

The fact that the truth had just come out didn't change the way Jules felt. He had spent years in prison hating Zya for her betrayal, and he was determined to make her pay. He saw that she was deep in thought, and jumped on the opportunity. He hit the gun out of Zya's hand, and it flew over to the corner. He then struck Zya across the face with his fist. Zya fell onto the ground, and Jules stood above her with his gun pointed to her head. Zya had no weapon and no chance.

A single shot rang out and echoed through the whole house. Zya's face was full of blood. But not her own blood. It was Jules's. Vita had scuffled to Zya's gun and put a bullet through Jules's head, causing him to die on impact. Jules's body fell on top of Zya, and she quickly pushed him off of her. Zya looked over at her friend, barely holding up the gun.

"Vita!" Zya yelled as her friend collapsed onto the floor. Zya went over to her dying friend and held her hand as the blood poured out of her chest.

"We have to get you to the hospital," Zya said as she tried to apply pressure to the wound. Zya quickly pulled away from Vita, remembering that she had HIV.

Vita grabbed Zya's hand and whispered, "No, it's okay, Zy. It doesn't even hurt anymore. I can't feel anything. Zya, you are my sister, and I will always love you. Please forgive me and remember our bond. I love you," Vita said before she stared into space and stopped breathing.

Zya ran her hand over Vita's face to close her eyes. Zya whispered, "I love you too."

Zya gently let Vita's body rest on the floor, and that's when her phone began to vibrate. She looked at the ID and recognized the number. It was Lonnie Wade.

Chapter 17

Loyalty or Supremacy

"**F**uck is your problem? Why did you take off the wire?" Wade yelled as he gripped Zya's arm firmly.

Zya looked at the detective like he was crazy, and she snatched her arm away from him. "Look, you aren't the one sitting in a room full of killers. If I'm gon' do this, it has to be my way! I'm not wearing a wire into those meetings. That's like sending me into a death trap," she stated firmly, standing toe to toe with Lonnie Wade.

"Fuck! I had them. She was getting ready to talk herself right into a conviction," he said in a frustrated tone.

Zya put her hands on her hips and sighed deeply. "Look, I can tell you whatever you need to know about Anari and her involvement in Supreme Clientele."

She paused for a minute, hating the fact that she was getting ready to snitch on her friend and mentor.

"That won't work. You were just a fucking waitress. I need someone who was directly involved in Supreme Clientele."

"I am," Zya admitted hesitantly. "I'm a member of the roundtable."

Lonnie Wade's face dropped in disbelief. He couldn't believe what he had just heard. Here he was, chasing Anari when he had a member in his presence, admitting her involvement in the most notorious drug operation America had ever seen.

"Are you going to arrest me now?" Zya asked.

Lonnie seriously thought about it, but changed his mind when he realized exactly what she could do for him.

"You know you are going to have to testify. If you can't agree to that, I can't agree to help you out," Wade said as he stared down at her.

Zya closed her eyes. *I'm a fucking snitch,* she thought as she shook her head in dishonor.

"I know . . . I know," she said softly, opening her eyes and revealing her pain to Lonnie Wade. "What about Snow? When will he get out?" she asked.

"You fucked up his deal when you took off that wire."

"What!" Zya yelled. She put her hands on her face and shook her head. *I knew it. I knew I shouldn't have trusted him. That wasn't what we discussed.*

"That wasn't the deal. You said that if I got Anari—"

Zya was standing directly in his face, screaming at him. Wade grabbed her wrists just as she was getting ready to smack him. He grabbed her violently and pulled her close to him. She could smell his cologne, and she breathed heavily as she tried to free herself from his grasp.

"That wasn't the deal," she said between clenched teeth.

"Well, it is now. You can take it or leave it," he replied.

"Fuck you. I'm not doing it if Snow goes to prison."

Wade nodded his head, turned her around in one swift movement, and clamped the handcuffs around her wrists. "You have the right to remain silent. Anything you say can and will be used against you in the court of law. You have the right to an attorney. If you cannot afford an attorney, one will be provided . . ."

Zya turned around and stared coldly at Wade. "Okay, okay!" she shouted. Wade stared at her with a smirk on his face.

"Take off the damn cuffs!" she yelled.

"Torey Smith aka Snow is a done deal. You do what I want, or you will end up just like him, behind a cage."

She lowered her head to the ground and nodded in defeat. He spun her around and took off the handcuffs.

"What do I have to do?"

"Tell me all the security codes to the restaurant. You are going to lead me directly to Supreme Clientele and Anari Simpson. I'm going to arrest her in the middle of the meeting."

Zya walked into the restaurant, and she could hear her heartbeat in her ears. *Calm down. You're not wearing a wire, so there's nothing for them to find,* she thought. She walked down the hallway, and it felt like she was taking the walk of death.

There was an eerie feeling in the restaurant, and Zya began to have second thoughts about what she was doing. She stopped before entering the room and tried to gain some type of composure. Her mind was all over the place, and she couldn't stop herself from shaking. She reached for the handle and slowly opened the door. She gasped when she stepped inside. The meeting room looked completely different. Everything had been removed from it.

Where's all the charts . . . the documents . . . where are the guns and the safe? What the hell is going on? Anari was the only member that sat in the room, and she sat back at the head of the table with a drink in her hands. Her stare was deadly, and Zya knew that something was wrong. The room had been stripped, and the other members who were supposed to be present were not there.

It's as if Supreme Clientele never existed, Zya thought as she stood perfectly still, waiting for Anari to speak.

"Where is everyone?" Zya finally managed to say.

"We wouldn't want them to be a part of what is about to go down," Anari replied. "Sit down. Have a drink with me before I go to jail," Anari stated as she motioned for Zya to sit across from her. Zya's mouth dropped in astonishment.

She knows. She already knows about the set-up. Zya sat down reluctantly, at a loss for words. She didn't know what to say to Anari, but she could see the look of pain mixed with anger in her face.

"Remember when I told you that this day would

come? I told you that you would have to make a choice."

Zya took a deep breath. The fear in her heart slowly left as she realized that she was just as important as the woman who sat across from her. It finally hit her. She was a part of the same notorious organization as Anari. She held just as much power.

Her mind flashed back to the pictures of the people that Anari had double-crossed. *Fuck that. All of her other friends ended up dead. She would do the same to me if she was in my position.*

"You told me that I would have to choose between loyalty and supremacy. I'm following in your footsteps. I'm choosing supremacy," Zya said as she poured herself a drink.

Anari laughed and replied, "I didn't know that there was supremacy in snitching."

Zya didn't reply. She just shook her head. Although she no longer feared Anari, she did feel guilty about what she was doing. Anari had been a good friend to Zya. She had given her something that she would not have been able to get on her own: the world.

"We were friends," Anari stated. It had been a long time since Anari had befriended anyone. Her life had been one of business interactions only. Zya had been the first person to get close to her since best friend, Tanya, had died. She was hurt by Zya's betrayal.

"We were friends, but you predicted this, Anari. There isn't enough room in this game for both of us. I don't want to do this, but I don't have a choice. I'm doing what I have to do."

Anari nodded her head and replied, "Then do what you have to do. Let him in."

Zya looked toward the door and knew that Wade was approaching. She stood up and walked slowly to the door. She could hear the footsteps coming near, and when she looked back at Anari, a tear slipped from her eye. They had been good friends, and Zya knew that she was personally responsible for Anari's downfall.

Zya opened the door, and a team of SWAT agents stormed the room with their weapons drawn and aimed at Anari. Suit after suit filled the room, until there was no room left. Fifty agents came in full force for one person . . . one woman . . . Anari Simpson.

Anari stayed seated, with a calm but heated expression on her face. She crossed her legs and continued to sip her drink as she looked around at all the guns pointed in her direction.

She is fearless, Zya thought as she watched Lonnie Wade approach Anari with a piece of paper in his hand.

"Search the premises. Tear this place up until you find something," he ordered. He grabbed Anari up out of her seat and placed the handcuffs on her. He read her rights as he maneuvered her through the busy room. She stopped walking when she reached Zya.

"I trusted you," she said. "You could have been great."

Zya dropped her head, and Lonnie guided Anari out of the room. Agent Bryson Matthews aka Buggy walked up and grabbed Zya gently by her elbow. "Let's go. Wade wants you at the station," he said.

Zya knew that Wade wanted to keep her close so that she wouldn't skip town to avoid testifying against

Anari. Zya knew what she was about to get herself into. She was about to face off against the most powerful woman in the country, and she hoped that she could handle it.

It's all or nothing. It's her or me.

Chapter 18

Queen of New York

"This is Lisa Stewart, reporting live from the Foley Square Federal Courthouse, where the notorious Anari Simpson's trial is taking place. Ms. Simpson stands accused of running Supreme Clientele, a roundtable that consists of some of the most wanted drug lords in the United States.

"Although the rest of the roundtable members are unknown, Zya Miller, one of the roundtable's elite, is the key witness in the prosecution's case. She is speculated to be responsible for more than six percent of the cocaine imported into the United States.

"This may be the biggest drug trial since the infamous D.C. trial of Rayful Edmonds. The court marshals have been ordered to stand armed in front of the courthouse, and the federal government has provided a bulletproof glass for the jurors to sit behind.

These precautions prove that Anari Simpson really is a woman to be feared."

Lonnie Wade approached the courthouse, and couldn't believe his eyes when he saw how many people were congregated outside. There were thousands of people chanting and supporting Anari, and news reporters and cameras were scattered everywhere. They were calling this the trial of the century, and everybody wanted to be a part of it. Anari's case was the type that detectives, lawyers, and judges hoped their entire lives to receive. If convicted, her case was sure to boost everybody's career. Wade maneuvered his way through the crowd.

"Detective Wade . . . Detective Lonnie Wade!"

He turned around to see who was calling his name, and a microphone was shoved in his face. "Lisa Stewart with the *New York Post*. What do you think will be the outcome of this trial? As the arresting officer in the case, how much evidence do you actually have on Ms. Simpson?"

"No comment," Wade declared as he pushed the mic from his face and continued to make his way through the crowd. There was no way he was willing to make any type of statement. He didn't want to jeopardize the case by saying the wrong thing, so he kept his mouth shut. Wade walked through the crowded halls of the courthouse.

"Hey, Wade, have you seen the paper?" Agent Matthews aka Buggy asked as he approached him. He handed him a newspaper. Wade opened it up and read:

ANARI SIMPSON VS. ZYA MILLER: WHO IS THE QUEEN OF N.Y.?

"Keep flipping," Agent Matthews stated with amusement in his voice. Lonnie turned the page and saw headline after headline chronicling Anari's trial.

THE QUEEN BEE: A TIMELINE OF ANARI SIMPSON'S DRUG CAREER

IS THIS THE END OF THE BEAUTIFUL QUEEN PEN?

Lonnie Wade threw the paper to the ground and stomped toward the courtroom with Matthews by his side.

"That shit is going to sway the jury. They are making this seem like a fight for the title between Zya and Anari," Wade said as he entered the courtroom.

There was chatter in the courthouse, and everybody seemed to be whispering facts and falsehoods about the case. Every seat in the room was taken. People were bunched up on the wooden seats, just to get a peek at the woman who had reigned in the streets. This was the first time that people had been able to put a face to the name. Anari had been known as Tony throughout her reign, and everyone in the room was shocked to finally know the truth: Tony is a woman.

Anari sat next to Anderson Wallace and smiled for the cameras. She figured if she was going to be seen, she might as well be looking good. She wore a white, tailor-fitted, Ferragamo pantsuit. The diamonds that cluttered her ears, wrists, and neckline made her appear to sparkle for her new audience. She was more like a celebrity than a queen pen, and no one wanted to believe that the glamorous woman who sat before them was a cold-hearted killer.

Lonnie Wade was disgusted by how comfortable Anari looked as she sat in her seat and talked quietly with her lawyer. *This bitch is sitting up there like she's not on trial for her life,* he thought.

Anari turned around and met eyes with the detective. They stared each other down, but Anari ended the staring contest by turning away. In the first pew behind the defense section sat a row full of people. The rest of Supreme Clientele was scattered throughout the courtroom.

Everybody was at her trial. It was more like a red carpet event than a court case. Famous rappers and singers walked through the doors left and right. Hip Hop's finest were in attendance, and they had all come to support Anari and show her love throughout her case. The newspapers had been calling the trial a star-studded event and the place to be. Today was by far the most eventful day, because it was the day that Zya was supposed to take the stand. The reporters were having a field day.

It had been three months since Anari's arrest, and the world had waited patiently for her to be tried. Her face had been plastered on every news station in the world, and her story had been told and retold a thousand times. The novel *Dirty Money*, which was based on Anari's life, flew off the shelves and became a street classic. The media played on Anari's friendship with Zya, and had people picking sides on which woman they supported.

The other members of Supreme Clientele were safe and sound. Neither Zya nor Anari ever mentioned their names. All the media knew was that Zya and Anari had once been good friends and made money together through their drug empire. Now Zya and Anari were adversaries, each one fighting to stay on top. The streets called Zya a snitch, and she knew that she would have to leave the country right after the trial was over. Her face was national news, and anywhere she went, people would know what she had done.

After today, I won't be able to go anywhere without people knowing who I am. Lonnie might as well have burned an S in my forehead, because everybody is gonna know that I ratted Anari out, Zya thought as she waited in the prosecutor's office, tapping her foot nervously against the ground. Her heart was heavy, and over the past couple of months, she had been sick from stress. She had lost almost everybody in her life that she cared about.

It turned out that Jules hadn't even done anything wrong. She had turned her back on him because of a misunderstanding, and the guilt from that chewed at her every day. Vita was dead and had suffered miserably from her drug addiction. *I was so busy hustling that I wasn't there for her. I should have helped her.*

Snow was locked up for the rest of his life. She had visited him frequently, and her heart broke every time she saw him behind the glass. She was in love with him, but the fact that she would never be able to see him free again haunted her.

Now she was getting ready to send the only person she had left to prison. Anari had given Zya her friendship, and in return, Zya was giving her betrayal. Zya touched her stomach and thought about the baby that she was carrying. She was three months pregnant with Snow's seed, and it was the only piece of sanity she had left.

"You ready?" Lonnie Wade asked as he entered the room.

Zya nodded her head and whispered, "Yes."

Lonnie looked at Zya and could see the fatigue and worry in her face. It was the first time he thought about how the trial was affecting her. As she got up to walk by him, he grabbed her hand and stopped her from leaving the room.

"Zya, thank you. I couldn't have done this without you."

"Don't thank me. If you didn't have a murder over my head, I wouldn't have helped you do shit," she responded coldly.

Wade laughed and replied, "You still have some sort of allegiance to Anari. She is a murderer, so do yourself a favor. Don't feel too bad."

Zya frowned and replied, "You keep calling her a murderer, but she is on trial for a drug charge. Tell me. What do you have against her?"

Wade didn't reply. He didn't want to reveal his personal reasons for wanting Anari. He changed the subject and said, "Let's go." He grabbed Zya's arm and led the way to the courtroom.

"The prosecution would like to call Zya Miller to the stand." The doors to the courtroom opened, and Zya stood there as lights flashed in her face. Chatter and whispers erupted as everyone in the place turned to stare at Zya as she walked in. Her Manolo Blahniks clicked on the floor as she walked up the aisle, and her black Gucci dress suit complemented her slightly pregnant figure. Her hair was neatly pulled back in a bun, and she wore pearls to accessorize.

"Get a picture of her outfit. We'll run hers next to Anari's to see who was best dressed," instructed a reporter.

Wade shook his head in disgust and watched as

every head in the courtroom looked back and forth between Zya and Anari. Both women were strikingly beautiful, and they looked liked they should be on a runway rather than going against one another in a court of law.

The bailiff approached Zya and she lifted her right hand. "Do you solemnly swear to tell the truth, the whole truth, and nothing but the truth, so help you God?"

"I do," she agreed.

"You may take your seat, Ms. Miller," the judge instructed.

Zya closed her eyes and breathed deeply to calm her nerves. Anari looked at her, and could see that Zya was stressed. She smiled smugly to herself, knowing that she had caused Zya to lose sleep.

"Could you please state your name for the court's transcript?" Rachel Evans, the District Attorney of New York, asked.

"Zya Miller."

"Ms. Miller, were you directly involved with Supreme Clientele?"

"Yes," Zya answered as she sat poised in her seat, her eyes directly on the prosecutor.

"What was your involvement?"

"I was the member of the table that had the coke connect."

"Coke connect? By that you mean you got the cocaine for the table?"

"Yes," Zya replied.

"Approximately how much cocaine?"

"I transported five hundred kilos of coke every month from overseas to the United States," Zya admitted.

"Daaamn!!" someone shouted from the crowd. There were gasps and chatter throughout the room, and the judge banged his gavel to get the crowd under control.

Anari sat back in her chair, knowing that the jury was watching her every move. She stared intently at Zya and shook her head in contempt. She hated snitches, and couldn't believe that Zya was getting ready to give her up.

"Ms. Miller," the district attorney said as she walked over to the defense table. "What part did Anari Simpson play in this drug transaction?"

Anari looked at Zya, and as their eyes met, Zya felt the tears threaten to fall. They stared intently at one another, and Zya opened her mouth to speak, but no words came out.

"Ms. Miller, answer the question," the judge instructed.

"What part did Anari Simpson play in this drug transaction?" Ms. Evans repeated.

I can't do this. I'd rather go to prison than be a mu'fuckin' snitch, Zya thought.

Zya shook her head and replied, "None."

"Excuse me?" the district attorney asked as she looked from Lonnie Wade to Zya and then back to the judge.

"She played no role in the drug transaction. It was all me. I don't even know the defendant," Zya stated firmly.

The courtroom erupted in conversation, and Lonnie Wade stood up angrily and shouted, "What the fuck are you doing?"

"Ms. Miller, do you know the penalty for perjury?" the D.A. threatened.

Zya snapped back, "Yeah, bitch. It can't be any worse than the penalty for murder. I do not know the defendant. I was responsible for the drug transactions."

Rachel Evans turned red and yelled, "And Supreme Clientele?"

"Supreme Clientele consists of myself, Torey Smith aka Snow, Tyrone Watson aka Black Ty, Julius Carter aka Jules, Arvita Simmons, and Lonnie Wade. All of the members are now dead or doing life in jail—all except for myself and Detective Lonnie Wade. Say hi, Wade," Zya stated with a smirk as she waved at Lonnie Wade.

All of the people sitting in the courtroom looked back at the Lonnie Wade and began to speculate about what Zya had just said. With her statement, she had just exonerated Anari Simpson and all the other members of the table from any involvement in Supreme Clientele. She had just taken the fall for the whole cartel.

"And Ms. Simpson's involvement was?" Rachel Evans was pushing to connect the dots between Supreme Clientele and Anari. She could feel the case slipping right out of her hands.

"The defendant was not involved. I disguised my identity by using the name Tony when I conducted business," Zya said, taking the blame for all of the charges. News columnists wrote frantically, trying to keep up with every word, and the crowd was unable to contain their astonished comments.

Anari's expression remained cold as she stared at Zya sitting on the stand. She leaned over to Anderson Wallace and whispered, "Get Snow taken care of. Make sure the hit is right."

"Your Honor!" Ms. Evans yelled. "I would like to request a three-month hold on this trial. This witness has hurt our case significantly."

Anderson Wallace stood up and said, "Your Honor, I must object. My client is guaranteed a speedy trial by the United States Constitution. If Ms. Miller is the only witness that the prosecution has against Ms. Simpson, that is their mistake. In fact, I would like to ask for an immediate dismissal."

The judge shook his head in disgust as he realized that the trial had just taken a turn for the worse. "I'm sorry, Ms. Evans. I cannot grant your request. Mr. Wallace, I also deny your request for a dismissal. Ms. Simpson will still be tried based on the evidence that the State has presented, no matter how little."

He looked down at Zya and yelled, "Remove the witness from the stand!"

Lonnie Wade got up and walked over to Zya. He was livid. "You're going to rot underneath the jail by the time I'm finished with you," he threatened as he placed her in cuffs and shoved her out of the courtroom.

Torey Snow sat in the prison cell, staring at the letter he had received from Zya. She had told him everything about Lonnie Wade, and told him that she had decided not to snitch. She told him that she would include his name as a member of the roundtable, but it didn't matter since he had two consecutive life sentences.

Snow was proud of Zya for maintaining the code of the streets, but he was also worried about his unborn child. He knew that he wouldn't be able to be a part of his child's life, and was sure that Lonnie Wade was going to send Zya Upstate. They would be locked up for the remainder of their natural lives, and he didn't want his child to be thrown into the system. He contacted his mother, who decided that she would adopt the child right after Zya gave birth.

Snow thought about Zya often. She was his woman, and he loved her more than he loved himself. Thinking about her hurt him to the depths of his soul, so Snow quickly learned to block out all thoughts of his life on the outside. There was no point in thinking about what his life used to be like because it would never be like that again. He had to get used to life on the inside. He slept, ate, and even showered when another man told him to. He was truly state property, and he was slowly adjusting to the fucked up circumstances that his life had become.

Snow got up and followed the line of inmates from their cell blocks into the shower. He stepped into the foggy area and carried his soap on a rope to a shower head and began to wash his muscular body. The steam from the hot water made it hard to see. As he washed his body, he felt a sharp object puncture his body. He grabbed the hand that held the object and slammed the white man repeatedly against the hard brick wall. His fist pummeled the man's face, but he was restrained by prison guards quickly. The man took advantage of the opportunity. He picked the shank up from the shower floor and stuck Snow with it repeatedly, causing him to fall to the ground. Blood came from Snow's mouth as his naked body lost consciousness.

❖   ❖   ❖

Wade picked up the newspaper and read the front page headline. SUPREME CLIENTELE MEMBER TOREY SMITH STABBED IN PRISON FIGHT: BODY DISAPPEARS FROM HOSPITAL.

Wade smiled to himself. *I wonder if Zya's heard the news. Anari probably had her little boyfriend hit after she took the stand against her,* Wade thought. He was glad that Zya had gotten what was coming to her. *After that shit she pulled in the courtroom . . .*

His thoughts were interrupted as his Lieutenant came walking into the room with two rookie cops standing by his side.

"I warned you, Wade!" he yelled.

"What are you talking about?" Lonnie asked. The two officers walked around Wade's desk and pulled him to his feet. "What the fuck is going on?" Wade asked as his eyes bucked open.

"You're under arrest," one of the officers said.

"For what?" he yelled as he jerked wildly, trying to free himself.

"For your illegal participation in Supreme Clientele," the Lieutenant answered harshly as he threw pictures of Wade standing next to Zya on the table.

Jones continued, "We have your phone records, showing that you were contacting Zya Miller frequently. Calls that weren't authorized or documented."

"Wait! Lieutenant Jones!" Lonnie yelled as he was handcuffed and escorted out of the police station. "It's not what it looks like." Those were the last words Wade said before he was hit over the head with a billy club and was carried off.

* * *

Anari walked through the crowd that had accumulated outside the courthouse. Everyone was anxiously awaiting the jury's decision. Dozens of people followed her with cameras. Reporters from almost every news and entertainment station in the country were trying to get an exclusive interview.

"What up? This is Sway from *MTV News*, reporting live from the Anari Simpson court case in New York City. The courthouse is packed today as everyone waits to see what verdict the jury will come back with. As soon as the decision is in, you'll know first. We're going to keep you, the people at home, updated on what's going on here at the trial of the century," Sway said as he walked alongside Anari, her entourage, and the dozens of news reporters.

He looked to Anari and said, "I'm behind you all the way. Good luck."

Although Anari didn't know him personally, she smiled and replied, "Thank you." Anari made her way into the courtroom and took her seat at the defense table.

The judge entered the packed courtroom and an abundance of "shhh" echoed throughout the place. The jury filed in one by one, and Anari gripped Wallace's hand as she looked at the people who held her life in their hands. She was breathing erratically as she tried to remain calm. She crossed her fingers and looked back at Von, who was sitting in the back of the courtroom with their five-year-old daughter sitting on his lap. Anari smiled as her daughter, LaTanya, waved innocently. Anari had named her daughter after her best friend who had died at the hands of the game. She raised her head to the sky, knowing that Tanya was looking down on her.

"Will the defendant please rise?" the judge asked.

Anari stood, closed her eyes, and lowered her head to the table, beginning to pray.

Please, God, I have been through so much in the past seven years. My heart was broken with the death of my son, and it took me a long time to rebuild my life. I know that everything I do is not right, but no one is perfect. I know that I am not without sin, but I am asking You now to give me another chance. I played the hand that You dealt me, and did what I had to do to survive. Let no man judge me, because I feel that You are the only one great enough to do so.

Please . . . if I get out of this, I will retire from the game. I will never touch another drug in my life. I will sit back with my family and enjoy my life with them. I will leave the game alone and be a mother and wife to my family.

Anari raised her head, and tears graced her face. It was the first time in a long time that she had shown weakness. She had buried her emotions when her son was murdered and she first entered the game, but she had meant what she said. If she got off, she was going to get out of the game and leave the malicious, fucked up part of the world alone. She planned on enjoying her money and spending as much time as possible with her beautiful daughter and husband. *I'll let Von handle the drug game, and I'll finally be able to just be wifey,* she thought.

The foreman of the jury stood, and the courtroom was so silent you could hear a pin drop. "We, the people of this jury, find Anari Simpson . . ." Anari held her breath as she waited for the last words. An eternity seemed to pass before she heard the foreman say, "Not guilty on all counts."

Everyone in the courtroom roared in applause and congratulations. Anari fell back into her chair in disbelief, and a tear of joy slid down her face.

Anderson Wallace embraced her and said, "You really are untouchable."

Anari laughed and replied, "You really are as good as you say you are."

Lights and cameras flashed as everyone took picture after picture of her. She ran to the back of the room, where her daughter was waiting with her arms outstretched. She picked her up and kissed her cheeks a thousand times as Von wrapped his arm around his wife.

"I love you, Mommy," her daughter said sweetly.

Anari laughed to release some of the joy she felt and replied, "Mommy loves you too." She looked around at all the people cheering for her, and her heart was finally soothed. The cold front that she had to build after her son was murdered dissolved, and she finally felt a sense of healing and happiness. Her struggle and heartache was finally over. She didn't have to hide out or conceal her identity anymore, because the world already knew.

"You ready to get out of here?" Von asked her.

"Yeah, let's go," Anari replied. Anari made eye contact with all of the Supreme Clientele members.

Jimmy Ross from Miami nodded his head, acknowledging her acquittal.

Khadafi Langston from the Midwest smiled and slowly clapped as he watched her walk by.

Emilio Estes from the West Coast kept his serious expression, but the slight wink he gave her and the look in his eyes revealed his happiness for her.

Mr. Castello raised a cigar in the air and laughed heartily.

Anderson Wallace held up his briefcase and signaled for her to call him. The only member of the roundtable who was missing was Zya, and Anari knew exactly where she was headed. She looked back at the courtroom one last time and promised herself that she would never be put in that situation again.

I am done with the game. It's time for me to retire. I just have one more thing that I need to handle. One more score to settle, then I am out . . . for good.

Chapter 19

This Can't be Life

Federal Agent Matthews escorted Zya on the bus heading to Bedford Correctional Facility for Women. Zya couldn't stand the sight of the person she knew as Buggy. He seemed like he was enjoying every bit of Zya's incarceration.

Matthews stood at the steps as the future inmates loaded the bus. When Zya approached the steps, Matthews looked at her and said, "I wouldn't miss this for the world. I can't wait until you step inside your new, permanent home. Make sure you sit in the back, where I can keep my eyes on you!" He watched Zya load the bus with a pleased expression on his face. It was about time that she received what she had coming to her, and he was glad that he would be the one to introduce her to her fate.

Zya remained silent, but smirked as she stepped onto the bus. She knew that Matthews was upset because of what she had done to Wade. Detective Lonnie Wade had been kicked off the force, and was now under investigation for his involvement with the Supreme Clientele drug cartel.

She was the last one to board, so Matthews walked behind her with a shotgun. "Keep going until you reach the back seat, Miller," he ordered.

Zya didn't say anything to Matthews. She just followed his orders and sat at the back of the bus, where he stood posted with his weapon. Zya looked at the two guards standing at the front of the bus and then at Matthews, who stood next to her in the back.

I know he is itching to shoot me. I better not make any sudden movement. I would have paid a million bucks to see his face when Wade was arrested. I don't know why he's so angry, but I guess it's true what they say. All pigs stick together.

Zya rubbed her swollen stomach and wished that she could have made things different. She was seven months pregnant and on her way to prison.

Zya looked around at the other women on the bus. She was surrounded by killers and thieves. Her only crime was that she was a born hustler. It wasn't her fault. It was what the streets had raised. She was a product of her environment, and this little Harlem girl turned into one of the most notorious drug lords of her time. She was sentenced to a life sentence, with no chance of parole for her involvement with the murder of Keyshawn King and her admittance to her involvement with Supreme Clientele. Zya not only ruined the lives of Snow and herself, she had ruined the life of their unborn child.

My son will have to be born behind bars, and I will never have a chance to raise him. I can never teach my child not to make the same mistakes that I have made. This can't be life. They are going to take my baby away from me. I'll never get the chance to be his mother.

Zya dropped her head while she caressed her belly. She closed her eyes and began to cry, hoping that her unborn child would have a better life than she did.

All of a sudden, she felt the bus jerk, and she heard the sound of the tires screeching. Matthews fell down from the jerk, and the whole bus was in chaos. The guards immediately pointed their guns on the inmates and yelled, "Remain calm! We caught a flat. Any unauthorized movement by the inmates will result in you being shot!" That comment quieted the bus down almost instantly, and the guards regained control.

Matthews got back to his feet and looked at Zya. "Do not fucking move!" he warned as he pointed his shotgun. Matthews took his gun off of Zya and exited the bus to see what the problem was.

Boom! An explosion blew up the front half of the bus, instantly killing the occupants that sat in the front, including the guards.

Oh God, my baby, Zya thought as she clenched her stomach and held her breath, not trying to breathe in the fumes from the explosion. Her only thought was to protect her unborn child. She dropped to the floor, trying to find some oxygen.

Zya tried to breathe, but every time she inhaled, she sucked in more smoke. Her heart began to pound harder and harder as she began to slip in and out of consciousness. Zya knew she wouldn't make it. She saw her whole life flash before her eyes. She thought about when she left her foster mother's home to run away with Jules. She saw Jules shoot King in the hotel. She saw when Jules was being escorted to jail. She saw herself sitting at the Supreme Clientele roundtable. She saw the boxes full of money, stacked up to her ceiling. She saw Vita, lying on the floor, life-less, her soul-less eyes staring up at her, haunting her with a junkie's gaze. She saw a baby boy that looked just like Snow, with gray eyes and a dark complexion. She saw her casket being closed, with no one at the funeral.

Zya felt her eyelids begin to close, and when she saw the bright white light, she knew her time was up. *God, please have mercy on me,* Zya thought as she closed her eyes unwillingly.

The bright, white light wasn't heaven. It was the light from the sun. Someone had opened the rear emergency door.

She felt a hand pull her from the bus and drag her away. Just as they got fifteen feet away from the bus, it exploded, sending burning debris flying every-where. Zya was dazed from the smoke inhalation, and her heart was beating erratically. She looked at the person who had come to her rescue and noticed it was Matthews.

"Buggy?" she stated in confusion as he continued to drag her up the road. A black car pulled up, and Agent Matthews shoved Zya into the vehicle. He jumped in next to her. "Nothing is going to stop you from going where you are supposed to go," he said as the driver sped off.

Somebody put a bomb underneath the bus. Anari is trying to kill me. I know it, Zya thought as she coughed uncontrollably.

Zya was somewhat happy that Matthews had instructed her to sit in the back. If she were in the front, she would have died from the explosion. She had never been so happy to see Matthews than when he pulled her out of the back of the bus.

Zya felt the car stop, and she noticed that they were in a big field with a jet sitting in the middle of it. "What the fuck is going on?" Zya asked as she looked out of the window.

"I told you nothing was going to stop you from getting where you were supposed to go." Matthews exposed an infrequent smile as he removed the handcuffs from Zya's wrists. "Come on," he said as he stepped out of the car.

What the hell is going on? Zya thought as she was about to get out of the car. Just before she stepped out, the tinted window that separated the driver from the passengers rolled down. When she saw the face of the driver, her heart nearly skipped a beat. It was Emilio Estes.

Anari set this up. They are taking me to this field to kill me, she thought as she saw Emilio smiling at her. What she heard from Emilio was totally unexpected.

"Thank you, Zya," Emilio said graciously just before he rolled up his window.

Matthews pulled Zya out of the car and nearly dragged her to the helicopter. Zya was kicking and screaming with all her might, but to no avail. He was much too strong for her.

Just as they reached the jet, the door swung open. Anari appeared, along with Sammy, the pilot, in the front. Zya couldn't believe what she was seeing. She completely froze up, trying to decipher what was going on. Anari pulled out a briefcase from under her seat and gave it to Agent Matthews.

"One million dollars. Enjoy," Anari said as Matthews grabbed the suitcase.

Zya looked at Matthews and then at Anari. Anari looked at Zya with welcome eyes and smiled at her. At that moment, it all came to Zya, and the fear that she felt left her heart. Zya smiled, knowing that Anari had set up her escape.

"You were working with her all along," she said to Matthews as she playfully hit him.

"Sorry for being so rude. I had to play the role, ya know? You have a good life, Zya. I am about to sit back and enjoy mine with my new wife," he said as he patted the briefcase and returned to the limo.

Zya watched as the limo took off and then turned back to Anari. "You knew all along that Buggy was a cop, huh?"

"I told you. I know everything. I knew you would have to make a decision between loyalty and supremacy. I trusted you from the beginning, and I don't do that with most people. You became like a little sister to me. I knew deep in my heart that you wouldn't turn on me," Anari said as she extended her hand and helped Zya in.

Anari continued to talk. "I want to thank you for taking the fall for us. It showed a lot of courage. I have another surprise for you."

"What?"

"Turn around."

Zya turned around and saw Snow sitting in the seat behind her. She immediately embraced him tightly and screamed, "Oh my God, baby!"

Snow cringed when Zya brushed against the stab wound in his waist. "Damn, girl," he said as he held his sore body.

"I'm sorry. What happened?" Zya asked as she examined Snow's bandaged mid-section and tenderly touched his face as if she couldn't believe he was sitting in front of her.

"Your clever friend over here set me up to get stabbed, so they could transport me to the hospital. Then she had one of her men sneak me out unnoticed, and here I am," he said as he winked his eye at Anari.

"Yeah, sorry about that. That was the only way to get you out."

"I'll take a hit in the stomach to be with Zya any day. You almost had me scared, though. The doctor said it was inches away from my liver," Snow said as he patted his side.

"I made sure that the stabbing was precise and in a spot that wouldn't cause any permanent damage. The attacker was a professional. Believe me, Boss Sparks is so good that he almost had me hit."

Zya turned to Anari and hugged her tightly. "Thank you, Anari. I thought you wanted to kill me. After what I did to you . . ." Zya's voice trailed off before she finished her sentence.

"How could I do that? You are right. You did do something to me, Zya. You took all of the weight off of my shoulders and put it on yours. I beat the charge because of you, Zya. I can't be charged for any of my past crimes. According to you, I was never involved in any illegal activity. This is the least I could do. We will always be friends."

"Always," Zya said as she smiled at Anari and placed her hands on her bulging belly.

"Oh my goodness. I have been so pre-occupied with everything that I didn't even notice. What do we have here?" Anari asked as she rubbed Zya's stomach gently.

"It's a boy," Zya said softly with a smile.

"What are you going to name him?"

Zya looked back at Snow to see what he was going to say, but he just shrugged his shoulders, not knowing the answer.

"Maurice," Zya said as she looked down at her belly and placed her hand on it.

"I like that name," Anari added, knowing that Zya had chosen the name as a tribute to Anari's late son. Anari's eyes became glossy. "Thank you," she whispered.

She was honored by the tribute, and began to wave her hands over her face to prevent a tear from falling. "You can take this jet anywhere you want in the world and live your life with your family. There is twenty-five million dollars in the back, and it's untraceable. I'm going to miss you, Zya."

"I'm going to miss you too," Zya replied as they embraced each other. Their bond had surpassed a friendship. They were alike in so many ways and had grown so close that they really were like sisters.

Anari hugged Snow then stepped out of the helicopter as a limo came up.

Zya looked down at Anari and said jokingly, "We need a book wrote about our story. I think it would be hot."

"I know just the authors to write it, too," Anari said as she laughed and shut the door to the aircraft. Zya and Snow disappeared into the clouds, on a one-way flight to paradise.

Epilogue

Zya and Snow watched as their four-year-old son boarded the helicopter alongside Anari. It was the first time that their child would be away from them. Anari had convinced them to let her godson stay with her for the weekend. Zya didn't want to admit it, but she did need some alone time with Snow. For the last five years, they had been living in seclusion in a small town in Jamaica under phony names.

"There goes our baby boy," Zya said as she waved to her son while the aircraft lifted from the ground.

"He's only gon' be gone for a couple days. We need some time to ourselves anyway. It'll be fun. I'll even take you to that maze of mirrors you been bugging me about. Since little Maurice is terrified of them, now is the perfect time to go," Snow replied as he threw his arms around Zya's waist. They walked back to their villa, which was about a hundred yards away from the open field, and prepared for their well deserved night out.

"Where you at, Snow? I'm gon' find you," Zya said as she placed both of her hands in front of her to avoid bumping into the deceptive mirrors. Zya turned her head as she saw his reflection brush past her. Zya laughed out loud as she stepped straight into a mirror.

"You'll never catch me," Snow said as he continued to make his way through the tricky maze. Zya could see him, but couldn't tell exactly which direction he was headed. There were so many mirrors that she couldn't decipher what was real and what was a reflection.

Got him, Zya thought as she noticed Snow tiptoeing through the maze. She knew that he didn't see her, so it was the perfect opportunity for her to tag him.

"I know where you at," Zya said in between her laughter. She spotted him, and she knew that he couldn't see her. She crept up on him, only to find that it was another mirror.

Damn, I can see him, but I can't get to him. Zya's heart dropped as she looked into the mirror and saw a raggedy-looking bum with dread-locks approach Snow from behind.

"Snow!" she yelled as the face of the man became clear. It was Lonnie Wade. "Baby watch ou—" Before she could get the words out of her mouth, Lonnie Wade had grabbed Snow from behind and placed a gun to his temple.

"Zya, where you at, bitch?" Wade yelled as he maneuvered through the maze with a struggling Snow in his grasp. He was choking Snow so hard that he couldn't breathe.

"Run, Zya, run!" Snow managed to let out. His voice roared through the soundproof house of mirrors. He was helpless against Wade because he had left his pistol at home.

"Wade, let him go. He has nothing to with this," she stated. Zya's heart was pounding frantically as she made her way through the mirrors, trying to find their exact location.

Wade strengthened his grasp, almost causing Snow to lose consciousness, with nothing but revenge on his mind.

"Do you know what it's like being a cop in prison? Do you, bitch?" Wade began to cry, and Zya felt fear creep into her heart when she saw the crazed look in his eye. He was like a madman.

Zya was speechless. She hadn't even thought of Wade since the trial, and now here he was, threatening to destroy her like he had always planned.

"Please, let's just talk about this," she pleaded as she continued to search for them. She could no longer see their reflections, and the fear of the unknown gripped her. "Wade, please," she cried out as she pulled her gun from its ankle holster. Zya could only hear his voice.

"Every day I got raped like a woman. My manhood was stripped from me, and it was all because of you." As he talked, he jammed the gun against Snow's temple. "All because you lied. I have been waiting on this day for four years, and now you will pay."

Before Zya could even respond, she heard a single gunshot ring throughout the entire maze, causing the mirrors to rattle.

"Snow!" she screamed as she frantically searched for her man. She turned corner after corner, and she found Snow's lifeless body lying in a pool of his own blood. "Snow! Please, God . . . no," she begged as she kneeled next to him. Her knees were soaked in his blood, and she struggled to pick him up in her arms. "Baby, please," she cried as she rocked him back and forth, staring into his lifeless eyes.

Wade escaped, and his mission was accomplished. He knew that by taking the life of Snow, Zya would come back for him to seek revenge.

And when she does, I am going to put her where she belongs . . . in a grave.

Zya woke up in a cold sweat, desperately gasping for air. Her heart ached, and she breathed heavily while gripping her chest. She looked over at her new-born baby in the corner of her room, and then over to Snow, who lay sleeping peacefully next to her. She then realized that it was only a nightmare and Snow was alive and well.

Her tensions settled as Zya got out of bed and slowly walked over to the balcony that overlooked the ocean. She took a deep breath of relief and watched as the tides gently washed up on the shore.

"It was all a dream," Zya whispered as she realized that she was finally at peace. She knew that it was not the last nightmare she would have, but it was a small price to pay for all the wrong she had done.

The baby began to cry, and Zya walked over to her son and gently scooped him in her arms. She rocked softly back and forth while returning to the balcony.

Snow crept up behind them and held Zya while she held their baby. Snow noticed Zya had been sweating. "What's wrong?" he asked.

"I just had another nightmare, that's all," she replied.

"You don't have to worry about anything, Zya. I will not let anything happen to my family. You're safe here." Snow kissed Zya and then his son. "I love you."

"I love you too."

THE END . . . FOR NOW